RHEN

By Charity W. Kelly

Copyright © 2017 Charity W. Kelly

All rights reserved. No part of this publication may be reproduced, distributed or transmitted in any form or by any means, including photocopying, recording or other electronic or mechanical methods, without the prior written permission of the author.

This is a work of fiction. Any resemblance to real persons or entities is coincidental.

Table of Contents

Chapter 1 1
Chapter 2 4
Chapter 3 7
Chapter 4 14
Chapter 5 19
Chapter 6 22
Chapter 7 39
Chapter 8 47
Chapter 9 76
Chapter 10 81
Chapter 11 93
Chapter 12 95
Chapter 13 107
Chapter 14 122
Chapter 15 126
Chapter 16 134
Chapter 17 146
Chapter 18 157
Chapter 19 197
Chapter 20 222
Chapter 21 241
Chapter 22 268
Chapter 23 289
Chapter 24 311
Chapter 25 339
Chapter 26 354
Chapter 27 365
Chapter 28 381
Chapter 29 386
Chapter 30 391
Chapter 31 400
Acknowledgments 404

Chapter 1

Rhen stared down into the frightened eyes of the attacking Thestran Royal, before striking the man's head with the hilt of his sword, gouging the expensive, gold plating on the Thestran's helmet and knocking the Royal unconscious. Under normal circumstances, Surpen's military forces didn't fight for other planets, but the Surpen King had lent Rhen and his men to their allies to stop Thestran's colonial spread.

"Seriously?" Rhen's Lieutenant, Jet, asked.

Rhen turned to find his men had knocked out the second Thestran Royal. He shook his head and glanced about the battlefield. Now that Rhen and his men had rendered Thestran's Royals unconscious, the rest of Thestran's army had given up. "That was easy," Rhen murmured.

"It was a joke," Jet called out to him. "Did you see the lame way the Thestrans were using their powers? They didn't even hit you once."

Rhen snorted. He, too, had been surprised. The Thestrans had more powers than any other planet in the Universe, which was part of the reason why they were so successful at colonizing planets. Everyone was terrified of their powers. Rhen stepped over the Thestran Royal at his feet. He had fought in enough battles to know that these Thestrans had been weaker than most. Rhen wondered if he was fighting one of Thestran's training crews. He made his way into Rowan's Capital to check in with their King before heading home.

Three hours later, Rhen strolled into his small, private chamber on the Surpen spacejet that had arrived to take him home. He and his soldiers had finished with the formalities of assigning their victory to the King of Rowan and accepting the King's gifts of gratitude. The spacejet vibrated under Rhen's feet, as it rose in the air. Rhen had four hours of down time before they landed on Surpen. He planned on using it to get some rest. Rhen tossed his steel helmet onto the shelf to his right and reached up to unbuckle the leather straps on his metal shoulder plates.

"Unbelievable!" someone said in the open doorway to Rhen's chamber.

Rhen turned to find a short, muscular soldier with mismatched teeth grinning at him. The man's red and black military tunic was still heavy with gore from the battle they had just completed.

Glancing towards the communicator on the wall, Rhen snapped, "Lieutenant Jet!" He crossed the tiny chamber, grabbing a half tunic, as he approached the communicator.

Jet followed Rhen's progress with his eyes. He waited, a light smile on his lips, for his friend to wrap the tunic around the communicator's speaker.

"Continue," Rhen replied, bending over to check that he had fully covered the device.

Jet twirled his bloody helmet in his right hand, his quick, grey eyes flashing with amusement.

"Unbelievable! I mean, can you believe it, because I certainly can't. What was up with those Thestrans? They fought like babies! I thought they were supposed to be warriors. Isn't that why everyone's scared of them? Isn't that how they've colonized so many planets? They have the powers of the Gods. But those Thestrans back there, it was like they didn't even know how to use their own powers!"

Although Rhen agreed with Jet's assessment of the Thestran's fighting skills, being the Surpen King's son, he had to be careful about what he said. There were too many cycs and cars on board the spacejet for him to risk such a casual conversation, even with the communications speaker covered.

"They are dangerous warriors," Rhen replied, with a nod towards the speaker to tell Jet that he was speaking officially. "We must've been facing one of their training crews. I guess they thought Rowan was theirs for the taking and sent less experienced men to claim their victory."

Jet shook his head. A moment later, he laughed, "Did you see that Thestran Royal's eyes, before you knocked him unconscious?"

Rhen raised his hand to hide his own grin. The entitled look on the face of Thestran Royal he had fought had quickly changed to fear, when Rhen had dodged the man's power blasts and rushed him.

"I bet that Royal wet himself, when you maneuvered around his blast," Jet remarked. "I don't think he'd ever seen anyone do that before." Jet chuckled. "How is it that you always seem to know when to jump when someone throws their powers at you?"

Rhen pulled off his shoulder plates and tossed them onto the shelf below his helmet. "Practice. That's all. You'd be able to do it too, if you'd had as much training as I've had."

Jet disagreed, but he didn't counter Rhen's comment. "Do you really think the Thestrans sent a bunch of novices to Rowan? I'm still in shock over how easy it was to beat them."

"Jet, we know the Thestrans are strong. If they were weak, Surpen or another member of the Convention would've attacked them years ago. We were lucky today. That's all." Rhen reached up to unbuckle his chest plate, adding, "I have a feeling Thestran will be back on Rowan with their top warriors within a week. They want Rowan and they aren't going to give it up after only one battle."

Jet nodded, contemplating Rhen's words. "I'd be honored if you'd include me on the next mission to protect Rowan."

Rhen tossed his chest plate onto the shelf with his shoulder armor and turned to face his friend. "I can't think of anyone I'd rather have by my side."

"Thank you, Commander," Jet replied, sounding official. He came to attention, offering Rhen a quick salute, before lifting his chin in goodbye and walking off.

Rhen pulled the tunic off the communicator, before bending over to remove his shin guards. He threw his shin guards onto the bottom shelf, with the rest of his armor, then sat down on his cot. Rhen stared at his bloody, black boots. If he didn't remove the blood from his boots soon, they'd be stained. He liked these boots and didn't want them streaked. Rhen considered getting up to clean them, but then he remembered that his father would want to see the Thestrans' blood. Both his father, and his father's advisor, hated the Thestrans with a passion. It was disturbing to see how much pleasure they got from hurting Thestrans.

Without thinking, Rhen reached for the fingers on his left hand and rubbed them, easing away an upsetting memory. He had once been a Thestran. The Surpen King had adopted him when he was eight. Rhen remembered the pleasure he had felt at giving up his Thestran heritage to become Surpen. He used to hate the fact that he looked Thestran, that he didn't blend in with the Surpens and their classic grey eyes and brown hair. Rhen released his fingers and leaned over to unlace his boots. Even though he still despised the Thestrans, he didn't mind his looks anymore. He knew he was Surpen, and so did the rest of the Universe, which was all that mattered.

Chapter 2

Her Royal Highness Kate of Thestran rushed into the hospital room in the Thestran Royal Castle. Her graying, blond hair looked disheveled, as she stopped by the bed where her eldest son, James, was sitting. "My word!" she declared, while glancing at the purple and blue bruises on her son's face and chest. "What happened? The Rowanians should have been easy for you to defeat. They don't have any powers."

James shook his head and glanced behind him at his brother Reed, who sat in the next hospital bed. His father, His Royal Highness Henry of Thestran, was standing next to Reed, his hand on Reed's shoulder.

"It would've been an easy victory," James told his mother, while turning back to her. Her blue eyes were shadowed with concern. "But the Surpens decided to show up."

Kate swore and glanced towards Henry.

James narrowed his eyes at their exchange. 'What was that all about?' he wondered.

"Did you see any of the Surpen's faces?" Kate asked.

With furrowed a brow, James opened his mouth to ask his mother why she wanted to know if he had seen the Surpen's faces, when Reed answered, "No, their helmets covered them, only their eyes were visible."

Reed's wife, Lilo, followed by her father, Estan, the King of the Wood Elves, entered the room. Lilo's shoes made a loud, clacking sound on the white tiles of the medical room floor, as she ran over to Reed to embrace him, while Estan bowed before James.

"Your majesty," he said. "Are you alright?"

King James of Thestran nodded his head. "The Surpens were on Rowan," he told Estan, feeling satisfied, when the elfin king gasped with surprise.

Lilo's arms tightened around Reed. "I'm fine," he told her, stroking her blond hair. "They knocked us out, but Rachel will be here in a minute to heal our wounds. We'll be fine."

Henry moved over to Kate's side to give Reed and Lilo some privacy.

"Does this mean that Rowan is a part of Surpen's territory now?" Estan asked James.

"No," James replied, reaching up to scratch at the sho his chin. "Oddly enough, when Reed and I woke up, the Rowa to meet, to discuss possible trade routes. We have a Council me arranged for tomorrow."

"Well, that's a relief," Kate declared. "Let's get Rowan to join our Council. That will put a thorn in the Surpen King's side."

"Speaking of Surpen," James began. "Mom, you might want to bring our little brother, Max, home from that Surpen school he's attending. I can't see how his studying on a planet that's a part of the Convention would benefit him."

Kate's blue eyes grew larger. She glanced up at Henry, who gave a little laugh, before replying, "We've asked Max to return, but he seems adamant on continuing his education on Surpen."

"Well then force him to come home," James told his parents. "Surpen is no place for a Thestran elf."

Estan and Reed snorted in agreement. "Elves need to stay together," Estan declared. He looked over at his daughter, as she hugged Prince Reed. "It's in our nature." He was pleased that Lilo had fallen in love with an elf. While she had been at the Elfin University, she had mentioned she was dating a member of the Thestran Royal Family. Estan had been worried that she might have been dating one of the non-elves in Kate and Henry's brood. He was relieved to find out it was Kate and Henry's elfin son Reed.

"The next time we visit Max, we'll ask him to come home," Henry told James.

"Is he coming to Sage's wedding?" Lilo asked her in-laws. "I wish he had been able to make our wedding."

Kate and Henry shifted their feet in preparation to leave. "Not sure yet," Henry threw out over his shoulder, as the two of them moved towards the exit.

Before James could question Kate and Henry further on Max, his sisters, Rachel and Lilly, rushed into the room. "I'm so sorry we couldn't get here sooner," Rachel declared. She stopped next to James' bed to heal his bruises with her powers. "I brought Lilly to heal you Reed, so you wouldn't have to wait." Rachel lifted her hands and swirled them about in the air, feeling her cooling powers rush to her fingertips. When her powers were strong enough, she reached out and touched James' bare shoulders. He flinched from the coolness of her touch but remained seated, as her healing powers flowed through his body, healing the bruises he had received at the hands of the Surpens.

"I need a vacation," James declared, when Rachel was done. He glanced ...nd him. Lilly had already finished healing Reed. Her cold, healing powers .ad left white fingertip marks on Reed's shoulders. James reached up to rub the cold marks that Rachel had left behind on his body.

"I hear you," Reed agreed. He jumped off the bed and reached out for Lilo, scooping her up into his arms and making her giggle.

"Where's Susan?" Rachel asked her brother.

"My wife and kids went on a trip with her family," James told them, while pulling on his black shirt and gold jacket. "I told her she should stay with them. I wasn't hurt and I didn't want her to end her trip prematurely."

"Where did they go?" his sister, Lilly, asked. She reached up push her bangs out of her eyes.

"I think it was called a ranch? Something with...cowboys, I think?" James told them.

"You should join her tomorrow after the meeting with the Rowans," Reed told his brother. He pulled on his brown and green Wood Elf cape that matched his father-in-law's.

"You know," James commented. "Perhaps I will."

Chapter 3

Rhen stretched out his back, lifting his arms high in the air, before dropping his hands down into his lap. It'd been three months since his battle on Rowan, a battle that had been nothing but a waste of time. As soon as the Thestrans had regained consciousness, the Rowanians had made a deal with them, pledging their planet to Thestran, so they could be included in Thestran's trade routes. 'Typical,' Rhen thought with distaste. He shifted on the dusty ground, stretching his long legs out in front of him in the dark, empty room. Pushing his back against the cool, dirt wall, he considered his sullen mood.

This morning, his father had informed him that His and Her Royal Highnesses of Thestran would be arriving that night for an unprecedented meal with the Surpen Royal Family. Rhen didn't know what Andres and his advisor, Loreth, had arranged for this evening's event, but he was sure he wasn't going to like it.

Rhen shook with anger at the thought of Loreth. By God he hated that man. He rubbed his forehead with a rough, calloused hand, hoping to remove all thoughts of Loreth, then pressed his palms onto the cool tiles below him. Taking a deep breath, he savored the sweet scent of dry air. Above him, he could hear the loping sounds of the Surpen Beasts of War playing in the fields. Sighing, Rhen imagined himself flying off into the sky on his beast.

The soft, rhythmic sound of boots on dust covered tiles tickled his ear drums. Rhen turned his head to the right. He could tell from the way the person walked that it was Bosternd, his second in command and his best friend. Rhen listened to Bosternd, as he hesitated two chambers away. He heard a fingernail tapping on metal and groaned. "Stupid locating device," Rhen mumbled. "I never should have given it to him."

A few seconds later, Rhen saw Bosternd's flare light scan the room next to his. The light grew brighter as Bosternd moved towards him. Rhen turned his head from the doorway, when Bosternd's light grazed over his seated form. The dust particles danced around him in the air in its beam. Without speaking, Bosternd extinguished his light, tucked his locating device into his pocket and put his hand on the side of the wall. With care, he maneuvered around the room, using his hand as a guide. He stopped about three feet from Rhen, turned his back to the wall and slid to the ground to sit beside him.

Rhen listened to the sound of Bosternd breathing. He could smell the remains of Bosternd's lunch on his breath.

"I heard what Andres and Loreth are doing. Is it true you petitioned to leave, but they won't let you?" Bosternd asked.

"Yes," Rhen answered.

"I'm sorry," Bosternd sympathized. When Rhen didn't respond, he continued, "Have you spoken to Ceceta? I'm sure she's equally upset."

Rhen sighed before answering. "No, I haven't spoken with my wife."

"You should ask Andres to excuse her from this evening's meal. I'm sure she doesn't want to be reminded of her birth family any more than you do," Bosternd offered.

"You're right," Rhen agreed. He felt his body reacting as he thought about Ceceta and glanced towards Bosternd, thankful for the room's darkness. He didn't need Bosternd teasing him about his physical weakness for his wife.

Bosternd smiled in the dark, forgetting Rhen's abilities. "What's so funny?" Rhen asked with concern, when he saw Bosternd's grin.

"You're hiding," Bosternd told him. "What would our enemies say, if they knew Surpen's Military Commander was hiding in his own underground headquarters?"

"I'm not hiding," Rhen protested. "I'm thinking in the only quiet place there is on Surpen."

"Right," Bosternd teased. Rhen reached out his arm and pushed Bosternd, causing him to tumble over onto his right side with a grunt.

"Sorry," Rhen apologized, rising to his feet. "I forgot you couldn't see me. Let's go. I want to find out if Ceceta wishes to be excused from tonight's suffering."

"Okay," Bosternd said, while standing up and lighting his flare light.

They walked through the underground maze that comprised Surpen's Military Command Headquarters. The bunker was a labyrinth of hidden tunnels and passageways. It had been created by Rhen, when he had first become Commander of Surpen's Military Force. Any outsider would be lost forever in its dark tunnels. Only Surpen's soldiers could navigate its paths, and they kept to the tunnels they knew. Rhen tugged Bosternd into a hole on his left.

Bosternd was surprised to find himself near the main exit. "What passageway was that?" he asked, while eyeing the dark hole.

"That's the Ceceta Passage," Rhen commented. "When I want to get out of here in a hurry to find my wife, it takes me to the closest exit."

Bosternd laughed. After a few moments of silence, he asked, "Do you think she'll be upset, when she learns the Thestran Royals are coming?" They stepped into a bright room and were saluted by fifteen soldiers wearing red military tunics, black boots and black weapons belts. After returning the salute, they moved on to the next room, where they were again greeted by saluting soldiers.

"Yes," Rhen replied, sounding exasperated. "She's been cross a lot lately. I can't figure out what's bothering her."

Bosternd pinched his lips shut rather than state the obvious. It wasn't his place to get between his friend and his friend's wife.

They left Surpen's military headquarters through the main stone doorway, pausing to salute to three battalions of soldiers, who were waiting for General Nk to take them on drills. Rhen told the second lieutenant in charge to begin a Thestran training exercise and then he and Bosternd proceeded across the dry, brown field towards Surpen's Castle.

Suddenly, Rhen stopped so short that Bosternd bumped into him. "Everything okay?" Bosternd asked, when Rhen lowered his head and turned towards his right.

The Surpen Palace, with its high, stone walls, was right in front of them. It had been built as a place of refuge from attack and had little character. The outer wall was three stories tall. It was comprised of smooth, dark brown stones and had only three openings – the front gate, the rear exit and a new side exit that faced the entrance to Surpen's military headquarters. Inside the Castle's protective outer walls was the palace itself, a tall, dark, brown stone structure with multiple open archways and stone courtyards.

"Rhen?" Bosternd questioned again. "Is everything okay?" Rhen's head was still bent downward and his eyes were closed, as if he were listening for something.

With a shake of his head, Rhen opened his eyes and mumbled, "I thought I heard Loreth."

Bosternd nodded and turned to scan the horizon for the King's advisor. "I don't see him."

"Nor do I," Rhen answered, continuing towards the palace.

They entered the palace's side courtyard, saluting the soldiers on guard, before crossing the gravel pathway to the stone arch, where a side door into the castle was located. "Do you want me to come with you?" Bosternd asked, hesitating in the doorway.

"No," Rhen said. He nodded towards his friend, allowing him to return to the safety of their military headquarters. "I'm sure I'll see you before dinner tonight."

"Yup," Bosternd agreed, stepping backwards into the warm, Surpen sun. He glanced up at Rhen's eyes, which had turned almost pure white in the dark passageway. "Your eyes," he said, warning his friend. As soon as Bosternd spoke, Rhen's eyes turned black again.

"Thanks," Rhen told him. "I guess I have a lot on my mind."

"Who wouldn't," Bosternd replied, with laugh. "It's not like you're going to see your birth parents in a few hours, after years of being separated and being adopted by their mortal enemies, and you've been ordered not to speak in their presence or anything."

"You heard about that?"

"Yeah, it's making the rounds."

Rhen shook his head. "I think that one is courtesy of Loreth. Although, I'm not sure whether I should thank him for it or not. In all honesty, I have nothing to say to a stinking Thestran, no matter who they are."

Rhen turned on his heel and mounted the red, stone steps to the third floor. He passed several rooms painted in bright colors on his way towards Ceceta's bedroom. Unlike the outside of the castle, which was a muted tan color, the inside was an explosion of vibrant colors.

'Ceceta would be either in her bedroom or the Queen's sitting room,' Rhen thought to himself. 'The two places where Loreth would never show himself.'

Rhen paused outside the open, stone doorway to his wife's bedroom. He scanned the green and yellow room for Ceceta and saw she was missing. Turning, he took a short cut through the throne room to reach the Queen's sitting room. He was pleased to note that his father's throne room was empty. 'Loreth and Andres must be off plotting this evening's festivities,' he thought, as he jumped the three small stone steps out of the throne room. He sailed past several empty conference rooms and stopped outside of Orpel's sitting room. Although he was a man and could march into the room without announcing himself, he preferred to give his wife and mother some warning that he was there. Clearing his throat, he waited a moment, until the rustling in the room quieted down, before stepping through the open archway into the bright orange and blue room.

His mother, Orpel, dressed in robes of green, sat on her chaise smiling up at him, while working on one of Andres' tunics. Rhen returned the smile with warmth in his eyes. As soon as Orpel registered his smile, Rhen saw her lean back in her chair and relax. His smile was enough to tell her that he was alone. If he had been with anyone, she would have seen it on his face and dropped to the ground in a low bow before leaving the room. Knowing he wasn't there for her, Orpel pushed her gray hair back behind her ears and pointed over towards the small opening that served as the room's window.

Ceceta stood with her back to them as she gazed out over the City of Surpen. She had heard Rhen, but hadn't turned around. Orpel would have given her some indication, if he hadn't of been alone. If she had coughed, Ceceta would have dropped to the floor, like her mother in law and crawled out of the room. Instead, she stood with defiance, ignoring her husband's presence. Rhen crossed the room, stepping up behind her. Without speaking, he kissed Ceceta on the top of her head, before wrapping his arms around her body and pulling her into him.

Ceceta leaned back into Rhen's body, placing the back of her head against his chest, as she reached up with her hands to hold his arms where they crossed her. She could feel the warmth of the Surpen sun on his clothing and tightened her grasp with pleasure. Twisting, she brushed her cheek against his tunic. Rhen tightened his embrace, his body reacting to her attention. Ceceta smiled to herself, before shaking her head.

"What?" Rhen murmured, while bending down to nibble on her earlobe.

Ceceta was a typical Neptian with blond hair, dark brown eyes and blue skin. Her full lips were a darker shade of blue than the rest of her skin and Rhen found them intoxicating. "Love," he whispered, kissing her cheek.

Ceceta saw the shadow of a reflection of her mother-in-law behind her on the wall and flushed with embarrassment. She struggled to break free from Rhen's hold, but he held her a moment longer, before releasing her.

"I've heard the news," Ceceta announced. She walked over towards Orpel and picked up a yellow tunic that she had been sewing for Rhen. "Are you alright?"

Rhen nodded his head and turned to face them. His red, military tunic, with its black piping and black military bars on the sleeves, lay flat against his front. His black weapons belt, with its two long swords, remained still against his thighs. Only Rhen's black military boots looked out of place. They had a coating of dust on them from his walk across the field to the palace. Rhen ran a hand through his short, brown hair and studied them with his black eyes. "How are you?" he asked Ceceta.

"Fine," she replied, her lips thin with worry.

He gazed at her for a moment. "I'll ask Andres to excuse you."

Ceceta's blue skin flushed with anger. "Over my dead body," she snapped. "He's got something planned for tonight, and whatever it is, will put you in danger. I want to be there to help you in any way I can." Rhen nodded. She was right. Everyone knew something was going to happen tonight, they just didn't know what.

"Thanks," he told her. He wandered over to look at her work, hoping to find a way to change the subject. "That's beautiful my love," Rhen commented, while inspecting the black stitching that had been sewn into the cuffs of his new tunic.

Ceceta laughed and tossed a pillow at him. "Liar!" she declared. They both knew she was inept at stitching his tunics. Orpel had been doing his and Andres' tunics ever since they had arrived on Surpen.

"No, really mom," Rhen clarified, the side of his mouth rising, as he lifted the yellow tunic. "You really have out done yourself this time." He was pleased, when Orpel blushed from the compliment. Leaning over to give his mother a kiss, Orpel surprised Rhen, when she reached out and grabbed him, squeezing him tight. He could feel her body shaking with unspoken worry. "It's alright mom. I'll be fine."

When Orpel refused to release him, Rhen reached up to remove her arms. "Mom," he reassured her. "I'll be fine." Orpel nodded and let go of him, but she wrapped her arms around her own body to stop herself from shaking. Rhen reached out to take her chin in his hand. "Don't forget," he reminded her. "Andres loaned me out to the Rowans during their battle with Thestran. During that war, I met some Thestrans and bested them. They even had powers!"

When Orpel refused to meet his gaze, Rhen tried again. "Really mom. A Thestran threw his hands up to zap me with his powers, but before he could hit me, I knocked him unconscious. I'll be fine. I promise."

Orpel gave him a half-hearted smile, telling him she wanted to believe him.

Without hesitation, Rhen bent down to kiss her on the top of her head. "I love you," he whispered, before rising to go.

Ceceta lunged out to grab Rhen's hand as he turned. "Yes," she told him with determination. "You will be fine."

Rhen smiled at her strength. He debated snuggling up into her again, but decided against it. He needed to find Andres. He wanted to know what his father had planned for him tonight. He wasn't sure if Andres would tell him the truth, while Loreth was around, but perhaps he would get lucky.

Chapter 4

Her Royal Highness Kate of Thestran looked at her youngest son through swollen eyes. He was poised, holding her above the ground with one arm outstretched. His grip on her shirt was so tight that if he were to twist his wrist a little further, she would be strangled. Kate knew her right arm was broken and at least seven of her ribs felt cracked. Her right ankle was also shattered and blood flowed down her forehead into her eyes. Rhen had fought so fast and with such precision that she hadn't had a chance to defend herself.

Rhen was quiet. For that matter, everyone was quiet. The Surpen Royal family, along with most of the top ranking Surpen generals, had witnessed their fight. Andres, the Surpen King, had convinced Kate to enter a 'mock' battle with her son. He had implied that it would be a great way for her to bond with the boy. She knew now that he had wanted to see if Rhen had the ability to hurt her. He had wanted to prove to himself and the others that Rhen had no ties to Thestran. This battle had been Andres' victory.

Kate had been surprised, when Rhen had dodged her first power blast to land a crushing blow to her ribs. She had never seen anyone move with such speed before. Perhaps she had meant to miss him with that first blow. It was the first time she had seen him, since they had left him alone on Surpen all those years ago. She and Henry had been speechless at the sight of him. When Rhen had entered the room that evening, dressed in his finest Surpen attire, their mouths had dropped open. Rhen looked just like Henry, with his dark brown hair, dark eyes and rounded face. They couldn't wait to catch up with him, but Rhen had refused to speak to them the entire evening.

Their evening had started out pleasant enough. Andres and Loreth had seated them at the dining table. After they had taken their seats, Loreth had ordered a guard to fetch Rhen. He had entered the room, followed by his wife, and taken the seat across from them, while his wife had sat on the floor, with her head forward in a dismissive bow. Andres and Loreth had chatted with them about general topics. They had inquired about the Thestran Royal Family's health and had confessed their continued distrust of the Convention Members, a group of solar systems that Surpen belonged to, who opposed Thestran and her Council.

When Henry broached the subject, which had brought them there, Rhen's attending Sage's wedding, Rhen's eyes had widened, as Loreth's and Andres' had narrowed. Through clever banter, the two men had made a deal with Kate. If she were to fight Rhen in a 'mock' battle, they would allow Rhen to attend Sage's wedding. Rhen had opened his mouth to protest, but Loreth had silenced him with a wave of his hand.

Feeling confident with her multiple powers, Kate had gazed at Rhen's round cheeks and long lashes. She had run her eyes up and down his sculpted ears and had reminded herself that all Thestrans, with elfin blood, abhorred violence. Andres had continued to press her, telling her she would bond with Rhen during their fight. Kate had felt as if she had nothing to lose. Henry, though, had sensed that something was amiss. He had reached out his hand to warn his wife, but before he could touch her, Kate had accepted the challenge.

By the time that Kate had realized she was in over her head, it was too late to stop. Her first few power blasts had missed Rhen, and as the heel of his left boot slammed into her chest, breaking more of her ribs, she knew she was in trouble. Rhen had a way of striking a person's bones that caused them to shatter.

And now, here they were, Kate, defeated and dangling from Rhen's hand above the ground, and Rhen, his eyes trained on Andres, as he waited for permission from the Surpen King to end the fight. Kate could feel her healing powers rushing to her head. She blinked her eyes, hoping to remain conscious. Her powers weren't strong enough to heal these shattered bones tonight. It would take her some time to recover from this battle. She heard Andres yell out to Rhen in Surpen then winced, when Rhen released the collar of her shirt, allowing her to fall to the ground like a sack of potatoes. Kate cried out in pain, as her body hit the sand. Turning her head, she looked back up at her son. His black eyes glared at her with hatred.

Kate raised her right arm to wipe the blood from her forehead onto her sleeve. Once again, she had been made into a fool by this Surpen King. She had fallen right into his trap. She had no doubt that Andres would now refuse to allow Rhen to attend Sage's wedding. Her pain and suffering had been for nothing.

Following Surpen tradition, Rhen bowed to Kate to express his gratitude for the honor of fighting. He rose and turned on his heel to leave. Kate groaned, as she watched him march back to Andres' side. A flash of black and gold caught Kate's eye and she saw Henry squat down by her side. His graying, dark brown hair fell forward over his face, as his eyes spoke his concern for her well-being. "Can you self-heal these wounds? Do you need a doctor?" Henry asked, while keeping his voice low. He was all too aware of the Surpens, who were watching them. Kate looked horrible. He'd never seen his wife with so many injuries. Henry hoped the Surpens weren't planning on ambushing them, now that Kate was out of commission. It would be just their luck, and knowing Andres, Henry wouldn't put it past him. Henry could almost see James' face, when he received their ransom or death notice.

"I need a doctor," Kate whispered, the blood running down her throat making her voice hoarse. "He was stronger than I realized." Henry shifted his body upward, debating whether he should indicate to Andres that they needed help, but Kate placed her good hand onto his cheek. "No. Not here," she said.

"I'll be able to make it to the hospital on Neptian." Henry nodded that he understood and worked his arms around Kate, lifting her to her feet. Sand poured out of the wrinkles and creases in her evening clothes, filling the valleys that her body had created, when she had fallen to the ground.

Kate put most of her weight on Henry's shoulders. She was far too tired to use her powers to fly. Trying to draw as little attention as possible, the two of them shuffled towards the Surpen Castle. There was a portal in the castle they could use to return home. As they climbed the stairs to enter the building, Kate turned to look back at Rhen. He was wearing his formal dining tunic of red and gold. He had put his weapons belt back around his waist and reattached his royal cape to his shoulders. He wasn't wounded, tired or even taxed in any way that she could see. His battle with her had been nothing to him, as easy as a walk in the park.

They stepped into the Surpen Castle, moving out of sight of Andres and his guests. Kate, limping with every step, turned towards Henry. "I'm afraid the recent predictions we've been hearing might be true." She paused. Henry waited until she had caught her breath before urging her forward. "We need to get Rhen off of Surpen as soon as possible."

"I know," Henry murmured. "It became apparent during your fight."

"I just thought that since he doesn't have any powers, the predictions that he'd conquer the Universe couldn't be true."

Henry braced Kate, as they came to a new set of stairs. "He doesn't need powers to be dangerous. Kate, you didn't hit him once with your power blasts."

"I know," Kate said. She hunched over, as a fresh wave of pain hit. When it had dissipated, they continued.

"Right now, people aren't paying attention to the prophecies, because they feel secure. They know your powers will defeat Surpen. If word gets out that Rhen can beat you," Henry said, pulling Kate forward. "There'll be widespread panic." Kate nodded in agreement, while clutching onto Henry's arm for support.

They arrived in the round, open room that served as Surpen's portal room to find a soldier standing beside the large, majestic, golden frame that served as Surpen's portal. At the sight of the man, Henry stopped short. Was the soldier there to stop them? Could Henry defeat this man, if a fight were to break out? Kate squeezed Henry's hand to express to him the seriousness of her injuries. She needed to get to a hospital. Henry lifted his head and addressed the soldier in Thestran, "Would you please thank the King for his kindness tonight and apologize to him for us, but we have a pressing engagement on Thestran that we must attend to." Henry hoped the man could understand the Thestran language, as he added, "Please inform Andres that we will return in three weeks to take Rhen with us to his sister's wedding."

Bosternd hesitated. He surveyed Kate, assessing her injuries. He had been sent to the portal by Rhen to make sure that Kate and Henry didn't run into any of Andres' personal guards as they made their retreat. Bowing, Bosternd indicated to the Thestran Royals that he would pass along their message to the King.

Henry took in the short, stocky man. He had the classic black hair, grey eyes and tanned skin of a Surpen. His red, dress tunic was decorated with numerous black bars, indicating his high rank in Surpen's military. He was wearing a single dress sword in his weapons belt. There was no doubt that this soldier had been at the elaborate dinner party that Andres had thrown for them earlier this evening, but Henry had trouble telling the Surpens apart, let alone remembering their names.

Turning towards the portal, with a calm he wasn't feeling, Henry said, "Neptian Royal Castle." The portal, a massive, golden frame that appeared to be missing its picture, surged to life, as an electric, blue light filled the space inside the frame. A moment later, the blue light dissipated and they found themselves looking at the greeting room in the Neptian Royal Castle. Henry gave Kate a nod of reassurance, before stepping through the frame into the Neptian Royal Castle, while carrying her with him. The Neptians in the room rushed towards them, but Henry waved them away. When the portal behind him had faded and turned black, he nodded that they could approach. He hadn't wanted the Surpen soldier to see how much help Kate needed.

The blue skinned, blond haired Neptians carried Kate to the hospital wing of their royal castle, as the Neptian Delegate known as Te, joined Henry with a questioning look. Neptian was a part of Thestrans' Council and Te was their Delegate. While Kate was being attended to by the Neptian doctors, Henry explained the situation to Te. He stressed to him the importance of keeping silent regarding Kate's condition. The predictions, about Rhen's future Universal rampage, hadn't spread to this part of the Universe yet, so Te was unaware of the true meaning behind Rhen's effortless victory over Kate.

When Henry was finished with Te, he went to Kate's side and took her bandaged hand in his own. He bent over her and brushed his lips against her ear. From her light smile, he could tell she was finally feeling relief. The doctor's reports had indicated that her body was healing itself, even if it was taking a long time to do it. "We have him now," Henry whispered to Kate. "Andres told us in front of many of his top generals that we could take Rhen home with us for Sage's wedding. We left before he could go back on his claim. If he were to refuse us now, he would lose face with his soldiers."

"For the Universe's sake, I hope you're right," Kate replied, before relaxing into her pillow and falling asleep.

Henry kissed her again, then moved over to the windows. He had always loved Neptian. It was such a beautiful planet, so lush and warm. A massive waterfall could be seen in the distance.

Henry leaned his head against the window pane and watched his breath steam the glass. He wished that he and Kate had never visited Surpen all those years ago. He wished they had stayed on Neptian with their youngest son and ignored the desperate pleas for help from Surpen's King Andres.

Chapter 5

Rhen stormed into the throne room of the Surpen Castle. "What do you mean I have to go to Thestran for some idiotic wedding?" he demanded, approaching his father.

Loreth had left the castle right after Kate and Henry. He had been very pleased with the way things had gone that evening and had informed Andres that he was taking a vacation.

"I refuse! I will never go to Thestran!" Rhen barked.

"Rhen," Andres began. "Please. Let's not fight. We just had a marvelous evening, which ended delightfully with your defeating Kate with ease."

Rhen's frown deepened at the memory of the battle. It hadn't been delightful. It had been upsetting. At one point, he had thought that she was missing him with her power blasts on purpose, but then he remembered that Kate had abandoned him as a child years ago, without even a backward glance, so there was no reason for her to hold back. The battle had confused him. Kate was supposed to be the most powerful person in the Universe, but after he had broken her ankle, and she had flopped about on the ground trying to retreat from him looking pathetic, he'd wanted to call off the fight. He would have done it too, if it hadn't of been for the fact that in doing so, he would have been contradicting his father in public, a crime that was punishable by death in Loreth's presence.

"Father, please," Rhen begged.

"No, wait! Before you start, hear me out," Andres told Rhen. He walked over and placed his steady hands on Rhen's shoulders. Rhen gazed down into his father's grey eyes.

"As you know, Loreth wants us to attack Thestran. He has his heart set on making Thestran a part of Surpen's Territory. We weren't sure if we would be able to do it, but after tonight, it appears possible," Andres explained. He slapped Rhen on the arms with affection. "You bested Kate! Do you know how amazing that is?" As Rhen shook his head, Andres laughed and grabbed him in a tight hug. "It's huge," he breathed out, before releasing his son.

"So, when do we attack?" Rhen asked his father with a sigh.

"We're not quite ready yet," Andres informed him. "We know you can outmaneuver their power blasts, but you alone, against all of them…well, it's not ideal. You would eventually be brought down. We need to be sure our army can also defeat them. You need to go to Thestran to assess their strengths and weaknesses. After your little reconnaissance mission…"

"The girl's wedding?" Rhen interrupted for clarification.

"Yes," Andres agreed, with a wicked grin. "After Sage's wedding, you'll have gathered the information we need to attack. It's the perfect plan."

Rhen nodded his head with appreciation. It was a good plan. He had heard a lot about the Thestrans' powers and was curious to see them in action. How powerful were they? The Thestrans he had met on Rowan hadn't seemed that strong. At least, they weren't any stronger than the Zorthans he knew who had powers.

"You will go to Thestran in three weeks with Kate and Henry," Andres informed him, while walking across the room to his desk. "We will follow the same guidelines that we did tonight. You are not to speak to them or to socialize with them beyond eating your meals with them. If they ask you a question that must be answered, respond with as few words as possible. Don't do anything with them and don't encourage them in any way. I don't want them anywhere near you, if I can help it."

"Nor do I," Rhen agreed. He thought about all the years of abuse he had received at the hands of the other Convention members for the simple fact that he looked Thestran. What would they say, when they learned he had gone back to Thestran? They wouldn't let him off the hook with a simple, 'I was spying', excuse.

Andres glanced up at Rhen with a broad smile. He loved it whenever Rhen said something disrespectful towards the Thestrans. "Correct. You will go for one or two days, you will take Ceceta with you as your cover…"

"NO! I don't want to endanger her by bringing her on this mission."

"What mission?" Andres replied, with an innocent smile. "You're going to your long, lost sister's wedding."

Rhen grimaced. He could see from Andres' face that he wasn't going to get a choice in this matter. With reluctance, he nodded his head. He would bring Ceceta. "Sour?" he asked, trying to remember the name of the girl who was getting married.

Andres laughed with delight. "Her name is Sage and I hear she's marrying a merman?"

"Really?" Rhen asked. He had heard rumors about the Merpeople, who lived under Thestran's oceans. "They must not have much of a relationship."

Andres smiled again at Rhen's lack of knowledge about the Thestran Royals. "Actually, Sage is the only Thestran with elfin blood who has powers.

She can breathe underwater, communicate with ocean creatures and transform her fiancé Ryan into an above ground Thestran."

"Sour has powers?" Rhen asked with interest. He had thought that he was the only person with elfin blood in the Universe to have powers.

"Yes, like you, SAGE," Andres annunciated, to remind Rhen of the girl's name, "has powers. Now, besides my orders that you are not to speak with them or to socialize with them, except to attend meals and the wedding itself, it is imperative that you, under no circumstances, let any of them know that you have powers." Andres knew Rhen had healing powers. He had seen Rhen heal not only himself, but his soldiers on numerous occasions, and he didn't want the Thestrans to discover Rhen's secret.

Rhen nodded in agreement, as Andres stepped forward to embrace him again. Andres had heard the recent prophesies about Rhen, so he could only assume the Thestrans had heard them as well. Why else had Kate and Henry come to Surpen? It couldn't have been for something as silly as a wedding. Not after so many years of silence.

"I want you to come home immediately after the wedding," he told Rhen. "Do you understand? I don't trust those Thestrans. They're up to something."

"Of course, father," Rhen replied obediently. He bowed and turned towards the doorway to leave. He was tempted to ask his father for permission to sleep in the castle tonight, rather than in the barracks, but he decided against it. Andres looked tired, so Rhen didn't want to distress him further by begging to sleep in the castle with Ceceta. The one perk of going to Thestran for 'Sage's' wedding was that he would be with his wife, and the two of them would be able to spend an entire day, possibly two, together. Two whole days on Thestran with orders not to speak to or socialize with anyone but Ceceta. He could hardly wait.

"We'll talk about this in greater detail later," Andres called out, as Rhen waved his hand behind him in a dismissive gesture and walked out of the room. Andres chuckled, recognizing the gesture as his own.

Chapter 6

Sage glanced out across the Thestran castle's lawn at the many tables filling up with guests for her pre-wedding feast. The golden tablecloths glowed in the setting sun and the crystal glasses sparkled from the many candles that were being lit in preparation for sundown. She had invited only her family members to tonight's event, but her brother, Thestran's King James, had forced her to include the Thestran Council Delegates as well as the Elfin Royals for political peace. Sage sighed, as she watched the Delegates, dressed in stylish clothing, stroll about the lawn, while finding their seats.

Her fiancé, Ryan, took her hand and squeezed it. "Don't worry, I'm sure your parents will be here soon."

"They'd better be, after dropping that bombshell on us two weeks ago. I mean, really? Baby brother Max is supposed to conquer the Universe and murder all of us?!"

"That will only happen, if he isn't removed from Surpen."

"Come on, Ryan. That's ridiculous! Max has elfin blood. Elves are pacifists. The whole idea is absurd."

"He's not just a school boy like we thought Sage," James commented, while taking the seat of honor beside her, the black cowboy hat that he had picked up on vacation sat high on his head. "You heard Mom and Dad."

"Right," Sage replied with sarcasm. "I find it hard to believe he's the head of Surpen's military. He's an elf, so what's he doing? Research? The whole thing sounds off." She paused to take a drink and watched her remaining siblings find their seats. "I mean," she continued, placing her goblet back on the table. "How old is Max anyway?"

James shrugged his shoulders. "Younger than Charlie," he answered with a grin. They watched their younger brother stumble into the back of his chair and fall onto the floor, before popping back up with a goofy laugh and tumbling into his seat at the foot of the table.

"I remember Max as a tiny boy, who liked to draw dragons," their sister, Lilly, said from half way down the table.

"According to mom, he's a soldier now. Not only that, but he's good. He beat her in a mock battle on Surpen," James reminded them.

"Not possible," Sage stated, shaking her head with disbelief. "No one can beat mom."

Rhen turned his head towards them and noticed the commotion. He barked out something in Surpen. Immediately, Ceceta took the seat beside him. She sat erect, then turned to her left and right, while raising and lowering her hands. The next moment, she shrank down in her seat, but a second later, she was sitting sideways and wiggling.

"What the Hell is going on?" James demanded.

"Nothing," Kate snapped, watching Ceceta sink down in her chair again, as if she wanted to disappear under the table. Kate reached out to pat Rhen on his shoulder. He turned towards her and glared up at her with angry, hate-filled eyes, so she dropped her hand down to her side.

"*She's patting me like I'm her pet. Should I be disobedient and bite her hand?*" Rhen asked Ceceta in Surpen. Ceceta giggled nervously and sank even lower in her chair.

Turning, Kate walked back towards the head of the table. "Alright, we got him here. Now we need to find a way to keep him here. Better yet, let's find a way to keep him here that will not include Surpen declaring war on us."

"This whole thing is ridiculous," Sage announced. "Max doesn't have any powers…"

"Rhen!" Henry barked. "Don't call him Max. His name is Rhen." He looked down the table to find Rhen staring at him, so he nodded to his son and raised his glass in salute.

Rhen leaned over towards Ceceta. "*Want to see something funny?*" he asked. Without waiting for a response, he placed his hands over his face, covering his nose and forehead, just as his helmet would have covered his face in battle.

James and Reed, who had been staring at Rhen, gasped in recognition. Rhen had been the Surpen soldier, who had defeated them on Rowan, that was why he looked familiar to them.

Rhen chuckled at their discomfort and leaned over towards Ceceta, dropping one of his hands into her lap. "*They aren't that special,*" he told her. "*Andres told me they were powerful, but I think he might have been misinformed. Half of them are short and lack muscular build and the other half look…effeminate, don't you think?*" Ceceta nodded in agreement.

"*And what's with the elves?*" Rhen continued. "*They're all so anemic looking.*" Ceceta chuckled. Rhen took a deep breath, smelling the sweet, moist Thestran air. He found it curious that he didn't remember anything about Thestran. He had thought there would be some part of this world that would jog

Ignoring Charlie, Kate reached out and took Rhen's hand to guide him to his seat. She stopped short, when he jerked out of her grasp. Rhen glared at Kate for a moment, before reaching for Ceceta's hand.

When Rhen looked back at her, Kate said, "Follow me." She led them around the table, until they reached the two empty seats between Charlie and Chaster, the King of the Air Elves. "Here Rhen, why don't you sit here," she gestured towards the chairs and back at Rhen to indicate to him that he and his wife should sit down.

Rhen released his wife's hand and took the seat next to Charlie, while Ceceta moved to stand behind him.

"No, that won't do," Kate said with frustration. She snatched Ceceta's hand and pulled her towards the empty seat.

Ceceta gasped and shook her head, while fighting against Kate, as she tried to remain behind Rhen.

"What's wrong? What's she doing?" Sage asked.

"She's refusing to sit down," Kate explained, while giving Ceceta's arm a sharp tug. Kate glanced towards Rhen for support, but he was ignoring them, his eyes on Thestran's Castle.

"Don't make her sit at the table," Sage told her mother. "She can remain with the staff."

Kate stared at her daughter with disbelief. "You're going to make his wife sit with the staff?"

"That's his wife!" Sage exclaimed. "I had thought it was his interpreter."

"Rhen has a wife?" James asked. He stared at Ceceta with interest. "When did he get married? Why didn't you tell us?"

"Why weren't we invited to the wedding?" Lilly asked.

Kate hesitated a moment, before releasing Ceceta's arm. She looked away from them, her shoulders sagging.

"Mom," Sage began. "Maybe you'd better explain."

Instead of answering, Kate turned towards Ceceta and grabbed her arm again. She jerked it, while yelling, "Sit at the table!".

everything from the manicured lawns and ocean to their right to the woods, stables and mountains on the opposite sides.

When finished, he turned his gaze to James, staring at the Thestran King until James was forced to look away. As soon as James looked down, Max leaned over to make a comment in Surpen to the woman beside him. The two of them chuckled, before lifting their now expressionless faces to the Thestrans.

"I feel as if I've just been sized up and didn't make the cut," Reed remarked, while placing his princely Wood Elf cape of green and brown on the back of his chair.

"Yeah," James agreed. He hadn't expected his brother to be so confrontational.

Reed noticed Max's eyes were focused on him. He wondered if his baby brother remembered that he had been invited to his wedding. They had been so busy with the preparations, that it hadn't been until after Reed's marriage, that they'd realized Max hadn't come.

"Does he look familiar to you?" James asked, interrupting Reed's thoughts.

"Of course, he does," Sage answered. "He looks like you and Dad."

"Yes," James agreed. "But, there's something else about him, something that makes me feel as if I've seen him before."

At that moment, Kate stepped forward and gestured out, towards the guests at the main table. "By now, you've all guessed who this is," she swung her hands around towards Max. "So, there's no need to make a formal introduction. However, there are a few things you need to be made aware of. First, Max doesn't remember how to speak Thestran, so he can't understand us. When we arrived, I offered him a universal translating device, but he refused it. Secondly, Max is no longer known as 'Max'. He's decided to use his middle name, Rhen, so use that instead, and thirdly, please don't be surprised when he calls Henry and me by our first names."

"Okay Kate!" her second youngest son, Charlie, yelled out, his pale blue eyes peeking up at her from under his mane of tussled blond hair. Kate raised an eyebrow. Her expression caused Charlie to burst into a fit of laughter, in which he swung his arm out and bumped into one of the serving trays beside him, dumping most of the food off the tray onto his lap.

"Ohhh," he exclaimed with surprise, taking in the mess he had made.

"An elf who fights," her brother, Reed, piped out, while placing his daughter into the chair beside him. "What would our Genister God Themrock say if he knew?"

"I know!" Sage shouted in agreement. "It's preposterous!"

"Relax," Ryan told Sage. He reached over to rub her tight neck and shoulders. "It'll be alright."

"It had better be," James stated. He used his powers to lift a pitcher of water to fill his glass. "After Mom and Dad returned from Surpen, I did some research on the predictions they mentioned, and they seem to be valid. We need to connect with Max right away, if we want to stop a Universal war." He shook his hand twice to remove the chill he always got from using his powers.

Kendeth, James' advisor, rose from his seat, his eyes on the south pathway to the Thestran Palace. The others turned to see what had drawn his attention. In the distance, they could see Kate and Henry strolling towards them with a tall, elfin man in a red tunic that ended at his knees. He had two swords in his weapons belt and beside him walked a Neptian woman. The Thestrans were surprised to note that the Neptian woman was dressed like a Surpen, with long, colorful, flowing robes of emerald green that wrapped around her body. She wore no jewelry but there was a single, white clip holding her blond hair up on top of her head. Instead of a purse, she carried a dark brown, leather bag slung across one of her shoulders in such a way that it rested on her back.

"They got him," Kendeth breathed out with relief, as the foursome navigated the tables on the lawn on their way to the main table.

"Thank Themrock," James whispered. He rolled his shoulders back and leaned his head to the left and right to relax the tension that had built up. He hadn't told the others, but he had already decided to attack Surpen and remove Max by force, if Andres didn't release the boy tonight.

Kate brought Max and the Neptian woman to James' side, but before she could introduce them to the current Thestran King, Sage blurted out, "This is Max?" Her eyes darted back and forth between Henry, Max and James, noting their similar dark eyes, brown hair and round faces.

Kate laughed with forced cheer. "Yes," she replied. "This is your little brother Max." Stepping closer to Max, she placed her hand on his sleeve, but he jerked his arm away from her.

"That was rude," Lilly exclaimed from her spot at the table. She watched as a cold, angry look settled on her youngest brother's face. He narrowed his eyes and scanned the guests at the table, before turning with a derisive snort to study the Thestran Castle and its surroundings, taking in his memory, but the people, the landscape and even the smells were foreign to him. Rhen decided he preferred the hot, dry climate of Surpen with its flat, rough countryside. He liked the Surpen people better, too. The Thestrans seemed very full of themselves. He would describe them to his mother, when he returned home tomorrow, as a noisy, obnoxious crowd.

Kate's daughter Lilly cleared her throat. "Are you sure he's going to kill all of us? I can't pick up any thoughts coming from his or his wife's minds. It's like their minds are totally blank. Besides, Max doesn't have any powers."

"Rhen," Henry reminded her.

Lilly smiled at Henry, acknowledging her father's words, and continued. "He can't kill us, if he doesn't have any powers."

"First of all, Lilly," Kate began. "One of them must have powers, because they're blocking us from reading their minds. I was hoping you'd be able to see past their block, but I guess they're stronger than us. Also, even if Rhen doesn't have powers, he can still beat us. Don't forget, he beat me, when I fought him on Surpen three weeks ago."

"Yeah, but you said that was a 'mock' fight, so you were holding back, right?"

"He can defeat all of us," King James told the table.

"How do you know?" Lilly asked.

"Because, he's the Surpen solider, who defeated us on Rowan," James answered.

"Oh, Hell," Kendeth swore.

"He's evil," Sage declared, while glaring down the table at her little brother.

"No, Sage," Kate replied. She took a sip of wine. "He's not evil. He's Surpen, a very, talented Surpen soldier. Under different circumstances, I'd be enormously proud of him."

"But he beat the crap out of all three of you," Charlie cried out. "How can you be proud of that?"

"Mom?" James asked. "Why did you send Rhen to a Surpen school in the first place? Why didn't you have him attend our Thestran schools?"

Kate picked up her fork and began to eat, while Henry drank from his wineglass.

"Mother," James said, after a few minutes. "You never told us why you left Rhen in a boarding school on Surpen in the first place. Please explain."

Kate turned towards Henry and the two of them began talking to each other.

"Mom," Sage tried. "Are you going to answer James?"

"Excuse me, what dear?" Kate asked, but before Sage could repeat her question, Kate turned towards a servant to ask for more bread.

"Mom. You've got to tell us. You can't keep ignoring us," James told her. "If you want us to find a way to keep Rhen on Thestran, we have to know what happened. Why did you send him to a Surpen school?"

Kate glanced down the table at Rhen, who was watching Charlie suck up the last piece of pasta from his plate through pursed fish lips. When the strand disappeared into Charlie's mouth, he smiled at Rhen, displaying pieces of vegetable and chewed, white chunks of pasta in his teeth, a drop of oil dangled from the edge of Charlie's chin.

Rhen turned his head away from Charlie to stop himself from laughing.

"Mom, Dad, you have to tell us what's going on. Why did you leave Max at a Surpen school?" James repeated.

"His name is Rhen and this isn't the time or place for this conversation," Henry began.

"Yes, it is!" James barked.

"Don't speak to your father that way!" Kate snapped.

"I'm worried about the future of our planet! We need to understand Rhen's past, if we're going to find a way to get him to stay on Thestran, short of locking him in the dungeon, which I'll do if I have…"

"You'll have to kill him," Kendeth interrupted. "Rhen won't stand for being placed under arrest. He's a Surpen. He'll fight us, killing as many of us as possible before dying himself." Kendeth rubbed his hands together, looking for warmth. "He won't allow you to lock him up."

Turning back to his parents, James asked, "What's going on? Tell us."

"Alright," Kate began with hesitation. "In truth, we didn't leave him in a boarding school on Surpen. We left him in the care of the Surpen King and Queen."

"What?" Reed questioned. "What do you mean?"

"Why don't you start from the beginning," James told her, his face looking strained.

Kate sighed and glanced at Henry. "Eventually, we're going to have to tell them what happened. They'll need to know, since it will help us find a way to keep Rhen on Thestran," Henry whispered. "Why not now?" Kate gave a quick nod and turned to face the table.

"When we left on our trip with Max..." she began, but corrected herself. "Rhen, all those years ago, we stopped first on Neptian to conduct some business. Rhen had reached the Neptian age of marriage, and while we were there, he met and married his wife..." Kate glanced at her lap, as she remembered that fiasco, but she didn't want to get into that one right now, so she continued. "Immediately after Rhen's wedding, we received an urgent communication from the Surpen King, Andres. He asked us for our help with his war on Etsaw and hinted that if we were to help him, he would leave the Convention."

"Wow!" Reed exclaimed. "That would have been enough incentive to make any of us rush to Surpen. Can you imagine the ramifications of removing Surpen from the Convention?"

Kate smiled with gratitude towards Reed. "At the time, we had felt the same way. We helped Andres with his war on Etsaw. Afterwards, he claimed we needed to help him with his war on Roundet, before he would join Thestran's Council. After Roundet, he informed us that he'd 'changed his mind'. When we returned to Surpen to collect Rhen, we discovered that during the time we were gone, Surpen's laws had declared Rhen an 'abandoned' child and Andres and his wife, Orpel, had legally adopted him." Kate stopped talking to take a drink.

"Excuse me?" James asked, his eyes narrowed in disbelief, while the table remained silent.

"Rhen is the legal son of the King and Queen of Surpen. Although he shares your blood, he's technically no longer your brother," Henry clarified.

Kate shook her head. "That's not what James is asking. He wants to know how it happened, and honestly James, I don't know. It was such a stressful time. Andres tricked us completely. From the very beginning, he had been plotting to steal Rhen. We've been asking ourselves why ever since. Why would he do such a thing? Why didn't he just adopt a Surpen? Why did he need Rhen?" Kate rubbed her eyes. "We just don't know the answer. I wish we did."

Charlie surprised everyone by leaning over and putting his arm around Rhen. "Hey, little brother!" he said, while pulling Rhen towards him in a sideways hug. "How's it going?"

Rhen stared at Charlie with an unreadable expression.

"You a Surpen dude now?" Charlie asked. He released Rhen and leaned over to rest his head against Rhen's shoulder.

Instead of shaking him off, Rhen smiled at Charlie. *"This one's funny,"* he told Ceceta. *"He reminds me of Nk. But his breath smells thousands of times worse."* Ceceta giggled, as she stared at her lap.

Ignoring them, Sage asked, "So, what did you do, when you found out Andres had adopted Rhen?"

"What do you think?" Kate snapped. "We argued with Andres, but he made it clear that we couldn't do anything about it. He had already informed the Convention members of the situation and they were poised, ready to attack, should we declare war on Surpen. What could we do?"

"Go to war," James answered. He glanced over at his son, Henry Jr., who was just turning six. He couldn't imagine letting someone take his son away from him.

"We couldn't do that to you," Kate protested. "If we'd gone to war against the Convention, we might have lost. We couldn't risk it. We wanted to protect you, all of you."

"You could have stolen him back," Reed suggested. "You have powers. You should have flown into the Surpen Palace and snatched him back."

"I tried," Kate snapped.

"Themrock!" James swore. "And you think he's going to agree to live on Thestran? Why the hell would he? He's the Surpen Prince! You might have saved us from a war then, but you've certainly doomed us to it now. By the Genister Gods, this is a hell of a mess you've put us in."

"ENOUGH!" Henry yelled. "We made a terrible mistake. We know that. Today, though, we've had a victory. We've removed Rhen from Surpen and returned him to Thestran. After dinner, we'll retire to my chambers to discuss how we're going to accomplish the task of keeping Rhen here. Understood?" Henry paused and reached for Kate's hand. "Tonight's celebration is for Sage and Ryan. Let's honor them and discuss this no further at the table."

After a tense moment, James nodded in agreement and the guests began to talk about the upcoming wedding.

Towards the end of the meal, Kate glanced down the table to see that neither Rhen nor Ceceta had eaten anything. It confused her for a moment, until she remembered that Surpens had special diets. "Oh no," Kate breathed out.

his throat. Stepping back for safety, Henry tripped over the edge of Charlie's empty chair and fell. Instead of crashing to the ground, he felt the wind rush through his hair as Rhen caught him and swung him back up into a standing position.

"Um, thanks," Henry said. He smiled at Rhen and patted his hands on his legs for a minute feeling confused. 'Why had he come down here to see Rhen?' he thought.

"Oh," Henry said, as he remembered what Kate had asked him to do. He gestured up towards the castle with his hand. "Going to show you to your room now," he told his son, with an encouraging smile. Rhen nodded and tossed the black dagger he was holding onto the table. It landed next to his plate with a thud. Rhen held out his hand to Ceceta, then followed Henry across the lawn past the waiting servants.

After they had left, Sarah, the Water Elf Princess, leaned over to pick up Rhen's dagger. It was black and heavy for its size. Aaron, the son of the Fire Elf King, reached over and brushed his fingers gently against the back of Sarah's hand, as he took the dagger from her. Sarah glanced up into his face and winked.

"This is a nasty weapon," Aaron commented, when he noticed the jagged edge along one side of the dagger and the curved tip. Sarah nodded but leaned away from Aaron, when she saw her parents watching.

Across the lawn, Henry took Rhen and Ceceta past several elaborate fountains depicting artists' renderings of the Genister Gods. He explained to Rhen that the Genisters were a species from a different dimension. "They created our Universe and everything in it," he remarked. "When the Genisters finished making the Universe, they decided to take elfin forms and live among us. The Universe was a magnificent place during the Genisters' time. Unfortunately, they're gone now, but they did leave behind a small taste of their amazing powers. Only a few lucky people seem to be born with powers. Your mother's unusual, because she has more powers than anyone else in the Universe," Henry informed Rhen.

They walked up a set of marble stairs, past sculptures of the Genisters. Henry chatted about everything they passed, giving his son a complete explanation of the elves' and Thestrans' beliefs. Out of kindness, Rhen and his wife nodded their heads during the appropriate pauses, as if they understood.

When they entered the Thestran castle, Henry pointed to their left to show them the visitors' office. He explained to Rhen and Ceceta that the palace was shaped like a star with five points or wings. Each wing had a different function – apartments and hotel rooms, offices and meeting rooms for the Council Delgates and the Thestran Royal Family's private living quarters.

Just when it looked like things were about to get out of hand, Ceceta picked up her plate and handed it to Charlie. She smiled at him and bowed once before sitting down again. Charlie looked astonished. He held the plate away from him with disgust.

Rhen nodded. It seemed to him that Ceceta had resolved the issue. He released the hilt of his sword, pushed his plate towards his wife, so they could share, and sat down.

"What? Why did she give me her plate?" Charlie asked, as he turned his head away from the offensive food.

The Air Elf King, Chaster, stood up, his white and blue cape falling to the floor, as he snatched the plate from Charlie. "I think, Charlie, that they thought you were trying to take their food. Rhen was ready to kick your butt, but his wife has kindly saved your neck by giving you her dinner instead."

"What? I don't want their food! I want to get rid of it!"

Chaster looped his hand under Charlie's armpit and forced him to turn away from the table. "We'll be right back," he told the other guests. "I need to explain to Charlie that you don't come between a wild animal and its food." With a jerk, he pulled Charlie towards the castle, as the others settled back into their seats.

Rhen watched the Thestrans. When no one was looking, winked at his wife to thank her for handling the situation.

"Well," Reed's wife, Lilo, commented in a chipper voice. "I think that was enough fun for one night. Come along children. Time for bed." She rose with Susan, James' wife, and together they walked their children towards the palace.

As the evening progressed, Kendeth watched Rhen and his wife murmuring to each other, while ignoring the rest of the table. Rhen had placed his arm around her shoulders. Every now and then, he would lean in towards his wife and brush his lips against her cheek.

When most of the guests had left and Rhen and Ceceta were no longer eating, Kate asked Henry to show them to their bedroom. Rising from his seat, Henry stretched and yawned before walking down the length of the table towards Rhen. He found Rhen and his wife staring into each other's eyes and giggling. Henry stood behind them for a moment feeling awkward, before reaching out to touch Rhen on the shoulder.

Rhen shot out of his chair like a bullet, a small, jagged dagger appeared out of nowhere in his left hand. Henry was surprised to find the dagger poised at

Charlie's eyes grew wide at the sight of Rhen eating meat. He pushed his chair back from the table, turned and vomited onto the ground behind him, making the children squeal.

Rhen glanced over at Charlie. *"Yes,"* he told Ceceta. "*He definitely reminds me of Nk. No doubt about it."* After a moment's hesitation, Rhen added, *"Please eat. We aren't on Surpen. You don't have to wait until I'm finished."* Ceceta hesitated, but hunger won out. She pulled some of the raw meat onto her plate.

While the children at the table shrieked, Rhen, keeping his face expressionless, pulled the brains out of the head of the pig in front of him then sliced some intestines into strips and slurped them down like spaghetti.

Reed suppressed the urge to vomit himself and complained, "I think he's doing that on purpose just to excite the children."

"That would be a good sign," Kendeth replied. "Maybe there's some Thestran left in him."

Charlie vomited again. "Ugh! How can an elf eat meat? What's the matter with him?" he announced, as he wiped his sleeve across his mouth. He turned and glared at Rhen. Leaning over to point his finger at Rhen's food, Charlie yelled, "NO! BAD! DON'T EAT MEAT!"

Rhen rose to his feet, his face an expressionless mask.

"Oh, my God," Kate gasped. "CHARLIE SIT DOWN!"

"CHARLIE STOP!" Henry screamed.

"NO!" Charlie yelled at Rhen again. "NO, MEAT! BAD ELF!" He shook his finger in Rhen's face as one would a disobedient dog.

Rhen frowned at Charlie, before turning towards his wife and asking her in Surpen, *"What's the matter with him? Does he want to fight?"* Ceceta shrugged. She didn't have any idea what Charlie was doing. Placing his right hand on the hilt of his sword, Rhen began to pull it from its sheath.

"IT'S NOT NORMAL FOR ELVES TO EAT MEAT!" Charlie yelled at Rhen. "YOU'RE STRANGE IN THE HEAD! ELVES ARE VEGETARIANS FOR GOD'S SAKE! OUR BODIES CAN'T PROCESS MEAT!"

Henry was screaming at the head of the table for Charlie to sit down, while Kate was running around the table to try to stop him. Many of the children had started to cry.

"Quick," she called out to a servant. "Bring Rhen and his wife the uncooked head of a pig, as well as a cow's heart, intestines and liver. And pour them blood to drink, absolutely nothing else."

"What are you doing?" Reed asked. "He's an elf."

"They're Surpens," Kate told him.

When she didn't elaborate, Reed added, "And?"

"Surpens only eat meat. Flavored meat and..."

"WHAT!" several of the elves at the table exclaimed.

"It will kill Rhen," Reed added. "Elves can't eat meat."

"Well, I guess they actually can," Kate snapped. "It's just your religion that stops you from eating meat, not your body."

Sage dropped her head into her hands. "He goes against all of the teachings of the Genister Gods! They'd be furious if they knew about this."

"He isn't an elf," Chaster, the Air Elf King, declared, as the other elfin royals nodded in agreement.

"Please tell me you don't eat meat," Charlie howled next to Rhen.

Rhen looked at him and replied in Surpen, *"What's the matter with you? Did a cow sit on your head at birth?"*

"It's nice to meet you too!" Charlie replied with a smile, forgetting what had upset him earlier. He tried to repeat the Surpen words that Rhen had just spoken. Rhen put his head down next to Ceceta's, as he tried to hide his mirth at Charlie's attempt to speak Surpen. Poor Ceceta couldn't help herself. She burst out laughing.

"They're laughing at us," Kate declared. "Mocking us for forgetting to give them food they can eat."

"Now, Kate," Henry told her. "We don't know that." Although it was clear, he wasn't sure.

The Thestran's liveried servants rushed forth with platters of raw meat, which they placed in front of Rhen and Ceceta. They poured blood into the Surpen's goblets and stepped back to wait for further instructions. At the sight of the uncooked meat and animal brains on the table, the children in attendance giggled and groaned, but they continued to look on with morbid curiosity, as Rhen took a bite of raw food.

Henry gestured in front of them down the Grand Hallway of the Family's wing. Rhen and his wife nodded with appreciation. The corridor was long and decorated with murals and portraits. Individuals from different planets hurried past them on their way to events and meetings. There were numerous carved, wooden doors along the sides of the hallway. About a quarter of the way down the hallway, Henry stopped to show them one of the stairways to the Royal Family's private section of the castle. The stairway was wide and painted in the Royal Family's colors of gold and black. It had golden handrails that were full of intricate carvings and decorated with rare jewels. Four guards in black and gold military outfits stood on either side of the entrance. "I must confess," Henry told Rhen. "The guards are really just for show. The Genisters placed a spell on our family's staircases. It's impossible for anyone to enter our private residence, unless they are related to us by blood or have been given special permission to enter by a family member."

Henry started up the stairs but paused. "You know, this has been fun. Let me show you more of the castle." Turning around, he motioned for Rhen and Ceceta to follow him down the hallway. He opened some of the wooden doors, to show them Thestran's Council Chamber, various meeting rooms, restaurants, cafés, an enormous concert hall and the formal, master dining room. "The biggest fountain in the Universe is in the center of our castle," Henry informed Rhen and Ceceta, as he took them up the main staircase into the Thestran Royal Family's private wing of the castle. "The first floor of our wing contains our family's private living chambers, several common rooms, the family library, a private music room and the family's private dining room. The second floor contains our bedrooms and a private medical facility. The third floor is our activity floor and the fourth floor has our theater plus additional activity rooms and a pool."

Henry continued up the stairs until he reached the second floor. The white hallway was decorated with elaborate wall sconces, artists' pictures of the Genisters and various side tables and chairs. The floor of the hallway was covered with a thick, golden carpet that had black trim. Henry stopped in front of a bedroom door made of mahogany and stained a dark brown. Every door on the second floor looked the same. Rhen wondered why they were alike, but he couldn't figure out how to ask Henry his question in Thestran, so he assumed the doors were similar to act as a form of camouflage, protecting the Royal Family members, in case intruders entered their home while they slept.

"Here it is my boy," Henry announced. He opened Rhen's bedroom door and motioned for them to go in. Out of politeness, Rhen and his wife indicated to Henry that he should enter first, so he stepped into the room. "Do you remember your old bedroom?" Henry asked Rhen, as he waved his hand about.

Rhen and Ceceta gazed about the room, taking in the elaborate Thestran decorations. They both felt the room was too cluttered. Henry stared at his son's face with a wistful expression, as Rhen's eyes scanned the living room with its sofas, chairs, tables, lamps, portraits, toys, books and childhood knickknacks.

"I guess you don't," Henry commented, when he realized Rhen was seeing his bedroom for what seemed to be the first time. "Well, just so you know, all of the bedrooms are the same," he explained. "You have your entrance area, your living area, the bedroom off to one side, the closets for both you and your wife, the bathroom, a small eating area and the bar," he added, pointing to a fully stocked bar in the corner. Henry laughed without humor. "I guess in your case, we need to remove the liquor and bring in different flavors of blood." He shook his head feeling wretched and continued talking to himself. "We haven't done very well with either of our youngest boys. Charlie's out of control. He drinks so much we had to remove the bar area in his room and you..." Henry glanced up at Rhen with a concerned expression. "You're a completely different problem. If the oracles weren't screaming at us to do something about you, we probably would've left you alone on Surpen." Henry searched Rhen's face, and for a moment, he caught a glimpse of a memory of his son during happier times. Sighing, he added somberly, "I wonder what's going to happen to you."

For the next hour, Henry continued to talk to Rhen and his wife. When Ceceta yawned, he realized it was time to go. He rose from the chair he had been sitting on and bid them good night, reaching out to give Rhen a quick hug, as he passed by where he sat on the sofa. Rhen remained still in Henry's arms. Henry glanced into his son's face and found it devoid of expression. "You're a good boy Rhen," he told his son in parting. "I know we'll find you in there somewhere." With a wave of his hand, he left for the night.

As soon as Henry was gone, Ceceta started to laugh. "You let him hug you," she teased Rhen in Surpen.

Rhen grabbed Ceceta up into his arms and kissed her. He had been waiting all night to get her alone. "Yeah," he admitted, as he kissed Ceceta's face and neck. She felt good in his arms. He was ready to move on with their evening.

"Are we alone?" Ceceta asked with concern in Surpen. "Are they watching us?"

Rhen closed his eyes. He opened them a moment later. "We're alone. They aren't listening to us."

"So," Ceceta began, as Rhen took her hand and pulled her into the bedroom. "Tell me why we're here and why we're alone." Rhen hadn't had a chance to explain things to her before they had left Surpen. She was dying to know why they had been sent to Thestran without an escort. Rhen laughed, picked her up into his arms and tossed her onto the bed. He unhitched his weapons belt and dropped it to the floor before jumping onto the bed and reaching out for her. Ceceta wiggled away from him asking, "Why did your father send us here?"

"Later, Ceceta," Rhen replied, as he kicked off one of his military boots.

"NOW," she demanded. Ceceta spun to her right and got off the bed.

With a heavy sigh, Rhen dropped his other boot onto the floor and said, "We're spying on them. Dad sent us here so that I could examine their castle and assess its weak points…"

"For future attack purposes?" Ceceta interrupted.

"Yes," Rhen agreed, as he began to pull off his tunic. "I've already pinpointed where we should attack. I just need to discover the extent of their forces and we can go."

"Why did he send us here alone?" Ceceta asked.

"He thought we'd have more success in spying, if we came alone, and he was right. Henry just gave us a complete tour of the castle." Rhen paused to search Ceceta's face. "Are you worried? You know nothing will happen to us. The Thestrans are too insipid to go after me. They still consider me to be a part of their 'family'," he commented with derision.

Ceceta shook her head in disagreement. This was a sore point between them. "Rhen," she began with hesitation. "You are a part of their family. You look exactly like James and Henry, you're built like Reed and you have sculpted ears."

"CECETA!" Rhen snapped. "I can't understand why you're always harping on this issue. My family is Andres and Orpel, the Surpen King and Queen. The Thestrans mean nothing to me."

The two of them stared at each other in silence for a tense moment.

"I'm sorry honey," Ceceta began. "I just…you still have your birth family and mine is gone. I wish I had had the opportunity to at least see them again before they died."

"I'm sorry my love," Rhen replied, feeling remorseful. He reached out for her hand. Ceceta's family had tried to rescue her two years after Kate and Henry had left them on Surpen. The Surpens had massacred them. She didn't have anyone left.

Ceceta slid onto the bed next to Rhen. He folded her up into his arms and held her. "I'm sorry. Let's not talk about it anymore," he told her, as he lifted her chin up and bent his head down to kiss her. Ceceta wrapped her arms around him and held on tight.

Chapter 7

Lilly walked into the sitting room that adjoined her parents' bedroom. After last night's unproductive meeting, James had asked his family and the elfin royals to study up on Surpen, so they could discuss ways to keep Rhen on Thestran before breakfast. Lilly tapped the leather binding on the old, black book she had received from James. At first, she had been skeptical about studying Surpen. She didn't think there would be anything useful in these books that James was handing out, but once she'd started to read about Surpen's backward, male-dominated society, she had become fascinated and had stayed up until 3:00 in the morning. Lilly had made an important discovery last night. She couldn't wait to discuss it with the others.

As Lilly walked across the plush, beige carpet to get herself a cup of tea from the table near the back wall, she nodded to the other people in the room. Her sister, Rachel, was pouring herself some coffee. They kissed hello as Charlie strolled into the room sipping his morning cocktail. Charlie flopped down onto one of the three sofas in front of the fireplace and announced, "Since I didn't sleep last night, I was able to spot Rhen leaving the castle at 4:00 in the morning. So... how about that? Rhen was running around at 4:00 in the morning."

"Charlie," Kate replied with fatigue. "He runs the entire Surpen military force in a world where the strongest man is king and the weakest man is a slave." Charlie gave her a blank look. "All Surpen men work out in the morning for two to three hours before their morning prayers."

"Seriously?" Charlie gasped. "Do you think Rhen's in good shape?"

Lilly couldn't help but laugh, as Reed reached across the back of the couch to smack Charlie on the head.

"What?" he asked, a goofy smile on his face.

James cleared his throat, so they quieted down. Rising to stand in front of the stone hearth on the left side of the room, James began their meeting by discussing the Surpen's belief in one God. He informed them about Surpen's Debrino Codes, which were the current rules the Surpens lived by. "Over a hundred years ago, a powerful man, by the name of Debrino, convinced the Surpen King to install his Codes, in order to make Surpen successful. The King, at that time, had been weak, so to protect himself from Debrino, he gave Debrino complete control over Surpen. Once Debrino's Codes were in place, Surpen's open, free, egalitarian culture turned into an obedient, slave driven, closed society," James explained.

"Not only did Debrino introduce slaves into Surpen's culture, but he also banned education for women and stripped them of their once equal power to men.

Debrino's Codes of Order are a long list of rules the Surpens must follow. If any Surpen is found breaking the Codes, they're punished rather harshly in the manner laid out by Debrino himself. Due to the seriousness of the punishments, most Surpens follow Debrino's Codes without exception," James concluded.

As soon as James was finished, Lilly raised her hand to get everyone's attention. "Right, right, right, we all know this. I'm sure it was in all your books, along with the fact that Surpen's only eat meat, they don't allow music, dancing, art…blah, blah, blah. We all know this, right?" Glancing about the room, she noticed that most of her family had blank faces. Lilly narrowed her eyes. "You did read your books, didn't you?" There was a collective murmur in the room and Lilly shook her head. It seemed obvious they hadn't even scanned their books last night. Lilly grinned. Her news was going to come as a shock.

"So," she said, her eyes glinting mischievously. "You all know why the King of Surpen has latched onto our little brother, right?" No one answered. With care, Lilly opened her book. It was very old and the pages were brown along the edges. Trying to keep the ancient book in one piece, she placed it on the wooden coffee table in front of the fireplace.

Pointing at an artist's sketch of a green, dragon like creature, Lilly asked, "What do you think that is?"

James stepped forward to look at the beast. It was a greenish lizard, almost triple the size of a horse. The creature had pointy ears, sharp teeth, long talons on its front and back feet and small, strong looking wings.

"That my dear family," Lilly told them, after everyone had had a chance to see the book. "Is Rhen, the Surpen God of War!"

"What!" James exclaimed.

"Hell," Reed hissed through his teeth.

"Holy Crap!" Charlie laughed out.

When Lilly saw her mother shake her head in denial, she added, "You heard me correctly. This creature is Rhen, the Surpen God of War. Five hundred years ago, Surpen's oracles predicted their Supreme God would send them Rhen, a creature of such massive power and strength, he would be known as the Surpen God of War. During his time on Surpen, he would conquer the Universe, making Surpen the greatest, most powerful civilization of all time. Mom, when you left Max with the King of Surpen, did you by any chance mention to him that Max's middle name was Rhen?"

Kate shook her head and mumbled, "He seemed to know it already."

"If that's the case, his 'adoption' was definitely pre-meditated. The Surpen King was probably planning Max's abduction…adoption, whatever you want to call it, from the moment he first discovered that Max, 'Rhen', had been born to the most powerful Queen since the Genisters' time."

"I bet," Lilly added, "that after he heard Max's full name, he decided the oracles' predictions were finally coming true, and with proper Surpen grooming, he would be able to fine tune this Thestran child, through brainwashing or what have you, into becoming Rhen, the Surpen God of War. The King of Surpen has been grooming Max to take over the Universe and our current oracles are predicting that he's going to do it."

Charlie coughed in the silence after Lilly's monologue. "But, he doesn't look anything like that," he protested, while pointing at the picture in the book.

Rachel rolled her blue eyes at him. "Charlie," she told him with fatigue. "Anyone with the right powers could change Max into this God of War creature. Just look at Sage. She's changed Ryan completely for the wedding."

"I have not!" Sage protested.

"You know what I mean," Rachel told her. "You've genetically altered him to stay on land."

"But I haven't changed HIM!" Sage snapped back. "He's still the same."

"Technically..." Rachel began.

"STOP IT!" Kate yelled at them. She snatched up Lilly's book and walked around the couch towards Henry, who was standing beside Reed. Holding the book out to him, she asked, "What have we done Henry?"

"Not you mom," Sage blurted out. "The King of Surpen. You didn't do anything wrong, he did."

"I guess we now know what the Surpen King has planned for Rhen. He wants to turn him into this creature," James stated. He ran his fingertips along the top of the mantle, touching the cool, rounded, grey stones. "I doubt if anyone on Surpen has the power to do it, but their fellow Convention members certainly do, and there are a lot of oracles, who are predicting they'll be successful. We also know, from these same oracles, that if we keep Rhen here on Thestran, and bring him back to our ways, we'll stop him and save the Universe. Obviously, we know what we must do. The question is how? I open the discussion to all. What are we going to do about Rhen?"

The room was silent. It appeared no one had any idea what to do with Rhen.

"He's been gone for so long," Rachel remarked. "We don't know anything about him. We can't relate to him. I have no idea how to convince him to stay."

"Could we explain the situation to him?" Reed asked the others. "Do you think he'd agree to stay here to stop Universal warfare?"

"Unlikely," Kendeth remarked. "Surpens thrive on war. They conquer new planets all the time to sustain their way of life. They just don't have enough natural resources to support themselves on their desert planet without taking others."

Charlie burped then asked, "Why do we need to change Rhen to our school system? I thought he liked his boarding school?"

"Charlie, you imbecile," his brother, William, snarled. "We found out last night that he was never at a boarding school on Surpen. It was all a hoax. Rhen was adopted by the…"

"THAT'S IT!" Lilly yelled, interrupting William. She jumped up out of her seat. "Charlie, you're a genius! We'll enroll Rhen at the Elfin University."

"He'll never go for it," Reed told his sister, before turning back to his book, hoping to get some ideas.

"No," Kate contradicted. "He's not the problem, it's Andres. The Surpen King would never allow it."

"How much power does Andres have over Rhen?" Kendeth asked.

"He controls him completely," Kate replied.

"Perhaps not," Kendeth suggested. "Rhen's the head of Surpen's Military. Perhaps Andres doesn't have complete control over him. If that's the case, then Lilly," he said as he glanced over at her, "you're on!"

"Your plan?" James prompted.

Kendeth moved over to stand next to James by the hearth. He was an old man, who had lived with the Royal Family for years. Kate's children had grown up calling him 'grandfather'. When Kate was young and hadn't known her path in life, Kendeth had helped her find her way.

When all eyes were upon him, Kendeth began, "Here's a man, no, he's a boy. Let's not forget, Rhen is a boy. He's only 16 years old. He has grown up in an oppressive, over-bearing society. What are 16-year-old Thestran boys like? Do you remember? They're defiant, disobedient, stubborn, out to prove themselves, wouldn't you agree? Rhen's angry at us now. I say let's turn his anger towards the King of Surpen. Let's make Surpen the one he wants to rebel against."

"That's a great idea, but what does it have to do with sending him to school?" Reed asked.

"Last night, I noticed that Rhen is very much in love with his wife. She appears to hold a lot of power over him. Let's focus our efforts on his wife. James has just informed us that Surpen women are not allowed to be educated. That's great! What Neptian woman would stand for that? Let's pit Rhen against Andres. Let's convince his wife to go to the Elfin University. If my gut instinct is correct, he won't want to refuse her, nor will he want to leave her. We all know what Andres' reaction will be, when Rhen goes to him to ask for permission to go to school. Andres will tell him no, which will make Rhen mad. If Rhen has any Thestran in him at all, he'll fight his father." Kendeth smiled. "You know, the more I think about it, the more I believe it'll work. We will 'deprogram' Rhen, making him Thestran again, by sending him to the University."

"It'll never work," Kate declared. "You don't understand the Surpens. Women are subservient. Rhen would never give up his role as the Commander of the Surpen Military simply to return to school for his wife. Not only that, but even if Rhen did protest, even if we could get Rhen to want to go to the Elfin University with his wife, Andres would never let him."

"Kate?" Kendeth asked. He was surprised by her defeatist attitude. Kate turned away from him, refusing to meet his eyes. "I understand Surpen women are nothing more than property, but from my observations, I can assure you that Rhen loves his wife. If we can convince her to do this, I'm positive he'll tag along with or without Andres' blessing."

"No, he won't," Kate protested. "He will order her to return to Surpen immediately after Sage's wedding."

"Kate, listen to yourself," Kendeth urged. "You're giving up before we've even started. Remember, we're talking about young love. Children, who are Rhen's age, will disobey their parents over love. We've seen it a thousand times. Our job is to convince Rhen's wife to go to the Elfin University. If we can do that, I'm gambling Rhen will make sure she's given permission to go and he'll go with her. He won't want to be parted from her. If Rhen agrees to go to school, we have a chance of saving the Universe. If he doesn't, we'll need to stop him from returning to Surpen, even if it means we have to kill him."

The room erupted into conversation after Kendeth's last sentence.

"It's the truth," he told them, when things quieted down. "If Rhen refuses to go to the Elfin University, we'll have no choice but to kill him. He can't return to Surpen or he'll take over the Universe. We must stop him here. This is our only chance."

Okay," James said. "We understand the importance of this. Let's take a vote. All in favor of convincing Rhen's wife to go to the University, raise your hand." Every hand in the room went up into the air.

"So, you agree too," Charlie asked William, when he saw William's hand above his head.

"It's not like we had any other plan to vote for, did we?" he replied in a whisper.

"Great," James continued. "Lilly and Rachel, you focus on Rhen's wife during breakfast. Tell her all about the superior education she would get at the Elfin University. Oh, and speak in Neptian so she understands. Reed, you and William tell Rhen about the amazing sports available at school. Perhaps you can peak his competitive interest. The rest of us will try to maintain some semblance of normalcy by talking about Sage's wedding. That's it for now. This meeting is officially adjourned."

As they walked downstairs to the family's private dining chamber, Lilly and Rachel discussed their strategy for convincing Rhen's wife to go to the Elfin University. Entering the large, rectangular room, they found James' and Reed's wives and children already seated at the formally set table in the center of the room, along with many of the wedding guests. "Good," Lilly commented, while glancing over the seats. "Rhen isn't here yet. Let's try to finish our breakfast before he and his wife arrive, so we can focus on her." Rachel nodded in agreement and the two of them moved over to the buffet table that the staff had arranged under the windows on the left side of the room.

When James entered the room, he informed everyone about the Royal Family's decision to convince Rhen and his wife to attend the Elfin University. The wedding guests were eager to help them with their efforts.

Lilly approached her usual seat at the table but hesitated. "James, where should I sit? I want to be close to them, when I talk about the Elfin University, but since Rhen is a traveling dignitary, he should be up next to you at the head of the table."

"We want Rhen to realize he's a part of your family, he's not Surpen, so he should be seated half way down the table between Rachel and the Wood Elf King, Estan," Kendeth told her.

"Okay," Lilly agreed, taking her seat. "Mom, what's the name of Rhen's wife?"

Kate blanched and glanced over at Henry, who appeared embarrassed. "We...we don't remember," he told Lilly. "We feel dreadful about forgetting her name. Rhen's wedding on Neptian was so sudden and quick. We departed less than two days after it for Surpen. We didn't get the opportunity to really meet Rhen's wife or her family. And then, once we were on Surpen, well, things just fell apart."

"You don't remember the name of Rhen's wife?" Sage asked her parents sounding shocked.

"Well, we were only with her for two days," Kate began. She stopped speaking, when she saw the horrified looks on her children's faces.

"What about her family?" Reed asked his parents. "Can you find out her name from them?"

"They're dead," Henry answered.

"Dead?" Reed asked. "Her entire family is dead?"

"Yes," Henry agreed with a nod, hoping they wouldn't ask how her family had died.

"That's too bad," Sage said. She reached out for her fiancé's hand and squeezed it.

"That's worse than bad," Lilly commented with chagrin. "That's horrible! How are we supposed to talk to her, if we don't know her name?"

"Just pretend you forgot it," William told his sister.

Lilly shook her head. "That doesn't feel right. I can't ask my sister-in-law what her name is! I should know it. We all should know it."

A servant approached Kate to ask what he should prepare Rhen for breakfast. "Oh, thank you for asking. I keep forgetting Surpens have dietary restrictions. He won't be eating pancakes or toast, will he?" she said with a laugh, before turning to Henry. "Actually, I'm not really sure what Surpens eat for breakfast. Do you remember Henry?"

"Bloodworms," Henry responded with a grimace. "I'll never forget our first day on Surpen, when we learned that all Surpen children were required to eat bloodworms. I should have known something was wrong that first morning, when bloodworms were placed into the two bowls at the breakfast table for Max and his wife." He turned towards the servant. "Do we have any bloodworms?"

"No, sir," the man replied.

"Well," Kate began. "Let's see if he'll enjoy fish. Why don't you bring out a bowl with four live fish, some bloody, uncooked meat and maybe some uncooked chicken pieces?" The servant nodded and turned to go, but Kate called after him, "And don't forget, they only drink blood." A shiver of disgust passed through the man, as he bowed to Kate in response and left.

James' son looked up at Kate and asked, "Is Uncle Rhen a vampire?"

Everyone chuckled. "No, sweetie," she told him. "Vampires don't exist. They are just stories."

Chapter 8

Rhen hummed a tune that was playing in his head, as he and Ceceta walked down the empty hallway towards the Thestran Royal Family's Dining Chamber. He couldn't remember the last time he had felt so happy. After his workout this morning, Ceceta had surprised him in the bathroom. They had made out in the bathtub and then a short while later on the couch. It had been an exceptional morning.

Rhen stopped before the doorway to the dining room just long enough to finish the song he was humming. Ceceta beamed up at him, a light blush on her cheeks. She nodded with approval, when he finished, and Rhen, on impulse, leaned down to give her a quick kiss. Reaching out, he opened the dark wooden door to the dining room. It was heavy and Rhen was tempted to hold it open for Ceceta, as he had seen some of the Thestran men do for their women, but he knew he needed to be careful. You never knew who could be spying for whom, and the last thing he needed, was for Andres to find out he was treating Ceceta like an equal. He didn't want to be banned from seeing her as punishment for disobeying Surpen's laws regarding women. Rhen stepped through the doorway quickly, hoping Ceceta would follow him before the door swung shut. Keeping his face expressionless, he scanned the crowded table before him. There were a lot of elves in the room. From their dress, he could tell the royals from all four elfin tribes were present. 'Good,' he thought. There were some things he needed to learn about them.

Most of the people at the table were staring at them. Rhen was pleased to see from their faces that they were impressed. He knew the royal blue tunic he was wearing was quite beautiful. It had an intricate pattern of green and gold piping around the collar and sleeves and a single row of golden triangles were outlined in the same piping along the bottom hem by his knees. He had chosen to wear a necklace of braided gold and silver around his neck that was very valuable and he had polished his four swords, while Ceceta was dressing, so he knew they shined in the morning sun as they hung from his weapons belt.

Rhen also knew his wife looked stunning today. Ceceta had worn a gorgeous assortment of soft, orange robes that were decorated with red and yellow piping. She had left her long, blond hair unbound and it hung loosely around her, covering, in part, the leather bag that was hung over her left shoulder.

Rhen was tempted to read the Thestran's thoughts, but years ago, he had promised Ceceta he would never, ever, ever read anyone's thoughts. Fortunately, it appeared he didn't need to read their thoughts, because Lilly announced them.

"Well, one thing is for sure, those Surpens have beautiful clothing," Lilly told the room, as several people nodded their heads in agreement, while gazing at Rhen and Ceceta.

To keep himself from laughing, Rhen thought about his mission. He scanned the room to make sure it was secure then moved over towards the buffet table. Ceceta followed along behind him. Rhen's swords rested against his thighs, as he strode across the room. Years of practice had shown him how to walk in such a way as to keep them from bouncing about. It was a skill he needed in battle. Rhen noted with pleasure that King James' eyes never left his swords. He wondered what James was thinking. Was he remembering their fight on Rowan? Was he embarrassed that he had succumbed to Rhen's skills? Rhen was tempted to read James' mind, but he didn't. A promise was a promise, and the last thing he wanted to do was to make Ceceta mad at him for breaking his vow. Today was their last day alone together. He wanted to enjoy it as much as possible.

Rhen picked up a golden plate and peered into the first serving tray on the buffet table. Inside it was a mushy, white food that assaulted his nostrils. Cream of wheat. 'It has to be,' he thought. He had seen it before on the Planet of Tgarus. Ceceta looked up at him hopefully, as she picked up her plate, but Rhen shook his head. They couldn't eat it.

Rhen and Ceceta proceeded down the buffet table peering into each tray. Nothing was edible. When they reached the end of the line, they noticed a few smaller plates of meat and a round bowl with fish swimming in it, shoved behind a platter of green fruit. They both gave a tired sort of sigh. "*Clearly our meal was an afterthought,*" Rhen whispered to Ceceta in Surpen. "*And what's with the fish? Don't they realize fish are revered on Surpen?*"

"*Do you think they expect us to eat them?*" Ceceta whispered.

"*My God!*" Rhen replied, sounding horrified. "*You think?*" Ceceta's round eyes looked up at him confirming the idea and the two of them started to laugh. When they had stopped, Rhen added, "*They really know nothing about us, do they?*"

"*No,*" Ceceta agreed. The two of them watched the fish in silence for a few minutes, as they swam around in circles in the glass bowl. "*They're so beautiful,*" Ceceta whispered in Surpen, as the four, orange and white fish completed another circle of the bowl.

"*Yes, my love, they are.*"

After several more minutes had passed, and Rhen and Ceceta still hadn't moved, William said, "Perhaps they don't know they can eat the fish? Maybe they think it's an arrangement?"

Rhen's ears twitched, as he picked up William's words. Henry had spoken with them at such length last night that he had learned the Thestran's language. Languages had always been easy for him. He was pleased to know Thestran. It would help his father, when they conquered this planet.

Out of the corner of his eye, Rhen watched Kate shrug in response. He could feel William's eyes on his body. "Do you think he wears anything under that tunic or do you think he just lets it hang in the breeze?" William asked the room.

A small boy, who was sitting beside James, piped up, "The Quinxos, Jenpers and Mericoles all wear underwear under their skirts but the Ameripans and Fawstars don't."

James gave the boy a loving look and patted his head. Rhen watched the exchange out of the corner of his eye. "That's right," James agreed with pride.

Rhen made special note of the child. They would have to kill him, when they conquered Thestran, so there could be no disputes over the throne. Although he abhorred the idea of killing children, Rhen had gotten used to it. All of the members of the Convention followed the practice and it had served them well.

While Rhen was committing James' child to memory, a small, blond-haired girl in a green dress, with green ribbons in her hair, marched over to the buffet table. She paused beside Rhen, as she gazed at the platter of green fruit next to the fish. Rhen watched her push down on her dress to smooth it. She picked up a muffin from one of the platters on the table and looked up at him. Rhen stared at her without any expression on his face. Foreign children made him nervous. They were unpredictable. The girl gave him her brightest smile, so Rhen responded with a curt nod, before turning back to look at the fish bowl. He figured it was best to dismiss her.

Realizing that she was being ignored, the girl bent over to look underneath Rhen's tunic. She wanted to be the one to answer William's question. As she leaned over, she touched the trim on the bottom hem of Rhen's tunic. He felt it and spun around, grabbing her arm with his hand then flinging her about and twisting her arm up behind her back. The movement sent her muffin flying across the room, where it smacked into the side of the Wood Elf King's head, before landing on the ground in a pile of crumbs. The girl cried out, more in shock than in pain at Rhen's handling of her.

Rhen glared at the room full of people, while holding the child immobile. As he stared at their faces, he noticed the overt concern on Reed's face and the empty seat beside Reed's wife, Lilo. The child must be Reed's. From their expressions, he gathered they hadn't asked her to approach him. Satisfied, Rhen shoved the girl away from his body. She stumbled forward and fell to the ground but got up without crying and ran back to her mother. Lilo kissed the girl's hands, elbows and knees then told her to sit back down. The room was silent as the girl took her seat.

"Dude, you didn't have to shove her," Charlie told Rhen.

Rhen glanced at Charlie, debating whether he should say something, but changed his mind and turned back to the fishbowl, dismissing the incident.

As soon as Rhen's back was turned, the table erupted, as everyone started to talk at once: 'He's so rude', 'I hate it when he dismisses us like we are nothing', 'Rhen was unduly harsh to Alexa', 'Someone should shove Rhen so he can see what it feels like', 'How did he know she was there, she barely touched him', 'Rhen can't be very smart or else he wouldn't need to resort to violence with a child'.

As their comments filled in the room, Rhen smiled to himself. Good. It was better if they felt this way about him. He didn't like them, so he wouldn't have expected them to like him. Besides, it would make it easier for him to conquer their planet if they hated him.

When the room calmed down, Rhen and his wife were still standing in front of the fish bowl. "Why aren't they moving?" Rachel asked Lilly, who shrugged.

"Maybe it's because his balls are cold," William mumbled to himself, but Rachel heard him.

"Jeez, William," Rachel snapped. "If you're so curious to know what's under his tunic, why don't you just go ask!"

"Hmm," William said. He looked up from his plate and noticed everyone staring at him. "Why not? It's not like he'll understand me." Rising from his seat, William tossed his napkin onto his chair and sauntered over to the buffet table.

Rhen sensed his approach and turned towards him. He didn't like William. William was one of Kate and Henry's younger sons, therefore he would never rise to a position of power. Whether it was for this reason or not, there was an undercurrent of uncontrollable rage within William that made him cruel. He reminded Rhen of Aul, the Surpe who had been Commander of Surpen's military before him. Aul used to torture prisoners for pleasure.

"Assuming he could understand what I'm saying," William addressed the dining room, while stroking his red and brown flecked goatee. "How would you suppose I should ask?" Keeping his eyes on the main table, while leaning his trim backside up against the buffet table, William said, "Excuse me little brother, how's it hanging or do you feel a bit of a breeze under there? You know you're tall enough that short people can look right up your skirt, is that a problem? I like your jewelry. Do you always dress in drag, and if so, are you wearing women's underwear?" William smiled triumphantly as several people laughed. Feeling inspired, he continued, "Or maybe I should just ask…so, little brother, do you get hair in your ass when you ride a horse?"

"Sit down William!" James barked. He'd had enough. There was no need for William to mock Rhen, simply because he didn't speak Thestran.

William chuckled, but it was clear that he was now uncomfortable. He had lost his audience. Turning, he found Rhen staring at him with an odd, confused expression on his face. Feeling a rush of anger towards his youngest brother, William reached over and grabbed a fish out of the fishbowl. He slapped it down onto Rhen's plate. "You eat it," he snarled, while miming the motion of eating.

Rhen continued to stare at William, only now his face was expressionless.

Tiring of the situation, William returned to his seat.

Rhen watched William until he had placed his napkin back in his lap. After William was settled, Rhen picked up the fish on his plate and handed it to Ceceta. *"Put it in your bag,"* he told her in Surpen. When Ceceta looked up at him with concern, he added, *"Don't worry. I'll keep them alive until we can release them at home."* Ceceta nodded and waited, as Rhen handed her the rest of the fish from the bowl.

"I can't believe they were serving us fish," Ceceta murmured in Surpen with disapproval.

"Why are they doing that?" Sage asked, as they watched Ceceta take the fish from Rhen and put them in her bag. Her question was answered with silence. No one knew.

"Her bag is going to stink when the fish die," Ryan stated.

After Rhen and Ceceta had placed all of the fish into Ceceta's bag, they filled their plates with raw meat and walked over towards the main table. A member of the staff stepped forward to pull out a chair for Ceceta. Without any hesitation, Rhen sat down in it, his swords slipping between the back rails of the chair, as he pulled it closer to the table to eat. The confused servant turned to pull out another chair for Ceceta, but found she was already seated. Last night, Rhen had given Ceceta permission to sit with him during their meals on Thestran. She was delighted to be included and smiled, as she pulled her chair up to the fancy table with its white table cloth, gold silverware and crystal glasses.

"We need to switch seats," Rhen mumbled in Surpen, before Ceceta had picked up her fork. Ceceta nodded and stood up to change seats with her husband.

"Do I smell?" the Wood Elf King, Estan, asked his wife, Ralis, in a teasing voice, when Rhen moved away from him.

"No," Henry answered. Rhen's eyes glanced over at him. He was curious to hear Henry's explanation. "Surpen custom dictates that a man's wife must always be below him. Rhen and his wife switched places to mark that distinction. He's closer to the head of the table now, so he's in the superior seat." Everyone at the table nodded their heads, as Rhen shoved his first bite into his mouth. He was impressed with Henry's explanation, even if it wasn't correct. Surpen women weren't allowed to sit at a table with men, so Henry's clarification for why they had changed seats was wrong. No, they had changed seats simply to give Rhen a better view of the Thestrans in power. He was working and needed to see them to study them.

Rhen motioned for Ceceta to begin eating. She tore into her food. Their morning activities had left her famished. With her fingers, Ceceta ripped apart the thick piece of beef on her plate and shoved a chunk of the meat into her mouth, savoring the rich juices as they rolled down her throat.

Rhen caught site of James nodding to Reed. 'What's that all about?' he wondered. Reed opened his mouth to discuss with William the amazing sports that were offered at the Elfin University. Reed compared the University's athletes to the Gods and mocked other solar systems for their attempts to beat them in competitions. Rhen tilted his head to the left, when he heard Lilly clear her throat to tell Rachel in Neptian about the wonderful education they had received at the Elfin University.

'What are they doing?' Rhen thought to himself. Their conversations were downright comical. Had they lost their minds? He was there to scout out their territory for future invasion and they were talking about…school? Rhen put his hand over his face to cover his eyes, as he rolled them with disbelief. He was about to make fun of the Thestrans to Ceceta but stopped, when he caught sight of her hopeful face. She understood Lilly and Rachel and was desperate to talk to them. From her furtive glances in their direction, it was obvious she was intrigued by their conversation and wanted to join in. Rhen dropped his hand down and used his fork to stab a chunk of meat with force. Damn them. They were trying to get to him through his wife. It was so blatant. He remembered his father telling him that the Thestrans were tricky. His Dad was right.

After twenty torturous minutes of Ceceta begging him with her eyes for permission to speak, Rhen conceded and nodded his approval. 'Fine,' he thought to himself, as he watched Ceceta's face light up with pure joy. He didn't care if they wanted to play underhanded. It meant that the Thestrans had already lost the war and they knew it. Rhen smiled to himself. How could they not know it? It had been James and Reed he had bested on Rowan. Rhen wanted to shout with glee. And to think he had been worried about their 'super' powers. They were nothing, these Thestrans. He had beaten Kate with ease only three weeks ago.

Thestran was as good as Surpen's. His army would have no trouble defeating them.

Rhen listened to his wife talk to Lilly, Rachel and the Wood Elf Queen, Ralis, in rusty Neptian. Ceceta wanted to hear everything about the Elfin University. She was fascinated by their stories and couldn't wait to learn more. As they spoke to her, Ceceta listened to every detail. Although she had permission to speak, she remained, for the most part, quiet during their conversation, because she was embarrassed by her Neptian. The Thestrans were gracious about it, but Ceceta could see they found it difficult to understand her.

"Do you think he understands them?" Kate whispered to James at the far end of the table.

Rhen kept his eyes on his plate but his ears were trained on the King of Thestran. 'What did Kate mean? Who was he supposed to understand?' There were only two conversations occurring right now, Reed and William's, and Lilly, Rachel and Ceceta's. James shrugged in response. Kate turned in her chair and a royal servant approached. "Please get us one of the translating devices for Rhen to wear in his ear," she told the man.

Rhen furrowed his brow. He was supposed to be listening to these conversations? He would have expected the opposite. Wouldn't it be easier for them to manipulate him through his wife? By now, he had figured out that they wanted her to go to the Elfin University. Why they wanted her to go there was beyond him, but that seemed to be their objective. Meanwhile, Reed and William seemed to be bragging about their people's athleticism, but Rhen already knew that was a joke.

When the servant returned to the room with the translating device, Rhen heard Ceceta tell Lilly in broken Neptian that she had adored her school experience on Neptian and she wanted to finish her education at the Elfin University. The Thestran women seemed beside themselves with joy at this announcement and promised to enroll Ceceta that very day. She could begin right away. As they described to her which classes she could expect her first year, Kate walked down the side of the table towards Rhen. She held out the translating device to him and said in broken Surpen, "*Wear. This do will translate understand say.*"

Rhen couldn't believe it. First of all, what was Ceceta doing? She couldn't go to the Elfin University, and secondly, Kate was a woman. She had no right to address him without permission. It was very inappropriate. Rhen debated what he should do. He put down his fork and leaned back in his chair, staring at his plate with a blank expression. Surpen law dictated he ignore Kate, so that was what he was going to do.

Kate stood beside Rhen, waiting. She tried to tell him again in Surpen to put the device in his ear, but he remained focused on his plate. Feeling defeated and angry, Kate slammed the earpiece onto the table next to Rhen's glass before returning to her seat. When she had sat down, Rhen leaned forward and picked up his fork to finish his meal.

"Why won't he wear the translating device?" Reed asked.

"I don't know," Kate replied with frustration. "He's being difficult."

"He's being stubborn," James corrected. Several people nodded their heads in agreement.

Ten minutes later, the Wood Elf Queen, Ralis, asked Rhen's wife her name. Before Ceceta could answer, Rhen replied in perfect Neptian, "You don't need to know her name. She's my wife and that's her role." His voice was cold and there was a warning tone to it. Everyone at the table turned to stare at him. They were shocked to discover he could speak Neptian.

Rhen stared at the Wood Elf King, Estan, as he added, "And, I would appreciate it, if you would stop speaking to my wife about going to the Elfin University, because it's not going to happen." He was making it clear to Lilly, Rachel and Ralis that their conversation with his wife was now over. The table became silent. Their hopes to convince Rhen's wife to go to the Elfin University seemed shattered.

Ceceta knew she had lost permission to speak. She dropped her head down and continued to eat her meal, as Rhen glared at her. He wasn't mad at her, but he didn't want Andres to hear he hadn't disciplined her for agreeing to go to the University. When Rhen was finished glaring, he picked up his glass and drank the rest of the blood in it. His eye caught sight of the translating device. Rhen smiled and slammed his glass down on top of it, smashing it.

"Damn Rhen, you're a jerk," Charlie exclaimed in the heavy silence that followed.

Rhen was confused by Charlie. Something about him didn't add up. Rhen put his elbows on the table and clasped his hands together, as he gazed at Charlie over the top of his fingers. He was about to comment on Charlie's 'drunkenness', when James cleared his throat and spoke in Neptian. "Rhen, part of our family tradition is to attend the Elfin University. We thought you might like to follow in our paths and finish your education there."

'Oh, my God!' Rhen thought with disbelief. Had he heard James correctly? He gave James a thin smile. After a brief hesitation, he replied in Thestran, "Well, I suppose I would've considered attending your University, if I had been raised as a part of your family, but since you're no longer my family, I'm under no obligation to follow in your traditions."

William started to cough and choke into his napkin. Charlie slapped him on the back with a little too much force to be meant as helpful.

Lilly stared at Rhen in shock. "Can you speak Thestran?"

Rhen glanced over at her, sizing her up. She was a short woman with large bones. She would have appeared too husky, if it wasn't for her thin face. Her medium length brown hair suited the pearl shape of her face and made her intelligent, blue eyes look stunning. Since he couldn't speak to Lilly, without breaking Surpen etiquette, Rhen turned towards Charlie, who was sitting beside her, and said with scorn, "Obviously."

"Could you speak it before you came to Thestran?" Sage asked Rhen from farther up the table.

Rhen turned to inspect Sage. She was very thin and tall. Her black hair was long and stringy, but it looked attractive. Her green eyes were striking and Rhen wondered if they had been enhanced, since he had never seen eyes that green before. When he was finished with his observation, he turned towards Ryan and answered, "No." He liked looking at Ryan. Ryan mystified him. The idea of a merman was intriguing, especially coming from the desert planet of Surpen. He loved the fact that Ryan, who was really nothing more than a glorified fish, could live out of water. If he had had more time, Rhen would have cornered Ryan to study him. Ryan looked like Sage, only his eyes weren't quite as green. The two of them seemed to suit each other well.

"But how did you learn it so fast?" Reed asked Rhen.

Rhen narrowed his eyes, as he turned towards Reed. He wasn't sure what to make of this tall elf with reddish, blond hair. If they had been Surpens, not Thestrans, Reed would have been King. He was bigger and stronger than James, and although it was reported he didn't have powers, there was no doubt in Rhen's mind that Reed could have defeated James years ago to claim the throne. "You're Reed, right?" Rhen asked, staring into Reed's dark blue eyes. "Why aren't you King?"

Reed was stunned by the question. No one had ever implied before that he take the throne from James. It had never occurred to him. He turned towards James, who seemed just as shocked by the question. "I will become King of the Wood Elves, when my wife's father Estan retires," Reed replied, wondering if Rhen would think less of him for his answer and finding himself angry for caring. "I have no desire to be King of Thestran."

Rhen stared at Reed in silence, before asking, "How large is the Wood Elf army?"

The reason for his visit became clear. Andres had allowed Rhen to attend Sage's wedding to gain information on Thestran. Rhen was there on a fact-finding mission, and he didn't seem to care if they knew it, which meant he had already decided they weren't a threat. If Rhen had been worried about defeating them, he wouldn't have told them his objective.

"The Wood Elves have no army," Reed stated with reluctance. For the first time in his life, he wished they did.

Rhen was satisfied with the answer and gave Reed a curt nod, before looking away.

"Rhen," James said. "You didn't answer Reed's question. How did you learn Thestran so quickly?"

Rhen stared at James, until the Thestran King squirmed. After James had looked away, Rhen answered, "Henry was good enough to speak a great deal of Thestran to me last night. The language became clear to me by the time he left."

Henry laughed, sounding embarrassed. "Well, I, I guess I was a little long winded last night. Sorry about that son."

Rhen stiffened, when Henry called him 'son'. "No apology necessary," he answered. He had been pleased to learn the Thestran language. Turning his head, Rhen glared down the table at Naci. "You're the King of the Fire Elves," he stated, taking in Naci's red coat and black cape. The man was small but very sturdy and he seemed filled with anger. Naci reminded Rhen of one of his old weapons teachers. His black hair was quite short and his beady, brown eyes stared back at Rhen with hostility. Rhen decided to have some fun, so he asked Naci in a mocking voice, "Do you have an army?" He already knew the answer, but he wanted to see Naci squirm.

Naci narrowed his eyes, as he glared back at Rhen. "Our army isn't something that concerns you," he replied, his fury over the question obvious.

Rhen chuckled outright at Naci's blatant bluff. "Very well," he told Naci. "I appreciate your honesty. It's nice to know that none of the elves have trained armies." Naci's eyes flashed with anger, as Rhen grinned at him. Rhen knew he had an enemy in Naci, but he had expected as much. In fact, he had expected to feel hatred from all of the Thestrans. He had been surprised last night, when none of them had challenged him to a fight. Their insipid smiles were driving him crazy. Didn't they know he was their enemy? Wasn't it obvious their planets would soon be at war? What was wrong with them? Rhen liked Naci's anger, because he could relate to it. He disliked Naci as much as Naci loathed him. Naci would have made a fine Surpen.

Having finished both his meal and his final assessment of the Thestrans' fighting capabilities, Rhen was ready to go. Sage's wedding wasn't until later that afternoon, which meant he had all morning with Ceceta. Rhen shoved his chair back from the table and stood up. Focusing on William, he said, "In answer to your question, Surpen men wear military shorts during their battles and competitions," he paused to be dramatic, adding a moment later, "and when assholes like you are visiting our planet."

Rhen jerked his wife's chair away from the table, as she was in mid-bite and helped her to her feet. Ceceta dropped the food she was holding onto her plate and followed him towards the exit.

"Rhen," James called out. "Would you please reconsider my suggestion about going to the Elfin University? You can get back to me about it tonight?"

Rhen paused, as he opened the heavy, wooden door, allowing Ceceta to sneak out into the hallway. "No need James. I have about as much interest in attending your University, as William has in bedding my wife." With that, he stepped out of the room, letting the door slam shut behind him.

"What's that supposed to mean?" William cried out, while Susan and Lilo whisked their children away from the table, so the family could discuss Rhen.

"You must kill him before he returns to Surpen," Kendeth announced, after the children had left.

Naci grinned. He couldn't wait to beat the smile off that young, impudent face. The nerve of that boy mocking him. How dare he!

"Not today!" Sage yelled, interrupting the chatter of worried voices. "My wedding is today. Tomorrow." She nodded her head, as if it had already been decided.

"Yes," Kate agreed. "There's a chance the oracles are wrong. They've been wrong before."

"Kate," Kendeth remarked, with concern. "They aren't wrong. You know that. Over 137 oracles have predicted his victory over the Universe." Several people at the table gasped. They were stunned by the number. "Rhen will conquer us, killing most of us in the process. The only way to stop him is if we keep him here on Thestran or kill him before he returns to Surpen." Kendeth could see that Kate was having second thoughts. They needed her for this battle. He hoped she would make the right decision. Turning to address the rest of the members of the Royal Family, Kendeth said, "You must work together to stop him, before he can return to Surpen and come back with his army."

Kate stood up, knocking over her chair. "We'll talk about it tomorrow," she told the room. "After, Sage's wedding. Today, we'll celebrate. Perhaps Rhen will be more amenable to our suggestion tonight."

Kendeth closed his eyes. "You're making a mistake. Rhen isn't going to change his mind. The sooner we do this, the better."

"No, Mom is right," Sage said. "It should be put off until after my wedding."

A servant leaned over and whispered something into James' ear. "Oh, Themrock no!" James barked, turning to the servant. "Are you sure?" he asked the man. The servant nodded his head and backed away. Everyone watched James, waiting for him to explain what had just happened. "I'm sorry Sage," James apologized, turning back to the table. "I'm afraid we can't put it off. Rhen informed the servants this morning that he'll be leaving us as soon as the wedding is over. He isn't even planning on staying for the reception."

Kate gasped and raised her hands to her mouth, her eyes brimmed with tears.

"Ooooh, that stinks," Charlie breathed out, before knocking over his morning martini.

"We must kill Rhen before the wedding," Kendeth announced, with a calm he wasn't feeling. "We certainly can't do it during the ceremony. Hundreds of peaceful dignitaries are coming from all over the Universe to see Sage get married. If we tried to eliminate Rhen during the service, it would be a blood bath. We can't let our allies walk into that. I suggest you fight Rhen during the family photo session, before the wedding. We could tell the guests there was a terrible accident and the wedding could be rescheduled." Sage and Ryan looked at each other. They didn't want to delay their wedding, but Kendeth's plan seemed to be their best option to stop Universal warfare.

Kate cried out and collapsed to the floor sobbing. Henry rushed over and pulled her up onto his lap, as she wailed onto his shoulder. Her scene made the others uncomfortable and most of the remaining guests snuck out of the room. When Kate could speak, she said, "He...he's mmmy son. I cccan't do it. I cccan't kkkill him."

Fear spread like wildfire through Kate's children. They couldn't kill Rhen without her. She had more power than all of them combined. She also had the most battle experience. "Mom," Lilly began, "if he's as strong as you say he is, you have to fight with us or you will lose more than one son today."

Kate struggled to keep from crying. She could hear the worry in Lilly's voice. Dabbing at her red eyes with Henry's handkerchief, she looked up at her family. Lilly wasn't the only one afraid, they all were. The oracles were right. Rhen had to be stopped. For the greater good, she'd have to help them. She had to save as many of her children as possible. Feeling sick with sorrow, Kate nodded her head.

Kendeth and the others sighed with relief. "We will…'take care' of Rhen in two hours at the family photo session," Kendeth instructed the room. "Since Rhen is a trained fighter, I suggest we arrange to have the photo session in the main stadium. It's the best location, in which to contain the battle, and should provide you with an advantage. We'll be able to hide soldiers within the stadium, so they can rush out to assist you, once the battle has begun."

No one objected to Kendeth's plan, so they rose to leave. They had to prepare themselves for battle.

Kate and Henry spent what was left of their morning, sitting in their bedroom going over old photo albums. They were surprised to find that Rhen wasn't in any of their family pictures. In one picture, he was hiding behind his nanny. In another, they could see his foot, as he was running out of the frame. There was a photo, where just the top of his head was visible behind a large gown that Lilly was wearing. They had another picture of Rhen, in which he was dressed like a girl, but he was crying with such abandon that Sage was holding something in front of his face to keep him quiet.

When it came time to go to the stadium, Kate showed her family the photos she had of Rhen. "Since I don't own any photos of his face, I'd like to have someone take our family picture before we…"

"Of course," James interrupted, giving his mother a quick hug. He couldn't understand why they didn't have any pictures of Max. Hadn't Max lived in the palace for the first eight years of his life? There had to be some photos of him somewhere.

In the stadium, the Thestran Royal Family hid their weapons behind the seats closest to the stage, where the pictures were to be taken. The Elfin Royals, along with many elves, had joined Thestran's soldiers in hiding, while a rather robust, military man was on stage with the Royal Family, working to set up the camera for their 'photo shoot'.

Charlie was having trouble with his nerves. He rushed up into the stands to vomit.

"What an idiot," William laughed out with scorn, when Charlie staggered back down towards the stage, tripping over his own feet.

"Be quiet William," Lilly snapped.

"I'm sorry," Charlie groaned.

Lilly pulled Charlie down to sit on the step beside her. "It's okay, Charlie," she told him, while smoothing back his long, blond hair. "We're all nervous. But you don't have to worry. If things get out of hand, I'm sure the Black Angel will swoop down to help us out."

A second later, Charlie's glum expression had changed to joy. He jumped to his feet exclaiming, "Yeah! I mean, with that many oracles predicting Rhen's evilness, certainly the Black Angel won't let us fight him alone. He's definitely going to help us defeat him." Charlie stepped forward, but forgot he was still on the stairs. He tumbled down into Reed's arms. Once Reed had righted him, Charlie laughed and turned to the soldier with the camera. "Be sure to take a picture of the Black Angel before he disappears," he instructed the man.

Kate frowned, as she considered Charlie's words. For years, this mysterious individual, with superior powers, had been appearing around the Universe rescuing people. Whoever it was dressed in black, thus the name the Black Angel. The Black Angel never spoke, but used his or her powers to save people in trouble and then disappeared. "You need to do more to find out who it is," Kate told James. "A person with such extraordinary powers would be dangerous, if they fell into the hands of the Convention members. If the Black Angel's identity is known, it would be difficult for someone to manipulate them. Everyone would be on watch, making sure the Angel was safe."

"I know mom. We've been working on it for years. The Angel hasn't left us any clues to go on."

"But there has to be..."

James interrupted her, "Let's just focus on the matter at hand, please? One thing at a time."

Kate sighed, as the reason for their presence in the stadium returned to the forefront of her mind. She looked at her children and prayed to Themrock that he would find a way to save Max and stop this impending battle.

As the hour for the family photo came and went, James became concerned. "Where's Rhen? Do you think he knows about our plan? Could he be hiding outside the stadium, waiting to ambush us?" he asked Reed. Naci marched up onto the stage. "Naci, what're you doing up here? What if Rhen arrives late?"

"That's why I'm here. Where is he?" Naci demanded.

"If I knew," James began, but Charlie's sudden laugh was so loud it interrupted him.

"I bet the Black Angel has already taken care of him for us," he told them. "Thank you, Black Angel!" he shouted into the air, before dancing across the stage.

James shook his head and motioned for one of his soldiers to approach. "Go find Rhen," he told the man.

Ten minutes later, the soldier returned. "Sir, Rhen entered his bedroom after breakfast and has yet to leave it."

"What?" James exclaimed. Turning to Kate, he asked, "Why is he avoiding us?"

Kate grabbed Charlie by the arm, in the middle of his dance. "You did tell Rhen to meet us in the stadium an hour ago for a family photo, didn't you Charlie?"

Charlie appeared confused. "No, you didn't ask me to. I thought Reed was going to tell him."

"Neptian's Balls!" Reed swore.

"You mean, Rhen had no idea he was supposed to meet us?" James asked.

"That appears to be the case," Kate confirmed.

"Kendeth is going to kill us for this one," James remarked. He turned to dismiss the stadium full of soldiers and inform the Elfin Royals about the situation.

Together, the Thestran Royal Family and Elfin Royals walked back to the castle for lunch. After dropping their weapons in one of the private meeting rooms on the first floor of the castle, they walked to the dining room. When James opened the door to the dining room, he found the room silent, except for two people arguing with each other in another language by the windows. The people, who were arguing, were hidden from view behind one of the window's long, golden curtains.

Kendeth, Lilo, Susan, and a few of the other wedding guests, were sitting with worried expressions, as they watched the two people argue. When they saw the Royal Family and Elfin Royals enter the room, relief spread across their faces. "By the Genister Gods," Lilo breathed out. "We were waiting to hear about the results from the stadium, when Rhen and his wife strolled into the room. We weren't sure why he was here or what had happened to you. We feared the worse."

"What happened?" Susan asked her husband, when James bent over to kiss her.

"Don't ask," he replied with rue, keeping his eyes away from Kendeth. He didn't need to look at the man to know he was livid. He hoped Kate would explain the situation to him before he had to.

James glanced over at the windows. Rhen and his wife were arguing in hushed tones. He was debating whether to get a translating device, so he could eavesdrop on their conversation, when a waiter caught his eye. The man wanted to know if he should have the servants deliver lunch to the table. James peeked over at Rhen. Nothing had changed, so James nodded yes. The servants rushed into the room, carrying trays laden with food. They walked around the table, offering food to the guests, before placing the trays on the table.

As the Royal Family began their meal, Rhen yelled at his wife and marched over to the table. He jerked his chair out and dropped down into it, an angry scowl on his face. Rhen was still staring at his plate, when his wife stepped up to the table to join him. She sat down next to him looking very demure. Her blond hair cascaded down across her face, so she pushed it back behind her ears, as she kept her eyes on her plate.

Deciding it would be best to ignore them, James began to eat his lunch. The others at the table followed his lead, eating their meals in silence. It had been a nerve-racking morning and none of them felt like conversing.

After a few minutes had passed, during which the only sound was that of people eating and the occasional clink of silverware on plates, Rhen cleared his throat and turned to face James. Most of the people at the table paused, waiting to hear what Rhen had to say. "It appears," he began, with hesitation in Thestran. "That I'll be taking you up on a..." Rhen paused and took a deep, frustrated breath, before continuing, "on your offer of schooling," he finished, growling out the word 'school'.

James was shocked. He hadn't expected this at all. Even more surprising was Rhen's wife. She lifted her hands up into the air behind Rhen's back to give the thumbs up sign to Lilly and Rachel and then did a little victory dance, waving her raised thumbs around in front of her face.

Kendeth was right, James realized, the woman could control Rhen.

James glanced back at Rhen's narrow, defiant eyes. Rhen was waiting to see if James would challenge him on his change of heart regarding school. James realized he would blow it, if he seemed too excited about Rhen's new plan, so he gave his little brother a brief nod, as if Rhen's decision wasn't of any great importance, and went back to his meal.

James' simple gesture diffused the anger that had built up inside of Rhen. He snapped his head around and heard Lilly gasp. 'What's up with her?' Rhen wondered, before glancing at his wife. Ceceta's hands rested on her lap, as she sat without moving, while staring at her plate, a blank expression on her face.

James couldn't believe how skilled Rhen's wife was at acting obedient. He wanted to laugh, but he was afraid he'd put her in danger. She was something else, sitting there so quiet and innocent looking.

The tension that had been in the air, dissipated almost at once, as the realization that they had won, dawned on everyone. They didn't have to kill Rhen! They'd be able to keep him on Thestran and save the Universe!

With a sudden shriek of joy, Kate rushed down the side of the table to hug Rhen.

Rhen pushed Kate off him, causing her to stumble backwards a few feet, before regaining her balance. He ran his hands through his short, brown hair and grumble in Surpen, *"That woman has got to learn to keep her damn hands off me, if I'm going to stay on this planet."* Ceceta nodded in agreement, while staring at her plate.

With the problem of Rhen behind them, everyone began to talk about the wedding. They had been so preoccupied with Rhen, they hadn't finished preparing. As soon as lunch was over, the Royal Family rushed about the castle, shouting out orders and working with determination, to finalize a wedding they had thought was going to be canceled.

Their last-minute rush paid off. Sage's wedding, on the public balcony of the castle overlooking the ocean and the Merpeople, was beautiful. No one could remember a more perfect ceremony. The reception was held on the castle's lawn. Rhen and his wife were seated at a table with his siblings. As the other guests moved about, conversing and dancing, Rhen and his wife sat in their seats until they were finished with their meal. As soon as they were done, they rose to leave. The party was still in full swing, so Charlie called out to them to stay, but Rhen shook his head, as he and his wife walked towards Sage and Ryan.

James needed to talk to Rhen, before he left for the night. He jumped from his chair and dashed around three tables to catch him. "Will you be spending the night on Thestran?" James asked Rhen as he approached.

"Why do you wish to know?" Rhen replied.

"Well, Sage planned her wedding for today on purpose, because she wanted Charlie to be able to attend. You see the new school year at the Elfin University begins tomorrow, and if Sage had had her wedding any later, it might have interfered with Charlie's education." James laughed without mirth, adding, "Not that any of us think he does a lot of studying, but it's still nice to be considerate."

"Tomorrow?" Rhen asked with surprise. "You want me to start at this Elfin University tomorrow?" He had thought he'd be able to return to Surpen and gradually break the news of his attending the University to his father. If he had to start tomorrow, it would make things difficult for him.

"Yes, tomorrow," James nodded in agreement. Reed walked up to stand next to James, in case he needed help with Rhen.

Rhen turned to look at his wife. She was staring at her shoes, like a proper Surpen woman. He didn't want to go to the University. He knew he could force Ceceta to return to Surpen. They could leave Thestran right now. In a few years, if she still wanted to go to the University, he would permit her to attend. By then, Surpen would have conquered Thestran and it would be a Surpen school. Rhen leaned over and placed his head against Ceceta's. He breathed in her sweet scent and sighed.

James and Reed, who were watching him, tried not to smile.

"Yes," Rhen told them, lifting his head. "We'll spend the night here, before going to the University."

They heard Ceceta exhale and realized she had been holding her breath, while Rhen had been debating what to do. It seemed she didn't realize the power she had over her husband.

"Good. You can go to the University with Charlie tomorrow. He'll be able to show you around," James told them.

Rhen seemed concerned. He stared over their heads at Charlie, who was dancing by himself, swinging his hips and arms around in strange, looping shapes.

James followed his gaze and laughed. "Perhaps we should consider finding someone else to show you around the University tomorrow," he offered. Rhen nodded his head in agreement. "Anyway, we'll see you in the morning."

Rhen made a quiet 'humph' sound and turned to walk towards Sage and Ryan's table. When they were ten feet away, Rhen paused and gestured towards Ceceta with his hand out. She pulled the bag that was resting on her back, around to her front, and reached into it, bringing out a small present wrapped in blue paper. Rhen took the gift and walked up to the newlyweds. He bowed before Ryan saying, "Congratulations. May you have a long, strong life together and may the one true God bless you with a bounty of children." Rhen offered Ryan his gift and gave him a Surpen military salute, his right hand crossed over to his left shoulder, his head dipped down, as he pounded his shoulder twice then swung his right hand down towards his left sword, before bringing it across his body and letting it rest on his right sword.

Ryan and Sage thanked Rhen and Ceceta several times for coming to their wedding and for their gift.

Rhen nodded in return, took Ceceta's arm and guided her back towards the Thestran Castle. As they passed the other wedding guests, everyone stared at them. Rhen knew they were curious about him. He also knew that many of them were laughing at him behind his back. They had no respect for Convention members. Rhen glanced at Ceceta to see how she felt about being mocked. If they were going to be laughed at here, there was no doubt they would be made fun of at the University. From the look on Ceceta's face, it appeared that she didn't care what the Thestrans thought of her. She was just happy to be going back to school. 'Well,' Rhen thought, 'I guess that's all that matters.'

When Rhen and Ceceta were out of sight, Sage ripped open the paper on their wedding gift to reveal a small, golden box that was engraved with odd writing. "A box," Lilly remarked by her side with a giggle. "Well, I guess that's better than a piece of meat." Sage grimaced as Lilly laughed at her.

"Maybe there's something inside it?" William suggested.

Sage opened the box to find it empty. William chuckled and reached out to take it from her. He turned it around in his hands and held it up above his head in the moonlight. It appeared to glow as the moon's rays hit it. "Well, now we know what Surpens give for gifts, empty boxes," William told his sister.

Sage shrugged. It didn't matter that there wasn't anything inside. She hadn't expected anything from Rhen. The box itself was pretty. She decided she would keep it on her desk.

The reflected moonlight from the box caught Kate's attention, as she danced with Henry. Patting Henry's shoulder, Kate indicated she wanted to go over to Sage and Ryan. As they approached the group, Kate asked, "May I see that William?"

"Sure," he replied, handing her the box. "It's not exciting, just an empty box. One of Sage's many wedding presents."

Kate nodded and took the box. 'Could it be?' she wondered. She turned it over a few times in her hands, inspecting the symbols on it, then held it up into the moonlight again. As soon as the light struck the box, Kate saw the writing on the box glow. "By the Genister Gods!" she exclaimed with astonishment. "Where did you get this? Who gave this to you?" Kate asked, running her fingers along the glowing words. Her excitement attracted the attention of several people, who were now walking over to see what was happening.

Naci, the Fire Elf King, stepped behind Kate and glanced down over her shoulder at the box. "Is that what I think it is? I've never seen one before. Is it real?"

Instead of answering Naci's question, Kate asked Sage, "Who gave this to you?"

"It's just a box," she answered. "What's so special about it? Rhen gave it to us as a wedding present."

"Rhen?" Kate repeated, sounding shocked. "Rhen gave this to you?" Kate held it up to the moonlight again.

"Is that what I think it is!" Plos, the Water Elf King, yelled as he jogged up to the group. "I saw you hold it up before, but I couldn't believe my eyes when it glowed. I thought I had imagined it. WOW!" he exclaimed, while gazing at the box in Kate's hands. His green eyes were sparkling with excitement. "WOW!" he repeated.

Kate laughed at his enthusiasm. "Yes!" she told him. "It's amazing. I can't believe I'm holding one in my hands."

"It belongs to the elves," Naci stated. He put out his hand to take the box.

"No Naci," Kate snapped. She jerked it out of his reach. "It belongs to Sage. Rhen gave it to her as a wedding present."

"Try it out!" Ralis, the Wood Elf Queen, exclaimed.

"May I?" Kate asked Sage.

"Sure," Sage said. She still wasn't sure what everyone was talking about. No one had explained the mystery of the box yet. It was attractive but that was all. She couldn't figure out why everyone wanted to touch it and examine it.

Kate ran her thin fingers over the box. Would it work? A shiver of anticipation raced through her, as she closed her eyes. "I wish I had 50 white diamonds," she said, while the silent crowd watched. The box didn't feel any different, so Kate started to doubt herself, but when she opened the lid and saw the diamonds, she laughed with delight. Kate turned the box upside down and poured 50 white diamonds onto the table beside her, while the guests, who had been watching, gasped.

"Themrock!" Naci exclaimed.

"You're the luckiest person in the Universe," Estan, the Wood Elf King, told Sage.

"Do it again!" Plos cried out. He tossed his blue and green Water Elf cape back over his shoulders. "I love Genister artifacts, do it again."

Kate handed the box to Plos and he froze. "Ahh," he breathed out with reverence. "I'm holding something made by a Genister." He laughed and turned to Sage. "Would you…would you mind if I had a go?"

"No," she answered.

Plos hesitated a moment before saying, "I wish I had 200 Luna moths." With care, he opened the lid on the box. Two hundred majestic, light green, Luna moths flew up into the night air. The crowd gasped with pleasure, while the moths fluttered back and forth above them. Kate smiled to herself, as she watched a moth fly towards the castle. She had known that Plos would wish for just the right thing.

"Let me try," William demanded. He grabbed the box from Plos and closed the lid. "I wish I had the fastest horse in the Universe." William opened the box and a white mist floated up into the air. It hovered over the ground, before turning into a black and brown stallion. The horse whinnied and threw its head. The crowd clapped. A servant ran over to throw a rope around the horse's neck before it could run off.

Kate took the box from William and handed it to Sage. "What is it?" Sage asked, cradling the box in her hands.

"It's a Genister Magic Box," Kate told her. "I've only ever seen them in pictures. I think there were once five of them in existence. They're priceless. Anything you wish for, within reason mind you, will appear in the box or float out of it, as William's new horse just did. What it gives you is real. The horse, the diamonds, the moths, they're all real. It's an incredible gift. I can't believe Rhen would part with it. No one would give away a Genister Magic Box. I wonder how Rhen came to own one?"

Kate pointed at the box and added, "You need to put a spell on it, so it'll only work for you and Ryan. It's the best way to make sure that no one will steal it." Sage nodded and gazed at the box in her hand. She heard her mother say, "I just can't believe he would give this away."

"For Rhen to give Sage such a valuable present, when he doesn't even know her," Kendeth remarked. "It makes you wonder what's important to him, what does he value? Clearly not material possessions or this box wouldn't have left his sight."

"What are the markings on the box?" Sage asked. The mysterious carvings on the box were beautiful, when they glowed in the moonlight.

"They're Genister markings," Kate answered.

"The Genister symbols on the box alone make it priceless," Plos, the Water Elf King, told Sage. "Especially if your box contains new symbols that were lost. If it does, it could help us decipher some of the writings on our temple walls."

"You should let the professors at the Elfin University examine it," Lilly told her sister. "It'd be wonderful, if your box held the key to decipher the Genister's language."

"Yes," Sage agreed.

"After you put a spell on it," Kate reminded her daughter, a stern look on her face. The band was playing a familiar tune, so Kate reached out to take Henry's hand. Before leaving to dance, she pointed at Sage and repeated, "You should lock it away now, before anyone gets any ideas. I don't think someone will steal your box, but it's better to be safe than sorry." She turned to a servant and pointed at the diamonds on the table. "Would you please donate these diamonds to the Family's charity."

"We'll be back," Sage told the guests around her, as she and Ryan headed off towards the castle to secure their gift.

Once they had arrived in their bedroom, Sage and Ryan inspected the box, before placing a spell on it and locking it away. As they were stepping out of their room to return to their party, they spotted a figure in orange walking down the stairs. "That must be Rhen's wife. Let's catch up to her to thank her," Sage said.

"Yes, I want to let them know how much we appreciate their gift," Ryan agreed.

Sage and Ryan hurried down the hallway towards the stairs, but Rhen's wife was moving fast. As they stepped out onto the Grand Hallway, they saw her duck into the Thestran Council Chamber.

"Why would she go in there?" Sage asked Ryan, who shrugged in response. They followed Ceceta, pushing open the door to walk into the Council Chamber.

The Thestran Council Chamber was where Thestran and her allies held their official proceedings. Delegates from Council planets attended daily Council meetings that covered everything from trade routes to individual planetary pollution programs. The Council Chamber was several stories high and dark brown in color. Ornate carvings, by artists throughout the Universe, marked the ancient wood that comprised the Chamber's walls. In the center of the room, on the bottom floor, was a raised crescent shaped dais that contained a long table of the same shape. When the Council was in session, the Thestran Royal Family sat in golden chairs on the dais.

Encircling the Thestran Royal Family's table, running in concentric circles around the room on three different levels, were long rows of simple, wooden tables painted in gold and black, along with upholstered chairs. Each planet had its own designated location. Blank screens were located on the walls above the tables. When the Council was in session, the screens would display the individual who was speaking, as well as the Delegates' votes. Located, above the screens, were a large assortment of Intergalactic Viewing Monitors. If a Delegate was unable to attend the Council session, they could watch the proceedings from their personal monitors. Above the monitors were public galleries, as well as several press boxes.

There were five, golden portal frames located on the ground level of the Chamber against the far, right wall. The portals had been installed to make it easier for the Delegates to travel back and forth to their planets.

After Sage entered the room, she hesitated. One of the portals was active. It cast a cold, blue light on the pillars in the room. Sage felt as if she were intruding. She considered waiting outside, but when Ryan bumped into her from behind, she changed her mind and stepped forward. The two of them tiptoed towards one of the massive, marble columns that encircled the room. They could hear men talking in a different language to their right. With care, they leaned around the column and saw Rhen's wife lying on the ground bowing. She was facing away from them and her arms were stretched out in front of her, as if she were praying.

Rhen was standing a few feet in front of her, bowing from the waist down towards a massive man, wearing a black, Surpen tunic. The man's large hands rested on his hips, as he stared at Rhen with disbelief. Sage nearly gasped at the sight of him. The man's facial profile was jagged and rough. His nose was long and a piece of it had been cut off about ¾ of the way down. His black hair was cut very short and there were numerous scars on his face and neck. His eyes were grey in color, and his legs were spread apart, as if he were about to attack. There was also an unpleasant odor emanating from him. Sage grimaced and pulled back. "That must be the King of Surpen," Ryan whispered to her. Sage nodded in agreement. She felt an overwhelming hatred for the man, and she was sure, from the look of him, that he deserved it.

Trying to be quiet, Sage leaned back around the pillar to watch. Andres didn't look pleased. His words to Rhen sounded harsh. The translating devices on the Delegates' tables were too far away for Sage to reach, so she tried to memorize the words the men were speaking, so Kate could pull the images out of her mind later and translate what was being said.

Andres bellowed at Rhen. Spittle flew from his mouth, landing on the floor in front of him. It was obvious that he was furious with his son. Sage didn't need a degree in linguistics to guess what he was angry about. It seemed Rhen had told his father he was going to the Elfin University, and Andres didn't agree with his decision. After a few minutes, Andres calmed down enough to stop screaming. He shook his head and stepped forward, placing one of his melon-sized hands on Rhen's shoulder. In response, Rhen stood up. The two men spoke to each other for a few minutes. Andres shook his head in disagreement. As he turned from Rhen, he spotted Rhen's wife and pointed his fat finger at her, while yelling with fury. Rhen stepped between them, getting hit in the face with a glob of spit from his father's diatribe. He ignored the saliva, as it dripped down his cheek, and put his hand on his father's shoulder. With a lazy smile, Rhen said something that made the Surpen King laugh.

Rhen stuck his hand out, behind his back, and snapped his fingers. Ceceta jumped to her feet and approached him with her leather bag. Rhen turned towards her and reached inside the bag, pulling out one of the fish he had taken from the buffet table that morning. Sage almost gasped, when she saw it squirming in his hands. She couldn't understand why it hadn't died. Andres smiled and nodded with approval at the sight of the fish. It struggled in Rhen's grasp, so he returned it to Ceceta's bag. A moment later, Rhen pulled a clear, plastic sack that contained all four of the fish from this morning's buffet table, out of Ceceta's bag. The fish swam around, inside the water-filled bag, looking content. Sage felt Ryan shake his head with wonder. Neither of them could figure out how Rhen had saved the fish.

Sage and Ryan watched, as Andres stepped forward to throw his sizeable arm around Rhen's shoulders. Rhen smiled at his father and together they walked back towards the glowing portal. Sage found herself straining to hear their words. At the portal, Andres hugged Rhen. When he released his son, Rhen handed him the bag of fish. Andres held the bag up into the air and laughed with delight, before stepping through the portal and disappearing.

The Council Chamber was silent after the Surpen King's departure. Rhen waited until the portal's light had gone out, before turning towards his wife. A smirk appeared on his face, as he strode towards her. Ceceta shouted with glee and jumped up into his arms, kissing him. "Well, I think that went rather well," she stated in Neptian, while Rhen lowered her back down to the ground.

"Right," he told her with sarcasm. "Two minutes ago, you were about to be killed by the most powerful King in the Universe and now you're joking about it." Rhen ran his long fingers through his hair, stopping at the base of his neck to rub at a sore spot.

"Thank you for saving my life," Ceceta told him.

"Any time love," Rhen replied taking her hand. Together they walked towards the main doorway, which was located behind Ryan and Sage. "So, you got your wish," Rhen added.

Ceceta shrieked with joy and again jumped up into Rhen's arms. "I'm so happy!" she cried out. Rhen pulled Ceceta into his chest and felt his body respond at once. A smile passed over his lips, as he thought about the alone time he was now going to have with his wife. Maybe this 'school' thing wouldn't be so bad after all.

Rhen continued walking towards the door, holding Ceceta in his arms. "Ceceta, I'm really glad you're excited, but tell me, why do you really want to go to school? You can't do anything with your education back on Surpen? What's the point?"

"I know, but it's still going to be great," she answered. "All of the things that I feel are just out of reach, will now fall into place. I'll finally understand the Universe and what's going on. I think my getting an education will help you, too."

Rhen laughed and answered in a teasing voice, "Right. I have no interest in going to school. I'm not going to get anything out of this experience, and you know it. I can't believe I let you talk me into it. This is going to be pure hell."

Ceceta dropped her legs down from Rhen's waist, so he released her. "It's not going to be hell. As we already discussed, I'll do all the work," she assured him.

"You better," Rhen mumbled. He pushed down on his tunic, to flatten it in the front.

Ceceta paused. "Do you want me to teach you to..."

"NO," Rhen interrupted.

Ceceta stared at her husband in silence for a moment then nodded her head. "If you change your mind, just let me know."

"Sure," Rhen agreed. He tucked her hand into the crook of his arm. "You're going to owe me big time for this one."

"I'll start to repay you tonight love," she whispered, a smile on her face.

It wasn't what he had meant, but Rhen liked her thinking. He gave Ceceta a look that made her blush a deep blue and they continued towards the exit.

As they approached the column, where Sage and Ryan were hiding, Rhen asked in Thestran, without turning his head, "So, do you enjoy spying on people?"

"What?" Ceceta responded in Neptian, as Sage and Ryan stepped out from behind the pillar looking flustered. The minute that Ceceta saw them, she dropped Rhen's hand and stepped behind him, lowering her eyes to the ground.

Sage felt guilty for being caught and went on the defensive. "We weren't spying. We were looking for you to thank you for the Genister Box. It's truly amazing."

Rhen nodded to Ryan, ignoring Sage. "We're glad you like it." He wasn't used to being addressed by women. Something about it made him feel odd. All communication between him and Sage would have to be done through Ryan, as was proper Surpen etiquette.

Rhen continued walking with Ceceta trailing along behind him in a submissive manner. As Sage watched him, she realized she didn't want him to leave. She wanted to talk to him the way he had been talking with his wife earlier. She wanted to get to know him. She liked the casual Rhen, the one that had been in the room a few minutes ago. He seemed...sweet. Sage knew she could be friends with that Rhen. Trying to draw him out, she asked, "Are you sure you want to give it to us?"

Rhen stopped and turned to look at her with one eyebrow raised. His black eyes scanned her facial features, trying to read her hidden meaning. Turning towards Ryan, Rhen said, "Yes, why not?"

Determined to have her brother acknowledge her in person, Sage stepped in front of Ryan and replied, "Because it's so valuable and rare. Why would you want to part with such a priceless item?"

Rhen's face was expressionless for a moment. He turned and said something in Surpen to his wife that made her giggle. Looking back at Sage and Ryan, he replied, with dripping sarcasm, "A priceless item for a priceless couple." Rhen laughed and walked out of the room with Ceceta following along behind him.

Sage knew Rhen was joking, but his words had a strange effect on her. As Rhen left the Chamber, she realized they had never spoken to each other before. When Rhen was born, she was already at boarding school. During her school vacations, Rhen was never around, because he was always with his nanny. In her youth, Sage wasn't fond of babies, so she'd never sought him out, as Lilly had done countless times. Sage felt her heart ache with sadness. She reached out for Ryan's hand. Together they returned to their party.

Sage gestured for Kate to follow them, as she and Ryan walked over towards James and Reed, who were listening to a bunch of Delegates tell stories about the Black Angel. They weren't surprised by the conversation. The Black Angel was everyone's favorite topic.

"I swear, out of nowhere, the Black Angel showed up. My spacejet was just about to crash into the heart of the city during rush hour. He must have saved at least 3,000 people, when he stopped us. It was incredible," one of the Delegates remarked.

"Like the time he saved my aunt and her family from those pirates on Jenpers," another Delegate commented. "We have to find a way to contact the Black Angel. He should be a part of the Council."

"Gentlemen, there's no way to contact the Black Angel," James informed them with fatigue. "We've been trying to get in touch with him or her for years. We even went so far as to stage a fake crisis, but the Angel knew it was a hoax and didn't show up. The Angel is a mystery, and we should thank Themrock that he or she exists." James reached up to rub his temples. He sure wished he knew who this super power was.

"Are we still tracking the Angel? Do we know where he comes from?" a Delegate asked.

"We aren't tracking the Angel per se," Reed informed them. "We chart the locations of where the Angel saves people's lives to see if there's a pattern to the movements. That's all. We have no idea where he or she comes from or where the Angel goes after saving someone."

"Do you see a pattern to the Angel's movements?" another Delegate inquired.

"Yeah," James laughed, without humor. "The Black Angel always seems to go to the parts of the Universe that are in the most turmoil. Big shock!"

James glanced up, when Sage touched his shoulder. Like Lilly and Kate, he could read minds. His powers weren't as strong as theirs, but he could still find out what someone five feet away from him was thinking. Sage rolled her eyes upward, to indicate to him to read her mind, as she thought, 'James, come with me. I want to show you something. Tell Reed to come too'.

"Excuse me gentlemen," James told the group. He stood up, shaking the chill of using his mental powers from his bones. "I need to have a word with my sister. Reed," he indicated with a nod that Reed should join them.

"Do you think the guests can hear us here?" Sage asked Kate, when she stopped near the stables.

"No, we're too far away," Kate replied. "Why did you want to see us?"

Sage told them about Rhen's visit with the King of Surpen in the Council Chamber. Kate motioned for Kendeth to join them. William and Lilly followed along behind him to see what was going on. When everyone was ready, Kate closed her eyes and felt the chill of reaching into Sage's mind. She watched Sage's memory, while transmitting it to the small group around her.

"Did you understand what they were saying?" Sage asked her mother, when Kate opened her eyes.

"Not all of it," Kate replied. She rubbed her arms to warm them. "I've always found Surpen to be a difficult language, but I think I understood most of what was going on. It seems Andres was very angry with Rhen for agreeing to go to the Elfin University. He felt Rhen was betraying his Surpen duties, and he threatened Rhen with a Debrino Code punishment. But..." Kate swallowed. It was hard for her to say the next part.

"Go on mom," James nudged her. "We need to know what they decided. We can't risk letting Rhen leave Thestran. If Andres has told him to return to Surpen, we must mobilize our army immediately."

"Andres told Rhen that...that as his father he couldn't punish him. He said something about education being a weak person's ambition and Rhen being a soldier, so he didn't need an education. Rhen answered that he would only be spying on us to learn our weaknesses." Kate paused, trying to remember her Surpen. "Oh," she said, opening her blue eyes. "Andres verbally attacked Rhen's wife, until Rhen stepped in front of his father and made some comment along the lines of...no woman could ever control him."

James and Reed snickered, since it was obvious that Rhen's wife could control him.

"Was that it?" Kendeth asked.

"For the most part," Kate replied. "I didn't get anything about the fish. Andres told Rhen he had to follow Surpen's rules, while he was here."

"Well," replied Kendeth. "That's very interesting."

William looked aghast. "We should arrest Rhen for spying on us!"

"William," Kendeth began. "I believe Rhen said that so he would receive permission to stay with his wife. It's rather clever. He knows we don't trust him. He knows we won't teach him anything valuable at school. It was simply an excuse to get permission from his father to stay with his wife. I think this entire conversation was a good sign. It shows the Surpen King doesn't completely control Rhen. Our prospects for success grow with each new encounter."

Chapter 9

Kate and Henry entered the dining room the next morning to find Rhen and his wife finishing their meal. The two of them were smiling and chatting rapidly together in Surpen. Kate watched her son's easy manner with his wife and noticed, for the first time, that he was quite handsome. The smooth planes of his face, when not screwed up in anger, were breathtaking. The shape and color of his eyes made him appear rather exotic. Kate wondered why she hadn't noticed the differences between Henry and Rhen's eyes before.

Rhen nodded his head at something his wife said and Kate cursed herself for not remembering the woman's name. Did it begin with an 's' or was it a 'j'? She watched as Rhen reached into the bowl in front of him and picked something up. He raised his fingers to his mouth and Kate shuddered with disgust at the sight of the pure white, night-crawler sized worm that had a hard, red cap for a head. Bloodworms. Rhen popped the worm into his mouth and chewed. A drop of blood from the worm appeared on his lips. He licked it up with his tongue, before reaching down into his bowl again.

Rhen chuckled at the squeals that were coming from the children at the table. Whispering to his wife, the two of them shoved the last few worms that were in their bowls into their mouths, making sure to leave a few of the bloodworms' tail and head sections sticking out from between their lips. The worms wiggled in protest, as Rhen and his wife sucked them into their mouths, before crunching their red capped heads between their teeth. The children, who were watching the show, shrieked with horrified laughter.

"I see you received your bloodworms from Surpen," Kate commented. "My servant mentioned a large shipment of Surpen food had arrived this morning. Would you like me to send it along to the University?"

Rhen had lost his napkin under the table, so he dried his mouth with the napkin that was in front of Rachel's seat. His lips left behind a thin smear of bloodworm blood on the white napkin. Rachel frowned and leaned back in her chair, as Rhen tossed her napkin beside her plate. With a groan, Rachel flicked the offensive napkin onto the floor with her knife. Even though she was a doctor, the bloodworms disgusted her. They looked too much like parasites.

"Yes," Rhen replied to Kate's question, although he was looking at Henry when he spoke.

Henry waved his hand to indicate they would take care of it, so Rhen turned back towards his wife.

Kate spotted Sage and Ryan kissing. "Congratulations again you two. I know you'll have a wonderful time on your honeymoon. Neptian is beautiful this time of year."

Rhen's wife began to cough. Kate's eyes flicked over towards her. Rhen was rubbing her back, as she held a napkin to her mouth. The woman seemed fine, so Kate turned away from her to ask James about his business trip later that day. Before she could open her mouth, Kate felt Kendeth's powers push a spoon against her hand. Like James, Kendeth had the ability to move objects, but he rarely used his powers. Kate was curious to know what he wanted. She placed the spoon next to her coffee cup and used her own powers to telecommunicate with him.

'Rhen's wife seems homesick,' Kendeth thought in response to Kate's question. 'Draw her out. Continue talking about Neptian. If we can get her to embrace Thestran, Rhen will follow.' Kate released her powers with a slight shiver. Although she loved her abilities, she could do without the cold.

"Don't forget," Kate began, while glancing back at Sage. "You must visit the Ldastar waterfalls, with their warming mists. The beaches of Jengas are also quite enjoyable and rather beautiful this time of year. I know you'll have a wonderful time." With a nod from Kendeth, Kate looked down the table at Rhen's wife and asked in Neptian, "Tell me dear, where in Neptian was your family from again?"

Rhen's wife stared at her plate, as Kate waited for an answer.

"*Go ahead and answer*," Rhen whispered in Surpen to Ceceta. "*I've scanned the area. Andres doesn't have any spies here.*"

"Do I have permission?"

"Yes, love," Rhen whispered back, before kissing her on the side of her head.

Ceceta grinned and turned towards Kate. In her best Neptian, she responded, "We lived near the Ldastar Falls, in a town called Ngignik."

Kate smiled, when she heard the name of the town. "I know Ngignik well," she replied, thinking she had found something in common with Rhen's wife. "That's where the current Neptian Delegate to the Royal Council lives. I've visited him and his family several times. It's a lovely town."

Ceceta cleared her throat and asked with hesitation, "You…you've been there? Not many people go to Ngignik. Most tourists stay on the other side of the falls, where the shops are located."

"Yes," Kate replied. "I've been there. In fact, after our last trip to Surpen to see you, we spent some time in Ngignik." She didn't add the fact that she went to Ngignik to stay at the Council Delegates' home, while she recovered from the injuries Rhen had given her.

"May I ask who the Neptian Delegate is? Perhaps I'll know him," Ceceta inquired. Her family had been moderately wealthy, so she knew most of the families from Ngignik, who might have been appointed as Delegates to the Thestran Council.

"Yes," Kate replied with a smile. She was overjoyed with her success in speaking to Rhen's wife. "The Neptian Delegate is Te of Ngignik."

Rhen's wife's eyes grew very large and she gasped. Tears welled up and rolled down her cheeks, as her lower lip quivered. Rhen stood up so fast he knocked his chair over and banged into the table, causing most of the glasses to fall. "Is this some kind of sick joke!" he demanded in Thestran. He was shaking with fury.

Everyone went on alert. They had been doing so well with him, but now it appeared as if they might have lost everything.

"Rhen, I don't understand," Kate replied. She rose from her chair. "How did I offend you? What did I say?"

With a look of pure hatred, Rhen turned from Kate. He reached over to help his wife out of her chair. Together, they walked towards the door to leave.

"Rhen," Henry called out with concern. "What did Kate say that's upset you so much?" Rhen looked angry enough to kill. Like everyone at the table, Henry was worried that Rhen and his wife would leave for Surpen.

When they reached the door, Rhen leaned over to whisper something to Ceceta. She nodded yes and left. Turning to face Henry, Rhen shook his head with dismay. He couldn't believe the stupidity of his so called 'family'. "What the hell's the matter with you? Don't you know anything about..." he paused and took a deep breath. Rhen's break seemed to calm him, and after a moment, he looked back at Henry and said in a matter-of-fact voice, "Te's son Yfetb was betrothed to Ceceta when they were born. She was deeply in love with him. Unfortunately for Ceceta, he decided he was too good for her on their wedding night and he left her...how do you say it...at the altar? The entire town knew of her disgrace, and they took her family's lands away from them, before kicking them out of Ngignik."

Everyone appeared confused. Rhen sighed, before laughing in bitterness at their blank faces. They had no idea who he was talking about. Turning to rest his forehead on the wooden door that he was holding, Rhen said in a tired, annoyed voice, "I met Ceceta and her family two days after the incident, while her family was at the Neptian Royal palace asking for new lands." Rhen glanced over at his parents. "You were there. You don't remember, do you?" With a shrug, he added, "What else is new? I agreed to marry Ceceta. Since I was your son at the time, the Neptian King returned Ceceta's family's lands to them. Although their disgrace was never completely lifted, they at least had a home to live in. Now that they're dead, I guess it doesn't really matter. Does it?" Rhen didn't wait for a response but walked out, letting the door swing shut behind him.

The room was silent, as everyone sat looking horrified. "Well, Ceceta it is then," Charlie remarked with a triumphant smile. "We now know her name!"

"CHARLIE!" Rachel yelled.

"What?" he asked. "Weren't we trying to figure out her name? Didn't we just score?"

"Shut up," William snapped. He smacked his brother on the arm.

"I thought he married her out of love. You never told me it was an arranged marriage," Kendeth remarked with accusation, while glaring at Kate and Henry.

Henry looked bewildered, as he tried to come to grips with what Rhen had just told them. "It wasn't. I don't think...I mean. Was it? He insisted on marrying the girl. We were focused on other issues at the time and just went along with it." Henry glanced up at his family with a distressed look. "I never knew he did it to help out her family."

"Of course, he married her out of love," Kate told Kendeth with conviction. "If he hadn't, he'd be divorced by now. He doesn't gain anything by staying married to a powerless, Neptian girl." Kate nodded to assure herself that she was correct. "Yes, he was in love."

"It's no wonder they lost him, when they arrived on Surpen," Naci whispered to his wife. "They couldn't even keep track of their youngest son, when he was on friendly territory."

"Well," Rachel began. "If he wasn't in love then, he certainly is now."

Reed's wife, Lilo, placed her hand in his. She felt sorry for Rhen. When she had married into the Thestran Royal Family, she had found them to be a very close and supportive group. Their odd detachment from Max had always seemed wrong to her, but before she could confront her husband about it, she had become pregnant and had gotten caught up in her own issues. Now, she wished she had followed through and contacted Rhen or at least pushed Reed to reach out to him earlier. Her in laws' actions were abominable.

"I never asked him to marry that girl," Kate mumbled. "What did he mean by 'he agreed to marry Ceceta'?" She glanced at Henry. "Do you think the Neptians asked him to clean up their dirty laundry for them by marrying her? I can't believe they would have done that behind our backs." Henry shrugged in response.

"We'll never know," James remarked. "Because the people, who were in power back then, are dead. Te and his son, Yfetb, are the current rulers of Neptian, and they'd only give us their side of the story."

Chapter 10

Rhen spent the morning consoling his distraught wife. By lunch time, Ceceta was feeling better, but Rhen was still angry with the Thestrans, so when Ceceta rose to go to the dining room, he told her to sit down. Instead of meeting the Thestrans for lunch, Rhen used his powers to make a lunch appear for them in their bedroom. He had no interest in spending any more time with the Thestran Royal Family.

A servant arrived at their door a short time later to inform them that it was time to go to the Elfin University. They were expected to meet Charlie at the portal in the Council Chamber. Rhen grunted an affirmative response in Thestran and closed the door, leaning his head against the dark wood. "Are you sure you want to do this? They aren't going to make it easy for us."

"What do you mean?" Ceceta questioned him from the couch.

"Surpen is a member of the Convention," Rhen answered. "We're their enemies."

"But they haven't treated us as their enemy."

"I know Cece," Rhen replied with tenderness. "They want something from me. I'm not sure what it is yet, but they'll make it obvious soon enough. Whatever it is that they want, I won't give it to them, so they'll either kick us out of the University or they'll make our lives there so miserable, we'll leave on our own."

Ceceta thought for a minute. "Do you have any idea what it is that they want?"

"No," Rhen answered.

"Couldn't they just miss you," she suggested.

Rhen gave a short bark of laughter and stepped away from the door. "No," he told her with certainty. "They don't miss me. They don't care about me at all. They want something, and they'll pester us until they realize they can't get it. At which point, they'll make our lives hell."

Ceceta stood up and straightened her violet robes. She strode over to Rhen's side and pulled down on his tunic. When his head was close to hers, she gave him a peck on the lips and said, "Then it'll be just like living on Surpen, only not as hot." Without waiting for a response, she pulled open the door and stepped out into the hallway.

"Surpen isn't hell," she heard Rhen call out, as he jogged down the hallway to catch up to her. "It's our home."

"It isn't hell for you," Ceceta replied. She paused, before stepping out into the Grand Hallway. She had to be the appropriate distance behind Rhen, in case there were any spies watching. "But it is for me." A large group of tourists opened the door beside them and entered the hallway. Ceceta dropped her head down to stare at her shoes, as she followed her husband to the Council Chamber. She could tell by the length of his stride that he was angry with her. Fortunately for Ceceta, he wasn't going to do anything about it. Thank Themrock Andres had sent her on this trip to Thestran with Rhen. It had opened a whole new world for her.

When they reached the Council Chamber, Rhen threw open the door with enough strength that Ceceta could slip into the room without touching it. Rhen had been good about doing things like that for her and she appreciated it.

They found Kate, Henry and Charlie standing before the portals waiting for them. Kate smiled at them as they approached, so Ceceta smiled back. She knew her husband wasn't going to respond to Kate, but she didn't feel there was any need for her to be rude. Ceceta was overjoyed that the Thestrans had found a way for her to escape Surpen. This University idea was fantastic. She couldn't wait. Perhaps, if things went well, she could extend her four-year stay, maybe even get an advanced degree? Ceceta shook her head. 'Slow down girl,' she thought. 'One step at a time.'

They stood in front of the Thestrans in silence. It appeared that Kate and Henry wanted to talk, but Rhen wasn't in the mood. He stared at them with one of his blank expressions that unnerved people. When Kate realized she wasn't going to get anywhere with him, she said, "Alright, shall we go?" Rhen didn't respond, so Kate turned to the portal and said, "Portal, open to the Elfin University." The inside of the portal frame flickered, as a blue light filled the empty space. A moment later, the light faded and they saw a lawn, with several institutional buildings in the distance. "After you," Kate told Rhen.

Rhen debated taking Ceceta's hand but decided against it. He should do a thorough scan of the University, before breaking Surpen protocol. Rhen stepped through the portal and the others followed. Charlie stumbled, as he crossed over. As usual, he had had his celebratory drink that morning before returning to school for the new session.

In front of them was a modern building made completely out of glass. It was shaped as an octagon and glittered like a gem with the sunlight sparkling off the window panes. There were several brick buildings on either side of the main school. To the right of the school were student dormitories and to its left was the Teachers' Residence Hall. As Rhen and Ceceta looked past the student dorms, they saw an enormous lake surrounded by rocky cliffs. Turning around, they discovered the Wood Elf Forest behind them. To their left was a sloping hill and behind the main school building were more student dormitories, a stadium and another sloping hill. Everywhere you looked, students rushed around the grounds with their families.

"Normally, the school's portal is located within the main building," Henry informed them. "But on the first day of school, the Headmaster always sets up several portals outside to handle the heavy demand." As if on cue, students and their families began to emerge from the portals beside them.

"Not everyone arrives through the portals," Charlie mumbled, sounding cross. "Many of my friends come in their spacejets." Kate gave Charlie a stern look. After Charlie had crashed his last spacejet, she had refused to buy him a new one. He had been grounded for two years now. "If you want to bring your spacejet to school," Charlie suggested to Rhen, when it occurred to him that he could use Rhen's spacejet while Rhen was at school. "I'll fill out the paperwork for you, so you can have a docking station in the jetport at the back of the school."

Rhen frowned. "That won't be necessary," he replied. He didn't have a spacejet either. In fact, he'd been banned from flying spacejets for the same reason that Charlie had, but neither of them knew about the other's situation.

Charlie looked crestfallen, when Rhen declined his offer. He assumed the Surpens had something against spacejets. Spotting some of his friends, he called out to them.

Charlie was in his last year at the school. Most of his friends had arrived without their parents. He was a little embarrassed to be standing next to his and wanted to get away from them. As his friends walked over towards them, Charlie introduced them to his parents and to his brother and sister-in-law. His friends were surprised to meet Rhen. From their History of the Thestran Royal Family class, they knew Rhen existed, but they hadn't learned anything about him. As soon as Charlie was finished introducing them, they started to ask Rhen questions: "Why did you choose to live on Surpen?" "When did you get married?" "What's the Convention like?" "Have you been living at the Surpen boarding school this whole time?"

Rhen stared at the boy named Stanley, who had asked this last question. 'Had he been living at a Surpen Boarding School?' What was the kid talking about? Before Rhen could open his mouth to inquire, Charlie ushered his friends away. Over his shoulder, Charlie called out, "See you around little brother," while he and his friends ran off towards the student dormitories.

"Come along then," Kate said. The four of them headed to the Headmaster's office. When they entered, they were greeted by a secretary, who directed them into the Headmaster's personal rooms. The Headmaster was a round, short, old man with a cheery face and graying brown hair. He was wearing a pin-striped suit with a red bowtie. The minute he saw Kate and Henry, he jumped up and ran over to greet them. "Well, well, well, to what do I owe this pleasure," he said, embracing them. He had educated all of Kate and Henry's children and had found their patronage of the University very rewarding.

Kate pointed towards Rhen. "I don't believe you've met my youngest son, Rhen. He'll be enrolling as a freshman this year."

The Headmaster's head jerked backwards, as he stared at Rhen, taking in his physical similarities to Henry and his odd clothing. He had never seen Rhen before, and he wondered why Kate wasn't calling him by his first name, Max. Not wanting to be rude, and knowing he'd be able to grill Kate about the name change later, he smiled and marched over to Rhen with his hand out in greeting.

Rather than taking the Headmaster's hand, Rhen performed a Surpen military salute. "Well," the Headmaster declared, while lowering his hand. "I haven't seen that one before. It's nice to meet you too. You'll like our University. We have many students from different planets and solar systems here." He leaned in towards Rhen to whisper, "Most of the students from other planets are like you. They don't shake hands." He nodded and turned back towards his desk. "Yes, not to worry," he pontificated, as his mind raced over what he could remember of little Max. "You'll like our University. For one thing, it was designed for elves. As you know, elves are all very tall, so you'll find the furniture has been built to accommodate your shape." He turned to look at Rhen's large frame. "Yes, you'll feel comfortable here. Also, we have a diverse student body. Many of our students are from different solar systems and planets. Our Elfin University seems to have become a favorite with the Kings and Queens abroad. What planet have you been living on?" he inquired, while looking at Rhen's green and purple tunic, his tight leather necklace with turquoise stones, his military belt complete with seven daggers and his black military boots.

"Surpen," Rhen snapped. The only teachers he'd met in his life were nasty. He assumed the Headmaster would soon turn on him.

"Ah," the Headmaster breathed out, while nodding his head. "Surpen, a member of the Convention." He glanced over at Kate and Henry with curiosity, as he wondered why they had allowed their son to live on an enemy planet. "That's one culture we know very little about," the Headmaster added. "Come to think of it, you might be our very first Surpen student. Perhaps you'd be kind enough to teach a class on Surpen to those students, who are interested in learning about Surpen and its language? We give extra credit points to students, who help round out our curriculum by teaching others on subjects they know a lot about."

Without giving the suggestion any thought, Rhen replied, "No." He turned away from the Headmaster and studied the room. The Headmaster was surprised by his behavior. New students tended to bend over backwards to please him. He lost his train of thought, as he regarded Rhen's back. Before he could remember what he had been talking about, Ceceta stepped over and nudged Rhen's arm. Rhen gazed down at her and nodded. Ceceta smiled and turned towards the Headmaster. In a soft voice and using broken Thestran, she said, "Ah touch clz Supen."

The Headmaster stepped back to take a better look at Ceceta. She was dressed in long, violet robes and was carrying a brown, leather bag that rested on her back. Although she was dressed like a Surpen woman, it was obvious she wasn't Surpen. The Headmaster laughed, when he saw a wisp of her blond hair peeking out from underneath her scarf. Blue skin, blond hair and dark eyes, she was a Neptian. "Ah ha! A Neptian," he stated. "You're bound to be very clever if you're Neptian. Yes, we'd love to have you teach our students. I'll have my scheduler arrange a time."

Ceceta bowed to the Headmaster and informed him in Neptian, "The class can only be held between five and six in the morning, while Rhen is exercising and before Surpen prayers. Would that be acceptable?" The Headmaster hesitated. How many students would wake up early for a class on a planet they couldn't care less about? He wanted to reject her offer, but decided it wouldn't be polite, so he nodded in agreement. If nothing else, it'd be one more item to add to their school brochure for interested parents.

"Very well," the Headmaster agreed. He turned back to Rhen. "As your parents may have mentioned, my name is Professor Dewey. If you need anything, please let me know. In the meantime," he added, while walking back to his desk and picking up some papers. "Here is our Code of Conduct and the Rules of the University. We operate just like any other school. If you are found breaking our rules, you'll be expelled."

Professor Dewey walked over to his office door and opened it. He gestured towards Rhen with the papers. "Now, I need to chat with your parents. Why don't the two of you take a walk around the grounds, and we'll catch up with you when we're done."

Rhen debated informing the Headmaster that Kate and Henry were not his parents but decided against it. He stepped out of the room, as Ceceta took the papers the Headmaster was holding. When Professor Dewey shut the door behind them, they could hear him asking Kate and Henry, in a strict tone of voice, "So, would you mind telling me what the hell is going on?"

Rhen smiled at Ceceta and said in Surpen, so the Headmaster's secretary wouldn't understand, "*Oooo, they're in trouble!*" Ceceta giggled. The two of them walked out of the Headmaster's waiting room. They wandered down the school's carpeted passageways, opening doors and inspecting classrooms. One teacher, who was setting up his room, asked them if they were in his class.

"I don't know," Rhen answered.

"What year are you?" the professor asked.

"I guess, first year," Rhen informed him.

"Oh, then you'll be taking Mr. Balot's History of the Thestran Royal Family. First year students are required to learn about the Thestran Royal Family. Second year students must pass History of Thestran and her Solar Systems and third year students are assigned History of the Universe. I'll see you in three years," he told them, dismissing them with a nod.

"Right," Rhen mumbled. He and Ceceta left the classroom.

After they had walked down the hallway in silence for a few minutes, Rhen asked Ceceta, "Do you think I'm included in the History of the Thestran Royal Family or have they 'accidentally' left me out?" Ceceta gave him a sad smile and reached up to touch his face. Rhen took her hand in his and kissed it, but winced and rubbed at the back of his head.

"What is it?" Ceceta asked. Reaching up, she felt the back of Rhen's head. She found a bump located two inches from his right ear at the base of his skull. "What's that?" she asked, her fingers probing it.

"I don't know," Rhen told her. "It started hurting when we arrived on Thestran and it's gotten bigger over the last two days."

Ceceta shuddered. "Could it be something you got on the Island?"

Rhen looked thoughtful. "Let's hope not," he told her, patting down his brown hair to make it lay flat.

They decided to go outside for some fresh air but had to wait ten minutes for a procession of tiny Nosduh students to cross from one side of the hallway to the other. Nosduh's were only an inch tall at full height. Having small legs, they took forever to move about. It was against Universal law to step over a Nosduh, doing so was punishable by death or life imprisonment. Nosduh's were an angry lot and they made sure to enforce this law whenever it was broken.

When the Nosduh's had cleared the hallway, Rhen and Ceceta made their way outside. As Rhen stepped out into the warm sunshine, he smiled. He didn't like being inside. His work on Surpen kept him under the desert sun most of day, and he preferred it that way.

In the distance, Rhen could see the Wood Elf Castle. Its tallest spires peaked out over the top of the Wood Elf Forest. "Do Reed and Lilo live in that castle? Is that the Wood Elf Castle?" Ceceta asked him.

"Yes," Rhen answered. He had asked one of the servants in the Thestran Castle about Reed and had learned all about the Wood Elves and their Castle. It appeared the four elfin tribes were having financial problems, so the Elfin Royals spent most of their time with the Thestran Royal Family, in the hopes of receiving favors from them. The Wood Elves were the richest tribe, since their princess had married the son of the Thestran Royal Family. Rhen tried to remember where the Wood Elf Castle was in relationship to the Thestran Royal Palace, but he couldn't recall. He thought it was in the middle of the planet, roughly a four-hour jet flight from the Thestran Castle, but he wasn't certain.

"Look," Ceceta said, bumping into his back.

Rhen glanced over and saw Charlie sitting under a tree smoking cigarettes and drinking with his friends. Charlie waved to them. Rhen returned the gesture with a hesitant wave. He heard Ceceta giggling behind him. "Was that painful dear?" she teased.

Rhen laughed and turned around, picking her up in his arms. "Absolutely," he replied, before kissing her and placing her back on the ground. "Actually, I didn't mean to wave back. It was kind of an involuntary reaction," he admitted. Ceceta smiled and took his hand. They walked over to a row of apple trees and sat down to watch the other students.

"I assume everything checks out?" Ceceta asked, when Rhen pulled her up against him.

"Yup," he replied, nuzzling his face into her hair.

"There aren't any Surpen spies at the University?" Ceceta prompted.

"Nope," Rhen mumbled. "No Surpen spies, no Convention spies, no Loreth spies and no annoying Genisters." He chuckled into her hair and the heat of his breath sent a shiver of desire down her back.

Ceceta considered asking him to phase them away to a secret location where they could get intimate, but at the last minute, she changed her mind. There was too much to see at the University and she didn't want to miss it. She'd spent her entire life in the Surpen Palace and now she was out. She couldn't get over all of the strange species of people that existed and she asked Rhen to educate her on everyone's home planet. As they watched the other students, they noticed that most of them were wearing shirts or carrying bags that had pictures or drawings of the Black Angel on them. A bunch of kids also had shirts that said B.A.C. on them. On the back of their shirts, it explained that the B.A.C. was the Black Angel Club. "Who knew the Black Angel had a Club?" Rhen stated amusement. Ceceta giggled.

Most of the students, who passed them, were discussing their course schedules, dorm rooms and the friends they hadn't seen all summer, but there were also a lot of students, who were discussing the latest adventures of the Black Angel. He appeared to be quite the celebrity. Rhen and Ceceta found this very amusing.

"Can I hear some music?" Ceceta asked Rhen, after they'd been sitting in silence for a while.

"Sure," he replied. Rhen used his powers to transmit the song that was playing in his head to her.

"Oh, that's beautiful," Ceceta commented. She closed her eyes to focus on the melody. "You always have the most beautiful songs playing in your mind."

"Beautiful to you, annoying to me," Rhen grumbled. He lay down on the soft, green grass to watch the spacejets. "That's one power I could do without." Ceceta patted Rhen on the arm and lay down beside him to watch the sky.

"You probably wouldn't mind it as much, if music was allowed on Surpen," she told him softly.

"Perhaps," Rhen answered, pulling her in towards him.

An hour before dinner, Professor Dewey, Kate and Henry found them under the apple tree. Rhen was lying on his back, looking up at the clouds, with Ceceta next to him. Her head was resting on his stomach. When the adults arrived, Rhen and Ceceta rose to their feet. Professor Dewey apologized to them for taking so long. He dismissed Kate and Henry, telling them they had to leave, so he could get down to business with his newest students. Kate and Henry wanted to hug Rhen goodbye, but they knew he'd get angry with them for touching him, so they attempted to give him a Surpen military salute. Rhen seemed to have no reaction to their efforts, although he did bow to them, when they were done. Kate and Henry laughed with embarrassment and turned to leave.

After they had left, Professor Dewey took Rhen and Ceceta to their apartment, which was in the Teachers' Residence Hall. "Because you're married," he explained. "You won't have to stay in the students' dormitories." As they entered their apartment, Ceceta and Rhen found a small, walk-in kitchen located immediately to their right. Professor Dewey flicked on the kitchen's fluorescent lights to show them the space. There was a refrigerator, dishwasher and numerous white, laminate cabinets. The left wall, in front of the sink, was open, so they could look through to the living room.

Walking down the hallway, they noticed that the other side of the half wall had been made into a bar area and there were four, bar chairs lined up underneath the counter. Rhen walked over to inspect a wooden bookcase that lined the left wall of the living room, while Ceceta touched the tired looking blue couch and chairs that were set in a semicircle around a brown coffee table in the living area. Beyond the couch was a worn looking oak desk, where they could do their homework, and above the desk, were two windows. A simple, white door was located on the left side of the room, before the bookcase. Rhen opened it and nodded, when he saw a bedroom and bathroom. Their bed was already made with white sheets and a white comforter. The apartment itself was painted in white and most of the furniture in it was a dull, brown color. Ceceta smiled at the bland décor.

"The University's staff will take care of any dishes, laundry and cleaning that needs to be done, so you can focus on your studies," Professor Dewey told them. "Also, even though you have a kitchen, you're required to eat your meals with the rest of the students, so you can make friends and form study groups for your more intense courses." Professor Dewey handed Rhen their course schedule, which Rhen passed over to Ceceta. She scanned the page and nodded in agreement. "Great," the Headmaster remarked. "Will you please accompany me to the main auditorium for the commencement services."

As they walked out of the apartment, one of the University's employees arrived, looking flustered. "Sir, Rhen's 'slaves' have arrived with their things."

Professor Dewey seemed concerned for a moment. "Rhen, would you mind not using your slaves, while you're here at the school?" he asked, with some trepidation. "We require the other students to leave theirs at home."

Rhen didn't care for slaves. He'd never liked the way they hung over him, so he nodded that it would be fine. "You'll find our staff can do everything your slaves do, sometimes faster and better," Professor Dewey assured him, as they walked off towards the auditorium, while the frazzled employee ran off to send the Surpen slaves home.

When they entered the main auditorium, a silence fell over the room. It appeared word had spread that Kate and Henry's youngest son was going to the University. The students were eager to see Max. Not a lot was known about him. They leaned over the balcony railings and stood up in the tiered seats to get a better view of him. Professor Dewey walked Rhen and Ceceta over to some seats in the front of the room and indicated to them that they should sit down. When they were settled, he moved over to the podium to welcome the students. He promised them a fun-filled academic year with many new challenges. He introduced the new teachers and talked about the special events the University would be hosting over the upcoming year.

Bowing his head towards Rhen, Professor Dewey introduced him to the student body. "It's an honor to include in our enrollment this year, the youngest Thestran Prince and...Surpen Prince, as well, of course," he added. "Kate and Henry's eighth child, Rhen. Rhen is now 16."

Rhen frowned and turned away from Professor Dewey.

The Headmaster hesitated. For some reason, the boy looked furious. Continuing, Professor Dewey said, "He will be joining our student body as a freshman. Prince Rhen lives on Surpen. He and his wife will be our first Surpen students. They've been kind enough to offer a course on Surpen for any interested students."

The room became noisy, as the students whispered among themselves. No one could understand why the Headmaster had called Max, Rhen; why a 16-year-old would be allowed to enter the University or why a member of the Convention would be allowed to attend a Thestran place of learning.

Professor Dewey brought the meeting to an abrupt end and strode across the stage towards Rhen. "I understand you have a special diet. Your planet's food arrived this afternoon." He paused and glanced up towards the balcony to wave at some students, who were calling out his name, before looking back at Rhen. "You're not the first student to require a special diet. Would you mind sitting in some pre-arranged seats for a few weeks, so the staff can learn who you are and the students can get used to the foods you eat?" Rhen nodded his head in agreement. "Don't worry, it's only for a few weeks. After our first break, you can sit wherever you want."

Rhen didn't respond but stared at him with a blank expression that the Headmaster found unnerving.

"Great," Professor Dewey said. He nodded and turned to leave. Before he could step away, Rhen grabbed his upper arm. The gesture wasn't meant to be an attack, but Professor Dewey was frightened, after his talk with Kate and Henry, so he cried out in alarm.

Most of the students and teachers were still in the auditorium. They turned, when they heard someone yell, and were shocked to see their Headmaster struggling in Rhen's grasp.

Rhen was surprised by Professor Dewey's reaction. The man looked like a frightened animal, struggling and fighting against Rhen's grip. Rhen released his hold on the Headmaster's upper arm and watched, as Professor Dewey jumped away from him.

"I am not 16. I am 17," Rhen told Professor Dewey, who was rubbing his arm, where Rhen had held it.

"What?" the Headmaster asked. He had no idea what Rhen was talking about.

"I am 17," Rhen told him.

"Huh," the Headmaster grunted, as it dawned on him that this was the reason why Rhen had appeared angry. "But, your parents said you were 16."

"Yes, I was last year. But this year, I am 17."

"I think your mother would know how old you are, after all...." the Headmaster began, but the look of hatred that spread across Rhen's face brought him to an abrupt halt.

Ceceta stepped forward and placed her hand on Rhen's shoulder. She stared at Rhen with piercing eyes, until he nodded that she could speak. "Right," she said in Neptian, while turning towards the Headmaster. "Kate seems to have lost track of the years. I can assure you my husband is 17-years-old. In fact, he will be 18 before the end of this school year. Does that mean you should bump us up one grade?"

Professor Dewey's arm ached. He was having trouble concentrating. He had never experienced someone like Rhen before. Students, who planned on entering the military, always did so after graduating from the University, not the other way around. Before he could think of what to say to Ceceta, Charlie stood up from his chair in the top of the balcony. "Let's all raise a glass to Rhen for his 17th birthday, which slipped away before we even got to celebrate it! Happy Birthday Baby Brother!" he cried out. Charlie raised the drink in his right hand up towards Rhen then swung his red, plastic cup downward, hitting the top edge of the chair in front of him and spilling the remains of his drink everywhere.

For the first time in his life, Professor Dewey was happy to discipline Charlie. The boy had given him something else to focus on. Rhen was going to be more of a problem than he had realized. Even though Kate and Henry had warned him about Rhen, he had had trouble imagining one of their children as dangerous. Now, he understood what they had been trying to say, and he knew he needed more of the Royal Family members to watch over Rhen, while he was at the University. Charlie wouldn't be able to help, since he was inebriated most of the time.

"Charlie go to my office! Immediately!" Professor Dewey yelled. Turning back to Ceceta, he said, "You and Rhen are in the correct grade level. All of the students in the freshman year are either 18 or soon to be turning 18."

Ceceta nodded and reached out to take Rhen's hand. *"Come, let's go eat,"* she whispered in Surpen.

Still frustrated, but for the most part at himself for his inexplicable feelings of anger over the fact that his birth mother had no idea how old he was, Rhen nodded and they walked off to the dining hall.

When Rhen and Ceceta entered the dining room, a University staff member indicated a table in the far, right corner of the room, where they should sit. The room looked very institutional with its white walls and white-tiled floor. There were numerous rectangular, grey, metal tables with benches and several doors that connected the room to the cafeteria, where students received their food. On the right wall was a row of small windows that looked out over the school's main lawn.

Rhen sat down at their assigned table, as Ceceta sat across from him. The staff placed plates of raw meat onto the table in front of them and disappeared.

"*Well, that's a blessing,*" Rhen mumbled in Surpen, when they were gone.

"*What?*" Ceceta asked.

"*I was worried they were going to hang over us while we ate,*" Rhen answered. Ceceta nodded, even though that hadn't occurred to her. She ate her meals alone with the Surpen Queen, after Andres had finished and left the room. The castle's slaves never hung around them. "*The more they leave us alone, the better,*" Rhen added. He forked a large chunk of meat into his mouth.

Ceceta disagreed. Although she couldn't wait to spend more alone time with Rhen, she wanted to get involved in life at the University. She hoped to meet the Thestrans and learn more about them. She had forgotten much of her earlier life before Surpen, and she wanted to know what she was missing. Her eyes glowed with excitement, as the students came off the cafeteria line and headed towards their table. It appeared most of them were eager to meet the youngest Thestran Prince. But, as soon as they caught sight of what Rhen and Ceceta were eating, they groaned and turned away.

Rhen finished his meal feeling quite content, as Ceceta picked at the remains of her dinner. She hadn't expected the Thestrans to turn on them quite so fast and was beginning to have doubts about her school experience.

Chapter 11

Andres drummed his fingers on the arm of his throne. Loreth would be arriving at any minute. He was worried what his advisor would say, when he learned that Rhen had enrolled at the Elfin University on Thestran.

Loreth had helped Andres further Surpen's goals. Together, they had conquered countless planets using Rhen's skills. Loreth's temper was notorious, though, and Andres feared he had made a mistake in allowing Rhen to stay on Thestran.

What would Loreth say about Andres' decision to let Rhen remain on Thestran? Andres shuddered at the memory of his last disagreement with Loreth, as he rose from his throne. His right hand would never be the same. Granted, Loreth had healed the bones he had broken, after Andres had apologized for disobeying him, but his joints still ached from the wounds Loreth had inflicted.

Andres strode over to one of the open windows and looked out over the military barracks. Rhen had asked him to appoint his friend Bosternd to be Military Commander in his absence and Andres had followed his wishes. He liked Bosternd. The man was loyal and obedient. He would serve Andres well until Rhen returned.

A splash startled Andres. He turned to face the room, searching for Loreth. Andres leaned to his left to check behind the massive columns that supported the vaulted ceiling. As far as he could tell, he was still alone. He walked towards the main entrance, passing several arched openings and paused by the small, sunken pool near the main doorway. The beige stones at his feet had dark circles on them. One of the fish that Rhen had given to him must have splashed water onto the floor. Bending down, Andres gazed into the pool at the four, orange and white fish that were swimming before him. It was quiet in the room. The setting sun basked everything with a golden light. He smiled, as one of the fish paused below him, looking for a handout, its tail fin fanned the water beneath it. 'How peaceful,' he thought to himself, before every muscle in his body clenched in pain. Andres dropped to the ground beside the pool, whimpering in agony.

"Where's Rhen?" Loreth asked, materializing by Andres' throne.

The pain was so intense that Andres couldn't speak. Loreth smiled and regarded his nails with bemusement. He left Andres on the ground for a good five minutes, before releasing him from his powers. Andres gasped for breath and crawled onto his hands and knees. He knew he needed to respond to Loreth right away or Loreth would punish him again. "He's…he's trying to learn more…by…by spying on them longer," Andres gasped out, as Loreth waved his hand in Andres' direction, making Andres forgot about the pain he had been feeling.

Andres stood up and approached Loreth, stopping five feet away to bow. "He doesn't trust the elves and is enrolling at the Elfin University to learn more about their armies," Andres added.

"Armies?" Loreth asked with mirth. "The elves don't have armies. They're pacifists."

"Rhen felt that might be a front. He wants to investigate the elves further. There may be a possibility they have hidden armies at Thestran's disposal," Andres informed him.

Loreth laughed. He gazed down on Andres, who was still bowing before him. "I know elves. I know them better than anyone. Elves are pacifists. Rhen's on a fool's mission. Tell him to return home at once." Loreth wanted Rhen on Surpen, so he could prepare their military to attack Thestran.

"Yes, sir," Andres replied, standing up to go. As he walked towards the exit that would take him to Surpen's portal, he bumped into an invisible wall blocking the doorway. Loreth had done this to him before, so Andres knew the drill. "Was there something else," he asked, while turning towards his advisor.

Loreth appeared pensive. He gazed down at Andres' fish. "Rhen is at the Elfin University?" he asked.

"Yes," Andres confirmed.

"His birth family wanted him to go?"

"I don't know," Andres admitted. "They didn't object to it."

Reaching up to stroke his chin, Loreth gave Andres an evil smile. "Leave him," he told the King. "I'll enjoy our victory over Thestran even more, if they fall in love with our Rhen. How delightful to watch the horror on their faces, when they see his betrayal. Yes," Loreth said with a laugh. "Let's leave him for now. I want to conquer Thestran after those fools learn to trust and adore him. Once they consider him to be theirs, we will strike."

"As you wish sir," Andres replied, feeling relieved. His own pleasure at the thought of hurting Rhen's birth family was lifting his mood.

Chapter 12

Rhen and Ceceta walked into the student dining hall the next morning to find Rhen's sister Lilly, and a few of the University's teachers, eating breakfast at a table in the back of the room. Lilly waved hello to them as soon as they entered, while the teachers sitting with her turned their heads to stare. It was obvious, from their expressions, that Lilly had been talking about them. Ceceta waved back, as Rhen leaned over and whispered, "*I guess we're the freak-show attraction.*"

"*Did you think things would change here on Thestran?*" she responded, as Rhen chuckled and poked her in the ribs. Ceceta smiled and sat down across from him at their assigned table. As soon as they were seated, the University's staff placed bowls of bloodworms in front of them. "*They're good,*" Ceceta remarked, of the school's employees. She had been impressed at the speed with which they had met her needs. Rhen nodded in agreement, as a staff member filled his glass with blood and placed the pitcher onto the table in front of him.

Overnight, a few of the elfin students had decided they would sit with the youngest Thestran Prince at breakfast, no matter what he was eating. To Rhen's chagrin, seven students placed their trays onto the table around them. They greeted Rhen and Ceceta and held out their hands to shake. Rhen ignored them, as he drank from his glass. He had no desire to meet any Thestrans. Ceceta was desperate to respond, but dropped her head down to look at her bowl, since Rhen hadn't given her permission to speak yet.

The elves remained at their table, chatting about various upcoming sporting events, while encouraging Rhen to get involved. Rhen's response to their dialogue was to pick up a few of the wiggling bloodworms from his bowl and pop them into his mouth. As he crunched their red-capped heads, the bloodworms emitted a thick, warm, rusty, blood smell. The elfin students gagged, and within minutes, they had all moved to different tables. Rhen smiled with triumph, revealing blood-soaked teeth, as Ceceta kicked him under the table. He knew it was for the best. The Thestrans should learn to stay away from him. When Ceceta kicked him again under the table, Rhen grimaced, knowing the moment he gave her permission to speak, he was done for. She'd be all over him. For the rest of their breakfast, Rhen ate at a snail's pace, enjoying the silence before the maelstrom.

The classes that Kate and Henry had chosen for Rhen and Ceceta were History of the Thestran Royal Family, Writing Composition, Women in Interuniversal Politics, Astronomy and Math Level 1. Professor Dewey had suggested giving them a language class, but Kate and Henry had told him not to bother. Rhen could already speak more languages than most people. As Rhen and Ceceta moved from classroom to classroom, they noticed they had the same students in most of their classes. It seemed the freshmen class had been broken into groups and each group stayed together throughout the day.

Most of Rhen's teachers found him infuriating. He would gaze out the windows or flip through his textbooks, looking at their pictures, during the lectures. It was obvious he had no interest in being at the University. Professor Dewey had told Rhen's teachers that they were not allowed to discipline him, nor could they fail him. They had to give Rhen passing grades, no matter what work he did. It was a nightmare situation for them.

"*I'm bored*," Rhen moaned, when he and Ceceta entered their math class after lunch.

Ceceta refused to answer him. She was still angry at him for scaring away the students, who had approached them during breakfast. Rhen plopped down into the seat beside hers and glanced up at the young man who was teaching math. He couldn't have been much older than they were. He was a dark-skinned elf with shoulder length black hair and a warm, inviting expression.

Professor DiGrego had heard, from the other teachers at lunch, that Rhen was disrespectful. He didn't mind, as long as Rhen didn't take away instruction time from the other students. "Okay class," he began, while beaming at his students, as he wrote an equation on the screen in the front of the room. Several of the students smiled at his apparent enthusiasm. "If any of you can figure out the equation I wrote on the screen, you'll receive an A in this class, and you'll be excused from taking math for the rest of your time here at the University." He smiled with contentment, while watching the students' eager expressions, as they read the equation on the board. He knew the problem was far beyond their years. It was too advanced for even the graduate students.

Rhen sighed and glanced up at the screen. Within seconds, the answer to Mr. DiGrego's question popped into his mind. He debated whether he should answer it. He wanted to stay with Ceceta, but the idea of escaping these horrible Thestran classes, for even a few minutes, made him lift his hand to get Mr. DiGrego's attention. "75.75," he told the teacher, while giving Ceceta a triumphant smile. He was ready to go. In fact, he wanted to go home. He'd had enough school to last him a lifetime.

"Excuse me?" Professor DiGrego asked. He wasn't sure he'd heard right. He had been teaching math for ten years and no one had ever figured out one of his opening equations.

"75.75," Rhen repeated, with annoyance.

DiGrego gave a surprised laugh. He couldn't believe it. Rhen had figured out his equation. "Was that a lucky guess?" he asked. Instead of answering, Rhen stared at him without any expression on his face. Professor

DiGrego walked back to the screen and wrote out another equation. Turning to Rhen, he said, "If you can get this one, I'll give you an A in the class."

Rhen felt himself flush with anger. "You already said that I was getting an A. Why do I have to continue? Were you lying before?"

"No," Professor DiGrego replied, hoping to keep Rhen calm. "It's just that I've never had a student, who could answer that equation before. In case you were told about it before coming to the University, I want proof you solved it yourself."

"So," Rhen said, shifting in his seat. "You're calling me a liar."

Now, Professor DiGrego realized why the other teachers had found Rhen difficult. It was because he was difficult. "Rhen," he said, in an appeasing tone of voice. "You get an A in this class for the year. Would you please amuse me by answering this equation?"

"And I never have to take math at this University again?" Rhen prompted.

Professor DiGrego squirmed. That promise was beyond his power, but he'd made it, so he had to uphold it. "Okay," he agreed. "But first, you need to answer a few other equations, so when I go to the Math Department to petition for your removal from the Math Program, I'll have the data I need to have you released."

Rhen glanced up at the screen and said, "235.678."

Professor DiGrego looked back at the equation. "Correct," he said over his shoulder. He wrote out a new equation. "Try this one." Before he could turn around, Rhen answered, "0.56734."

Without responding, Professor DiGrego continued to write equations on the screen. Rhen gave the correct answer to each of them, before Mr. DiGrego could remove his hand. Soon Professor DiGrego was pulling math books off his bookcase. He copied down equation after equation onto the screen, while Rhen answered each of them as soon as he had finished writing them down.

When he'd reached the end of the book he was holding, Professor DiGrego slammed it shut and placed it onto his desk. "You're a genius!" he shouted. "A mathematical genius! How'd you know the answers to these equations? I didn't even know the answers to some of them. I had to look them up in the back of the book, after you'd given me your answer." Rhen shrugged.

Professor DiGrego walked over to stand in front of Rhen's desk. He gazed down at him with awe. "You're a genius," he repeated. "Would you consider joining the University's Math Club? We try to discover answers to the Universe's greatest math problems."

"No," Rhen replied.

"Please," Mr. DiGrego begged. "With your knowledge, we'd be able to advance the field of mathematics to new heights. It'd be amazing what we could do!"

Rhen shook his head. He had no interest in becoming involved in the University. He wanted to leave it as soon as possible, without upsetting Ceceta.

Professor DiGrego sighed. "Perhaps we'll be able to entice you into joining us later in the year. It'd be a shame not to tap into your innate skills and knowledge." Rhen glanced over towards the door. It was clear what he wanted. "Alright," Mr. DiGrego said, stepping away from Rhen's desk. "You can go. Would you like me to have the Headmaster find you another class during this period?"

"NO!" Ceceta yelled out, startling everyone.

"Okay," Professor DiGrego said, while taking a moment to study Ceceta. He'd heard from the other teachers that Ceceta never spoke. As far as he knew, this was the first word she'd spoken all day. He found Rhen and Ceceta's behavior odd, and he wondered what life was like on Surpen.

Rhen stood up and leaned over to kiss Ceceta. *"I'll see you at our History of the Thestran Royal Family class,"* he told her. She nodded in agreement, as he walked towards the door.

At the Headmaster's request, Lilly had been attending Rhen's classes. She hesitated, watching Rhen walk towards the door. She wasn't sure if she should follow him or stay with Ceceta.

"Hey," Professor DiGrego called out to Rhen, when he opened the door. "If you change your mind about Math Club, let me know. We're always happy to have a brilliant mathematician join us." For a moment, it looked like Rhen was about to laugh, but he stepped out of the room, closing the door behind him.

Lilly decided it would be too obvious if she followed him, so she remained in her seat.

After math class, which the rest of the students found very difficult, Lilly walked with Ceceta towards her History of the Thestran Royal Family class. "So, Ceceta," she commented in Neptian. "How did Rhen know the answers to all of those equations?"

Ceceta shrugged. She could talk to other women, when there weren't any men present, so she added, "I don't know."

"He must've had a wonderful math teacher on Surpen," Lilly remarked, increasing her speed to keep up.

Ceceta laughed out loud. "No," she replied, while reaching out to open the door to her history class. "He's never taken math."

Lilly stared at Ceceta with raised eyebrows, but before she could ask her to explain, several male students walked up behind them. Ceceta dropped her head down and walked into the classroom, taking one of the seats in the front. A few minutes later, Rhen strode into the room looking very pleased. Ceceta could smell the scent of the Surpen Beasts of War on his tunic, and she realized he had popped home for a quick visit, while she was in math class. Ceceta reached out to touch Rhen's arm. His skin was still warm from the Surpen sun. *"Bad boy,"* she whispered under her breath. Rhen gave her one of his mischievous smiles, before their history teacher began.

Professor Balot closed the door to the classroom. "I love teaching this class, because I find the Royal Family fascinating. Don't you?"

The students murmured in agreement, as Mr. Balot walked to the front of the room. "Occasionally, we're lucky enough to have a member of the Royal Family join us, but now," he said, while turning towards Lilly and Rhen. "For the first time, we have two members of the Royal Family in attendance. Does anyone want to get their autographs before we begin?"

The students weren't sure if he was serious or not. They wanted Lilly and Rhen's autographs, but they hesitated. They'd heard rumors about Mr. Balot. He wasn't supposed to be nice. Mr. Balot laughed at their indecision and added, "Maybe you can get them after class." Turning towards Rhen, he remarked, "I believe this will be the most interesting class I've ever taught. In the past, we've spoken about the members of the Thestran Royal Family in detail, but we've only ever mentioned Kate and Henry's youngest son, Max, briefly. Now Max is in our classroom and..."

"My name is Rhen," Rhen said, interrupting him.

Mr. Balot paused to regard him. "Yes, of course," he commented. He glanced back at the rest of his students. "It appears I've been teaching Max's history incorrectly. It's time," he stated, staring down at Rhen, "for you to tell us your story." Rhen remained quiet, so Professor Balot continued. "You've always been just a side note in my students' education. My bonus question on tests, if you please. 'Do you know what planet Max is currently living on?'"

Rhen remained focused on his desk. He could tell Professor Balot was baiting him. He'd met men like him before. There was always someone out there who wanted to test themselves against him, someone who wanted to prove they were stronger than him.

"I do hope you'll tell us what you've been doing with your life," Mr. Balot said. "For example," he added, while leaning so close to Rhen that their faces almost touched. "How did it come to pass that you can eat meat? Was it hard being the only Thestran on a Convention run world? What was it like to be forced to call King Andres dad?"

Rhen was going to have to fight him. There wasn't any way around it. Mr. Balot wasn't going to leave him alone. Rhen raised his eyes to Balot's. "It's none of your business," he told the man.

"Oh, yes, it is Max. You're a part of the Thestran Royal Family. What you do IS our business. We have a right to know about your life. You owe it to us Max."

Professor Balot was so close that Rhen could smell the fish he had had for lunch. Gritting his teeth, Rhen decided to give the man one more chance. "I am not a Thestran," he told Professor Balot. "I am a Surpen. Therefore, I don't owe YOU anything. Should YOU move to Surpen, I would be happy to tell you what I have been doing with my life."

Mr. Balot chuckled. Rhen felt his hot, stinky breath blowing against his cheeks. "You don't look like a Surpen to me," Professor Balot replied. "You look like a plain, old, Thestran elf."

Rhen thrust himself forward, head butting Professor Balot. The man fell to the ground unconscious. Standing up, Rhen surveyed the shocked students around him. "Class dismissed," he announced, before walking out the door without looking back.

The room erupted, as everyone began to talk at once. No one could believe what Rhen had done. He was sure to be expelled. The students rushed out into the hallway, telling everyone they met about what had happened to Mr. Balot.

Lilly bent down over the fallen professor. She had never liked the man. Mr. Balot had deserved it. He'd been antagonizing Rhen. Reaching out, she used her powers to wake up Professor Balot. Without a word of thanks, he rose and rushed out of the room to inform the Headmaster.

Lilly sat down on the floor and rubbed her chilled arms. She glanced back at the desks and noticed Ceceta sitting alone, staring out into space.

"He was asking for it you know," Ceceta mumbled in Neptian. "I thought this school experience was going to be fun, but it's been miserable. And now," she added with a sigh. "I guess it's over."

Lilly wanted to tell Ceceta she wasn't going to be expelled, but she had no idea what the Headmaster was going to do.

"What was I thinking?" Ceceta continued. "You can't ask a wild tiger to watch babies, without at least one of them getting killed."

Lilly laughed. Ceceta gave her a sad smile and ran her fingers over the covers of her textbooks. "I guess I'll just leave them here and go pack," she said, while reaching up to take the translating device out of her ear.

"NO!" Lilly exclaimed, rising to her feet. "I'm not going to let him get away with this! Professor Balot is not going to get Rhen expelled. Don't worry Ceceta, I'll take care of it." Without waiting for a response, Lilly rushed from the room.

An hour later, Rhen lay under the apple trees on the hill near the Teachers' Residence Hall. He had apologized to Ceceta for his behavior, and it seemed as if she had forgiven him. Professor Dewey, Lilly, Mr. Balot, Kate and Henry were meeting to discuss his fate. He didn't care what they decided. He was going home. He had had enough of this whole 'school' thing and he wanted out. He would insist Ceceta accompany him back to Surpen this evening.

A gorgeous, blue butterfly fluttered by Rhen, making looping shapes as it searched for food. Its wings matched the color of Ceceta's cheeks. As Rhen watched the butterfly move from flower to flower, he was suddenly hit with guilt. He had agreed to let Ceceta attend this University and now he was ruining it for her. They hadn't even gotten through one complete day, and he was already forcing her to go home. Ceceta. His beautiful, loving, supportive wife.

A group of students approached him to thank him for putting Mr. Balot in his place. They were the seventh group to stop by, since he had sat down under this tree. Rhen gave them his usual nod and watched as they ran off, laughing at his balls for knocking out a teacher. Earlier, Charlie had sat down next to him to tell him that he should've knocked out Mr. Balot in secret, so he wouldn't have gotten in trouble. Rhen had assured Charlie that the next time he would be more careful.

'The next time,' Rhen thought. He groaned. He felt terrible for Ceceta. The excitement on her face, when they had gotten out of bed this morning had thrilled him. He loved it when she was happy. She was the only thing in the Universe that he cared about and now, he was letting her down. Rhen closed his eyes and made a promise. If Professor Dewey didn't expel him, he would behave himself and support Ceceta for as long as she intended to stay at this school. It was the least he could do for her, after the years of support she had given to him.

Rhen heard someone approaching and opened his eyes. An honor student stared down at him. She smiled, but waited for the large spacejet to pass over their heads, before speaking. Once the noise had diminished, she said, "The Headmaster wants to see you in his office now." Rhen nodded and stood up.

He walked into the Headmaster's waiting room and was ushered into his office. Professor Dewey was sitting alone behind his desk. As Rhen entered the room, he indicated that Rhen should sit down.

Professor Dewey watched Rhen for a few minutes. He seemed somber, which the Headmaster took as a good sign. If Rhen had marched into the room laughing, he would've been forced to change his mind about Rhen's punishment. Picking up some papers from his desk, Professor Dewey decided to make Rhen wait. He wanted Rhen to know he was displeased with him, his decision was a difficult one.

Fifteen minutes later, Professor Dewey put down the papers he was holding and looked at Rhen. The boy hadn't moved. Most students would've spoken to him by now, either begging him for forgiveness or blaming the teacher for the incident. At the very least, they would've been shifting in their chair. Rhen was so calm it seemed wrong. Professor Dewey shook his head, feeling sad for the boy. Rhen must've learned to control himself in the army. Whatever this child had seen in his life was more than he wanted to know. Rhen had been disciplined well, too well for a Thestran Prince.

"This has been an exciting first day of school for you," Professor Dewey commented. Rhen nodded in agreement. "Well, I won't beat around the bush. You should be expelled for what you did, but it seems your sister feels you did it in self-defense."

Rhen snorted. Was that what Lilly had called it? Self-defense?

The Headmaster paused. "I had to agree with her, since she hasn't anything to gain from lying, so you won't be expelled. BUT!" Professor Dewey yelled. "IF YOU EVER SO MUCH AS BRUSH AGAINST ANOTHER TEACHER, YOU WILL BE EXPELLED. DO YOU UNDERSTAND?"

"Yes, sir," Rhen replied.

Professor Dewey felt he had made his point. "You can go."

Rhen stood up and walked towards the door. "And please," Professor Dewey added, as Rhen opened the door, "try not to cause any additional incidents."

"I'm sorry sir. It won't happen again," Rhen told him. He bowed and left the room, closing the door behind him.

Professor Dewey stared at his closed door for a few minutes, before going back to work.

Both the teachers and the students at the University were surprised, when they learned Rhen hadn't been expelled. At dinner, the students joked that they were going to start slapping the teachers around, if they gave out too much homework.

Lilly entered the dining room and sat down next to Rhen. She was pleased she'd been able to help him and Ceceta. Rhen gave her a look and grinned. Dropping his gaze to his plate, so it wouldn't seem as if he were addressing her, Rhen said, "Self-defense?" He laughed and shook his head in disbelief.

Lilly's heart skipped a beat. Rhen had just addressed her. He wasn't doing it openly, but he was still doing it. "Well it was!" she protested, hoping to keep their conversation going. "Mr. Balot was belittling you, and you couldn't even move away from him. He was blocking you. I told the Headmaster that if he'd kept a proper distance, you wouldn't have been able to head butt him. It was his own fault."

Rhen laughed again. He scanned the room for spies. When he was sure it was safe, he looked into Lilly's eyes. "Self defense?" he asked her. Lilly smiled at him with encouragement. With a disbelieving shake of his head, Rhen leaned over towards her and bumped her with his shoulder. Lilly was shocked by the gesture and almost missed hearing him add, "I'm going to get walloped for that back in the barracks."

A shiver ran through Lilly's body at the magnitude of their exchange. Rhen had not only spoken to her, but he had bumped into her, as if they were friends. She couldn't wait to tell the others. She gazed up into his relaxed, laughing face and felt her heart stutter. Rhen was gorgeous. Why hadn't she noticed it before? "I think I'm going to get something to eat," she mumbled, while rising to her feet. She paused, when she noticed Ceceta watching her like a hawk. Lilly smiled at her sister in law, but Ceceta only blinked in response. With a shrug, Lilly turned and left to get her meal.

Ceceta had seen her husband touch his mother and the wives of other soldiers but never an unmarried woman. It was against Surpen law for a man to touch a woman, who wasn't a part of his family. His unexpected familiarity with Lilly confused and annoyed her. For the first time, Ceceta wondered if it had been a mistake for her to take Rhen off Surpen. He had an aura that people were attracted to. If he were free from Surpen's laws, would he notice other women?

Standing up, Ceceta moved around the table to sit down beside Rhen, as he rubbed at the sore spot on the back of his head. She wrapped her arm around his waist and leaned up to kiss him on the check. Rhen returned the gesture. "Thank you for fixing everything," she told him in Thestran. To express his remorse, Rhen had given her the ability to understand, as well as to read and write in Thestran, and she no longer needed permission from him to speak.

"My pleasure," he told her. "I promise to behave."

Professor Dewey came up behind them. "Ceceta," he said, holding out a sheet of paper for her to take. "We've had two students sign up for your Surpen class. Crystam, the daughter of the Ventarian Queen, and Latsoh, the daughter of the King and Queen of the Fire Elves."

"Really?" Ceceta asked, her eyes lighting up with excitement. "That's wonderful."

"What's wonderful?" Lilly inquired, placing her tray of food on the table. "And how can you speak in Thestran?"

"Two people signed up for my Surpen class," Ceceta began. "And I remember my Thestran now. It just took me a few days to brush up," she lied. A moment later, Ceceta started to give Lilly a run down on her ideas for the class she was teaching. She spoke for a long time, occasionally stopping to ask Rhen his opinion.

Rhen grew tired of listening to her. He grunted in response to her questions and rubbed at the back of his head. After a while, Rhen waved his hand at Ceceta to tell her to be quiet, but Ceceta ignored him. Looking for relief, Rhen left the table to go to the bathroom.

Pushing open the wooden door to the bathroom, Rhen walked over to stand in front of a urinal to relieve himself. He paused, when he heard some noises coming from one of the stalls. Glancing behind him, Rhen saw a short kid being suspended over one of the toilets by four older boys. The bigger kids had stopped their tormenting, when Rhen had entered the bathroom, and were now staring at him with apprehension, their eyes darting to the 15 small daggers he wore around his waist. When Rhen ignored them and turned back to the wall, they breathed a sigh of relief, but they remained silent until he left. Outside the bathroom, Rhen paused, as he debated whether he should return to help the small boy. He decided to move on. He really didn't want to get involved with the Thestrans.

Returning to the student dining hall, Rhen discovered that Ceceta had picked up some more 'friends'. It appeared as if she hadn't stopped talking the entire time he had been gone. Rhen sent a prayer to the Surpen God that he wasn't going to regret his decision of allowing her to talk whenever she wanted to. He closed his eyes and rubbed at the back of his head. Feeling like he just couldn't handle any more Thestrans for the night, he turned around and walked out of the building.

Making his way to the University's lake, Rhen sat down on the lush grass, pulled his knees up to his chest and slumped his shoulders over them, so he could rub at the back of his head with both of his hands.

The night was alive with wild creatures. Their evening songs played in his ears, complimenting the music that had popped into his mind when he had sat down.

A small, pale-skinned boy was sitting just a few yards away from him with his eyes closed. The boy's skin shimmered in the moonlight, making Rhen wonder where he was from.

The two of them sat in silence for half an hour. Eventually, the boy opened his eyes and rose to his feet. Turning, he made his way to Rhen. Although he was wearing traditional Thestran clothing, his large, brown eyes and soft features were not Thestran. "Sorry about that," he apologized. "I didn't mean to ignore you. I didn't even hear you arrive."

Rhen paused in rubbing his head and shrugged in response.

"You're Kate's son Rhen, right?" the boy asked, even though he already knew the answer.

Rhen nodded yes but remained silent. He figured, if he didn't engage the boy, the kid would leave him alone.

"My name is Erfce. I'm from Ponto. My family has ruled Ponto for 1,000 years." Erfce stepped sideways and sat down next to Rhen, his hand brushing against Rhen's sleeve by accident. Rhen glared at him and moved two feet away.

"Sorry, again," Erfce apologized, before looking up at the moon. "I know how you feel. I've been coming to the Thestran's schools for three years now, and I still don't feel comfortable." He glanced back at Rhen. "I'm an oracle," he stated. Rhen didn't answer, so Erfce continued, "most of the kids don't bother with me. It's no fun having a friend who can see the future. I know who they're going to marry, if they'll have children, and whether they'll live long enough to become kings themselves."

Erfce paused to stare at Rhen. "You know what?" he asked. Rhen didn't respond. "The funny thing is...I can't read you," Erfce admitted. He shook his head in confusion then gazed at Rhen, searching for an answer.

Rhen ignored him. Reaching to his waist, he took a knife from his belt and started to pick at a rock, the tip of which was sticking out of the ground.

"I've never not been able to read someone before," Erfce told him. "You may find this odd, but I find it very peaceful to be with you. I find a calmness in your presence that I can't reach around others. Their futures are always blaring in my mind, whether I want them to or not. The teachers here are trying to help me control my powers, but it's hard for them, since none of them are oracles, and they don't know what I'm dealing with. When I'm near you, everything just chills out and I can block the waves of knowledge that flood over me." Erfce peered at Rhen. "Do you have any idea why that would happen?"

Rhen didn't answer. He continued to pick at a new rock with his knife. Erfce decided to respect his silence and stopped talking. He closed his eyes and leaned his head back against the grass. They sat in silence for an hour. The only sound was the night creatures, and Rhen picking at an obstinate rock in the ground.

When Rhen got up to walk away, Erfce opened his eyes. "I'm not going to tell anyone about what you do to my powers, about the fact that they're under control or perhaps even gone in your presence," he mentioned, wondering which one it was. Rhen paused with his back to Erfce. "I enjoy the peace you give me. In fact, it's such a relief that I'm planning on being next to you as much as possible this year. I've already asked the three of our teachers, if I can sit next to you." Erfce laughed. "They didn't have any problem with it, since it seems all of the other students have requested not to sit next to you. Anyway, I just wanted you to know why I'm going to be following you around for the rest of the year."

Erfce seemed to be finished, so Rhen walked away without saying anything. He heard the boy groan in discomfort, as the distance he put between them, caused the thoughts and futures of the students in the area to rush back into his mind like a tidal wave.

Rhen considered using his powers to help Erfce but decided against it. The only people, who knew about his powers, were Ceceta and the Genisters. He had mentioned his powers to Bosternd a couple of times but never in any detail. It was best for everyone, if he kept his powers hidden.

Chapter 13

The next morning, as Rhen was exercising, Ceceta walked into the small classroom that Professor Dewey had assigned to her. She stopped short at the sight of the gorgeous, young, blond woman sitting at a desk in front of her. The woman's deep blue eyes left Ceceta speechless. "My name is Crystam," the woman told her, when she saw Ceceta's stunned expression. "The Queen of Ventar is my mother."

"Oh," Ceceta said, nodding her head in comprehension. The Queen of Ventar, also known as the Goddess of Love, was known to be the most beautiful woman in the Universe. "So, Crystam, my papers say you're a freshman. Out of curiosity, why did you decide to take this class? Your planet is aligned with Thestran's Council, not the Convention."

Crystam hesitated. "Well, to be honest. People don't always respect me. They can't see past," she held up her hand to indicate her face. "I hate it. I hear on Surpen the men treat their women the same way, like objects. I can relate to that, so I thought I'd learn about your planet to see if I could do anything to help Surpen's women change their situation."

"I love you," Ceceta told her. There was a moment of silence and then Ceceta and Crystam laughed. "Sadly, I don't think you'll be able to do anything to change our circumstances," Ceceta told Crystam. "But we, Surpen women, appreciate your thoughts."

Turning, Ceceta took in the green-eyed, red-haired beauty sitting beside Crystam. The girl was very pretty, but her looks paled next to Crystam's. "Hello. My papers indicate you're the daughter of King Naci and Queen Reman, the King and Queen of the Fire Elves."

"Yes, my name is Latsoh and I'm also a freshman. I'd like to learn about Surpen's Debrino Codes. I think they might be helpful to my father. From what I've read, it seems as if Debrino's Codes provided your people with a strong base from which they could repair their society. The elves were devastated after Lord Themrock's disappearance. I think a strong set of rules might help us repair our culture."

"Hmm," Ceceta said. "Well, I'm not sure what you've read about the Codes, but I don't think they'll work for the elves. The Codes are a form of control over the people, and their effects have been, for the most part, negative. Although they do bring order, it's a stifling order that isn't natural. Before Debrino put his Codes into effect, Surpen's culture was peaceful and well-rounded. All of that changed, due to the Codes."

For the next few minutes, Ceceta spoke about the Codes in detail with Latsoh. When she felt she had answered all of Latsoh's questions, she asked, "Do you still want to take the course?"

"Will you teach us how to speak and write the Surpen language?" Latsoh inquired.

"Yes, of course, if you would like me to," Ceceta replied.

"Then I will take your class. Surpen controls six solar systems. That's more than any other planet in the Universe. It may prove to be a valuable language to learn."

"Yes," Ceceta agreed, with a knowing smile. "I believe you're right." She rose from the seat she had taken beside Latsoh and moved to a metal desk near the front of the classroom to begin the day's lesson.

At the end of the period, Ceceta closed her book and looked up at her new friends. "Well, if you'll excuse me, I need to join Rhen for morning prayers."

"Can we come?" Latsoh asked.

"Maybe in a few weeks," Ceceta told her. "If you came today, Rhen would think you were mocking our prayers. He needs to get to know you first." She paused and added, "Why don't you join us at our table for breakfast?"

"That'd be great," Crystam said, as Latsoh nodded. "Rhen can keep all of my annoying suitors at bay. I'd appreciate even a few minutes of peace."

"Me too, from the Fire Elves," Latsoh added. "I love my people, but sometimes I just need a break from their constant attention."

"Great! We'll see you at breakfast."

Later that morning, when Rhen and Ceceta entered the dining hall for breakfast, they found not only Crystam and Latsoh at their table but Erfce as well. The young Pontian Prince was chatting with both women, when Rhen plopped down onto the bench beside him.

"Good morning!" Erfce said to Rhen.

Rhen grunted in response and grabbed a bloodworm from his bowl. Popping the worm into his mouth, he turned his head away from the Thestrans at the table.

Ceceta sat down between Crystam and Latsoh, on the opposite side of the table. "I hope you liked my class," she said in greeting, while grabbing her bowl of bloodworms from the center of the table.

"Of course, we did!" Latsoh told her. "It was very interesting."

"Completely fascinating," Crystam agreed. "I can't wait until tomorrow." Turning, she caught Rhen's eye. "Hi, I'm Crystam. I'm taking Ceceta's class."

Rhen froze. "Uh," Ceceta began, as she looked at Rhen. "You see Crystam, it's against Surpen etiquette for Rhen to speak to you." Crystam looked taken aback. "But, he should," Ceceta added, with a growl, "break from that archaic attitude and learn to speak to women, while he's here on Thestran."

Rhen sighed and reached down for another bloodworm.

"*Git mngn*," Latsoh greeted Rhen in Surpen. She butchered the words making him laugh. He glanced up at her and dipped his head in greeting, before turning to nod at Crystam.

Erfce rose from his seat and leaned over the table with his hand out in Ceceta's direction. "Good Mo..." he began. Rhen backhanded him in the stomach, knocking the wind out of him and forcing him to sit back down.

"You are NOT allowed to touch a Surpen woman, unless you are married to her," he barked at Erfce.

Rubbing his aching stomach, while giving Rhen a pained look, Erfce apologized, "I'm sorry Rhen. I didn't know about that custom." He turned back to Ceceta. "My name is Erfce. I'm the Prince of Ponto. We're a small planet in Thestran's solar system."

"It's nice to meet you Erfce. When did you meet Rhen?" Ceceta asked, trying to move past Rhen's rudeness. She couldn't believe he had just struck the only student in the University, who had wanted to become friends with him.

"We met last night by the lake, although yesterday I sat two rows behind you in Women in Interuniversal Politics," Erfce told her. He took a drink of milk, before adding, "Our politics teacher may move my seat, so I can sit next to you for today's lesson." With a quick glance towards Rhen, he added, "I had trouble hearing him yesterday." Erfce wondered if Rhen would call him out on his lie, but Rhen was ignoring him. That was just fine with Erfce. He didn't need to be friends with Rhen. He just needed to be near him.

"Great," Ceceta said. "If you're in our politcs class, you must be in our other classes too?"

"Yes," Erfce confirmed with a nod.

"Well, you'll have to sit next to us in all of our classes," Ceceta added, happy to have a new Thestran friend.

Erfce smiled at the idea. "I'd like that very much," he admitted.

"Me too," Latsoh agreed.

"I'll join you in Astronomy. That seems to be the only class I have with you," Crystam informed them.

For the rest of the meal, everyone, except for Rhen, chatted about their classes. At one point, Latsoh leaned over towards Ceceta's bowl of bloodworms. She snatched a bloodworm up with her fingers and stared at it as it wiggled about. "Is it any good?" she asked.

Rhen stopped chewing. His eyes focused on the worm in her hand.

Ceceta, who had been talking with Crystam, turned her head towards Latsoh. "Is what any good? Do you mean the bloodworms? No, they're terrible. But we're not allowed to eat anything else for breakfast." When her eyes passed over Rhen, she noted the concentration on his face and realized Latsoh was in danger. Jerking her head about, she screamed, 'NO!' at the top of her lungs, while lunging forward to grab the worm out of Latsoh's hand. In her rush, she knocked Latsoh to the floor.

The entire dining hall became quiet, as everyone stared at Ceceta, who was turning a darker shade of blue, as she glared at Rhen.

"What was that all about?" Erfce asked, while Latsoh got up off the floor.

"Were you going to let her eat it?" Ceceta yelled at Rhen. "How could you? Why are you being so mean?"

Ignoring his wife's outburst, Rhen dropped his gaze to his bowl and reached down, lifting out another bloodworm.

Ceceta took a few deep breaths, before turning towards her new friends. "It's very, very, very important that you never, ever eat a bloodworm! Ever! Promise me. Okay?"

"Okay," Latsoh said. "We promise. But, you have to tell us why. What's wrong with eating them?"

Ceceta pushed the blond hair that had fallen out of her ponytail back behind her ears and sat down. Her voice sounded drained, as she told them,

"Bloodworms don't leave your body after you eat them. They're parasites, controlling parasites. These are babies." She pointed down at the wiggling worms in her bowl. "After you eat them, they transform into their adult shape and adhere to your intestinal track."

"Disgusting," Erfce said with a grimace.

"Surpens feed their children bloodworms to make sure they'll only ever eat meat. You see, over time, your intestines become thick with the bloodworms that you've eaten. They clog your throat, your stomach…everything. Bloodworms will only eat meat. They go crazy, if any other form of food enters your system. If you eat meat, the bloodworms will digest it for you giving you the nutrients. But, if you try to eat anything else, they'll kill you by thrashing about inside your body to get away from the food. I saw a woman eat a piece of fruit once and the bloodworms clogged her throat in protest, so she couldn't breathe. She suffocated to death. Another time, there was a boy who ate some candy. The bloodworms went mad, bursting out of his intestines in protest. You can imagine what that did to his body." Ccceta shuddered at the memory.

"But why?" Crystam asked. "Why do the Surpens do that to their children? Why do they only eat meat?"

"It's the Surpen way," Ceceta responded, as if the reason were obvious.

"Can you remove the bloodworms?" Erfce asked, sounding worried.

"We don't think so," Ceceta answered, while glancing at Rhen, who was rubbing at the back of his head. Her anger faded and she found herself feeling sorry for him. He didn't want to be there, but he had come for her. His head had been hurting him for days, and he missed his soldier friends. Ceceta reached across the table for Rhen's hand. "We tried to find a way once, when we were younger, but it didn't work," she told Erfce, grasping Rhen's fingers with hers. Rhen smiled at her in a way that said he was sorry about Latsoh. Ceceta nodded back to tell him she understood. She knew he would've stopped Latsoh before she had eaten the worm.

"But why do you still eat them? Surely you don't want to put more of them into your body?" Latsoh asked with horror.

"We're considered children until we turn 18," Ceceta said, letting go of Rhen's hand and sitting up straight. "All children are required to eat bloodworms."

Rhen stood up and left the dining hall without saying goodbye. Ceceta gave her new friends a hopeful smile to apologize for his rude departure. "He's a little rough around the edges, but when you get to know him, you'll find he's incredibly funny and good natured."

Lilly, who had moved closer to their table to listen to Ceceta, leaned forward. "My brother? Rhen? Funny and good natured? Surely you must be speaking about someone else in my family? Charlie for example?"

Across the room, Charlie was chugging a gallon of milk; it spilled down his face, while the boys around him cheered him on. "No" Ceceta said, glancing back at Lilly. "Funny and charming as Charlie can be. He's no Rhen."

"No," Lilly agreed, with a shake of her head. "He is no Rhen." There was a weightiness to her voice that caused the conversation to end. As one, the group rose to go to their class. Lilly decided to accompany them part of the way. She needed to use the school's portal to go to the Royal Palace to update her family about the bloodworms. As they left through the same door Rhen had taken earlier, they bumped into him almost at once. He was staring up at the ceiling, while rubbing at the back of his head. They looked up to see what had caught his attention and found a small student, who was wearing a B.A.C. shirt, chained to the main chandelier in the room.

"Oh, that poor kid," Crystam commented, while taking in the tiny, blond-haired boy.

"You are getting him down, aren't you Rhen?" Ceceta snapped. She wasn't sure why Rhen hadn't already saved the student.

"Do I have to?" Rhen complained. When he had first entered the room, he had thought the student was dead, but his hearing had picked up the kid's rapid heartbeat, so he assumed the boy was too terrified to move. The mechanism that raised and lowered the chandelier had been vandalized, therefore they couldn't lower the student down, nor did there seem to be any ladders in the area. Rhen felt sorry for the kid. It appeared to be the same boy he had seen being bullied in the bathroom before.

"Can you get him down?" Erfce remarked. "That's the question. You'll have to scale the side of the wall, crawl across the ceiling, holding onto the molding and shimmy down the chandelier. Assuming it can hold both of your weights and doesn't crash to the floor, you'll then have to chop off the chains and carry the boy back down the same way you went up. Nope. It can't be done. We need to get the teachers to help us."

As if they had heard him, a group of teachers walked into the room on their way to class. When they noticed the student chained to the chandelier, they rushed to the chandelier's lowering mechanism. Discovering it was broken, a few of the teachers ran off to find someone to help, while the others tried to call out to the student.

Ceceta smacked Rhen on his back, surprising Lilly and the others. "MOVE IT!" she commanded.

They expected Rhen to turn on Ceceta, but instead, he asked Lilly, "Can you fly?"

She hesitated a moment, before answering. "No, I never got that power. Only mom can fly. Can you?"

Instead of replying to her question, Rhen moved over to the wall. He tested the molding, to see if it would support his weight, then climbed up the wall with incredible speed. When he reached the ceiling, he paused again to test the ceiling's moldings with his right hand. Satisfied that it would hold him, Rhen swung from molding to molding, hand over hand, like he had been doing it all his life, until he reached the chandelier. Rhen lifted his knees up, to use them to hold onto the molding, and dropped the upper half of his body down, so that he could grab the chandelier chord, which he used to pull the heavy chandelier up towards him.

When Rhen's tunic dropped downward, Ceceta was relieved to see he was still wearing his military shorts from his morning's work out.

Holding the chandelier chord with his left hand, Rhen pulled a dagger from somewhere near his leg and slashed at the boy's chains. The force he used, in wielding the knife, was great enough that the chains broke and crashed to the floor. Rhen moved fast, catching the boy with his knife hand, before the student could fall to the ground.

When the boy was secure, Rhen lowered the chandelier. Once it was down, he grabbed the ceiling's moldings with his hands, and in one swift movement, shifted the boy onto his back, while dropping his legs down. Rhen swung back across the ceiling like a monkey. Just as he reached the wall, he let go of the ceiling and dropped to the ground. As he was falling, a few of the teachers screamed out, thinking he had lost his grip, but Rhen landed on his feet, as if he'd only dropped a short distance.

Turning to face everyone, Rhen found his new 'friends' had their mouths open, but they weren't speaking. He gave them a questioning look, before walking over towards Ceceta, while pulling the shaking kid off his back. Rhen placed the boy down on the ground and Ceceta, as well as a few of the teachers, bent over him to see if he was injured. Glancing back at his 'friends', Rhen laughed. "Well," he told them, sounding amused. "If I'd known you'd shut up after seeing me climb a wall, I would've done it hours ago." Rhen turned towards Ceceta, who was tugging on his sleeve.

"His name is Tgfhi. He's the son of the King of Tgarus," Ceceta told Rhen. "The planet Tgarus is near Surpen, isn't it? Don't we own Tgarus?" she asked. Being a Surpen woman, she had never been informed on what planets and solar systems Surpen controlled.

"Yes," Rhen replied with surprise. He grinned down at the tiny student. He couldn't believe that one of his people was attending the Elfin University. "Tgarus is a great planet. Good strong military force. I've fought with your people often. Nice to meet you Tgfhi," he told the boy, slapping him on the back. The boy stumbled forward from the force of his blow. Rhen grabbed the kid's thin arm to steady him. "Sorry," he added with a guilty look. "I'm used to dealing with your military."

Without a word, the boy lunged forward to hug Rhen. Rhen stepped back, his hands in the air, as the tiny child clung to his waist.

"Thank you, thank you, thank you!" the little boy named Tgfhi cried out. His blond hair was wet with sweat and his blue eyes looked haggard from his suffering.

"It's over," Rhen told him. He pulled Tgfhi off him. "Come on Ceceta, we're late." Rhen took her arm and together they left the room.

"I was *joking,* when I said he'd have to scale the wall," Erfce commented, his eyes still wide after watching Rhen's rescue mission. He looked up at the ceiling again, before turning towards Lilly. "Did you know he could do that?"

Lilly's mouth was hanging open. She closed it and shook her head no. "I thought he was strong, since he's the head of Surpen's military, but I've never seen him in action. That was really...something else, wasn't it?"

"Yeah. It was amazing! He's so big, but he can move so fast. Can you imagine the strength he must have in his arms to do that?" Latsoh remarked. "Themrock! We're going to be late for class," she added, when she noticed the time. Grabbing Crystam and Erfce, she dragged them out of the room.

That afternoon, when Rhen and Ceceta sat down for lunch, they discovered Tgfhi had joined them at their table. "I'm so happy you're feeling better," Ceceta told him. "You're welcome to join us for every meal."

"Yes, please," Tgfhi accepted, before adding at a rapid speed, "that would be amazing! It's been very hard for me here. The bigger kids enjoy torturing us smaller ones. When they learned I could turn into water, they decided to make me their number one target. I hate it. Everywhere I go there's always some big kid waiting for me. I've missed most of my classes, and I can't go anywhere without feeling afraid. You know, it's not my fault I'm so tiny. Tgarian men don't grow until they turn 19. Once I reach the age of 19, my body will shoot up and my muscle mass will double in size. I'm 18 now, and I'm stuck in the body of a typical Thestran 10-year-old boy. Can you imagine anything more frustrating? Probably not. But then, if you really think about it, you can come up with some..."

"Whoa," Erfce interrupted. "Slow down there Tgfhi."

"Sorry," he apologized. "I don't mean to be this way. Normally I'm much more calm, but this school has left me frazzled."

"Do you have classes with any of us?" Latsoh asked.

For once, Tgfhi was quiet. He raised his big, blue eyes, his cheeks flushed, and he glanced at Crystam.

"Of course," Crystam mumbled, before looking down at her salad and stabbing it with her fork.

"I'm sure Crystam would be happy to escort you to your classes," Latsoh told Tgfhi, while hiding a smile.

"Indeed," Crystam agreed halfheartedly.

"And we'll protect you in Astronomy," Latsoh added.

"That would be great!" Tgfhi cried out. "I can't tell you how upsetting it is to be picked on by the kids at this school. I think I'm actually older than a bunch of them, if you can believe that. I've complained to the Headmaster, but Professor Dewey hasn't done a thing." After a brief pause, he added, "I know! We should form a Club! Speaking of Clubs, I see that none of you have a B.A.C. shirt. Do you want to join the Black Angel Club?"

"That's such a load of crap," Rhen sneered.

Tgfhi looked crestfallen. "What do you mean?" he asked, in a small voice. His blue eyes seemed almost as large as Erfce's, as he waited for Rhen's explanation.

"The Black Angel Club?" Rhen replied with sarcasm. "What do you do? Sit around dressed like him thinking happy thoughts?" He laughed until Ceceta shoved her plate into his with a loud bang.

"Here honey!" she snarled, through clenched teeth. "I don't think you've put enough into your mouth yet."

It was clear that Tgfhi was wounded by Rhen's words. He hunched up his little shoulders and dropped his head down. Rhen had saved his life. Rhen was his Prince. Rhen was his hero. "Well," he whispered. "We...we don't dress like him or her. But we do sit around discussing the Angel. We try to figure out who it is and where the Angel comes from. We want to discover the truth about the Angel, before anyone else does." Tgfhi turned to Latsoh. "You were at our last meeting, weren't you?" he asked in a tiny voice.

Latsoh almost choked on her apple. "Um, uh, yeah, I was."

"Did you enjoy it?"

Latsoh squirmed. She had enjoyed it. She'd thought it was a blast, but she was embarrassed to say so in front of Rhen. "It was okay," she murmured, while glancing away from the table.

Tgfhi stared down at his plate, his eyes filling with tears. He was still so young looking that it was hard for them to believe he was 18. "We'd love to join your Club," Ceceta announced. She smiled, as the joy returned to his baby face.

"No, we wouldn't!" Rhen snarled.

"I'd love to join your Club!" she clarified, while staring at Rhen to see if he would forbid her. "When is your next meeting?"

"Tonight, after dinner, in the library. Can you come?"

"I'd be delighted to come," Ceceta told him. "And I'll bring along a few of our friends," she added, glancing at Latsoh.

"Do you want to join the Movie Club," Crystam asked her.

"Yes," Ceceta agreed. "Why not? It sounds like fun." Rhen rolled his eyes and rubbed at the back of his head, as they rose to go to class.

"Do you want me to carry your books," Tgfhi asked Crystam.

"Sure Tgfhi, that'd be nice," Crystam replied tonelessly.

Tgfhi beamed with pleasure, as he struggled along behind Crystam, carrying her books as if they were a treasure.

When they met later for dinner, it was clear to everyone that Tgfhi was smitten with Crystam. He followed her everywhere and did whatever she did. He even went so far as to pick the same foods she was choosing on the cafeteria line. "You shouldn't lead him along Crystam," Latsoh whispered to her, when Tgfhi started to talk to Erfce about their astronomy class.

"I'm not," Crystam denied. "He's grown on me. He's really very cute."

"He's 18 Crystam," Latsoh warned her. "He may look like a little boy, but he's a man, and he has a man's urges."

"He's still innocent. I always wanted a little brother and he's perfect," Crystam replied. Latsoh snorted. "Don't worry. I'll handle it when he grows."

Latsoh shook her head. No doubt about it, Tgfhi was going to have his heart broken.

"So, what did you think of astronomy class today?" Erfce asked Rhen, trying to draw him into his and Tgfhi's conversation. Rhen shrugged.

"I thought it was great," Latsoh replied.

Erfce blushed at Latsoh's answer, causing Rhen to roll his eyes. Rhen caught Ceceta smiling at him and nodded.

"Our astronomy teacher is one of the best in the Universe," Erfce informed Latsoh.

"Really?" she asked. "How do you know that?"

"I read his biography. Did you know he's studied and lived in over eight solar systems?"

"Is that all?" Rhen asked mockingly, while scratching at the back of his head with his right hand.

"What do you mean, 'is that all'? That's a huge number of solar systems to live on," Erfce responded.

Rhen shrugged in response and turned away. He was finished with dinner and had had enough of his 'friends' for today. He wanted to get his wife alone for the night. Standing up, he nodded towards Ceceta. She grinned and rose to her feet. "Good night! We will see you tomorrow," she told them.

"I think Ceceta forgot about the B.A.C. meeting tonight," Tgfhi said, after they had left. "I'm going to go tell her. I think she really wanted to attend the meeting. It'd be a shame if she missed it, simply because she forgot about it."

"We'll come with you," Latsoh offered. "We want to see their apartment."

Later, as they walked up the cement stairs to the Teachers' Residence Hall, they bumped into Professor DiGrego. "Hello!" he cried out, while holding open the door. "Where are you going?"

"To Rhen and Ceceta's apartment," Latsoh replied.

"Are you going to study with them? I'd like to join you, if you're discussing math."

"No," Tgfhi told him. "We're just reminding them about the B.A.C. meeting tonight."

"Great! I hope they'll come. Our last meeting was very productive. Maybe I will ask Rhen to reconsider joining the Math Club at the meeting. See you there."

"Bye," Tgfhi called out.

"Mr. DiGrego goes to the B.A.C. meetings?" Crystam asked, as they continued up the stairs to the second floor.

"Yes," Tgfhi told her. "He's the only teacher who comes. He's really nice. Everyone likes him."

"He's great," Erfce agreed, stopping in front of Rhen and Ceceta's apartment door.

Latsoh knocked on the door and Ceceta opened it almost at once. "Hi!" she exclaimed. "I was just in the kitchen, when I heard you knock. What're you doing here?"

Pointing at his shirt, Tgfhi said, "I think you may have forgotten about the B.A.C. meeting tonight and I wanted to remind you."

"Oh," Ceceta breathed out, while eyeing Tgfhi's shirt. From the expression on her face, they could tell she didn't feel like going anymore.

They stood in the doorway for a minute, feeling awkward, while Ceceta stared at them, her brow furrowed. A moment later, she threw the door wide open. "Well, come on in and check out our place before we head over to the meeting." Tgfhi let out the breath he was holding, and the four of them entered Ceceta's apartment.

"This is much better than a dorm room!" Crystam declared. She walked into the living room and scanned the bookcase for anything Surpen.

"Yeah," Erfce agreed. He sat down on the sofa beside Latsoh.

"It is," Latsoh said. "But if you're a teacher, and you live here all year long, it's kind of small. Don't you think?"

"Well," Erfce replied. "I still think it's much better than our dorm rooms. In fact, it's awesome. We should have our study sessions here like Mr. DiGrego suggested."

"That'd be great!" Ceceta exclaimed. "I'll get the staff to stock our kitchen with foods you can eat. We can make this our study room." The others perked up at the idea and agreed they would start studying in Ceceta's apartment tomorrow night.

As they were discussing their plans, Rhen walked out of his bedroom into the living room, on his way to the kitchen, wearing only his black military shorts. Crystam gasped at the sight of him, while Latsoh's mouth dropped open.

Rhen ignored them. He opened the refrigerator and grabbed a pitcher from the top shelf. With his arm on the refrigerator door, he drank from the pitcher, before putting it back on the shelf and closing the door. "Would you please stop drinking from the pitcher!" Ceceta yelled. "It disgusts me!"

Rhen glanced at Ceceta and waved his hand in a dismissive gesture, telling her to leave him alone, while he walked back into his bedroom and closed the door behind him.

"Wow," Latsoh whispered.

"What?" Ceceta asked, sounding defensive. "It's disgusting when he drinks from the pitcher," she added, slapping the armrests on her chair for emphasis.

"Yeah," Latsoh agreed. "Disgusting!"

"Can I study with you guys too?" Tgfhi asked the others. "I mean, I'm only in your Astronomy class, and technically I should be finding other study partners, but I would prefer to study with you guys."

"Of course! We'll both study with them," Crystam answered. "We have the same classes, so we can test each other on our material as well." She gave Tgfhi an affectionate pat on the shoulder and was surprised, when he turned into a big puddle of water on the couch.

"TGFHI!" Erfce yelled, jumping up to shake out his wet pants. "Turn back you idiot."

A moment later, a flustered Tgfhi reappeared before them. His cheeks were red as he apologized, "I'm so sorry!"

"Get a grip on yourself," Erfce snarled. Tgfhi shrank down into the sofa.

"Erfce," Latsoh hissed. "It was just an accident. Relax."

Erfce's frown lifted and he peeked over at Latsoh. "Yeah." He turned to Tgfhi. "Sorry, I didn't mean to yell at you. Just, please...warn me the next time you use your powers."

"I will. I promise."

Tgfhi's power display jogged Crystam's memory. "I meant to ask you Ceceta, does Rhen have any powers like his brothers and sisters?"

"What?" Ceceta asked, appearing taken aback. "I...um..."

"NO," Rhen responded with authority, from where he was leaning against his bedroom door. He had put on a simple red tunic that had black geometric shapes stitched around the edges.

"Well, you have one," Ceceta conceded.

"It's not worth mentioning," Rhen replied. He walked over to sit down on the floor next to the coffee table.

Latsoh studied Rhen. If Rhen had a power, then he and Sage would be the only elves in the Universe with powers. "We elves had great powers once," she told the others. "When Themrock was free, he gave us more powers than any other species in the Universe."

"Themrock?" Tgfhi asked.

"Themrock!" Latsoh replied aghast. "Our Universal God, the Creator of our Universe and everything in it!"

"Oh," Tgfhi commented. "He's the Thestrans' God, right?"

"He's the God for all of us," Latsoh informed him, sounding cross. "Themrock was the strongest Genister. He created us. You can't worship anyone else. When Themrock returns from the prison he's been locked into, he'll restore everything."

"I've never heard of him before," Tgfhi told her. "If he's so powerful, how did he get locked into a prison?"

"He is powerful!" Latsoh seethed.

"Can't be that powerful," Tgfhi teased.

"Well, he is, damn you!" Latsoh snapped. "He created our Universe. He created all of us. We have songs passed down through generations that speak about it. He was so strong that his very essence held the other Genisters together. After he was tricked and imprisoned, the other Genisters just drifted away. Themrock promised us he would return one day, and when he does, you'll see. You'll bow before him as you should."

"Uh...yeah," Tgfhi replied. "Sure." He turned to Rhen. "The Surpens have a Universal God they worship. Don't they?"

Rhen nodded. His left hand rubbing at the back of his head.

"Is he also called Themrock?" Tgfhi asked.

"No," Ceceta replied. She watched her husband scratch at his head. "He doesn't have a name."

"Well, when you conquered our planet, you set up shrines to him, and we noticed that he looks very...strong."

Rhen smiled at Tgfhi's description of their God, before saying, "He is strong Tgfhi."

"Strong enough that he wouldn't be locked away in a prison, right?"

"Tgfhi!" Latsoh yelled.

"The Pontians believe another Genister locked Themrock away from us," Erfce interrupted. "Is that what you believe Latsoh?"

"Well," she began. "Some of us believe it was another Genister, who imprisoned Themrock. Others believe it was a force from a different dimension. I guess Themrock will tell us what happened when he returns."

"If, he returns," Tgfhi said.

Crystam kicked Tgfhi under the coffee table. "Aren't we going to be late for the B.A.C. meeting?" she asked.

"Yes!" Tgfhi exclaimed, jumping to his feet.

Everyone, except for Rhen, rose to go. "Don't you want to come? We'll be able to meet more students there," Ceceta asked him.

Rhen shook his head. "No. You go have fun. I'll see you later."

"Okay. See you soon." Ceceta leaned over to give him a kiss. "I can't wait to see what they do at the meeting," she whispered. She heard Rhen chuckling, as she followed the others to the Black Angel Club meeting.

Chapter 14

When Ceceta and her friends entered the University's library, they found most of the student body milling about. Tgfhi knew where to go, so they followed him through the lobby, down the right side of the stacks to the back wall and up a flight of stairs onto one of the library's many balconies. Three wooden tables had been turned sideways and placed against the metal balcony railing. The leaders of the Black Angel Club were standing around them talking.

"Ceceta!" Charlie cried out, when he saw her. He waved her over to where he was sitting at a table on the right. "Hey everybody, this is my sister-in-law Ceceta."

Ceceta blushed with embarrassment, but she was pleased, when the students around Charlie introduced themselves.

"Is Rhen here with you?" Charlie asked. "I want to introduce him to everyone before the meeting starts."

"No, he couldn't make it tonight. Maybe another time," she replied. Ceceta picked up the papers on the table before her. Most of them were about the Black Angel. She was surprised by their stories. She hadn't heard about some of the Angel's adventures and read them with interest.

"You came with Tgfhi?" Charlie asked.

"Yes."

"He's a good guy," Charlie told her. "He runs these meetings with Stanley."

"Really?" Ceceta turned to look for Tgfhi. She found him deep in conversation with Charlie's friend Stanley.

Stanley patted Tgfhi on the shoulder then climbed up on top of the tables to call the meeting to order. He told the newcomers about the purpose of the Black Angel Club and ran through the last five rescues the Black Angel had performed. After that, Stanley asked the room if anyone had information on rescues the Angel had performed yesterday that might not have been in the news.

Three students spoke up. One boy told them that his cousin's family had been attacked by Vivists on Solar System 35, while they were on their way to a conference. The Angel had saved them and sent the Vivists back to their own solar system. Another student announced that a mass murderer on her home planet had been caught by the Angel yesterday, before he could torture and kill her neighbor's son. The third student, a Nosduh, told everyone the Angel had rescued 12 Nosduh ships, which had gotten too close to their solar system's black hole and were being sucked in.

Everyone clapped for the Black Angel and Ceceta found herself giggling. Charlie gave her a look. "Why are you laughing?" he whispered.

"Oh, it's just that, you're all clapping for him right now and he doesn't even know it. It seems...silly. That's all."

"But the Black Angel does know it," Tgfhi said, from behind her. He stepped past Ceceta to climb on top of the table beside Stanley. "The Black Angel can hear and see everything. The Black Angel is a Universal God!" Tgfhi announced. The students broke out in applause.

"Now, Tgfhi," Stanley replied, in a placating tone, when the clapping had died down. "We haven't determined that yet. The Angel has more power than any other individual in our Universe, but the Angel is not a Universal God. There aren't any Universal Gods left. All of the Genisters are dead."

The students in the library murmured in agreement. Tgfhi frowned and crossed his arms over his chest, but he kept his mouth shut as Stanley moved on.

They ran through a list of the Black Angel's powers, then debated on what additional powers they thought he or she might have. The debate was followed by a dialogue on whether the Angel was a man or a woman. A discussion on the Angel's clothing came next. Stanley seemed to feel that if they could determine which planets the Angel got his or her clothes from, they could figure out where the Angel lived.

"The Angel's pants are Zorthan," a student yelled out.

"No, they're not. They're from Giaps," another student hollered back.

Twenty minutes later, Ceceta decided she was bored. She got up to leave, but Tgfhi stopped her. "Where are you going?"

"I'm sorry Tgfhi. I don't really need to know where he comes from. All I need to know is that he's going to save me if something bad happens."

"But don't you want to know who the Angel is?" Stanley asked her.

"No. He doesn't want us to know who he is, so I plan on respecting his privacy."

"Then why did you come to our meeting?" Stanley snapped.

"I'm not really sure why," Ceceta told him. "I guess I was curious to see why he's so famous."

"Because the Angel's a super power that saves people and won't let anyone know his or her identity," Charlie announced, as if it were obvious, while at the same time knocking the papers in front of him off the table.

"Yeah," Ceceta agreed, when Charlie sat back up with the papers in his hands. "And isn't it great? Don't you think he's amazing?" She paused to look at their confused faces. "Don't get me wrong. I'm glad you formed this Club. He should know people support him. Perhaps he won't stop doing it after all."

For the first time, Ceceta understood the expression, 'you could hear a pin drop'. No one was talking. Everyone was staring at her. She dropped her head down, letting her hair cover her face, as she studied her shoes.

"Ceceta, is there something you're not telling us? You keep calling the Angel a 'he'. Do the Surpens know the Black Angel's identity?" Stanley inquired, trying to sound casual.

Ceceta's forced laugh was dry. She lifted her head. "No, silly," she told him. "The Surpens don't know the Black Angel's identity. They assume he's a man, because that's their way."

"So, why do you think he might stop saving people?" Tgfhi asked her.

"Well, three months ago, he wasn't saving as many people as he had been, and I got the feeling he was getting tired of it. From what I heard tonight, though, I was clearly mistaken."

Tgfhi grinned. "I knew you were a fan! Only people, who follow the Angel, know that the Angel slowed down for awhile. The news companies never publicized it, but his fans knew."

"Well," Stanley remarked. "As you said, we need as many people as possible to join us, to show our support for the Angel. We don't want the Angel to stop saving people. You don't have to participate in our discussions about where the Angel comes from, but please come to our meetings, to show the Angel how much you appreciate everything he or she is doing."

"Okay," Ceceta agreed. She sat back down next to Charlie. "It's the least I can do for the Angel."

An hour later, Stanley brought the meeting to a close. Ceceta said good night to her friends and headed back to her apartment. She opened her apartment door and walked in, closing it behind her. Rhen was no longer sitting on the floor by the coffee table, so she went into her bedroom. Before she could reach for the light switch, someone thrust her up against the wall, pinning her. Ceceta shrieked then chuckled, her eyes adjusting enough for her to see that her captor was a tall person dressed in black clothing. He smelled like wet pine needles and his cape felt hard, as if it had been frozen.

Pulling her attacker in closer and smiling into his covered face, Ceceta said, "Hello, my Black Angel." From the chill of his clothing, she knew he had been rescuing people at a rapid rate in order to get back to her before she went to sleep.

"I sensed you needed to be saved," Rhen replied with complete seriousness.

Ceceta giggled. "Oh, I do," she agreed, nodding her head and pulling down on his black scarf to see his lips. The smooth, sloping lines of Rhen's lips looked enticing in the shadowed room. "I desperately do," Ceceta breathed out towards Rhen's ear.

Rhen threw back the icy hood of his cape and pulled off his scarf and sunglasses. He bent his head down, lowering his mouth to hers. They kissed, as if they'd been apart for years rather than hours. Rhen placed his palms against the wall on either side of Ceceta's head. When he lifted his head to break their kiss, Ceceta followed him with her lips, until she could no longer reach him.

"So? Are you saved now?" Rhen asked, his eyes searching her face, scanning the beauty of her perfect nose, intense, dark eyes and smooth, blue cheeks.

"Not quite yet," Ceceta teased. She reached out and unbuckled his black pants, allowing them to drop down to his knees. Rhen went to grab her hands, but she ducked under his arm, and laughing with glee, threw herself onto their bed. "Can you save me over here?" she asked, lowering her robes off her shoulders to show him more cleavage.

Rhen grinned, like a victorious warrior, and shrugged off the rest of his Black Angel outfit. As his clothes fell to the ground, they disappeared. He jumped onto the bed beside Ceceta and used his powers to make her clothes vanish as well, then pulled Ceceta on top of him.

"My, my, my," Ceceta breathed out. "You do take your job seriously Black Angel."

Chapter 15

The next morning, during Ceceta's class on Surpen, Latsoh and Crystam spent the entire time discussing the Black Angel. Ceceta couldn't seem to get them to concentrate on Surpen. She found it hard to assert herself, because she didn't want to alienate her new friends. Towards the end of class, Ceceta succeeded in teaching them a few phrases, so the lesson wasn't a total waste of time.

Later, during breakfast, Crystam decided to try out one of her new phrases on Rhen. Looking him straight in the eye, she declared, "*I have black hair in my ass.*"

Rhen's hand was half way up to his mouth with two wiggling bloodworms when he heard her. He dropped the worms back into his bowl and laughed, tumbling over sideways onto Erfce, who buckled under his weight. The two of them fell onto the floor.

"What? Did I say it wrong?" Crystam asked. "It's true!" she insisted.

Ceceta snorted at Crystam's announcement and dropped her head down onto the table as she laughed.

"What?" Crystam asked. "It's true. Didn't I say it right?" She glanced at Latsoh but Latsoh only shrugged.

"It sounds right to me," she replied. "*I have black hair in my ass,*" Latsoh repeated, using the words she had learned in Surpen class.

Rhen threw his hands out towards them, while climbing to his feet. "Stop! Please, just, stop," he told them. "Don't say anything else." He glanced at Ceceta, who was still giggling on the tabletop. "I can see my wife is an excellent teacher. It seems she's teaching you the most important Surpen phrases first." Walking over to Crystam and Latsoh's side of the table, Rhen said, "Tell me in Thestran what she was trying to teach you to say?"

"It looks cloudy outside today," Crystam and Latsoh parroted in Thestran.

Rhen bit down on his bottom lip, as Ceceta continued to giggle. "Great," he told them. "You have the words mixed up and you aren't quite pronouncing them correctly." Rhen paused. The easiest way for him to help them was if he touched their jaws as they spoke, but he didn't like the idea of touching them. He considered waiting for Ceceta to do it, but she was still laughing. With a sigh, Rhen made up his mind. He would touch Crystam and Latsoh briefly, just to show them how to move their mouths in the correct manner. Once they had learned the trick, they would have no trouble speaking

126

Surpen. Rhen straddled the bench between them, sitting down to face Crystam. "I'll show you the trick to Surpen," he told her, reaching out to take her face between his hands.

The minute Rhen's hands touched Crystam's face, she breathed in sharply. A wave of unexpected love coursed through her body. It caught her completely off guard. She wasn't even aware that she liked Rhen, but now, his closeness, his touch, his aroma, his soothing voice, the memory of his body and the feel of his warm skin against hers made it almost unbearable. She felt she should either fling herself on top of him or bow down at his feet.

Crystam's intense emotions brought a blush to her cheeks. She realized she had to get herself under control. She was lucky no one could see her change in color, because Rhen's hands were on her face. Rhen said the words in Surpen for '*it looks cloudy outside today*' and asked Crystam to repeat what he had said. Crystam said the same words back. As she was speaking, she could feel Rhen pushing on her jaw in certain spots to make her words come out sounding Surpen. Crystam could hear the mistakes she had made before and feel the difference in her mouth, as the words were spoken in the correct way.

"You got it?" Rhen asked, taking his hands away from her face. The redness from her blush was still apparent. Looking at her with concern, Rhen added, "Did I push on your cheeks too hard?"

"No," Crystam blurted out, while glancing away. "I got it." In perfect Surpen, she said, "*It looks cloudy outside today.*"

"That's it!" Rhen replied with satisfaction. He turned around to face Latsoh and reached out to take Latsoh's face in his hands the same way he had held Crystam's. Latsoh had the identical physical reaction to Rhen that Crystam had had. She looked at Crystam with surprise, as she felt love swelling up inside of her for Rhen. She had never felt that way before. Crystam gave Latsoh a slight nod, to tell her she had felt the same way. Knowing Crystam had experienced the same sensation, helped Latsoh relax. Rhen repeated with Latsoh, what he had done with Crystam, until Latsoh could say '*it looks cloudy outside today*' in Surpen.

"Now you both have it!" Rhen said with triumph. He stood up to leave, while reaching to rub at the back of his head with his right hand. Crystam and Latsoh rose at the same time. They giggled like school girls, when they bumped into Rhen by accident, while getting off the bench.

"They have crushes on him," Lilly whispered to Reed and Charlie from where they watched the scene across the room.

"Yeah," Charlie nodded in agreement. "The dude is like a sex magnet."

Reed laughed at Charlie's statement and replied with sarcasm, "Right. The evil Surpen God of War is a sex magnet. I don't think so."

Charlie glanced over at Lilly. She winked at him. The two of them had spent more time with Rhen than Reed had. They had noticed the way the female students watched him with more than just curiosity. "What do you think Crystam was saying that made them both laugh so hard?" Charlie asked, changing the subject. He stumbled after Reed and Lilly, who were making their way with haste to the portal to give their reports on Rhen's progress to James.

"I have no idea," Reed answered. He quickened his steps to follow Lilly through the school's portal into the Thestran Castle.

An invisible Loreth floated through the portal behind them. He was enjoying himself more than he had thought possible. He had arrived at the University to check in on Rhen and had found him holding onto an elf's cheeks while teaching her Surpen. At first, he had been livid, but then, when he had read the minds of the other students in the room, he had realized they were beginning to succumb to Rhen. He chuckled in silence, while floating above the Thestran Royals. Whether he knew it or not, Rhen had already succeeded in gaining the attention of most of the students at the University. Now he just needed to do the same thing with the elves and the Thestran Royal Family and then Loreth would be ready to strike. Loreth loved the idea of Rhen's family falling in love with him before the battle. How marvelous! He couldn't wait to see the shock on their faces when Rhen slit their throats. Their horror over Rhen's duplicity would make it worth this annoying wait.

Loreth flew into the room where James was receiving the latest report on Rhen's progress from his siblings. With a malicious grin, he made the room's temperature drop. The innocent lambs wrapped themselves in cloaks and lit a fire in the room's fireplace. It was easy enough for them to fix this little problem. How on Thestran were they going to rectify the colossal problem that was hurtling straight for them? Loreth chuckled in silence and flew away.

That night, after dinner, Ceceta heard someone knock on her apartment door. She ran over to open it and found her friends standing in the hallway. "Hey! I wasn't sure if you were serious about studying here." She stepped back and held the door open for them.

"Totally!" Erfce exclaimed. He brushed past Ceceta and walked into the room followed by the others. "Your apartment is much better than the library."

"I was hoping you'd show up. I had the staff stock the kitchen with refreshments for you."

"That's great!" Tgfhi called out, while putting Crystam's books on the coffee table.

As her friends settled into the chairs around the coffee table, Ceceta grabbed her books from her bedroom and joined them. They broke into groups and began discussing their homework.

An hour later, Rhen strolled into the apartment. He was wearing a dusty green tunic that had yellow and black piping. His military belt held only one sword and his boots were just as dusty as his tunic. Tgfhi and the others hadn't realized that he was out. Rhen stared at the group with curiosity, before walking over to kiss Ceceta on the head. She didn't have to look at him to know where he had been. She could tell from his smell that he had returned home to Surpen again.

Rhen went into his bedroom and came out, a few minutes later, wearing a clean, deep purple tunic. He strolled over towards the coffee table and flopped down onto the beige, carpeted floor beside it, closing his eyes. Fifteen minutes later, Tgfhi looked up from his textbook and asked, "Rhen, aren't you going to study?"

"I am studying."

Latsoh laughed. "Yeah?" she remarked in a sarcastic voice. "What're you studying? Blindness?"

Rhen opened one eye to look at her. Latsoh giggled, feeling nervous, as she remembered his touch from earlier that morning. She couldn't maintain his stare, so she glanced back at her book and flipped to a new page. Rhen closed his eye and continued to lie on the floor.

When they were finished working for the night, everyone got up to leave.

"Ceceta, thank you so much for allowing us to study in your apartment," Crystam told her.

"I love having you here. In fact, I wish you'd use our place as if it was yours. You can come and go anytime you want. We'll keep the door unlocked."

"That'd be fantastic," Tgfhi shouted with enthusiasm from the doorway, balancing Crystam's books in his arms. He glanced back towards the coffee table to say goodnight to Rhen, but the Surpen Prince appeared to be sleeping on the floor.

The next afternoon, Rhen was sitting at a desk in his History of the Thestran Royal Family class, while the teacher droned on about Queen Kate. He had no interest in what Mr. Balot was lecturing about, so he decided to check the Universe for trouble. With his eyes focused on the notebook in front of him, Rhen sent his mind out into the nearest solar systems. Things were calm in the immediate vicinity. He was about to send his mind further, to check Surpen's territories, when he heard someone nearby cry out in pain. Rhen pulled himself back into the classroom. Everyone seemed okay, with the exception of a boy two rows back who had partied too much last night and felt like throwing up.

Suddenly, Rhen heard it again. Someone cried out in pain. This time, he could tell it was coming from the University's main lawn. Rhen stood up and walked over to the classroom windows.

After his first encounter with Rhen, Professor Balot hadn't said one word to him. He gave Rhen a wary look and continued his lecture on Queen Kate.

Rhen opened the window and stuck his head out. In the distance, he saw several students surrounding a small boy. Without hesitation, he jumped out of the classroom's third-floor window. "Themrock!" a few of the students in the room shouted. They rushed over to the windows to see if he was alright.

Rhen was standing on the grass below them. They watched him pull a dagger from his belt. His eyes were fixed on a group of boys near the apple trees.

"Oh, my gosh, it's Tgfhi!" Latsoh cried out from the classroom windows. "Those boys over there are hurting Tgfhi!"

Rhen wondered if the boys would stop, after hearing Latsoh's remarks. He had his answer, when one of the boys grasped Tgfhi's arms behind his back, so he couldn't move. Tgfhi struggled against the boy, but it was no use. The sheer size of the other student was too much for him. The biggest kid in the group stepped forward and brought his hand back to punch Tgfhi in the face. As he swung his hand forward towards Tgfhi, Rhen released his dagger. The boy's arm flew out sideways and he screamed, when the dagger struck him in the center of his fist. His friends stared at him with surprise. They looked around to see where the dagger had come from. It didn't take long for them to spot Rhen standing next to the lower windows of the classroom building, smiling and waving at them.

"That son of a bitch!" the boy holding Tgfhi yelled out.

"This doesn't concern you," one of the boys hollered. He turned and lifted his hand to punch Tgfhi in the face.

Rhen moved faster, flinging another dagger from around his waist at the boy's hand and striking him in his fist. The kid screamed and dropped to his knees, clutching his wounded hand.

The boy holding Tgfhi let go, so he could help his friends.

Without hesitation, Tgfhi ran across the lawn as fast as he could towards Rhen.

"Are you okay?" Rhen asked, when Tgfhi ran up beside him panting.

"Yes," he gasped out.

Rhen turned back to the bullies. "Tgarus is under Surpen protection," he announced loudly enough for everyone to hear. "I know you understand what that means."

Without waiting for a response, Rhen picked Tgfhi up onto his side like you would a small child. "Which classroom is yours? I'll drop you off on the way to mine."

Tgfhi glanced up at the school building and saw that every window was open. The entire student body was watching them. Chills raced down his arms. He would never have to worry about being hurt again. No one would dare touch him now! He couldn't help himself from laughing. Rhen shifted underneath him, and Tgfhi sensed he was growing impatient. "The second window on the right over the dining hall," he told Rhen. Rhen swung Tgfhi about, so he was on Rhen's back then jumped up onto the building, scaling it like a squirrel on a tree.

The students in Tgfhi's classroom stepped back from the windows as Rhen appeared. Rhen reached behind him and pulled Tgfhi around his body, pushing him in through the open window. A few of the students inside the room helped Tgfhi down. As soon as he was safe, Tgfhi turned and said, "Thanks Rhen!"

"Don't mention it," Rhen replied with a shrug. He rubbed at the back of his head for a second, before continuing up the wall to his own classroom. As Rhen stepped in through the open window of his classroom, the students cheered. Turning, Rhen closed the window behind him and sat down in his chair. Professor Balot took a deep breath then picked up on his lecture, as if nothing had happened.

"How did you know Tgfhi was in trouble?" Erfce whispered to Rhen, once Mr. Balot's lecture was back in full swing.

"I heard him," Rhen said.

"You couldn't have heard him all the way up here with the windows closed," Erfce protested.

Rhen gave Erfce a blank look and picked up the book they were studying. He glanced down at it, while flipping through its pages of pictures on the Thestran Royal Family, none of which were of him.

Erfce shook his head. 'Impossible,' he thought. Rhen must've heard the bigger kids discussing their plans during lunch. There was no other explanation.

That evening, at dinner, Tgfhi marched up to Rhen's table with a huge smile on his face. He placed his tray of food on the table next to Rhen's and announced to the group, "No one bothered me all day long!" Tgfhi crawled up onto his knees on the metal bench beside Rhen and gave him a hug. "I love you!"

Everyone at the table laughed. "NO!" Tgfhi protested. "I really do love him."

"I heard those students," Erfce said, while nodding towards the opposite side of the room, where the kids who had attacked Tgfhi sat. "They tried to get Rhen expelled for using weapons on the school's grounds. Apparently, Professor Dewey saw the entire exchange and felt they got what they deserved."

"Really?" Latsoh asked.

"Really," Erfce confirmed.

"Tgarus is under Surpen protection!" Tgfhi exclaimed with pride. "I love that! Thank you for conquering my planet! Thank you! Thank you! Thank you! This has been the best day of my life!"

Ceceta and the others laughed again.

A small boy at the table behind theirs said, "Psst." Tgfhi glanced over at him, nodded once and turned back to Rhen. "Um, Rhen. My friends and I have been talking, and, well, I know you haven't conquered their planets yet, but these guys, well, they were wondering if you could give them Surpen protection as well?"

Rhen twisted his body around, so he could see the boys behind him. They were all small for their age. A few of them had purple bruises and cuts, and they seemed miserable. Turning back to the table, Rhen nodded yes. "Really?!" Tgfhi asked. Rhen nodded again, while taking a bite of meat.

The table of boys behind them erupted with cheers. Tgfhi jumped up onto his bench. "Let it be known that all of my friends are now under Surpen protection!" he shouted to the room full of students.

The dining hall was silent, until one student started to clap. A few minutes later, everyone was clapping.

"Damn," Reed whispered to his sisters, Lilly and Rachel, who were on Rhen duty for the evening. "Bullying has always been a problem here, but I guess Rhen just solved it. Who would've thought that he could be so nice?"

"The more I see of him Reed," Lilly commented. "The more I realize he's an amazing person. If we could just get him to like us, I'm sure we'd be able to enjoy him as much as they do."

Chapter 16

Reed ran into his brother's office and yelled, "He's back!"

James lifted his head from the papers he was working on at his desk. "Seriously?"

Rhen and Ceceta had gone back to Surpen for their first school vacation and James had been worried that Andres wouldn't let them return.

"Yes," Reed confirmed. He sat down in the chair opposite James' desk and stretched out his legs. "He returned just a few minutes ago."

"Thank the Genisters!"

"It's odd, don't you think?" Reed remarked. He reached up to scratch his nose.

"Very," James agreed. "I'm shocked Andres let Rhen return. It just doesn't add up. We know he wants to attack us, so why would he allow his son to be here? It's not to spy. Unless Rhen is providing Andres with false reports, but that doesn't seem like him. No, something is going on with Surpen. I just wish I knew what it was."

"Is there any possibility that Andres let Rhen return, because Rhen's having fun? He's been very active with his friend group. He was nasty to them at first, but that's all changed. He even attends the BAC meetings."

"He goes to the BAC meetings?" James asked. "From what I hear, the Surpen race seems to ignore the Black Angel."

"According to Charlie, Ceceta is dragging Rhen there. Rhen was angry with her at first, but now he just sleeps in a chair in the back of the balcony during the meetings."

"Charlie," James murmured at the mention of his little brother. He shook his head with disappointment.

"Come on, our little brother has been very helpful," Reed told James, while reaching for some of the papers on James' desk to see what he was working on. "Not only is he keeping Rhen busy, by having Rhen save his ass from his stupid pranks over and over, but his jump off Death Rock into the school's lake provided us with the knowledge that Rhen has healing powers. If he hadn't of missed the water and landed on those rocks, we never would have known that Rhen had the power to heal people."

"You're right," James conceded. "Charlie has gotten us more information on Rhen than anyone else has, in a round a bout way. Even Dad, who swings by to check in on Rhen once a month, barely speaks to him. They usually sit in silence and watch one of the school's games. By the way, I've asked the Elfin Royals to invite Rhen to their events. Maybe we can make a connection with him on the elfin front."

"Did they object to it?"

"No," James told his brother. He stood up and walked over to the door. "They were overjoyed with the idea of showing Rhen their new armies. Naci is still angry with him over that challenge at lunch."

"Yeah," Reed agreed, rising to follow his brother. "Are you heading to dinner?"

"Yes," James told him. He stepped out of the room. "Who's on Rhen duty tonight?"

Reed followed James into the hallway. "Lilly. She has a crush on Professor DiGrego, so she sits at his table. She doesn't seem to mind being on Rhen duty."

"DiGrego? He wasn't there when I was a student."

"He's new. He's also an elf," Reed told James, as they reached the family's dining room.

James frowned. "Oh, Lilly." He turned to look at Reed. "Is there any chance he'll date someone who isn't an elf?" Reed shook his head no. "Lilly and her crushes," James added with a sigh. They walked into the dining room, but James paused and held up his hand to stop Reed. "Can Lilly hear Rhen from the teacher's table in the cafeteria? Isn't that too far away from his table?" Reed shrugged. "I'll talk to her later," James said, turning to greet his wife.

"Hey, Ceceta! Rhen!" Lilly heard Latsoh call out, as Rhen and Ceceta arrived at their usual table in the dining hall. "How was your vacation?" Latsoh asked them. Lilly turned back to the teachers around her. Everything looked fine in 'Rhen World'. Now, where was her favorite math teacher?

"Terrible," Ceceta grumbled, while taking the seat between Latsoh and Crystam on the bench. She arranged her light green robes, so they wouldn't hit the floor.

"Why?" Crystam asked.

"First of all, I forgot that I had to bow to everyone, and my first day back, I was punished for not dropping to the floor to honor some stupid Surpen merchant; and secondly, we almost didn't get to return. When we got back to Surpen, King Andres informed us that we wouldn't be returning, because the Thestrans might corrupt us. Fortunately, his advisor talked him into letting us come back, but it was a tense couple of days, while we waited to see how the situation would resolve itself."

"That's horrible," Latsoh commiserated. She wondered what 'punishment' Ceceta might have been given but didn't feel right asking her about it.

"Bowing is such an annoying practice," Ceceta grumbled. Rhen glared at her. "I hate it," she admitted. "Surpens can be so backwards."

"CECETA!" Rhen barked, from his seat across the table. "Do not disgrace your people!"

Ceceta sneered at him. Furious, Rhen threw his napkin down and rose. He gave her a look, but when Ceceta stuck her tongue out at him, he turned and marched from the room.

"Don't worry about him," she reassured her friends, when she noticed they were still staring after Rhen. "He's just in a bad mood. Andres won't let us near each other, so he spent the entire week living in the barracks with his soldiers, running countless drills. He never got any sleep. In a few nights, he'll be back to normal. I'll give him a backrub tonight, which should start to improve his mood."

"Why won't the Surpen King let you be together?" Crystam asked.

Ceceta gave Crystam a wicked smile. "Because he thinks I'm a bad influence," she laughed then added, "He's kept us apart, on and off, for years. Now, tell me about your vacations!"

It was late when they finished their meal and walked back to their dorms. Ceceta had left their group earlier to check on Rhen. While they walked, Erfce stepped around a puddle and his fingers brushed against Latsoh's by accident. A vision of his future life with her appeared in his mind. "I can't wait," he blurted out.

"What?" Latsoh asked, while stopping to look at him.

Erfce blushed and turned away. Sometimes their future was so clear, he had trouble remembering that he had to wait for Latsoh to fall in love with him first. Looking for a reason to explain his words, Erfce jumped back to his vacation story. "You know when I told you my parents don't want me to be friends with Rhen, because they're scared of him? Well, in the future, we will spend a lot of time on Surpen."

"With Rhen?" Crystam asked. "I can't see myself on Surpen. Surpen's culture is too rigid for me. I don't think I would ever feel comfortable there."

Erfce shook his head. "I don't know. I can't see anything about his future. It's completely blocked from me. But, if we're spending time on Surpen, don't you think he's probably there."

"So, you can't wait to spend time on Surpen?" Latsoh asked him.

"Yes, I guess. I mean…I don't know…I," he was floundering here.

As luck would have it, Tgfhi interrupted. "My Dad is happy that I'm friends with Rhen."

"You're the only one," Crystam told him.

"It makes sense," Tgfhi continued. "He's our Surpen Prince. He's very powerful. Even though Surpen rules Tgarus, we don't know a lot about Rhen. My Dad thinks it can only help us, if I get to know the future king."

"Obviously," Latsoh snorted, before walking off towards her dorm room with Crystam and Tgfhi in tow.

"I can't wait," Erfce breathed out, while watching Latsoh's retreating ass. He sighed again, before heading towards his own dorm.

Later that night, Kate leaned back in her plush reading chair, propped her slippered feet onto the leather ottoman and took a sip from her espresso. "Excuse me, your highness," a servant said, approaching her. "Queen Chara's on the screen in your office. She would like to speak with you."

The servant watched as Kate's eyebrows rose. "Chara? What on Themrock would she want with me?"

"She didn't mention a topic," the servant replied.

"Okay," Kate said, with hesitation. She rose to go to her office. Sitting down before the viewing screen on her desk, Kate placed her espresso on the table and took a moment to straighten her hair, before telling the screen to commence. A moment later, Queen Chara of Ventar appeared before her. "Your majesty," Kate greeted her. She was careful to keep her eyes to the right of Chara's face lest she succumb to Chara's beauty.

"Your Royal Highness," Chara replied, looking perturbed. "I'll be brief, since I know you're busy. I heard from Erfce's parents that James has assured them the Surpen Prince is harmless, so I won't question you on that point. Certainly, if Erfce is in no danger then Crystam isn't either."

Kate racked her brain. Who were Erfce and Crystam?

"Regarding Crystam, though, I feel I need to touch base with you on the fact that I think she might be falling in love with said prince. I don't want to mention the subject to James...as you know, he has enough on his mind these days...so I thought I might touch base with you, to see if I should worry about Crystam and this Surpen Prince."

Kate was silent. It took Chara a moment to realize why.

"Kate, my daughter, 'Crystam'," she annunciated. "Is good friends with your son, 'Max', at the University. I believe she has also fallen in love with him. Is this going to be a problem?"

"Ohh," Kate said, putting two and two together. Crystam and Erfce were the friends of Rhen that Lilly had mentioned. "No, Chara, there's no need to be concerned. Rhen is completely in love with his wife. I'm sure Crystam will respect that bond."

"I'm not so sure about that Kate. Crystam is beginning to inherit some of my powers. She may use them to woo this prince and I can't have that. We are members of Thestran. Ventar will never join the Convention."

"Chara, I promise you. Crystam's infatuation will fade. She will not bring a Surpen boy home to meet you."

"Do I have your word on that?"

"Yes, your majesty."

"Very well. Thank you for your time."

"You're welcome and thank you for allowing your daughter to become friends with my son. We need him to make connections to Thestrans."

"I'd heard as much. It's not like I could stop her anyway. If I told her she was forbidden from being friends with the boy, I'm sure she would act very much like Latsoh is." Kate appeared confused and Chara found herself growing tired of their conversation. "Good night," she bid Kate, before signing off. The screen went black.

"What on Thestran was she talking about?" Kate wondered, taking a sip from her now lukewarm espresso.

A week later, King Tgonar of Tgarus sent a note to the Surpen King, informing him that he was going to visit his son, Tgfhi, at the Elfin University, and would Andres like Tgonar to check in on Rhen while he was there. "My lord!" Tgonar exclaimed, when he read Andres' response. He stopped walking and glanced up at his aides, who had followed him into the Royal Atrium. Holding up the monitor he had been reading, he shook it at them for emphasis while saying, "It appears King Andres and Prince Rhen might not communicate very well. I've been instructed to gather an enormous amount of information on Prince Rhen, while I'm at the University."

"King Andres will owe you, if you are successful," one of his aides told him.

"Indeed," Tgonar replied, sounding thoughtful. "Indeed, he will." He glanced up at a rare green humin bird that hovered near a yellow flower above his head. "This could be good for Tgarus," he told them, before turning to walk back to his office.

The next morning, King Tgonar's spacejet arrived at the Elfin University. He spent the first few hours of his day enjoying his son's company. At lunchtime, he asked Tgfhi if he could join him for lunch in the school's cafeteria.

"That'd be great Dad!" Tgfhi exclaimed. He grabbed his father's hand and tugged him towards the student dining hall.

Tgonar smiled and nodded to hide his disgust at the disturbing colored foods Tgfhi picked out for him. They didn't look at all appetizing, but Tgfhi assured him they were quite good. After they had gotten their meals, they entered the main dining hall. Tgfhi pointed towards a table on the far side of the room. "That's where I sit with my friends."

Glancing towards the table, it wasn't hard for Tgonar to identify the Surpen Prince. He was taller than everyone else at the table, and he was wearing a traditional Surpen tunic. Tgonar was instantly impressed by the sight of Rhen. The boy looked strong and formidable, which wasn't surprising. They walked over to the table, and Tgfhi sat down on the bench next to Rhen, while gesturing for his Dad to sit across from him by the female students.

"Hey everyone! My Dad came to visit me today, and he wanted to try out our cafeteria food."

"That's right," Tgonar agreed, taking the seat on the bench across from Rhen. Rhen glanced up at him with a blank stare that Tgonar found exhilarating. He liked this boy. He liked him a lot. Tgfhi had yet to learn how to control himself around others, how to intimidate others with a look. Rhen could teach Tgfhi a great deal.

"These are my friends, Crystam, Erfce, Ceceta and Latsoh," Tgfhi told his father, while gesturing around the table. "And this," he said, reaching up to pat Rhen's shoulder. "Is my savior, Rhen. He's the one I was telling you so much about! Rhen, this is my Dad, Tgonar, King of Tgarus."

Instead of speaking, Rhen gave Tgonar a quick nod in greeting. Tgonar wasn't sure what to make of the gesture. Even the King of Surpen would've said something to him. He wouldn't have just nodded. But a few seconds later, Tgfhi explained, "Dad, Rhen's awesome, but it takes him awhile to warm up to people. You'll see. In no time, the two of you will be talking about battles and showing each other your scars." He laughed at the idea, his big blue eyes looking hopeful. It appeared his son wanted him to like the Surpen Prince. Tgonar watched Rhen nudge Tgfhi with his elbow over his last comment. The gesture was meant in kindness, but it knocked Tgfhi into the pale-skinned, large eyed boy next to him named Erfce, who spilled his drink onto the table. The two of them laughed and threw their napkins onto the spill, as Rhen ignored them and rubbed at the back of his head.

"I'm sure we will," Tgonar replied with a smile. Rhen's gesture towards Tgfhi proved to Tgonar that Rhen did indeed like his son. It wasn't a one-sided relationship.

Tgonar glanced over at the woman named Crystam on his left. She had to be the daughter of the Queen of Ventar. She was breathtaking. Something about the color of her eyes and the smoothness of her pale skin was intoxicating. Tgonar wondered if she was as cold as her mother was rumored to be. He also wondered if the rumors about Crystam's Dad were true. He had been told that Crystam's Dad had died the night he had married and made love to her mother. Presumably, no one could survive making love to the Goddess of Love. 'What a way to go,' he thought to himself.

Tgonar turned his head back towards his meal and found Rhen staring at him. "You know my father," Rhen remarked. It wasn't a question, but Tgonar treated it like one.

"Yes, we're friends. I like your father. He's a good King. He cares a lot about his people and Surpen," Tgonar lied. Rhen nodded in response and looked down at his meal.

Following his glance, Tgonar saw that Rhen was eating typical Surpen food—uncooked animal body parts. The woman sitting on Tgonar's right was also eating the same meal. Tgonar looked over at her. What had his son called her? Ceta? Cesta? Ceceta? That was it. Ceceta. She must be Rhen's wife. She had been talking to the red-headed woman next to her, when he had arrived at the table, but now she was a vision of the perfect Surpen woman. She was waiting for her husband to finish eating, before eating herself. Her eyes were cast downward, and she was very still. Although he had never liked Surpen women, Tgonar could appreciate their self-control. He wondered why Rhen and Ceceta hadn't had any children yet. Surpens were known for their large families. By now, Rhen and his wife should have had at least three children, if not four. Tgonar shook his head, dismissing the thought and stared down at his own distasteful meal.

Tgfhi chatted throughout their lunch. He seemed oblivious to the fact that none of the other people at the table were saying much. Crystam, and the woman named Latsoh, kept watching Ceceta, who hadn't spoken or moved since Tgonar had sat down, and Erfce kept glancing over at Rhen, who was also very still. Tgonar realized his presence at the table had changed the usual dynamic of how the friends interacted.

"Who do we have here?" Tgonar heard someone say behind him.

He glanced up to see Thestran's Prince Reed and Princess Lilly walking up to the table. Tgonar hadn't realized there would be members of the Thestran Royal Family at the University. This must have been the reason why Andres wanted him to check up on Rhen. It seemed obvious the Thestrans were watching the Surpen Prince. Andres was not going to like it. Out of politeness, Tgonar rose from his seat and bowed to Reed and Lilly in greeting. The Thestran Royals meant nothing to him, his King was Andres, but there was no reason for him to be rude.

"This is my Dad," Tgfhi told the Thestran Royals.

"To what do we owe the pleasure of your visit today your majesty?" Reed asked, taking in Tgonar's broad shoulders, sharp jaw, graying hair and warm, brown eyes. He pulled down on his princely Wood Elf jacket of green and brown to make sure Tgonar noticed his status.

Tgonar smiled to himself. Of course, they wanted to know why he was there. He had never visited the University last year, when Tgfhi had taken some pre-University classes. The Thestrans must have figured out that he was there to check up on Rhen. Tgonar was happy to have the perfect excuse, one they couldn't question. Pointing to Tgfhi, he declared, "Well, I came to visit my son!" He laughed to himself at the irony, while adding, "We had so much fun on vacation that I wanted to see him again right away."

Reed and Lilly showed their emotions on their faces. Lilly believed his answer and Reed seemed to want to believe him. Tgonar glanced over at Rhen and caught sight of him hiding his smile, as he brought his glass to his mouth. Rhen knew he was lying.

Turning back to Reed and Lilly, Tgonar waited for Reed to finish his formal 'Welcome to Thestran' speech. When Reed had stopped talking, Tgonar saluted him. "Thank you very much," he told the Thestran Prince, before returning to his seat.

When Tgonar glanced back up at Rhen, he found him watching Reed and Lilly. He couldn't tell if Rhen liked them or not, but his glance suggested otherwise. This information would make the Surpen King happy. 'Yes,' Tgonar thought, everything he had seen so far, except for the presence of the Thestran Royals, would make Andres very happy.

The group finished their meal and rose to leave. As they were walking out of the dining hall, Tgonar reached out to put his hand on Rhen's arm. Rhen was taller and more muscular than he had realized. The Surpen King had done well in choosing his heir. "May I have a word with you before you return to class?" Tgonar asked Rhen. Rhen was expecting this and nodded yes. Tgonar turned to Tgfhi and thanked him for a wonderful visit. They hugged and Tgonar kissed his son on the top of his head before releasing him. "I'll stop by again," he promised.

"That'd be great Dad," Tgfhi replied. He turned to take Crystam's books from her. Tgonar watched Tgfhi and the others walked off towards their classes. When they were out of sight, he turned to Rhen. "Is there somewhere we can go to talk in private?"

With a nod, Rhen gestured for Tgonar to follow him. They walked out of the school building, down a brick pathway and up to a large, brick building that was named the Teacher's Residence Hall. Tgonar followed Rhen up the cement stairs into the building. They crossed a small lobby and went up more stairs, to the second floor, where they stopped in front of a plain, white, wooden door. Rhen leaned over and opened the door. He pushed it wide open, so Tgonar could enter. When Tgonar walked in, he found a quaint little kitchen and living room area. There were textbooks on the coffee table and a woman's shawl rested on the back of one of the blue chairs. Rhen had taken Tgonar to his apartment. Tgonar was pleased to see it. He could now report to Andres on Rhen's living conditions. He noticed Rhen was gesturing for him to sit down in one of the nicer chairs by the coffee table.

"Thank you," Tgonar said, taking a seat. Rhen sat down across from him.

"I guess by now, you've figured out that I'm not here just to visit Tgfhi," Tgonar confessed. He had decided to go with the truth. Rhen nodded his head in acknowledgement. "I came to see my son and to check up on you. I'm going to tell your father that you're being a perfect Surpen, amongst a flock of Thestran fools." Rhen smiled at the compliment and looked down at the floor. Tgonar wasn't sure how to read him. He was starting to find Rhen's lack of communication intimidating, and he wondered how Surpen would treat Tgarus when Rhen was King.

Out of the blue, Tgonar remembered something that twisted into a rather devious idea. Years ago, Andres had told him that his son had been a part of the invading force that had conquered Tgarus. If that was true, Tgonar might have a way to control Rhen. He grinned at the boy, while forming a dangerous plan. Looking Rhen in the eyes, Tgonar said, "I want to give you something to thank you for saving my son from public embarrassment, but I don't know what you want?"

"Tgfhi's friendship is all I need your majesty," Rhen replied with diplomacy.

Tgonar dipped his head at Rhen's words. Andres never would have said something so appropriate. It appeared Rhen was clever, which would make him even more dangerous than his blustering father. "You were a soldier during the war on Tgarus, right?" Tgonar asked with innocence.

"Yes, your men were some of the best I've ever had the pleasure to fight. It was an honor to be there."

"A true Surpen compliment. Thank you!" Tgonar replied. He stared at the boy for a few minutes, debating whether he should take the next step. If he was wrong, he might very well find himself assassinated by Andres later that night. If he was not, he would've hit a homerun that would ensure Tgarus' protection forever. Deciding to follow his instincts, Tgonar reached into his pocket and pulled out a small, plain, silver box. He offered to Rhen.

"No, thank you, your Highness," Rhen protested. "I do not need a gift for protecting Tgfhi."

"I insist on giving you this one," Tgonar said. He leaned over to hold the box closer to Rhen. "It's just a small token of my appreciation. I happened to have it with me, so I thought I would offer it to you."

Rhen hesitated, before reaching out to take it. "Thank you your majesty. You are very kind," he said. He placed the box onto his coffee table.

"Open it," Tgonar pushed. "The gift is inside."

Rhen reached out to pick up the box. He opened it to find a wad of Tgarus weed.

From Rhen's expression, Tgonar realized he was right. His gamble had paid off. Rhen was one of the Surpen soldiers that had been left on Tgarus too long with nothing to do after the war. In their boredom, they had all ended up trying Tgarus weed and every single one of them had become hooked. It had been a huge fiasco. The Surpen King had recalled his entire force and sent in new troops, which were under strict orders not to smoke the weed, but the damage had already been done. The strongest, bravest, meanest Surpen soldiers enjoyed smoking Tgarus weed, and they had brought their love of weed home to Surpen.

Ever since then, there had been a strong trade route between Tgarus and Surpen, and Tgonar had benefited from it royally.

Tgonar released the breath he had been holding, as Rhen closed the box with care and slipped it into a hidden pocket in his tunic. Looking back up at Tgonar, Rhen said, "Thank you for your generous gift. It is much appreciated."

As Tgonar rose to leave, he finalized his plan in his mind. He would have Tgfhi deliver weed to Rhen on a daily basis. Later, when Rhen became the future King of Surpen, Tgarus would be protected from whatever he decided to do. It would be safe. Their solar systems would always be at peace. And, if they played their cards right, perhaps someday Tgarus would find a way to rule Surpen. Tgonar smiled at the thought. This would be the only part of his visit that he would not mention to the Surpen King.

The next day after lunch, Tgfhi walked up to Rhen, who was coming out of the bathroom in the hallway outside the cafeteria. He tugged Rhen aside, so no one was near them. "My Dad told me to give this to you. He's got one for me to give to you every day that we're here at school." Tgfhi held up a small white envelope.

Rhen took the envelope and sniffed it. Tgarus weed. He smiled. "Your Dad is very kind," he told Tgfhi, while tucking the Tgarus weed into his military belt.

"Rhen, I didn't know you used Tgarus weed," Tgfhi whined.

"I don't!" Rhen denied. He glanced about, to make sure Ceceta couldn't see them.

"You shouldn't use it," Tgfhi moaned.

"Have you ever tried it?" Rhen asked with a sigh. Whatever Tgfhi wanted to tell him, he had already heard before from Ceceta and his mother. Tgarus weed wasn't illegal, so technically, he wasn't breaking any laws. Because of his bloodworms, he couldn't drink alcohol, so he used the weed to give himself a sense of peace for a couple of hours. It wasn't like he used it every day. He and Bosternd would imbibe on holidays, although Tgonar's gifts might change that now. He couldn't understand why Ceceta, his mom and now Tgfhi seemed so upset when he smoked it.

"Yes, I have tried it, but it doesn't have the same effect on our people that it seems to have on everyone else," Tgfhi told him.

"Listen," Rhen said. He leaned down to whisper into Tgfhi's ear. "Don't tell Ceceta what you're doing. Just give me the stuff and keep your mouth shut." Tgfhi nodded yes, his eyes welling with tears. He turned and ran off on his little legs towards his dorm room.

'How could this be happening,' he thought. After the war on Tgarus, he and his friends used to make fun of the Surpen soldiers who used Tgarus weed. They would lie around the city, mumbling and laughing to themselves. The Tgarians enjoyed seeing these strong, mean soldiers brought to their knees after the invasion. It was a source of great Tgarian pride. Many Tgarian farmers changed their crops to start producing Tgarian weed for the Surpens and all of them had become rich.

Tgfhi couldn't get over the realization that Rhen had been one of the invading soldiers on Tgarus. He was 13 when Surpen conquered Tgarus, which meant that Rhen had been fighting in battles before he had turned 13. At 13, Tgfhi had spent his days playing games with his friends and tormenting his parents, while Rhen had been a full-time soldier, killing people for a living. Had Rhen even had a childhood? "None of us know anything about Rhen," he said, while climbing up onto his bed. Tgfhi sat with his back against his pillow. "Well, that's about to change!" he declared to the empty room.

He stared down at the stack of white envelopes lying on the floor where he had dropped them. Jumping off his bed, Tgfhi leaned over and opened one of the envelopes. With care, he took out a chunk of weed and tucked it under his mattress. He wasn't going to let his Dad get away this. From now on, whenever he gave Rhen an envelope, he would remove more and more weed, until there wasn't enough for his friend to smoke.

As the weeks passed, Tgfhi kept his mouth shut about Rhen's use of Tgarus weed. He was surprised by Rhen's ability to hide it. He never seemed to be under the influence. Every day, Tgfhi would pull more weed out of Rhen's envelope and hide it in his room. Things were going great, until Charlie found his extra stash of weed and begged him to sell it, which Tgfhi did. He was happy to be rid of it. Unfortunately, Charlie told some other students where he had gotten his weed. It wasn't long before Tgfhi was approached daily, by students looking to buy Tgarus weed. He started to feel like a hypocrite, pulling weed away from Rhen and selling it for an exorbitant amount of money to the other students. Damn his father!

Chapter 17

"They're doing it all wrong," Erfce told the others at breakfast. "The Thestran Council has been fighting internally with Ustar for only three weeks and it's clear that they're in over their head. I wish they still had Kendeth."

"Who?" Rhen asked, while reaching over to take some meat off Ceceta's plate. She stuck her tongue out at him, causing him to smile.

"Kendeth," Erfce repeated. "Remember? King James' advisor who died." Rhen appeared confused. "Themrock!" Erfce swore. "Rhen, don't you remember? The Thestran Royal family came here and demanded that you go to his funeral, but you refused, because you said you weren't a part of their family anymore."

"Oh, yeah," Rhen said. "That old guy who died. They were pretty angry at me for not going with them."

"I remember," Ceceta told Erfce. "It was horrible. Charlie lived on our couch for two weeks. I think it's still wet from all his tears and snot."

"Ewww," Crystam said, scrunching her perfect face.

"The Thestran Royals were ridiculous about the whole thing," Ceceta added. "Kendeth was old and his death was honorable. What was there to cry about?"

Crystam laughed and put her arm over Ceceta's shoulders. "Really Ceceta, sometimes you can be so Surpen!"

"What?" Ceceta asked.

"Nothing," Crystam told her. She reached out to take one of the blue napkins that were on the table.

Ceceta glanced over at Rhen to see if he could explain, but he was less than helpful and just shrugged his shoulders.

"You're a member of the Council," Tgfhi told Erfce, while spearing a melon ball with his fork. "Why don't you go to their meetings and tell them they're doing it wrong?"

"My Dad's been doing that, but they won't listen."

"My Mom's doing the same thing," Crystam said. "This is the Council's first internal struggle in centuries and they're botching it."

"We could actually lose!" Erfce exclaimed, sounding worried.

"It should be okay," Latsoh told him. "Earlier this morning, James issued a decree that all of the Thestran Royals must join in the upcoming battle for Bunks Hill on Ustar."

"Themrock," Erfce swore again. "Have you been watching the feeds? We need more than just the Thestran Royals and their military on the battlefield. I've been plotting the entire war. If we lose Bunks Hill, Ustar will have no trouble finishing the war. They will conquer us and become the new rulers of the Council."

Latsoh shook her head in disagreement.

"My mom said the same thing last night," Crystam told them. She speared a melon ball off Tgfhi's plate. "She's offered to send our military to Ustar to help the Thestrans with the war. She'll even lead it herself," Crystam added, while gesticulating with her forked melon ball, "but the Council rejected her offer."

"Because they're being idiots," Erfce retorted. "They think your mom will turn around and say that she should rule the Council because her forces won the war."

"You think?" Crystam asked.

"Yes. They can't see beyond their own petty politics to the larger..." Erfce stopped speaking, when he spotted Sage and Lilly, wearing their black and gold military clothing, enter the room and walk towards their table.

"We're off to Ustar," Lilly announced. She swung her black and gold striped cape around, over her shoulders, hoping to catch Rhen's eye.

No one spoke.

"Will you join us Rhen?" Lilly asked, when he continued to keep his eyes averted.

Rhen turned towards Lilly and raised one eyebrow, an incredulous look on his face. When he realized she was waiting for a response, he said, "No."

Lilly nodded her head. She had expected him to refuse. "Will you at least come see us off? We aren't sure if Charlie will actually join us. Someone needs to force him through the portal. If he doesn't go, he'll be committing treason."

"We'll come," Ceceta told her. She stood up and held out her hand to Rhen. He rolled his eyes but rose and took her hand. The two of them followed the Thestran Royals to the school's portal.

When they arrived in the portal room, they found a large gathering of students milling about, waiting to see the Thestran Royals depart. The students spoke amongst themselves in hushed tones, while Lilly and Sage checked their weapons.

A few minutes passed before Stanley walked into the room dragging Charlie by his royal military collar. When Charlie saw the waiting portal, he shook himself free from Stanley and curled up into a fetal position on the grey-tiled floor.

Rhen couldn't believe the spectacle. "Poor Charlie," Ceceta whispered beside him.

"Seriously?" he asked her with disbelief.

"Rhen, come with us," Sage pleaded. "You're a part of our family. You're required to join our battle."

"Seriously!" Rhen snapped. When Sage remained in front of him, staring up at him with pleading eyes, Rhen shook his head and added, "What're you worried about? Use your water powers to give the Ustarians gills. None of them will be able to breath and you'll win without having to fight."

An odd look passed over Sage's face. "Even if I had that kind of power, I couldn't do that to someone."

Rhen shook his head in dismay. "And there's the problem."

"Rhen!" Charlie cried out, lifting himself up onto his knees. Snot rolled down his face and his eyes were swollen from crying. "Please help us!"

"God, Charlie," Rhen swore. "Certainly you, can use your powers to stop them."

"W...What?" he asked, looking stunned.

"In case you haven't noticed," Sage snapped. "Charlie doesn't have powers. You and I are the only elves in the Universe who have powers. The rest of the elves lost their powers when Themrock disappeared. They won't have them again until he returns."

"Huh?" Rhen murmured. He had sensed an enormous amount of power in Charlie, almost as much power as his father's advisor had. "I don't understand."

"Rhen, we don't have time to discuss our powers or lack thereof. Please, join us to protect Thestran and its solar systems. We need you. Thestran, your home planet, needs you!" Lilly pleaded.

"I...can't," Rhen replied. For some inexplicable reason, he was starting to feel guilty about not helping. It was obvious they were terrified. They would be lucky to live through today's battle.

Ceceta felt herself flush with anger. She didn't want anything to happen to the Thestran Royals. Turning on Rhen, she yelled in Surpen, *"Why not! They're your family! You're a Thestran elf for God's sake! Haven't you realized that by now? Get off your butt and go fight for them. It'll be easy for you."*

Rhen glared at her. She wasn't supposed to speak to him like that in public. She could say whatever she wanted to in private, but in public, she had to maintain the façade that he was the boss. Also, she had no idea what she was asking of him. If Ceceta knew, he was sure she wouldn't be telling him to go help the Thestrans. "No," he replied, crossing his arms in front of his chest.

Ceceta paused. She realized she was going to have to try another tactic to get Rhen to volunteer. *"You live on their planet, you take advantage of their hospitality and yet you won't lift a finger to help them protect their way of life? You're the best warrior in the Universe. You could end this thing in an hour, if you wanted to. Go, help them,"* Ceceta added in Surpen. *"Please."* She reached up to stroke the side of Rhen's face.

Rhen frowned and shook his head. "You don't know what you're asking."

Charlie could see Rhen was weakening. "Come on little brother. I need you to save my butt. Can you see me in a battle? I'm going to be killed for sure." He gave a rather morose sort of laugh.

"Please Rhen, join us. We wouldn't have been called into action, if the others weren't in trouble," Sage pleaded one last time.

"Please sweetie," Ceceta added. "Please go help them. No one knows war more than you do. No one can kill as well as you can." She stroked the bottom part of Rhen's earlobe. Rhen bent his head down towards her hand, and with that gesture, Ceceta knew she had him.

Closing his eyes and sighing, Rhen lifted his head up and nodded. The students in the room cheered. Rhen walked over and pulled Charlie to his feet. "Ready?" he asked, while Charlie wiped a long smear of glistening snot onto the sleeve of his black coat. Rhen rolled his eyes in disgust, before pulling two swords out of his weapons belt.

"Do you want to change into your war outfit?" Charlie asked, when he noticed the soft, blue dress tunic that Rhen was wearing.

"I'll be covered in blood, no matter what I wear, so it doesn't really matter."

Charlie shuddered at the thought.

"Thestran War Encampment on Ustar," Sage told the portal.

The golden frame filled with a blue light. When it dissipated, they could see an empty battlefield in front of them. Checking around them for danger, they stepped through the portal onto the bloody, torn Ustarian field in front of them. Just before their image faded and the portal closed, Rhen turned back to look at Ceceta. There was an unexpected sadness to his eyes that put her on alert.

Later that day, Erfce leaned across the table at lunch to look into Ceceta's eyes. She had been quiet ever since Rhen had left, and Erfce could see she was concerned. "Don't worry," he told her. "They're going to win. The Thestran Royal Family's future continues for a long time. I can see it clearly now."

"Yeah," Ceceta mumbled in response. Something about Rhen's last glance had worried her. She wondered if there was anything she could do to help him.

"How are you feeling Erfce?" Latsoh asked.

"About?"

"You told us a couple of months ago, that when Rhen was around you, you felt great, but when Rhen was gone, you got headaches. So, how are you feeling?"

"It's been okay," Erfce admitted. "I think the time that I've spent with Rhen has been...well, I guess helping my mind focus better. I seem to be able to block out some of the information I'm getting. It's like Rhen's been teaching me somehow."

"That's great!" Crystam told him.

"Yes," Erfce agreed. "It is."

"But how?" Latsoh asked. "How could spending time with Rhen, help your mind train itself?"

Erfce looked at Ceceta for an answer, but she wasn't listening.

On Ustar, Loreth chuckled with glee. He watched Rhen tire of the Council's incompetence and fling himself into battle. This was better than a Ventarian Delight, he thought to himself, while popping some cheese into his mouth and opening another bottle of wine.

He had been sitting on top of the Ustarians' castle for hours in his invisible state, watching the Thestran side of the battlefield. Their lame rulers couldn't seem to make any decisions on how to proceed. Loreth had used his powers to push the Ustarians into this war, and to his surprise, before Rhen had showed up, it had looked as if they might be victorious. The Thestrans and their Council members were such imbeciles.

Loreth drank from his green, wine bottle and gazed down on the battlefield. Rhen was nearing the Ustarians' command tent on his rampage. "Damn, but you are fast," he mumbled to himself. He had hoped that Rhen would join in this battle to help his 'fellow' Thestrans. How fortunate that the Surpen Prince had decided to oblige him. After this battle, the Thestrans' fate would be sealed. They would fall in love with Rhen, and then Loreth would pull him back to Surpen, so Andres could declare war. Perfect!

Loreth flew up into the air and stretched, arching his back, as Rhen sliced through the chest of the top Ustarian Military Commander with his sword. Loreth laughed at the look of horror on the Thestrans' faces, when Rhen decapitated the Ustarian King with his other sword.

'Well, that was fun,' Loreth thought, while flying up into space. Time to go to Surpen. Wait until Andres hears about today's activities. Loreth grinned, remembering the punishment for breaking Debrino's Code. How could Rhen have forgotten that Debrino prohibited Surpens from fighting for other planets. A purple, swirling vortex appeared three feet from Loreth. He zipped into it and disappeared.

The students at the Elfin University were just beginning their dinner, when Rhen startled everyone by walking into the dining hall covered in blood and carrying a heavy green, canvas bag over his back. His beautiful blue tunic was ruined. Blood had soaked through its light fabric, staining parts of it a mottled pattern. Rhen had blood across his left cheek and by his ear, and there was dirt smeared on his neck. He looked pleased and refreshed, as he strode up to Ceceta, who was rising to her feet with relief. Bending over, Rhen pulled her in towards him for a kiss. He released her and laughed, when he noticed the front of her yellow robes were now covered in blood.

Rhen pulled the bag that was hanging over his shoulder around in front of him. As he opened it, the other members of the Thestran Royal Family entered the room. Unlike Rhen, they appeared disheveled, dirty and morose.

Laughing and chatting to Ceceta in Surpen, Rhen put his hand into the bag he had been carrying. He pulled out the head of a man and dropped it onto the table in front him, where it knocked over a few of the dishes. Taking the hilt of one of his swords, Rhen cracked it down onto the man's skull until it opened. With care, he pried open the skull and pulled out the man's brains, putting them onto the plate in front of Ceceta. She grinned at him, as he sliced off a piece of the man's brain and popped it into his mouth.

Most of the students had fled the dining hall, when the man's skull had cracked under Rhen's sword, but when he started eating a person's brains, the entire room emptied out.

James cleared his throat and Rhen turned towards him. "Oh, sorry," Rhen said in Thestran. He walked over to James, fishing around in the bag he was holding. Rhen pulled out the head of the King of Ustar and gave it to James, who grimaced, while grabbing the King's head by its bloody black hair. Rhen pounded his left chest in salute. "Thank you, James! That was a lot of fun. They put up a good fight, don't you think? Nice sport!" he added, before turning and walking back to Ceceta.

"It was amazing!" Rhen told her in Thestran. "I forgot what it was like to just lay carnage and not have to worry about the overall game. We arrived on Ustar to find that James had no war plan, and the Council kept changing its mind about what to do. So, I got bored and took over. I just started killing Ustarians. I worked my way right up through the middle of their ranks into their main tents." He laughed and popped some more brain into his mouth, before adding, "The lower soldiers get to have all the fun, don't they?" Rhen paused in mid-bite, a confused look appeared on his face. Reaching up, he rubbed at the back of his head.

James put the head he was holding onto the nearest table, while Henry threw a napkin over it to cover it. "Um, Rhen, we need to speak with you in private, if that's alright," James said.

Rhen nodded and grabbed a fistful of brains, before following James and the other Thestran Royal Family members out of the room. They went down the hall, entering an empty side room that the students used for meditation. Rhen hesitated by the waterfall in the middle of the room to rub at the back of his head with his right hand, while the Thestran Royals sat down on the square cushions that were lined up across from him.

"Rhen, you were amazing out there. I've never seen anyone kill with such speed or efficiency before. There's no doubt in my mind that you're the most skilled fighter in the Universe. How you do it is a mystery to me," James stated. "But," he added. "You need to know that we end our wars differently than the Surpens do."

"We don't cut off their bloody heads and eat their brains!" Charlie yelled, as Rhen popped the last piece of brain that he was holding into his mouth. Rhen hesitated a moment, looking surprised by Charlie's outburst, before continuing to chew his victory prize.

James frowned at Charlie, warning him to be quiet. Turning back to Rhen, he said, "Actually, Charlie's right. We don't cut off our enemies' heads. We work with them to negotiate a settlement and to change their policies to bring peace."

Rhen frowned and bent his head over as he rubbed it. "Why?" he asked.

Kate held up her hand to silence Charlie before he could speak again, as James continued, "We feel it's kinder to work with the disagreeing parties to come to a compromise. If you work together, it'll ensure that any peaceful agreement you arrange will last much longer then, well, then any agreement that is reached when a conquering party cruelly murders the planet's leaders in front of their families and supporters."

"Are you sure it works better?" Rhen asked. "Fear is a powerful tool." He sat down on the plump, green cushion at his feet, so he could use both of his hands to rub at the back of his head.

"Yes, we're sure it works better and it's much kinder," Kate told him. "You Surpens should try it some time."

Rhen felt the hairs on his neck rise. He snorted with anger, stood up and walked to the door. Pausing by the door, he said, "Excuse me, but you sound like assholes. War is war. There's nothing 'kind' about war. If we hadn't won the war today, you wouldn't be sitting here telling me to play nicely, you'd be telling me to murder them in their sleep. You can afford to be jerks today, because you won. I don't think any of you truly understands the reality of war." Rhen opened the door to leave, but stopped to brace himself against the wall, as he rubbed at the back of his head. It was obvious something on his head was making him uncomfortable.

James took the opportunity to speak. "Yes, you're right. Perhaps we are acting like assholes. We've never had to fight such a violent, internal war before. In fact, without you, I'm not sure we would be here right now. You clearly won this war for us. Your joy at fighting inspired the troops. They followed you through the most dangerous fighting that I've ever seen. We kept thinking your moves would fail, but somehow, you always pulled it off. Let's just leave it like this. When you help us in the future, please win the war for us, but let us do the final negotiating. Okay?" He walked over to Rhen, who was still rubbing his head.

Rhen stopped what he was doing to stare at James. "I can't change my methods. If you don't like them, don't ask me to join you." Turning, he marched back to the dining room, where he found the students, who had returned, glaring at him. Rhen scooped up what was left of the brains, and with Ceceta following him, left. They went to their apartment, and for the first time, they locked their door.

Later that night, Rhen and Ceceta left their apartment to attend their Astronomy class. As they walked out their front door, they found most of the Thestran Royal Family waiting for them. The Thestrans accompanied them to their class, surrounding them as they sat down. Not only was Ceceta surprised by their actions but so were the other students and the Astronomy teacher. Rhen knew why they were keeping him separated from everyone else. It angered him that they didn't trust him.

When class was over, the Royal Family escorted Rhen and Ceceta back to their apartment in silence. Strolling down the school's hallways, Rhen and Ceceta heard some of the students whispering derogatory remarks about Rhen. They moved away from him, as if he were tainted, and stared at him with disapproval. Rhen shook his head. They had begged him to fight for them, but now they shunned him for his methods. 'How typically Thestran,' he thought. No wonder the Convention members despised these people. He remembered Loreth's overwhelming desire to attack the Thestrans and wondered if something similar to what he was experiencing had happened to the man. He had never asked his father why Loreth hated the Thestrans so much. Perhaps he had a good reason.

The Royal Family remained outside of Rhen and Ceceta's apartment after they returned. When their friends arrived for study group, the Thestran Royals turned them away. Disgruntled, the four friends wandered back to their dorm rooms. "I'm as pissed off now as I was when Professor Orisco informed me that he wouldn't teach me the drums, because I don't have rhythm," Tgfhi informed the others, stomping his little feet.

"Why won't they at least let us talk to Ceceta?" Latsoh asked. "She didn't decapitate anyone."

"They said they were tired," Crystam repeated James's words.

"They're not tired," Erfce replied. "I bet Ceceta and Rhen want company after a day like today."

"Yes," Tgfhi agreed. Several students ran by him talking in loud voices. One of the students bumped right into him, knocking him backwards. "HEY!" he yelled.

"Sorry," the student apologized, before running off with her friends. Tgfhi stared after her, taking in the large number of students, who were now running around the campus carrying papers and devices. "What's going on?" he asked. "Did the Black Angel do something?" His friends shrugged. "Hey," Tgfhi yelled at a passing group of students. "What's going on?"

"Rhen did it!" a boy responded, while looking at him with an awe-struck face.

"Did what?" Latsoh asked. She felt irritated that the other students knew something about Rhen that she didn't.

Charlie's friend Stanley approached. "Rhen single handedly won the war against Ustar for the Thestrans," he informed them. He handed each of them copies of the papers he was carrying. "I've printed some of the articles that are coming out. Rhen's a hero! We would all be Ustarian right now if it wasn't for him. The Royal Family did NOTHING during the war."

"Well, they did do something," another one of Charlie's friends remarked, while shaking the paper he was holding for emphasis. "They followed Rhen meekly as he cut a path through the Ustarian soldiers up to the King's main tent."

"It appears the Council members and the Thestran Royal Family stood around bickering over what to do, while their soldiers were dying in the fields. Rhen got pissed off and took charge. This isn't a victory for the Council or Thestran, it's a victory for Rhen," Stanley added. "Ustar is Rhen's."

"But he isn't claiming it," Charlie said in a quiet voice. He approached them from the direction of the Wood Elf Forest. "He's giving Ustar to us." Stanley and the others glared at Charlie. He shrugged. "Hey, the dude can fight. He has experience. What did you expect us to do?"

"You could have helped out our soldiers, while they were fighting for you," a nearby female student snapped. "Why did you leave them there with no orders and no direction?"

"We were working on it," Charlie snapped back.

"No. You and your family were squabbling, while our soldiers were dying," another student commented.

"No," Charlie told the kid. He pointed his finger at the papers they were holding. "The news companies are distorting the truth. We…we had a plan, but Rhen, after he heard what it was, showed us its weaknesses, and we realized he was right. Rhen suggested we follow his plan. The Council Members in the field were discussing it, James urged them to agree to it, but they were worried that

Rhen might have an ulterior motive, so they were examining it slowly. After three hours, the Council Members agreed to Rhen's plan, but Rhen told us his plan was now mute. It would no longer work. We had waited too long. As the Council Members tried to come up with a new plan, Rhen picked up his swords, yelled out to our generals to follow him and jumped into the battle. We couldn't see him. He was surrounded. Then, out of nowhere, we heard the Ustarians yelling to retreat, as Rhen ran along behind them, cutting them down with his swords. It was...." Charlie stopped speaking. He realized he had told them too much about the day's events.

"You don't deny that your family did nothing?" a student asked.

"We worked within the Council," Charlie informed him.

"Perhaps, in times of war," Stanley told Charlie. "You should reinstate James as full King and do away with the Council?"

Charlie's tired, blue eyes turned to Stanley. After a moment's hesitation, he nodded in agreement. "That would be a wise decision, but I have no power over Thestran politics and James is very lenient with his Delegates. I doubt anything will change after today's battle." He seemed depressed, and for the first time, sober. "Good night all," he said, turning to go to his dorm room, his shoulders hunched over from the day's events.

Chapter 18

When Rhen and Ceceta entered the dining hall the next morning, the students rose to cheer. Rhen gave them a small smile, acknowledging their thanks, and walked over to his table with Ceceta. As he approached, Erfce and Tgfhi jumped up from their seats and slapped him on the back. "We heard what you did! You're incredible!" Tgfhi exclaimed.

A group of students surrounded Rhen's table, the news reports glaring form their devices. A few of them were reading excerpts of his heroics aloud. Rhen smiled, while shaking his head at the news reports. He was dressed in a simple red tunic with no piping, and for the first time, he wasn't wearing his weapons belt.

"So, did you really win the war for us?" Crystam asked, when the crowd of students dispersed.

"Well, if that's what the news is saying, then it must be true," he told them with smirk. "You know how accurate they are."

"You were so covered in blood. It was gross," Latsoh remarked, scrunching up her face at the memory.

"Better theirs than mine."

"What's it like fighting in a war?" Crystam asked.

"You don't want to know," Rhen told her softly. He bent over and rubbed at the back of his head.

"Where are your swords today?" Erfce asked, while watching Rhen rub his head.

"I decided not to wear them."

"Why not?" Tgfhi asked.

"I'll be heading out soon, and I won't need them," Rhen responded.

"Where are you going?" Ceceta asked. They hadn't had a chance to talk last night before Rhen had left as the Black Angel. She knew something was wrong, but she hadn't figured out what it was yet.

"Home," Rhen whispered, rising to his feet.

The main double doors at the far end of the dining hall crashed open, making the walls and windows rattle. King Andres marched into the room with

20 soldiers in full military gear. The Headmaster followed along behind him calling out, "You must bring any issues to my office first. You can't just barge into the University's dining hall."

Andres growled at the Headmaster.

Professor Dewey pinched his lips and stepped backwards.

"I'm here to see my son. What I do with him, does not concern you," Andres told him in accented Thestran. The Surpen King turned. His eyes scanned the room, until they landed on Rhen. Rhen saluted his father, as Andres barked, "Front and center now!" Rhen ran around his table and down the aisle, stopping in front of Andres. He bowed to his father from the waist down.

"Rise," Andres barked. Rhen straightened in silence. "Is it true?" Andres asked, stepping forward, so he was almost touching Rhen. "Well, IS IT TRUE?" he shouted.

"Yes, my lord," Rhen replied, his face lacking expression.

Andres swung his enormous body backwards with distress, while yelling out, "FOR GOD'S BLOOD SON, WHAT THE HELL WERE YOU THINKING?" After a moment's hesitation, he turned back towards Rhen. "I thought I raised you better than that! You're proving that I'm a failure! You're demonstrating that I have no control over my own HOUSE! Were you a second son, I would have you killed!" A crack rang out, as Andres slapped Rhen across his face, drawing blood from his lip.

The students were shocked at the sight of someone abusing Rhen. Latsoh's temper boiled over. Rhen was a hero, yet his father was treating him like a traitor. She stepped forward to yell at the King, but Ceceta grabbed her arm and put her hand over Latsoh's mouth to keep her quiet. "Don't," she whispered. "You're a woman. Don't say anything or he'll kill you."

It was the Headmaster, who stepped forward to protect Rhen. "Now see here, there is no cause for you to abuse Rhen," he told Andres.

Instead of answering, the Surpen King glared at Professor Dewey, while two of his soldiers pushed Professor Dewey backwards, until he fell to the ground. Once the Headmaster was down, they smiled with satisfaction and turned back towards their King.

Andres faced Rhen again. "I am disgusted by this action and hurt by your betrayal! Didn't I tell you you would have to follow Debrino's Codes while here on Thestran! Any violation of his Code and you are to receive full punishment!" He pointed at one of his soldiers. The man had a Surpen's typical black hair and grey eyes. He also had a scar running down the side of his cheek.

The soldier opened up a parchment and read, "In sight of the Surpen God, you have been found guilty of violating Debrino's Code Rule Number 7. Any Surpen soldier found fighting for another planet must be lowered in rank by four stations and whipped 10 times the number of his previous station with the medusa whip."

Several of the students in the room gasped. The medusa whip was a vile instrument that had been banned in most solar systems. The tips of the nine leathers on the whip were fitted with a small, snake-like animal. When a person was whipped, the animal would bite at their flesh, tearing it, causing severe damage.

The soldier reading Rhen's sentence cleared his throat. "How do you plead?"

Without hesitation, Rhen replied, "Guilty."

Andres yelled out again and punched Rhen in the face. Rhen's body snapped backward from the blow, but he maintained his stance and didn't fall. "YOU STUPID IDIOT!" Andres yelled. "Do you know how many lashes you are to receive?" Rhen was silent. "Do you know child!"

"100," Rhen said, in a voice devoid of emotion.

Andres paced around Rhen fuming. "I have worked so hard to raise you and you repay me in this manner," he remarked with exasperation. He stopped in front of Rhen to look him in the eye. "I know you have amazing healing powers son, but my God." Reaching over, he grabbed Rhen's neck and pulled their foreheads together. "100 lashes," Andres murmured. "You could die, you know." After a moment of silence, Andres released Rhen and asked, "Why'd you do it?"

A smile formed on Rhen's lips. With laughter in his voice, he replied, "Have I ever said no to a good fight Dad?"

Andres chuckled. He stepped over to rub Rhen with affection on the head. When his hand touched the back of Rhen's head, he stopped and pulled Rhen downward, so he could inspect the area under his hand. Andres examined the bump on Rhen's head, as everyone waited. Eventually, Andres made a 'humph' sound and released his son. Turning, he marched towards the door asking, "Are you coming or do I need to have the guards drag you?"

At once, Rhen stepped forward to follow.

"Wait!" James cried out. Like Kate and Reed, he had been fetched the minute the Surpen King had arrived at the University. The three of them had witnessed most of the exchange between Rhen and his father.

Rhen paused and turned, as Andres walked back into the room to glare at the Royal Family.

"Rhen won the war for us on Ustar," James told the King, stepping forward. "You don't have to punish him. Ustar is his. We will give it to him."

"The Ustarian War was against Thestran, not Surpen. Rhen fought beside you. He fought for Thestran. He will be punished," Andres answered. He moved his body to block Rhen from James' view.

"No," James responded. "He shouldn't be punished. Ustar is his. Ask anyone. We did nothing during the battle."

"Your soldiers fought alongside Rhen," Andres replied. "He fought with Thestran. He knows he was wrong. He broke Debrino's Code. He will be punished."

"I broke our law," Rhen agreed. "I deserve to be punished."

James and Reed approached Rhen, stepping around Andres. The look on their faces was a mixture of pity and confusion. It was clear to all that Rhen had known this would happen, and yet he had still come to their aid. They owed him their lives, the fact that he might die because of it, was unthinkable. "You don't have to do this. You know that," James told him. "You're not Surpen, you're Thestran."

Rhen frowned. "But I am Surpen James? I keep telling you that."

Reed placed a tentative hand on Rhen's arm. "You were raised on Surpen, but your heritage and your people are Thestran. You don't need to follow Debrino's Code."

Rhen glanced at his father's back. "No," he answered. "I do. My life is on Surpen. My family is Surpen. It's all I know. I cannot desert my people. Would you desert them," he asked Reed, while gesturing towards the elfin students, "if I asked you to?"

Reed took in the worried faces on the elfin students in the room and dropped his shoulders. "Of course not. I could never abandon my people." Lifting his head, he squeezed his little brother's arm. "You will be a great ruler someday Rhen."

"If I live that long," Rhen laughed out. He turned to walk out of the room with his father's soldiers.

Andres remained a moment longer. He glared at James, his upper lip quivering in anger. "Thanks to you and your family I may lose my son today. If that happens, there will be retribution to pay." Reaching out, he pushed James on the shoulder, knocking him down. Andres debated kicking James, but changed his mind. He turned to follow Rhen back to Surpen. Ceceta dashed past the Thestran Royal Family in pursuit.

There was a stunned silence after they had left. The students were in shock. Rhen had saved their lives, and they had just sent him to his death.

James turned at the sound of people running down the hallway towards the dining hall. He lifted his hand, when the rest of the Thestran Royal Family ran into the room.

"We need to rescue him," Lilly declared, after James had told them what had happened. She couldn't believe her mother hadn't already left for Surpen.

They debated their next step and decided it would be best to visit Surpen on the chance that they might stop Rhen's punishment. James called out, 'Surpen!' at the school's portal, but instead of stepping through the frame, when it opened to Surpen, he paused.

The room, on the Surpen side of the portal, was full of soldiers in military gear.

Kate stepped past James and entered the Surpen palace, her children behind her. The Surpen soldiers in the room, were not only wearing their red and black military uniforms, but they also had black smudges on their cheeks. Their shields were held at waist level and their swords were raised and pointed towards the Thestrans. A tall, muscular soldier stepped forward from the side of the room. He looked like the other Surpens, with his short, black hair and gray eyes, but he had a rather large head, broad nose and full lips.

"The King said you would try to stop the punishment," he mentioned to James.

"Let us through," James demanded.

The man scoffed. "I don't think so. Just turn around and go back to Thestran. This situation doesn't concern you."

"Doesn't concern us!?" Kate yelled. "That's my son he's beating. I think it concerns us more than it concerns you!"

The man grunted. He had seen Kate speak before, so he wasn't impressed by her audacity. If she had been a Surpen woman, he would have had her arrested. "Then you don't know anything about us," he growled, as he stared at James. "There isn't a man in this room who wouldn't give his life for Rhen. We've grown up with him, we've fought with him and he's saved most of our lives on countless occasions. Had the King taken us, and not his Royal Guards to arrest Rhen, we would have issued the Oird Oath and taken Rhen's place. If he's so important to you, why didn't you do that for him?"

"Oird Oath?" Kate asked.

"We don't know an Oird Oath," Reed said.

"We don't know an Oird Oath," the soldier mocked, in a whiny voice. "It doesn't matter. Even if you had, you wouldn't have issued it. I can see from your faces that he's not a part of you." He turned his back on them and walked through the line of his men. "Leave now or we will kill you."

The Royal Family paused, considering the odds. After having watched Rhen fight on Ustar and Rowan, and knowing these men had been trained in battle the same way that Rhen had been trained, they weren't sure if they would be able to defeat them. James motioned for his family to retreat, so they walked back through the portal into Thestran.

Charlie paused by the Surpen side of the portal. He turned back to the man, who had spoken earlier. "Is he okay?"

The man lifted his head to regard Charlie. "We don't know yet," he replied, his eyes looking moister than they had been a minute ago.

Charlie nodded and stepped through the portal to return to Thestran. Before it closed, they heard someone yelling in Surpen to the soldiers. A great cheer went up among the men, and they banged the hilts of their swords on their shields, while chanting Rhen's name.

"I would take that as a good sign!" Charlie said, turning towards his family.

"I have to go back to Surpen," Kate announced. "I have to find him. I need to know that he's alright."

"How are you going to go back?" James asked. He took off his black cowboy hat and twirled it in his hand, while considering Kate's words. "They're guarding the portal entrance."

"There must be some way to return."

"Can we make a different portal opening to Surpen with the Genister Magic Box?" Sage asked.

Kate's face lit up. "Yes!"

"Let's go," James barked. He turned to the portal and said, "Thestran Royal Castle."

They followed Sage into her bedroom and waited in her living area, as she got the Magic Box from her safe. Holding the golden box with both hands out in front of her, Sage told it, "I wish I had a new portal connection to Surpen…"

"In the dungeon," Kate blurted out.

"A new portal frame that provides a single use visit from here in my bedroom to the Surpen Castle's dungeon," Sage clarified. She opened her box and they watched, as a white mist floated up out of it. It hovered in the air for a moment, before lowering and taking on the shape of a door. Within seconds, the mist evaporated and they were staring at a golden portal frame beside Sage's couch. Sage didn't waste any time. "Surpen," she yelled at the frame. A blue light filled the interior of the frame. When the light faded, they saw a dark, empty corridor on the opposite side.

"I have to go find him, but you don't," Kate told her family. "Please stay here where it's safe." She moved to step forward towards the new portal, but James grabbed her arm.

"You're kidding, right?" he asked his mother. "We're adults mom; we do what we want. Also, you wouldn't stand a chance alone in that male-dominated society." He moved past her through the portal into the Surpen Castle's dungeon, the rest of his family following along behind him.

When the portal closed, the dungeon became very dark. "Rachel, dear," Kate said. Rachel held up her hand and a small, white light glowed within the center of her palm. "I'm going to change your appearances," Kate told them. She moved from person to person, using her powers to change their looks, until they all resembled Surpen soldiers – muscular, black haired, grey eyed and dressed in traditional Surpen uniforms.

As a group, they walked up the first stairs they came to into the main portion of the castle. They wandered about, until they passed the room where the soldiers had stopped them earlier. Most of the men were gone. The ones who remained were celebrating with abandon. Continuing down a long corridor, they stopped, so Kate could ask a slave where Rhen was located. The slave pointed them through a doorway on their right. The room was empty, so they continued, entering the next room, where they found two slaves kneeling on the floor cleaning a pool of blood.

On either side of the slaves were blood splattered pillars. A pair of blood coated chains and wrist cuffs hung from the pillars and the black medusa whip, with its nine snarling, biting heads, growled from the hook on which it hung in the far, left corner of the room. "This must be where Andres had Rhen beaten," Lilly whispered.

Reed stepped forward and said Rhen's name to the slaves. They pointed him towards an archway on their right. As the Thestrans walked over to the archway, they noticed a trail of blood on the floor that went from the pillars through the doorway. "When in doubt, just follow the blood," Charlie piped out in Thestran. Sage elbowed him in the ribs. He slapped a hand over his mouth and glanced back at the slaves, to see if they had heard him. They were still at work, cleaning the blood, and didn't show any interest in Charlie or the others.

The trail of blood led them through one room into a spacious, oval room with multiple arched windows and two balconies on either side. Enormous blue curtains billowed inward from the wind. There were two rows of brown, stone columns holding up the vaulted ceiling and a small, blue pool located in the floor towards their left. In the pool, they noticed four, orange and white fish. "Are those the fish that Rhen took at breakfast the morning of Sage's wedding?" Lilly whispered.

Before anyone could answer, they heard a clinking sound and froze. When no one jumped out to attack, they peeked around one of the columns towards their right. On the far side of the room, they spotted Rhen sitting on a red, cushioned bench with no back to it. He was facing away from them and shivering. There was a thick, red blanket wrapped around his shoulders. An elderly woman dressed in blue and wearing a crown was hugging his left arm and whispering to him.

They heard another clink and saw Rhen throw something small and white into a twelve-inch-high, brass urn. Ceceta entered the room from the left, carrying two glass goblets filled with blood. A slave followed along behind her with what appeared to be clothing. Ceceta talked in a cheerful tone of voice to Rhen and the old woman in Surpen. Stopping beside Rhen, she handed him one of the goblets. When Rhen was finished with it, she took it and handed him the new one. After Rhen had emptied the second goblet, Ceceta placed them onto the low table in front of him and moved to his right side. With care, she pulled the blanket away from his back to look at his wound. Rhen's shivering increased, so Ceceta replaced the blanket. Holding her hand out behind her, they watched as one of the slaves moved forward to place the clothing he was carrying into Ceceta's palm. Ceceta stood in front of Rhen, shifting the thick red and black tunic around in her hands, so it would line up with his body. She dropped the tunic down over Rhen's head, and with the old woman's assistance, the two of them helped Rhen pull his arms through the sleeves.

When Rhen's tunic was in place, Ceceta pulled the blanket out from underneath it, before wrapping a new blanket around his body. Two slaves walked into the room carrying jewelry on trays. Ceceta took a necklace from one of the trays and placed it around Rhen's neck. Rhen threw his left hand out to bat her away, as he tossed another white object at the brass urn in front of him with his right hand. The white piece clinked on the urn's rim then fell into it.

The old woman placed a crown on Rhen's head. He barked something in Surpen, grabbed the crown and threw it behind him. The crown bounced and rolled across the room, stopping when it hit James's right foot. Without thinking, James bent over to pick it up.

The crown was made of gold with a varying array of multi-colored jewels that James didn't recognize. There were intricate, swirling carvings throughout the base of the crown. When James looked up, he jumped, because the old woman was right in front of him. Without saying a word, she knelt down onto the floor and bowed at his feet.

James didn't know what to do, so he placed the crown onto the floor by the old woman's hands. She snatched it up and crawled away from him, standing when she neared Rhen.

Ceceta, who had watched the exchange, kept her eyes on James. She appeared confused. Bending down, she whispered to Rhen.

Shivering, Rhen turned his head to look at the soldiers behind him. For a moment, he appeared puzzled, like Ceceta. He shifted his body further on the bench, to get a better view of the soldiers, and then started to laugh.

Rhen told the slaves in the room to leave. When they were gone, he said in Thestran, "I should be furious with you for breaking into my home, but I'm not. In fact, you're just in time. Reed and Charlie, can you come over here and help me? I need to meet my father on the balcony in a few minutes and I'm not sure I can go alone."

Startled by his words, no one moved.

"Seriously?" Ceceta asked. "It's the Thestran Royal Family?"

"Yes," Rhen told her. In Surpen, he explained the situation to Orpel, who was still standing beside him, holding the crown.

"You picked a clever disguise," Rhen told the Thestrans. "But you have a few things wrong. Your military bars are on the wrong shoulder and you need to add two more stripes, to be allowed into the castle. And," he added, while pointing at James, "no one, but the Royal Family, can touch my crown, so you owe Queen Orpel an apology."

James bent his head to the Surpen Queen. "I apologize."

The old woman moved over to a wooden desk located in the far, left corner of the room. She took a handful of small objects from one of the drawers and proceeded to hand them to the Thestrans. James sighed with relief, when he saw she had given him a translating device.

"You need help?" Charlie asked Rhen, walking over to him.

"Yes. Bend down." Rhen reached up to fix Charlie's uniform.

"Are you alright?" Reed asked, coming up beside them.

"Yeah, I'm fine," Rhen assured them. "I'm just having the shakes, but they'll be gone soon." He finished fixing Charlie's uniform and motioned for Reed to step closer so he could fix his. "Why are you here?"

"We were worried about you," Reed told him. Rhen smiled and shook his head. Reed opened his mouth to insist that they did indeed care about Rhen, but he realized his words would sound hollow.

Ceceta fixed the other solders' uniforms and grouped them in twos, placing them at the doorways around the room. "They should be marked in protest," Orpel told her, while glancing at their faces. Ceceta nodded and walked to the desk. She lifted a small pot of ash off the top shelf and returned to the soldier she had just moved.

"Dip your thumb in this and rub it in one stripe down your right cheek," she said.

"Why?" Sage asked, follwing Ceceta's command.

Ceceta laughed at the sound of her voice. "Sorry. I didn't know you were Sage. I thought you were William or James."

The soldier next to Sage spoke. "I'm William."

Ceceta laughed again. "You look funny as Surpens," she told them, while moving over to William, so he could mark his face. She crossed the room to hold the pot up for the soldiers located on that side. "Are you Rachel?" she asked.

"No, Kate," Kate replied. Ceceta chuckled.

"We don't have time Ceceta, hurry up," Orpel warned her. Ceceta brought the pot of ash to the remaining Thestrans, before returning it to the table.

As she placed the pot onto the desk, two soldiers, with black marks on their faces, entered the room. "Your presence is required your majesty," they informed Rhen. He nodded and raised his hands up to Charlie and Reed, indicating they should help him stand. While they lifted him up off the bench, he whispered, "Don't be nervous. I'm not hurt, just weak."

Supporting Rhen's weight between them, Reed and Charlie made their way over to the waiting soldiers. As they neared the men, the soldiers saluted

Rhen and turned to lead the way out of the room. Just as the tallest soldier reached the archway, he stopped and turned back towards Rhen. "Sir...I just wanted to say...I'm so sorry, I..." his eyes filled with tears. Without another word, he knelt before Rhen. The soldier beside him doing the same.

Rhen placed his hands on their heads. "Thank you."

"Sir!" they barked in unison, before rising to their feet, bowing to their prince and leading the way out of the room.

Before Rhen left, Orpel rushed over and placed the crown back on his head. "Thanks, mom," he told her, with dripping sarcasm, while walking out of the room.

Orpel shook her fist playfully at Rhen then turned towards Ceceta. The two of them whispered for a moment before approaching Kate. "You mustn't let anyone know who you are," Orpel told her. "The Debrino Code is very clear that impersonating a Surpen soldier is punishable by death, and our helping you with your impersonation will mean our deaths too."

Kate nodded. "We won't reveal ourselves until we're back on Thestran."

"Thank you," Orpel said. She hesitated before asking, "What do you want?"

"We came to make sure Rhen was okay. Now that we know he's fine, we'll bring him back to school."

"My husband won't let him return to your school. He's already told me this. His mind is made up," Orpel informed her. "Will you declare war on us, if he doesn't return?"

"No, why would you think that?" Kate responded.

"Because that's what a Surpen would do," Ceceta answered for her mother-in-law. "What will you do if we can't come back?"

"That depends on Rhen I guess. Do you think he wants to return?"

"I'm not sure. I think so."

Orpel smiled at Ceceta's answer and reached out to touch her chin. "It's for your sake. He's only at school for you, and we all know it."

Ceceta blushed. "No, he wants to learn and we've made some really good friends at school too."

Orpel laughed. "You can't fool me child. I raised the two of you. I know you better than you know yourselves."

Her words angered Ceceta. The Queen didn't know her at all. They spent a great deal of time together, but they never spoke openly. Since she didn't know anything about Orpel, how could Orpel know her so well? Ceceta was going to make a comment to that effect, when Orpel surprised her by asking, "Do they know everything?"

Ceceta stared at the Queen. What was she talking about? Did she know? Since Ceceta wasn't sure what Orpel knew, she kept her mouth shut and shook her head.

"You can't dangle that out there and not fill us in," James declared. "What's 'everything'?"

Orpel gave James a hard look then turned to Kate and said, "It's not my place to tell. If Rhen wants you to know, he'll tell you."

Choosing her words with care, Kate asked, "If there's something you feel we should know, something that would make Rhen's life easier, we hope you will tell us?"

Orpel laughed and shook her head. "Nothing will make Rhen's life easier. If he had been born without powers, he would've had a lovely life, but that's not to be his fate, is it?"

Ceceta's eyebrows shot up. Did the Queen know? Why else would she have said something like that? If Orpel knew, did that mean Andres knew Rhen had great powers too? And how had Orpel found out about Rhen's powers? Who would have told her? Was it possible she also knew that Rhen was the Black Angel?

"What powers does Rhen have?" James asked.

Before Orpel could respond, there was a sudden roar that echoed throughout the room.

Lilly glanced about with concern. "What's going on?"

"The King is speaking to the entire military force. He rarely does this, because there are so many soldiers. He's showing the men that not only is Rhen still alive, but he still supports his father. The soldiers' allegiance has always been to Rhen, not Andres. They love him." Ceceta paused, as another loud roar echoed through the room. "It's very important for Andres to make it clear to the soldiers that Rhen supports him, because for the first time ever, the soldiers are rebelling."

"Rebelling?" William asked, sounding worried.

Ceceta nodded in confirmation. "They're furious that the Debrino Code was enforced on Rhen. They heard Rhen beat the Ustarians without much help from you or your military, so they feel Ustar should be a part of Surpen's territory. Rhen won the war, not Thestran. Ustar is ours. The King, on the other hand, seems to have his own agenda. He's more interested in punishing Rhen than enlarging Surpen. The soldiers are very upset with him right now. He couldn't even ask Surpen's military to arrest Rhen. He had to use his own personal guard." Ceceta pointed at their faces and explained, "The soldiers are showing their anger by wearing a protest stripe down their cheeks."

"It's a historic moment," Orpel interrupted. "No one has ever protested the Debrino Code. Ever. Now, the entire military force, except for the King's personal guard, is showing defiance towards the law."

Outside, there was another loud roar as the soldiers cheered.

"None of us know what's going to happen next. If they're angry enough, they could overthrow the King and place Rhen in control. Although it's unlikely," Ceceta told them, when it had quieted down. "They would need some indication from Rhen that he would support them, but Rhen's never gone against his father."

"In public," Orpel mumbled. Ceceta raised an eyebrow. Orpel clarified, "He's never indicated to anyone, except to us in private, that he's unhappy with the King."

Ceceta gave Orpel a slow nod. She hadn't realized that Rhen had told his mother about his frustration with Andres and Loreth. Turning back to the Royal Family, Ceceta said, "Also, the Surpens follow rules. It's what they do best. The very fact that they're questioning a rule...it's astronomical!"

"You have no idea how amazing this event is in our history," Orpel emphasized.

Without warning, Andres strode into the room with ten soldiers who didn't have protest stripes on their cheeks. At the sight of him, Orpel and Ceceta dropped to the floor in low bows. Andres ignored them. He sat down on the bench near the low table and took a drink from the goblet he had received from one of the slaves, who had magically appeared in the room. "Move that bench over here," he told them, gesturing towards a red, cushioned bench that was against the far wall.

The slaves placed the second bench at a right angle to the one Andres was sitting on. Just as they finished, Charlie and Reed carried Rhen into the room. Rhen looked exhausted, his skin was pale and he was breathing heavily.

The trip to speak to the soldiers had clearly worn him out. Andres ordered Reed and Charlie to place Rhen on the bench next to his. They eased him down, catching Ceceta's eye when they stood back up. She indicated to them that they should walk over to guard one of the doorways.

A slave brought Rhen a goblet of blood, but he shook his head, so the man placed it on the center table in front of the two benches and backed away.

Andres dismissed his personal guards. Once they had left, he cleared his throat and said, "That went well." You could still hear the men cheering occasionally in the background. Andres stared at his son. "Not too tired, are you?" Rhen shook his head. "Drink something, it'll help."

"How do you know what would help?" Rhen replied, through clenched teeth. He moved his left arm up to cover his eyes. "Have you ever been punished with the Medusa whip?"

Andres decided not to answer. Getting up, he moved over to sit down on Rhen's bench, pushing Rhen's legs over to make more room for himself. He picked up Rhen's goblet with his massive hand and leaned forward, lifting the cup to Rhen's lips. Rhen removed his arm from his eyes and stared at his father without speaking.

After what seemed like a long time, Andres said, "Come on, drink some of this." He pushed the goblet against Rhen's bottom lip. Rhen opened his lips and Andres tilted the cup, pouring some of the red liquid into his mouth. When he felt Rhen had had enough, he lowered the goblet and returned it to the table. As Andres leaned back, he said, "Don't be mad at me Rhen. I wasn't the one who broke Debrino's Code. We had an agreement and...."

"I know all about our agreement Dad," Rhen snapped. "And I followed the rules, I accepted the punishment for my crime but...WHAT THE HELL!" He gritted his teeth with fury then added in a quieter voice, "Why did you choose Narseth to deliver the blows? You could've chosen Bosternd. I mean..." he sighed and pushed his body back against the bench with anger. "GOD! You can be such a Rasack's ass."

Andres' eyes narrowed, as he scowled at Rhen. "I needed to prove to everyone that I'm in control of my own house. You've been gone for months now, playing your little games on Thestran. The people wonder where your heart lies."

"No, they don't," Rhen protested. "They know I'm with them."

Andres grabbed Rhen's face, squeezing his cheeks. "I had to use Narseth," he growled. "He was the only one who could deliver the blows properly. Bosternd is your friend. No one would believe him capable of administering your punishment to its full extent."

"Let go of me," Rhen hissed.

Instead of releasing Rhen, Andres switched his grip to Rhen's tunic. He lifted Rhen a foot off the bench. Shaking him hard, he shouted, "I'm in control Rhen! Never forget that! I'M IN CONTROL! THIS IS MY PLANET. I'M THE RULER HERE. I'M IN CONTROL."

Rhen started to laugh, his limp body hanging from his father's hands. "Yeah, you sure look like you're in control Dad."

"Dammit!" Andres shouted, throwing Rhen back down onto the bench. He started to walk away from Rhen, but turned around and pointed at Rhen yelling, "NEVER FORGET THAT I'M IN CONTROL!"

"Yes, father," Rhen replied in a meek voice, but he couldn't help himself from chuckling again.

As soon as Andres heard him, he pulled his swords out of his weapons belt and rushed at Rhen, swinging them towards Rhen's head. Like lightning, Rhen pulled out a dagger, ducked under the King's swords, grabbed Andres by his hair and placed his dagger at his father's throat. After a tense moment, during which no one spoke or moved, Rhen said, "Leave the fighting to me Dad. That's my job. That's why I'm here. For once, I wish you'd believe me, when I tell you I don't want to be King." Rhen shoved his father away from him, causing Andres to stumble.

Andres turned and glared at Rhen, before putting his swords back into his belt. Rhen tossed his dagger onto the table and lay back down on his bench, placing his forearm over his eyes.

"I don't know why you care who swung the whip," Andres commented, while sitting down. "It's not like you don't heal instantly."

"It still hurts Dad!"

"Well, can't you get rid of the pain?"

"No," Rhen told him. "Only the wound."

"Is it hurting now?"

"No," Rhen admitted. "My system's drained, though." After a pause, he said in a teasing voice, "Where did your advisor go? He was in the room during my punishment. Did he leave once he got what he came for?"

171

"Shut up," Andres snapped. "Show some respect. Loreth's brought this planet farther than we could have ever hoped."

"Through bloodshed and tears," Rhen mumbled.

Andres jumped to his feet looking furious. He was about to walk over towards Rhen, when an enormous soldier, who could have been genetically engineered, entered the room, followed by a smaller soldier, whose cheek was marked in protest. Kate and Henry recognized the smaller soldier, he was the same man they had bumped into the night that Rhen had beaten Kate in hand to hand combat. Both men bowed before Andres and waited in silence. Andres sat down and motioned for a slave, who was holding a large box, to step forward. He opened the box the slave was carrying and took out a handful of gold coins. Rhen raised his arm off his eyes to watch his father. The King motioned for the large soldier to step forward. He handed the man the coins he was holding, saying, "Thank you. You're dismissed Narseth."

Before Narseth had even moved, Rhen scoffed and said, "So, Dad, since when do we provide extra payment for soldiers who are simply performing their duties?"

Infuriated, Andres lunged towards Rhen, hitting him hard on the head with his military wrist cuff and growling, "Don't you ever speak to me in that manner again!" He raised his hand to hit Rhen again, but the look his son gave him was so disturbing, he stepped back.

"Dismissed Narseth!" Andres yelled at the large soldier.

Addressing the smaller soldier, the King said, "Bosternd, you had something you wanted to speak to me about?"

Bosternd dropped to the floor in a bow. "Your majesty, I wish to inform you that since Rhen survived the punishment for breaking Debrino's Code, the soldiers feel his proper rank should be reinstated. As you know, Debrino's Code states you are innocent, if you survive a death penalty."

At Bosternd's words, Andres had a fit. He screamed and kicked at his bench, knocking it over. Bending down, he grabbed items off the table in front of him and threw them against the wall. Turning back to Bosternd, Andres held up his finger and yelled, "Rhen's punishment was NOT the death penalty, but a simple whipping, and Rhen's not innocent! He admitted his guilt."

Andres sat back down on his bench, which the slaves had returned to its proper location, and told Bosternd. "You're the acting head of Surpen's military. If you don't take control of the soldiers, I will replace you this instant and you can spend the rest of your time on the Island."

Without hesitation, Bosternd said he would take control of the situation. He saluted Andres and left as fast as he could.

When Bosternd was gone, Andres gestured for a slave to bring him a goblet. He snatched the glass and drank its contents, slamming it down onto the table in front of him when he was finished. A moment later, he moved over to sit down next to Rhen. Reaching out, he picked up Rhen's goblet and handed it to him. Rhen sat up to drink. When he was done, Andres took the goblet and put it down onto the table next to his. He leaned sideways against the bench to observe his son. The two men stared at each other in silence for a few minutes.

Andres surprised the Thestrans, when he said in a gentle voice, "You know how I feel about you son. Right?"

Rhen sighed and relaxed. "Yeah, I know." He motioned for a slave to move his brass urn back into place. After it was in position, he started to throw the white pieces that had been on the table into the urn. For five minutes, the only sound in the room was the clink of the white pieces as they struck the urn and fell in or bounced off.

"What are you up to?" Andres asked, breaking the silence.

"Seventeen," Rhen replied.

"Fantastic!" Andres cried out, slapping Rhen on the back and making the Thestrans in the room wince. "You really are amazing." He stared at the white pieces in Rhen's hand. "Whose bones are those?"

Sage coughed in shock at the question. She couldn't believe Rhen was using someone's bones for a game. Frowning, Andres turned around to stare at Sage. For the first time, he glanced around the room at the soldiers standing at attention. "Which battalion are these soldiers from? I don't recognize them?"

Rhen glanced up at the Thestrans, as if he hadn't noticed them before. "Legion 437," he replied with disinterest.

"Oh," Andres exhaled, perking up. "Your water troops?" Rhen nodded his head. "They did well on Tgarus. How did you get them to hold their breath for so long?"

Rhen threw another bone into the urn before answering, "Practice."

With a nod, Andres motioned for his wife to rise. She stood up and walked over to him, taking off his cape and military shoulder and breast plates. She handed his armor to a slave, who whisked it away. Leaning forward, she began to rub his back and neck.

"You know," the King told Rhen. "Your mother and I were thinking that you and your wife could move into the south side of the castle. I know you've always preferred that section."

"Thanks," Rhen replied indifferently, throwing a bone towards the urn. "After school is finished, we'd love to move into the south side."

Andres hesitated before saying, "Have you finished your surveillance? Have you determined the extent of the Thestran's forces and powers?"

Rhen gave Andres a crooked smile and lied. "Not yet. They're as powerful as you indicated, which will make it difficult for us."

Andres considered his words and replied, "I don't care anymore. You've done enough. You will not be returning to Thestran."

Rhen's arm was up in the air. He had been about to throw another bone towards the urn. Lowering his arm, he turned towards his father. "Excuse me?"

"It's in Surpen's best interest for you stay here. You know you can't trust the Thestran Royal Family. They're dangerous. They hate Surpen, and they're jealous of all we have. Eventually, they will try to conquer us, you know that. We've had countless oracles predict this. You cannot return to Thestran." There was a finality to his voice.

Rhen smiled. He turned back to the urn. Without speaking, he continued to throw bones at it. Andres wasn't sure what Rhen was thinking, so he continued, hoping to draw him out. "I've made up my mind Rhen. The only time you're allowed back on that filthy planet is when we're at war with them." He leaned to his left, as his wife continued to massage his shoulders. Rhen didn't respond, so Andres assumed he agreed, which pleased him, since he had thought the two of them were going to argue over this. With a cruel smile, Andres added, "I can't wait to see their faces when you're blowing up their castle and crushing in their skulls. That beastly woman I've had to negotiate with for years," he laughed. "She won't know what hit her."

"You mean my mother?" Rhen asked.

Orpel gasped, as Andres jumped to his feet. "WHAT DID YOU SAY!"

"My mother?" Rhen repeated, giving his father an innocent look.

Andres caught sight of the twinkle in Rhen's eye and laughed. "Oh, you had me for a moment. I thought you might actually," he waved his hand in a dismissive gesture towards Rhen. "Never mind," he said, sitting back down on the bench.

Rhen threw a new bone at the urn and missed. "I'm not debating the issue of school with you father."

Andres misunderstood his meaning and replied, "Good. I'm glad you'll stay. I had thought we were going to fight about this. I'm happy to see I was wrong." Orpel returned to rubbing Andres' shoulders. He dropped his head down, enjoying her massage.

For a while, the only sounds in the room were the bones, as they hit Rhen's brass urn, and Andres' grunts of pleasure, as his wife eased his aching muscles.

"Vivist's Tail!" Rhen shouted, startling everyone. He jumped to his feet. "Twenty in the pot! I'm good to go." He turned towards Ceceta and gestured for her to stand. "Come!" he ordered. Pointing at William and Sage, he said, "You." He turned and pointed at Kate, James and Henry, "You, and..." he nodded towards Lilly and Rachel, "You. Escort my wife back to the Thestran University. Use our main portal to go to the Thestran palace. She will show you how to proceed after that."

"STOP!" Andres bellowed. He rose from his bench so fast that he knocked his wife over backwards. "What the hell do you think you are doing? We just made an agreement."

Rhen stared at the soldiers he had just spoken to. "I GAVE YOU A DIRECT ORDER! MOVE OUT!" he hollered. At once, the Thestrans escorted Ceceta out of the room. Rhen pointed at Reed and Charlie. "You two are with me," he said, turning to walk out of the room.

"HALT NOW, BOY!" Andres screamed at the top of his lungs, while bits of spit flew from his mouth. "You're breaking our agreement. If you go back to that school, I will arrest you!"

Rhen marched over to his father. Dropping his voice, he said, "We do have an agreement. One we made months ago. I expect you to fulfill your part of the bargain, father."

Andres was shaking with rage. Rhen reached out to put his hand on his father's shoulder. "Dad, come on, let's not fight anymore. You know I'm your obedient son. I will do anything you want me to do. I will fight any war you want me to fight. I will turn the men to your will. I will follow Debrino's Codes. I will back you until the end of time," he paused to see if his father was listening. "But this, I need this. I need to return to this school. I can't explain why. I don't understand it myself. But I do know that if I don't return, I'll never be happy here. I wish I could explain it to you, but I can't. You have to trust me. You have to know that I am Surpen and nothing will ever change that." Rhen's speech diffused his father's anger.

Andres' shoulders dropped and his mouth curved downward. He knew he couldn't force Rhen to stay. The soldiers would never arrest him, and if he ordered his guards to arrest Rhen, there would be a civil war. He decided to try another tactic. In a forlorn voice, he said, "If you go back, they'll try to change you. They'll turn you away from Surpen. They'll start with small things and then it will get bigger and bigger. They'll trick you, to make you one of them. Will I be able to count on you when the war comes? Will you be able to slaughter them? Months ago, you would've drooled at the chance to take your knife to their throats. Do you still feel that way? Can you still annihilate them?"

Rhen didn't answer. His lack of response made Andres realize the answer was no. "I thought you might be softening towards them." Andres put his hand on Rhen's shoulder. "War is inevitable son. You're the deciding factor. Will it be Thestran or will it be Surpen? How do I know you'll stand by my side when the time comes? How do I know you'll take our men into battle with the intention of winning? How do I know you won't turn on me?"

Rhen reached out and hugged his father. As he held onto Andres, he whispered, "Never question my loyalty. I will never leave you. I will never betray my Surpen brothers. You can always count on me."

Andres struggled in Rhen's grasp, so Rhen released him. The Surpen King waved his hand to dismiss Rhen. It was clear he had heard enough. He didn't believe Rhen.

"I suppose it's too much to ask for your blessing?" Rhen asked.

Andres glanced up, his bushy, black eyebrows raised in surprise. Rhen thought his father might say something, but instead, he turned and marched out of the room.

Feeling disappointed, Rhen motioned towards Reed and Charlie. "Follow me!"

They walked through the castle until they reached a dark passageway that led to a heavy, metal door. Rhen stopped by the door and turned to face them. "First, I want to apologize to you for the way I behaved back there. Normally, Dad and I never fight. I was mad at him for choosing Narseth to perform my punishment." He shook his head adding, "On the bright side, at least it wasn't Aul. Secondly, my rank has dropped by four stations. There are a few top generals, who abuse their position. As a lower soldier, I am not allowed to…rebuff them. Do you understand?" Reed and Charlie stared at him. They didn't understand. Sighing Rhen continued, "I don't know how much you know about Surpen men or Surpen's military, but I will need you to…" he hesitated, scratching at the back of his head, feeling awkward.

"What?" Charlie asked.

Rhen pulled some additional military stripes from the pocket of his tunic. He added them to both Reed and Charlie's uniforms, while explaining, "Charlie, if a General, with the same number of bars that you have, approaches me and well, if he looks suspicious…then I need you to mark me as yours." Rhen couldn't believe he was asking for their help. But, he needed it. It had been years since he had held a low rank, and he wasn't willing to face its ramifications again without some sort of assistance.

If the Thestrans hadn't of followed him to Surpen, he would've asked one of the Genisters for help, but their help always came with strings attached. Rhen still hadn't figured out what the Thestrans wanted from him, but whatever it was, it couldn't be as bad as what the Genisters demanded.

Rhen inhaled sharply and lowered his head. He had just let his mind block slip. If Reed or Charlie had the power to read minds, they would've had quite the shock. He and Ceceta were the only ones in the Universe, who knew the Genisters were still around. If he didn't have pressing matters to attend to right now, he would've fallen on the ground laughing, not only at his own stupidity for letting his mind block drop, but also at what the Thestrans' reactions would've been to the news that the Genisters were alive and well.

When Rhen lifted his head, he found Charlie staring at him with an odd expression. A second later, Charlie's goofy look returned and he asked, "So, what do you mean, you want me to mark you? Like, should I pee on you?"

"NO!" Rhen barked, feeling exasperated.

Charlie laughed at Rhen's expression. "It's okay," he confessed. "I know what you mean." Rhen sighed and stepped forward to push the white, metal door in front of them open.

Reed put his hand on the metal door behind Rhen, to keep it open, and realized this had been the first door they had encountered in the Surpen Castle. There weren't any other doors or windows, just open doorways and arches. He wanted to ask Rhen why, but decided it'd be best to ask the question back on Thestran.

They followed Rhen across an attractive courtyard, down a stone pathway, through a guarded door in the outer wall that surrounded the castle and then out onto an enormous field. Everywhere they looked, they saw soldiers, thousands and thousands of soldiers. Reed couldn't help himself from whistling with appreciation at the enormity of Surpen's military force. Rhen smiled at him and said, "Thanks."

Of course, they were spotted by some of the soldiers. The men who saw Rhen cheered or waved flags in honor of their Prince. Rhen raised his hand to acknowledge them, while continuing across the field, down a small hill, towards a door located in the side of a rock cliff. When they reached the non-descript metal door in the cliff, two soldiers, who were guarding it, saluted Rhen. He nodded to them and stepped forward to open the door. Reed and Charlie were about to follow, but the Surpen soldiers put out their hands to stop them. "They're with me," Rhen told the guards. The soldiers dropped their hands and stepped back to allow Reed and Charlie to enter.

Reed and Charlie walked through the door and were startled to find themselves in a large, well lit room. The room was painted a brilliant, blue color and there was a mosaic of Andres, made from precious stones, on the floor. It was noisy and there were people bustling about. Placed evenly around the room were wooden desks with soldiers sitting behind them. At each desk were two chairs, many of which contained Surpen civilians, who were talking to the soldiers or filling out paperwork. At the sight of Rhen, the soldiers stood up to salute him and the women bowed down before him. Rhen saluted in return and crossed the room, entering one of the seven dark passageways that led out of it. "Civilians come to us to resolve any issues they might be having," Rhen explained to Reed and Charlie, walking into the darkness.

Reed put out his hand to feel the cool, stone wall. There was a lighted room ahead of them. "Is this your headquarters?" he asked.

Rhen stopped short. "No!" he barked, before chuckling. He was having fun with the Thestrans. He had already toured their military headquarters. One day, when Ceceta was taking Math, he had turned himself invisible and flown over to the Thestran Castle to inspect his competition. What he had seen there had made him throw his hands up in disbelief. The Thestrans were totally unprepared for invasion. Their headquarters was nothing more than a glorified doghouse. It'd be good for Prince Reed to see how a real military force operated.

"No, way!" Charlie exclaimed. "So, this is where Surpen plans its maneuvers and decides how to attack?"

"I never said that," Rhen replied, giving Charlie a friendly smack on the arm.

They walked through several rooms painted in bright colors and down multiple dark passageways. Whenever they passed soldiers, the men always greeted Rhen with warmth.

"It's a maze," Reed remarked. He was completely lost.

"Yup," Rhen confirmed, slipping into their fourth secret passageway. They walked down a small, unlit corridor, where they heard men's voices: "If we kill him, Rhen will be able to install the changes our society needs," "How do we know Rhen won't continue the current regime's policies," "Rhen is the true ruler, he's the stronger of the two," "The King must die for Rhen take charge."

Reaching the end of the corridor, Rhen pushed aside a dark, velvet curtain and stepped into a room. The room was round and bright, although smoke from the men's cigarettes had given the room a hazy appearance. Several Surpen generals were sitting at a round table filled with war plans. On the walls hung maps of solar systems, and underneath them, were wooden bookcases filled with books that had the names of the planets Surpen had conquered. On the far wall was a white, ceramic sink with a multitude of glasses around it. The generals in the room were in full uniform and carried two swords in their weapons belts. Their collective grey eyes swiveled towards the entrance where Rhen stood.

Bosternd was the first to recover from the surprise of being interrupted. "Rhen!" he shouted. Jumping up, he knocked over his chair in his rush to embrace his friend. Reed and Charlie saw the warmth in Rhen's eyes for this tiny general who ran towards him. The two men embraced, slapping each other on the backs and laughing.

Bosternd was a handsome Surpen. He had a Surpen's grey eyes, black hair and a strong jaw line. He was also quite short, which Reed and Charlie found interesting. For a short man to be in charge of Surpen's military, it could only mean that Bosternd was deadly in combat.

"Oh, sorry," Bosternd apologized, after he had slapped Rhen's back for the fifth time.

"It doesn't hurt," Rhen informed him. He reached over to tap Bosternd's head. "I've already healed."

The other generals were waiting for their chance to greet Rhen, so Bosternd stepped aside, allowing each of the remaining generals to greet their Prince. Reed and Charlie learned, from their greetings, that these men were Rhen's good friends. He had grown up with them and had spent every day of his life with them. They had fought in countless battles together and trusted each other. They were also the brains of Surpen's military force.

A tall, large-headed soldier approached. Reed and Charlie recognized him as the one who had barred them from entering Surpen earlier. When he stepped forward to hug Rhen, he brushed a tear from his eye. Rhen laughed. "Watch it Nk," he teased. "Or we'll have to kill you for being weak."

"I thought you were going to die," Nk told him with a haggard voice. He pulled Rhen into a tight embrace, before moving to the back wall to get control of his emotions.

"Like that could ever happen?" Rhen tossed out in a casual manner, hoping to make Nk feel better. The other generals nodded their heads in agreement.

The room grew quiet as the generals waited for Rhen to explain the presence of Reed and Charlie. Rhen shrugged his head in their direction, while pulling out a chair. "They're friends from Legion 437. You can trust them."

"I've never met one of Rhen's Legion 437 before," one of the generals declared. "We owe our victory over three solar systems to you men. Thank you!"

"Yes," Bosternd agreed. He raised his glass to salute Reed and Charlie. "Nice job on Yentar and Tgarus boys! We were in trouble until you came along. Thank you!" The other generals lifted their drinks as well, to salute Reed and Charlie, who were standing at attention on either side of the doorway. Reed and Charlie nodded in response.

Now that their presence in the room had been explained, everyone relaxed and the generals started to tease Rhen about going to school on Thestran. "What? Isn't our educational system good enough for you?" said a small general named Ngi, who was sitting next to Bosternd.

"How would he know," remarked another general. "He never did attend our Academy!"

"Yeah," said another man, from across the table. "Only special schooling for the king's son!" A few of the generals chuckled.

Gazing into his metal cup, Rhen replied in a solemn voice, "Yeah, special schooling. It was real special." He accentuated the word 'special' in an odd way that made Bosternd frown.

"We know the real reason why you're going to Thestran, Rhen," Ngi commented. "You want to taste some Thestran women before the war." Several of the generals hooted with approval.

"Yeah, before they become submissive like Surpen women," another general added.

"So, how do they taste?" Authe, the general sitting beside Nk, asked.

"I hear they're feisty and they actually talk back to you," one of the generals commented.

"Does that make them better in bed?" a general inquired as everyone laughed at him.

"We'll find out soon enough," Nk mumbled. "The King is itching to attack Thestran and gain her solar systems."

"He's wanted to attack Thestran ever since you joined our forces," Bosternd remarked, looking at Rhen.

"Maybe he thinks your Thestran family wants you back?" someone commented.

Rhen shrugged. "Who knows? But, he won't be attacking Thestran any time soon."

"Do they?" Bosternd asked out of the blue. Rhen looked at him with one eyebrow raised. "Do the Thestrans want you back?" Bosternd clarified.

"No, way!" Rhen laughed out. "Like they'd want the likes of me at their fancy social gatherings?" He chuckled at the idea as the others chimed in: "A little more blood with your tea sir?" "Biscuit or brains, sir?" "Can I check your bloody swords at the door or will you be wearing them inside the ballroom sir?" "That Rhen, he's always so cranky when he can't kill anyone before dinner!"

"Bosternd," Authe commented. "Why would you think the Thestrans want him back? They dropped him off when he was eight and didn't return to see him again until just a few months ago."

Reed and Charlie raised their eyebrows. Their parents had told them that they had visited Rhen while he was on Surpen. Although they now knew that Rhen had been abducted, they were still under the impression that their parents had visited with him upon occasion.

"Remember that retired Queen's reaction, when she saw you again for the first time?" one of the generals commented with a chuckle. "I thought her eyes were going to pop out of her head, and her husband, oh God, he was a trip."

"They were taken aback," Rhen agreed with a nod. "They weren't expecting me to look like King James. From the portraits of James that I've seen in the Thestran Castle, we didn't look alike as children."

Reed frowned. There were only two portraits of James as a child in the Thestran Castle, one was in James' private study, which was always locked and guarded, and the other was in James' bedroom. Was Rhen lying or had he gained access to those locations?

"If the Thestrans had wanted Rhen, they would've returned to get him like Ceceta's family did. Lot of good that did them in the end," a general remarked in a flippant voice.

The room became silent.

Rhen stood up to refill his drink.

"That was out of line," Bosternd snapped.

"I'm sorry," the man apologized. "I didn't mean to bring up your wife's misfortune. Rhen, please forgive me."

Rhen waved his hand in a dismissive gesture towards the man. "It's fine."

"I was only trying to emphasize the fact that her family cared about her and yours didn't. If they had, they would've attempted to rescue you from Punishment Island. Maybe Ceceta's family wouldn't have been slaughtered, if yours had helped. General Bondson told me your parents did nothing, when they were told on Roundet that Ceceta's family was trying to reclaim her," the man continued.

Rhen jerked around and glared at the man. The pupils of his eyes expanded, turning them black.

"GET OUT!" Bosternd bellowed. The general ran from the room.

Rhen closed his eyes and clenched his jaw, fighting to regain control of his anger.

"I will have him whipped and lower his rank by three stations," Bosternd told his Prince. "Is that acceptable?"

Rhen nodded his head once then downed his beverage. When he dropped his glass away from his face, they saw his eyes had returned to normal. "You..." Rhen cleared his throat. "You don't have to have him whipped. I, personally, don't find it very effective. It never stopped me." The generals chuckled. Rhen was trying to repair the mood in the room. He knew he had slipped. He had felt his anger change his eyes. Most of them had never seen him do that before. Rhen closed his eyes again, when he realized the Thestrans had seen it too. 'Rasack's puss,' he swore to himself. How was he going to handle that one?

"Are the Thestrans afraid of you Rhen?" a general asked, hoping to regain their earlier camaraderie. "Do they think you'll eat them?"

Before Rhen could answer, his friend Authe yelled out, "I'd eat them! I'll start with their women!" The generals laughed with ease, their relaxed natures returning.

"Like the Black Angel would let you eat a Thestran!" Ngi teased. He lit the Tgarian cigarette that was in his mouth.

"That guy is amazing!" the general beside Bosternd remarked. "Did you hear what he did to the Rasacks who attacked those missionaries!"

"Are the Convention members still trying to get in touch with him?" Rhen interrupted.

"More so now than ever," Ngi replied. "They believe he has God-like powers and they want to capture him."

"No, they want to worship him, as they do Therol," Bosternd corrected.

Reed narrowed his eyes. The Convention members worshipped someone named Therol? Who was he? Why hadn't they heard of him before?

"That's bound to anger Therol," Authe commented. "He likes to be the top dog. He's not going to want to share his throne."

"God-like powers?" Rhen scoffed, returning to Ngi's earlier comment. "You insult God by saying something like that." Ngi bowed his head in deference to Rhen's comment.

"If I could have one wish, it'd be to meet the Black Angel before I die," Ngi informed the room, the other generals agreeing with him.

"Oh, shut up!" Rhen snapped. The generals were startled by his reaction, so Rhen explained, "Before I left, we never discussed the Black Angel. What's happened to you guys?"

"Three months ago, the Black Angel saved Authe's family, as well as a hundred other Surpens from death," Bosternd explained. "It was the most amazing rescue anyone has ever seen. The way he wielded his powers...it was truly breathtaking. The event was caught on video, so everyone's seen it. The Surpen's have been talking about him ever since. You should see the footage."

"Hm," Rhen mumbled. "I'm glad your family is alive Authe. The Thestrans also have their belts tied too tightly on this subject. They spend hours trying to figure out who the Black Angel is. I guess I'm just sick of hearing about him all the time."

"No need to apologize, boss," Authe commented. "When you finally see him in action, you'll become obsessed with him, just like the rest of us." Rhen smiled, before nodding at Authe's words.

They continued to talk for a while. Rhen discovered that his father had set his sights on the Planet of Milow. The generals were expecting a declaration of war soon. "It rains a lot on Milow," Ngi remarked. "We might find this to be our most difficult battle yet."

"We'll do fine. I'll meet you there with Legion 437," Rhen told them, to ease their fears, but instead of calming them, it made them more anxious.

"Meet us?" Nk asked. He sat up straighter in his chair. "What do you mean?"

"Laugh all you want," Rhen told them, "but I'm going back to Thestran to finish that schooling." The generals didn't look happy with his announcement. Rhen rose and took his glass to the sink. He returned to the table to stand behind Bosternd. Placing his hands on Bosternd's shoulders, Rhen looked around at the generals. "I know, that while I'm gone, you'll offer the King every loyalty you would offer me," he stated. Everyone agreed. "Good," Rhen continued. "I would hate to return to Surpen to find Andres unhappy with his soldiers." Again, the generals assured Rhen that the King could count on them.

Rhen smiled and moved about the room, slapping each man on their arm or back to say good bye, before leaving with Reed and Charlie.

As the three of them walked up towards the Surpen castle, Reed and Charlie saw seven large, reptilian-like animals flying in towards a paddock in the distance.

"Are those dragons?" Charlie asked, his mouth dropping open in awe.

"No. They're Surpen Beasts of War. At this distance, they do look a little like dragons, I guess."

"I was going to say!" Charlie commented. "At the University, you study dragons in your fourth year. Every year the University hopes to capture at least one of the rare beasts for us to examine, but they haven't caught a dragon in ten years. If you had tame dragons working for you on Surpen, that would be...amazing!"

"Dragons are rare?" Rhen asked. "I thought they lived everywhere. When I was a child, I used to see so many of them, I had to yell at them to leave me alone."

Reed laughed. "Rhen, when you were little, you had imaginary dragons. You used to talk to them all the time. Once you even brought a dragon to dinner, but you told us he was invisible, so we couldn't see him."

"But," Rhen answered, in a faraway voice. "I don't remember them being imaginary."

"Rhen," Reed began. "In the bunker, your eyes turned completely black, why..."

"What are you talking about?" Rhen interrupted. He had given it some thought and had decided to deny it had ever happened.

"Really," Charlie agreed. "That white part in your eyes disappeared, when that General spoke about Ceceta's family." Charlie threw up his hand to point at Rhen's face and accidentally poked him in the left eye.

"Ow," Rhen said, placing a hand over his eye and rubbing it. "I don't know what you're talking about. That's impossible." Lowering his hand, he added, "Look at my eyes. They're perfectly normal."

"Well," Charlie mumbled. "They're not perfectly normal now. That one is black and red."

"Because you poked me," Rhen snapped.

"Was that true what they said?" Reed asked. "About Ceceta's family? Did they try to rescue Ceceta?"

Rhen stared off into the distance at the Surpen Beasts of War. He turned, gave Reed a nod and started to walk towards the castle again.

"Did Mom and Dad know about their attempt? Did they really refuse to come to their aid?" Reed asked, praying Rhen wouldn't nod his head again.

"They didn't like the fact that I got married at 8," Rhen said. He turned around to face them. "They said I was causing a scandal. Although they didn't stop my wedding, they ignored it, hoping it would go away. They turned their backs on Ceceta and snubbed her family."

"Why did Ceceta's family try to 'rescue' her?" Reed asked.

Charlie, feeling uncomfortable with the conversation, began to hum a tune.

Rhen struck Charlie across the face. "Don't sing," he admonished. "It's against the law." Charlie's eyebrows shot up, but before he could comment, Rhen inhaled at the sight of the three men, who were walking towards them. The soldier in front, with the scar on his face, was the same man, who had read Rhen's punishment at the University. "Aul," Rhen breathed out. "Charlie, it's one of the generals I warned you about," Rhen whispered. "Mark me!"

Aul was marching straight for them. The smile on his lips pulled the scar on his cheek tight, making a gruesome white line. Charlie froze at the sight.

"For God's sake Charlie, help me out!" Rhen pleaded.

Aul stopped a few feet away from Rhen. His smile widened so much it made him look almost comical. "Well, well, well," he began. "And what rank are you now, boy?" He leered at Rhen, as the men with him snickered. Aul leaned forward towards Rhen, making Rhen lean back, away from him.

Suddenly, Reed stepped forward. He pushed Aul, knocking him aside. Grabbing Rhen's head, Reed pulled him forward and kissed him. As soon as their lips connected, Reed felt a surge of adrenaline course through his body. He felt invincible. It was an incredible feeling and he couldn't figure out why he was experiencing it. Releasing Rhen, he stepped back to find his brother staring at him with astonishment. A thin smile crept across Rhen's lips, and it looked as if he were about to laugh. Reed nodded to his little brother then turned to face Aul.

Aul was livid. "How dare you! I was here first!" he screamed, while reaching down to draw his sword.

Still feeling the adrenaline rush from kissing Rhen, Reed struck Aul in the face, dropping him to the ground. Reaching behind him, Reed took Rhen's arm and jerked his brother forward, towards the castle. Charlie stumbled along behind them, barely keeping up.

They marched through the gate in the castle's perimeter wall and into the castle. As soon as they were alone in the darkened corridor, Rhen and Reed started to laugh, while wiping at their mouths with their hands. "That wasn't quite what I had meant," Rhen told Reed, "but it worked. Thanks! I owe you one." He turned on Charlie. "And you!" Rhen added, pointing at Charlie. "After everything I've done for you at school, all those times when I saved you, the fact that you can't help me out the one time when I need it, that's just plain wrong. Don't come knocking on my door at school for the rest of this semester."

Charlie shrugged looking sheepish. "Sorry! Aul was just so intimidating looking."

The smile faded from Rhen's face. "Yes, intimidating is the right word," he mumbled, before turning to walk off down the hallway.

Reed and Charlie followed Rhen through Surpen's castle until they arrived at the main portal. "Thestran Royal Castle," Rhen said, watching the portal come to life. He motioned for Reed and Charlie to go through first then paused, when he saw his mother running towards him. Orpel flung herself into his arms and hugged him. "It's okay Mom. I'll see you soon," Rhen reassured her. Bending over, he gave her a quick kiss on the top of her head.

"I'll miss you!" she called out, after his departing figure.

As Rhen stepped out of the portal onto Thestran, he turned and the world started to spin, an enormous amount of pain searing through the back of his skull. Reaching backwards, he clutched the portal with one hand and stumbled, his other hand rubbing at the back of his head.

"Are you okay?" Reed asked, from somewhere to his left. "Your face is white. Is your head bothering you?"

"Yeah, it's nothing...just a headache," Rhen whispered, his eyes squeezed shut from the pain. "I'm still recovering from earlier. It'll go away soon." After a moment, he released the portal and stepped forward towards the Thestran Council Chamber door. "So," he asked, straightening up and dropping his hand to his side. "Was that fun?" Reed and Charlie had lost their Surpen disguises the minute they had walked through the portal.

"Totally! You have so much power," Charlie told him. "I wish mom had left me on Surpen instead of you!"

"No, you don't."

They walked out of the Thestran Council Chamber into the Grand Hallway to find the rest of the Royal Family and the Elfin Royals waiting for them. Everyone cheered when they saw them. "You made it!" Kate exclaimed, her hands raised in the air for emphasis. "We weren't sure the King would let you go."

"He almost didn't," Charlie answered. "But then Rhen pulled some awesome moves on him. Rhen promised the King he would always be Surpen and never betray him. Then he told Surpen's generals that they had to obey his father. It was amazing. The power he has, it's so...alive. I love it! Mom, why didn't you take me to Surpen?"

Reed glared at Charlie. Hadn't Charlie heard anything the Surpen Generals had been saying? He was about to make a comment, when he noticed Rhen close his eyes and rub at the back of his head again. Maybe now wasn't the best time.

The Thestran Royal Family talked about what it was like to be Surpen soldiers, while they walked up the stairs into their personal quarters. "You've been through a lot," Kate mentioned, turning to Rhen. "Do you want to stay here for a couple of days before going back to school? I can contact the Headmaster requesting a vacation for you."

Rhen was rubbing the back of his head with vigor. Distracted, he told her, "No, we'll go back today." Ceceta's arm was around his waist. She watched him with concern.

"Is it back?" she whispered. Rhen nodded yes.

"Is what back?" Rachel inquired.

"Oh, uh, nothing," Ceceta lied.

"No, tell me," Rachel insisted. "I'm a doctor. I can see something is bothering him. I remember Rhen rubbing the back of his head after we returned from Ustar. What's going on?"

"He's got this bump kind of thing on the back of his head," Ceceta told her. "It shows up when we're on Thestran and goes away when we leave."

"Ceceta," Rhen grumbled.

"*Well, if she's a doctor, she may be able to help,*" Ceceta told him in Surpen. Rhen frowned in response.

"You never had it before you came to Thestran?" Rachel asked.

"No," Rhen replied.

"And it went away when we were back on Surpen," Ceceta informed her.

Rachel took Rhen's arm. "Come, I want to have a look at it."

Kate noticed Rachel holding onto Rhen's arm. She immediately reached out for his other arm. For the first time, Rhen didn't jerk free from her grasp, but he also didn't walk with them. Instead, Rhen stopped and refused to move. "It's okay," he told them. "I'm fine." From the look on his face, though, they could tell he wasn't 'fine'.

"A quick peek. What harm could it do?" Lilly said, from the side of the stairwell.

"Honey, I insist!" Ceceta told him in Surpen. "*I want Rachel to see your bump. Maybe she'll know what's causing it.*" She pushed on Rhen's back, and with reluctance, he walked with them into Kate's sitting room.

Rachel and Kate pulled Rhen over to one of the couches in front of the fireplace. With Ceceta's help, they pushed him down onto the couch. Rhen frowned as he sat down. Moving around to the back of the couch, Rachel said, "Lean your torso backwards, but bend your head forward." Rhen didn't move. "Lean your body back and your head forward," she told him again.

"No," he replied, placing his hands on the couch cushions to rise. "I don't think so."

Unexpectedly, Ceceta jumped over the couch and landed on Rhen's lap. In Surpen she whispered, "*You want this tonight? You do as Rachel asks.*"

Rhen grinned, then settled back into the couch, leaning his head forward. Rachel reached out to rub at the back of his head. "You definitely have something here. I think we should have Kate phase into your body to look."

"No," Rhen said. Again, he started to rise to his feet.

"*Remember what I just told you,*" Ceceta hummed in Surpen.

Sighing, Rhen sat back down on the couch and waited. Ceceta nodded to Kate, telling her to proceed. As Kate put her hands on either side of Rhen's head, he told her, "Just don't touch the bloodworms. They bite when they see you, and the damage they do to you in your phased state is real. Their wounds are difficult for a healer to heal."

Kate jerked her hands away from Rhen's head.

"What?" Rachel asked.

"I'll show you," Lilly told them. She closed her eyes and felt the coolness of her powers, as she transmitted her memory of Ceceta's explanation about the bloodworms to them. When she was finished, she shook from the cold.

"Wow!" Charlie remarked.

"I'll be careful," Kate assured Rhen. She put her hands on his head and closed her eyes. Her cold powers engulfed her body, while she pictured herself phasing into Rhen's head. When her body was ready, she lowered herself down, pushing her face into Rhen's head and disappearing within him. She was gone only a second, before she pulled herself out of him and vomited to her left onto Reed's foot.

"Nice, Mom," Reed commented. He walked towards the bathroom to clean off his shoe.

"Sorry," Kate apologized. She wiped at her mouth with her hand. "I didn't realize how disgusting the adult bloodworms were going to be. I'm sorry Rhen and Ceceta. I don't mean to insult you."

Ceceta laughed a hollow laugh. "No insults taken. We know all about those nasty, little bloodworms."

"Right," Kate agreed. She shook herself, to calm down. "Let's try that again." Kate held onto Rhen's head and repeated her actions to enter his body. Rhen sat very still with a blank expression on his face. About two minutes later, Kate pulled herself out of his head. She stepped back from him with a look of horror on her face, before turning towards the back wall. Walking away from everyone, Kate put her hands up to her cheeks.

"Is everything okay?" James asked.

Instead of responding, Kate gave herself a rough shake and turned around. She marched over to the couch and sat down next to Rhen. Reaching out, Kate patted Rhen on his thigh. He flinched from her gesture. "So?" Kate asked. "You don't know why your head hurts?"

"No, why?"

"You're sure, you don't know what's going on inside your head?"

"Do I get a prize if I guess?"

"You have a Zorthan robot in your skull," Kate informed Rhen. Rhen laughed at her with disbelief and started to rise, but Kate reached out to stop him. "I'm not joking," she insisted.

Rhen sighed and sat back down on the couch. In a tired, condescending tone of voice, he asked, "Wouldn't I know, if there was a robot in my brain?"

Kate paused. "That depends. Do you have any idea, when the robot was placed in your skull?"

Rhen and Ceceta's faces paled. It was obvious they both had some idea of when it might have happened. "What kind of robot is it?" Rhen asked.

"It's a Zorthan Mind Controlling Robot. Have you heard about them?" Kate inquired, while the rest of her family gasped.

Unlike the Thestrans, Rhen had never heard about the Zorthan's mind controlling robot.

James informed him that they had caught the Zorthans making this rather heinous device in the twelfth solar system about ten years ago. "The robot is placed into the base of your skull," James explained. "It's not very large, and it doesn't seem to bother its host. After a few years, it synchs to the host's body and the Zorthans can use it to control you."

"When it's being used, the host acts like a zombie," Rachel added. "The host will only eat, sleep or go to the bathroom when given permission."

"I thought we had completely destroyed this device and all of the information on how to create it," the Wood Elf King, Estan, commented. He gave Rhen a nervous glance, as if the Surpen Prince would attack him at any moment.

"We did," Kate assured him. "This one must have been placed into Rhen's mind, before we had a chance to destroy it."

"Nice," Charlie said with a laugh. "You have an out-of-date robot running your brain little brother." He laughed again and lifted his hand towards Rhen, pretending to hold a remote-control device. "Beep, beat up William, beep," he ordered Rhen in a mechanical voice.

"No, Charlie," Kate told him. "The robot hasn't been initiated yet. It's synched with Rhen, but it's not operational, although it appears to be shifting into place."

"Well, let's get it out," Rhen said. He phased his hands into his skull.

The Thestrans stared at him in shock. Rhen could phase? They had thought that Kate was the only person in the Universe who could phase, but Rhen was doing it right in front of them. He had healing powers and phasing powers.

Rhen closed his eyes and moved his hands around the device in the back of his head. His face contorted with pain, when his fingers became solid, while he pulled the robot towards the back of his skull. He gasped in agony and Ceceta yelled, "Help him!"

James and Charlie grabbed Rhen's forearms and pulled. There was a horrible, bone-cracking sound, as a part of Rhen's skull split open, and a loud, metallic hiss, when a small, black, stick-figured robot that was shaped like a dog, popped out of Rhen's head. The robot's joints hissed, as they were exposed to the air.

James and Charlie threw the robot across the room. It banged into the stone fireplace, before falling to the floor with a loud clank. During the commotion, the couch that Rhen had been sitting on, tipped over backwards, and Rhen tumbled off it onto the floor, holding together the back of his head, while his body worked to heal itself.

"Themrock! That thing is hideous!" James exclaimed. He stared with horror at the robot lying on the fireplace stones. "By the Genister Gods! It's moving!"

"Oh, no," Kate murmured. She watched the robot rise onto four legs. A red beam projected from its head area, as it scanned the room. "Quick, we must keep it away from Rhen. It's synched to him, so it'll be able to find him." Everyone in the room grabbed something with which to fight the robot.

Haltingly, the robot made its way across the floor towards the overturned couch and Rhen's prone body.

Sage smashed a lamp down on top of it, while James slashed at it with an ancient sword. Their efforts did nothing to stop it.

The elfin kings, Estan and Chaster, jerked Rhen to his feet and pulled him towards the exit.

"It's bloody evil," Lilly shrieked, when the robot jumped over the couch in pursuit of Rhen. She grabbed a vase of flowers and threw it at the robot, hoping the water would short circuit it or the weight of the vase would crush it, but nothing deterred the robot.

William and Rachel grabbed hold of it. The robot slashed out at their hands with its back legs, making Rachel cry out in pain and let go. William continued to hold on, but the blood from his hands made it difficult for him to get a good grip. The robot jerked to the right and William felt it slip free from his fingers.

Estan and Chaster moved Rhen towards a different exit to outmaneuver the robot. As they passed by the bathroom, Reed stepped out carrying his wet shoes. He stared at everyone with surprise, until he noticed the small robot walking towards him. "STOP IT," Lilly screeched. Reed jumped on top of the robot, covering it with his body. The robot cut him deeply in his chest. Despite the pain, he held on. Sage pulled a copy of a Genister whip off the wall and wrapped it around the robot's back legs. As soon as her whip was secure, Reed released the robot. Rachel rushed over to heal Reed's wounds with her powers, as Sage pulled back on the whip, the robot thrashing about on the opposite end.

A moment later, Sage cried out in pain, when the whip ripped through her hands, cutting them.

Free again, the robot turned and continued towards Rhen. As it passed the fireplace, Kate slammed it with a blast of her powers. The explosion caused it to tumble back against the hearth, but it recovered and charged past her straight for Rhen. "No!" Kate screamed, when the robot leapt into the air straight for Rhen's bent head.

At the sound of Kate's scream, Rhen looked up. He saw the robot flying at him and blinked. The robot stopped short, suspended in mid-air, inches from his face, before falling to the ground in a thousand tiny, hissing pieces. Rhen grunted and shook himself free from Estan and Chaster to walk towards the bathroom. His head had already healed, but there was blood all over his face and hair. He flung the door to the bathroom open and turned on the sink, filling it with water. Covering his mouth and nose with a towel, Rhen dunked his head under the water, rubbing at his hair to get the blood off. When he was done, he walked out of the bathroom.

The room was silent. No one had moved. Rhen could see confusion, fear and concern on their faces. As soon as he tossed the towel he was holding back into the bathroom, they all started talking at once: "What was that doing in your head?" "How come you never felt it in your head?" "How did you stop it without moving a muscle?" "Who put that in your head?"

"Punishment Island?" Ceceta asked quietly. She stepped up beside him and took his hand. Rhen nodded yes.

"What's Punishment Island?" James asked.

Reed and Charlie glanced at each other. This was the second time today that they had heard about Punishment Island.

Ceceta squeezed Rhen's hand. She wasn't going to answer. If Rhen wanted the Thestran King to know about Punishment Island, he would tell him.

After a long pause, during which Rhen debated what to say, he lifted his chin up and said, "It's nothing." Throwing his arm around Ceceta, he pulled her towards the door, calling out over his shoulder, "Thanks for your help. I didn't know that thing was in my head."

"Was the robot controlling him?" Reed asked the room, in the silence that lingered after Rhen's departure. He plopped down into the chair beside him and watched the others take seats.

"No. It was rotating around in his skull," Kate explained. "Positioning itself to take over. That was the pain he was feeling and the bump on the back of his head."

"So, whoever put that into him, was getting ready to take control of him," James commented. "It had to have been Andres. Clearly, he's having trouble controlling Rhen. We got that thing out of Rhen just in time."

"Yeah," Lilly agreed. "Andres was probably intending to use the robot as his insurance policy to keep Rhen in check, after he becomes the Surpen God of War on his 18th birthday."

"What?" James asked.

"Why do you think Rhen will become the God of War on his 18th birthday?" Reed asked.

"Seriously!" Lilly exclaimed. "Don't any of you pay attention? Eighteen is the age a Surpen boy becomes a man. It's obvious that Andres believes Rhen will turn into the God of War when he turns 18." She paused and glanced over at her mother. "When is his birthday?"

Kate flushed. "Um, it's in five months."

"I think," the Air Elf King, Chaster, remarked, rolling his royal ring around on his finger. "If Andres went so far as to put an experimental robot into Rhen's brain, then he may have taken other measures to control Rhen, in case the robot failed. We need to find out what else he might have done to Rhen and stop it."

"Punishment Island," James responded. "Whatever was done to Rhen must have taken place on Punishment Island. We need to find out what happened there."

"How?" William asked.

"Ceceta is the key," James replied. He thought of Kendeth, who had told them that from the very beginning. "Lilly, you, Sage and Rachel go to the University. Work on Ceceta. Get her to tell us about this place. Also, try to make more of an effort at convincing Rhen that he's a Thestran. The rest of us will stop by daily to further our goal of making him accept his Thestran heritage."

"That might be harder than you think," Reed stated.

"Why?" James asked.

Reed turned to stare at his parents. "Because he isn't Thestran, he's Surpen."

"Why would you say that," Henry asked his son.

"Because you made him so," Reed growled at his father. Henry opened his mouth to protest but Reed raised his hand to silence him. "While Charlie and I were on Surpen, we learned something about Rhen and Ceceta's past, something that you 'forgot' to tell us. Would you care to enlighten the rest of your family about Rhen's childhood?"

"We did at Sage's wedding," Kate responded.

"No," Reed said. "You told us a partial truth at Sage's wedding."

Henry and Kate glanced at each other. "Mom, Dad," James said. "What's going on? If you have information on Rhen, you need to share it."

"They don't have ANY information on Rhen," Reed snapped. "Because they didn't see or talk to him for the entire time he was on Surpen. The first time they saw Rhen again, after abandoning him on Surpen at the age of eight, was three weeks before Sage's wedding."

"No, Reed," Lilly corrected him. "They visited Rhen twice a year, every year, the week after Themrock Day and a month after the Summer Giy Flower Festival."

"No, they didn't. They were lying to us."

"They totally visited Rhen," Sage agreed with Lilly. "It was their routine."

"That's what they told us," Reed replied. "Not what they did."

"Mom, Dad?" James asked.

Henry took a deep breath and then blew it out. His silence confirmed Reed's words. "Oh, Themrock," the Wood Elf King, Estan, sighed, turning away from the Thestran Royals.

"Zorthan wart," James swore. His family glanced at him in surprise. James never swore in Convention terms.

"Mom," Lilly moaned. "How could you do that?"

"We tried to see him," Kate replied.

"And Ceceta?" Reed asked. "Did you try to see her too?" Henry shook his head no. "Why not?" Reed asked.

"Well, she had her own family..." Kate began.

"That you knew went on a rescue mission to save her from Punishment Island," Charlie said, sounding sober. "You did nothing to help them, and they were slaughtered." He stood up abruptly from his chair, and with uncharacteristic grace, strode out of the room.

"She wasn't elfin," Kate said in her defense, after Charlie had left. "Everyone knows how the elves feel about marrying out of their race. It's against their rules. If Ceceta's family wanted her to return to Neptian, it was for the best for Rhen."

"You can't blame your blatant neglect of your son and his wife on us," the Fire Elf King, Naci, declared. "He was a Thestran Prince. We would've accepted his decision without question."

"No, you wouldn't have!" Kate yelled.

"Let's not fight," the Water Elf King, Plos, told them. "We need to stop Universal warfare. Whatever mistakes were made in the past must be forgotten. Rhen hasn't had contact with us in years, but he's here now, so let's get to work to remedy the situation. Fighting amongst ourselves will be our downfall."

"Agreed," King James said with fatigue, rubbing his aching eyes. He would talk to his parents later about their abominable behavior towards his brother. "Get some rest," he told the group. "We have a lot of 'catching up' to do with Prince Rhen, starting tomorrow." Glancing over at the Elfin Royals, he added, "We'll need your help now, more than ever before." The Royals bowed their heads in agreement and left.

Back at the University, Ceceta sat down next to Rhen on their bed. "You couldn't feel it in your head?"

"No. After I received my powers, I felt something in my head, but I thought it was Layla. I had no idea they put a robot in my skull."

"Do you think Andres ordered it to be placed in your brain?"

"No," Rhen told her. "He wouldn't have done that. I doubt if he even knew it was there. In all probability, Loreth did it without Dad knowing."

"Love...Andres had to know," Ceceta pushed.

"Ceceta," Rhen began. "Andres loves me. He never would've done something like that to me. He's always been there for me, supporting me, helping me, encouraging me. Loreth has strained our relationship, but he hasn't destroyed it. Andres wouldn't have done that to me."

Ceceta was positive that Andres and Loreth had cooked up this entire scheme, but she didn't want to fight with Rhen about it. "It took you awhile to heal, after you pulled it out," she commented, changing the subject.

"Yeah," Rhen agreed, lying down on the bed. "My healing powers were still recovering from earlier. If I had used my full powers, I would have healed instantly."

"But you can't use your full powers yet," Ceceta warned him.

"I know," Rhen replied with a heavy sigh. "They tell me that constantly." He rolled over onto his side and pulled Ceceta in towards him. "Didn't you promise me something for letting Kate look inside my head?" he asked with a grin, using his powers to remove the robes from her luscious, blue body.

Chapter 19

The Thestran Royal Family found Rhen and Ceceta chatting with their friends at breakfast the next morning. They had already finished eating and were waiting for class to begin. "Mind if we barge in?" Rachel asked. She sat down next to Erfce with her tray of food. "I feel like I'm a student again," she announced, while opening a carton of milk.

Erfce blushed, as he watched her arrange her meal. He'd had a crush on Princess Rachel since he was 9. Latsoh kicked him under the table, making him jump. Erfce's heart soared, when he saw what appeared to be jealousy on his future wife's face. "You're drooling," Latsoh mouthed. Trying not to smile, Erfce dropped his eyes to his plate. He counted the months that were left before his and Latsoh's engagement. He couldn't wait for his life to catch up to his visions.

It wasn't long before the Thestran Royal Family found itself surrounded by adoring students. Rhen inched away from William, to give his fans more access. After yesterday's chaos, he didn't feel like dealing with the Thestran Royals. He knew they were there to pester him with questions.

Gulping down the last bit of blood in his glass to make a speedy get away, Rhen paused, when Tgfhi slapped a rectangular present, wrapped in red paper, down on the table in front of him. Placing his glass back on the table, Rhen glanced up. "What's this?" he asked. Surpens only gave gifts for marriages and births.

"I'm not telling, open it."

Rhen grinned and reached out for the present. He slid his finger under the tape, opening it. Inside, he found a pair of black, canvas, hi-top sneakers. "Oh," Rhen exhaled, holding them up in the air. He had admired an identical pair of green sneakers that Tgfhi had worn once before. "You remembered."

"And, I thought you could use them," Tgfhi replied.

Rhen turned around on the bench and kicked off his military boots. With care, he put on the sneakers.

"I hope they fit. Ceceta told me your size, but you never know," Tgfhi told him.

"They're soft inside," Rhen commented.

"Like, duh," Latsoh replied. "Everything's softer than military boots."

Rhen gave her a look before standing up. He walked around in a circle, keeping his eyes on his feet. "They're bouncy, too," he remarked, sounding surprised.

"They're sneakers," Tgfhi informed him, with a quirky smile. "Sneakers are soft and bouncy."

Rhen bent over to rub his hand against the sole of one of the sneakers to feel its traction.

"Why'd you give him sneakers?" Crystam asked.

With a twinkle in his eye, Tgfhi announced, "So, the next time his Dad shows up, he can run the hell away!" Everyone at the table laughed, including Rhen.

"Thanks, Tgfhi," Rhen told him. "I'll wear them forever."

Tgfhi lifted his little chin and beamed with pleasure.

As the days passed, the Thestran Royal Family and Elfin Royals adhered to their plan, following Rhen everywhere. They attended his classes, sat with him during his meals, tagged along behind him when he went to the library, out for a stroll or even to the bathroom. They dogged his every step. They were desperate to connect with him. They worked on Ceceta too, asking her thousands of questions which she always found some way not to answer.

The only time, when Rhen and Ceceta could be alone with their friends, was during their study sessions in their apartment. Rhen had asked the Thestran Royals not to attend those meetings, since their presence would distract them from their studying. Charlie still showed up occasionally, but he was often drunk or he fell asleep on Rhen's bed or he'd throw up in Rhen's toilet, instead of studying.

"This isn't working," the Air Elf King, Chaster, complained, walking away from Rhen and Ceceta's apartment door, after Ceceta had closed it in his face.

"It will," King James replied, from his spot on the stairs. "We just need to keep at it. We've ignored my brother's existence for years. It's going to take a little time for him to warm up to us."

"How can we connect with him, if he refuses to speak to us," the Wood Elf King, Estan, protested.

"But he is speaking," Sage countered. "Not in sentences, but at least he's not outright ignoring us, like he did before."

"Sage is right," James agreed. "We must have patience. Rhen will come around, eventually."

It was clear from their faces that the elfin kings didn't agree, but they held their tongues.

Charlie walked up the stairs, smelling like stale cigarettes and alcohol. He paused beside James. "I think you're just annoying the hell out of him," he remarked, before farting and continuing towards Rhen's apartment door. "Excuse me. Nature calls," he added, opening the door.

"Yuck," Sage complained, after Charlie had gone into Rhen's apartment.

A few seconds later, everyone, who had been in the apartment, was out in the hallway.

"Dear God," Tgfhi gasped. He shoved his and Crystam's textbooks into their bag. "What is wrong with him?"

"I don't know," Ceceta said, wiping at her tearing eyes.

Rhen appeared to be amused. He glanced towards the stairs, caught James' eye, and nodded towards James in greeting.

"Come on, we'll study in the library tonight," Ceceta told the others, as Erfce blew his nose to rid it of Charlie's smell. "Rhen, will you go back in and open the windows, so it won't smell when we return later?"

Rhen's eyes widened with horror, but he nodded his head yes. "Thanks love. We'll see you in the library," Ceceta added. She turned and walked down the stairs with her friends.

When they heard the downstairs door swing shut, James glanced over at his little brother. "I'll do it," he offered, pushing off from the stairwell banister and strolling towards Rhen's apartment.

"That's okay," Rhen told him. "I've got it."

"Hey, what's going on?" Lilly asked, mounting the stairs. James summarized what had happened and Lilly shook her head. "What are we going to do about Charlie?"

"Give him a job," Rhen told her.

"What?" James asked. "Give who a job?"

"Charlie," Rhen said. He turned and threw open the door to his apartment. The smell that seeped out into the hallway made them all step back.

"Charlie's too smart. He should have graduated years ago. He needs a purpose. Give him a job and he'll come around," Rhen added.

"Okay," James mumbled with surprise. He'd never considered Charlie to be smart. The boy was failing all his classes and would only be graduating this year because he was a Thestran Prince.

"You're very verbose tonight," Lilly told Rhen.

Rhen frowned. "Sorry," he apologized, before closing his eyes and rushing back into his apartment.

"Lilly! Why'd you say that?" Sage hissed.

"Well, he was talking, I was surprised," Lilly replied in defense. "That's all."

A moment later, Rhen ran out of his apartment. He stopped by the stairs and took several deep breaths, before laughing. Without looking behind him at the others, Rhen trotted down the stairs and out of the building. The Royals caught up to him on the lawn outside. They began to tell him about upcoming events he couldn't care less about. The Air Elf King, Chaster, was droning on about some Sunrise Ceremony, when Rhen heard a sound, like that of a Surpen Beast of War, out in the forest. "Quiet," he barked, trying to hear it again. From the look on Chaster's face, Rhen could tell he had offended the Air Elf King.

Rhen stepped to his right, towards the Wood Elf Forest. There. He heard the sound again. Without thinking, he ran into the woods. Behind him, he could hear the Royals shout, their heavy, pounding feet, hurried after him. Rhen went faster to lose them. He stopped beside a tree and waited, listening. A moment later, he heard the sound again. Rhen rushed off to his left. He slowed, coming to a halt beside a large boulder. On the ground, by a small patch of flowers near the boulder, was a beautiful, red and gold dragon. Rhen watched the majestic animal in silence, as it licked its claws to clean them.

In the distance, Rhen could hear the Thestrans calling out. They were making a great deal of noise. The dragon lifted its head and snorted. Rhen watched the red and gold scales shift, as the dragon took to the air, flying away to safety. "Wow," he breathed out. The dragon's scales blended into the setting sun, making it invisible.

The Thestrans were getting closer, so Rhen phased himself to the school's library door.

"He's not out here," Kate complained hours later. "We've searched everywhere."

"I'm going home," the Water Elf King, Plos, announced.

"Let's go back to the library," James said. "He'll show up eventually."

When they entered the library's main vestibule, they stopped short. Rhen was sitting in a chair next to Latsoh with his head on the table in front of him. There were bits of vegetation and dirt on his purple tunic, and his black sneakers were dirty. James walked over and sat down beside Rhen. "Hey, where'd you go?" he asked.

Opening his eyes, Rhen lifted his head to stare at the Thestrans. "Go?" he inquired, yawning in their faces.

"Yes," James said. "We left the Teacher's Residence Hall on our way to the library, when you ran off into the forest. We lost sight of you. We've been looking for you ever since. Where did you go?"

Rhen shrugged and yawned again.

"Well, how did you get back here?" Lilly asked Rhen. "We would have seen you leaving the forest."

Rhen shrugged again and put his head back down on the desk, ignoring them.

With his apparent lack of interest in them draining on their nerves, the Royals bid everyone good night and left.

After they were gone, Ceceta threw a pencil at Rhen. It bounced off his head and landed on the desk. Lifting his face up to her, Rhen yawned, as Ceceta asked, "You went into the forest? Why?"

"I heard something," he replied, placing his head down onto the table again and getting a whiff of the tangy scent of dried glue and cleanser that had been left over from a student's homework.

"What did you hear?" Ceceta asked.

"A dragon, but he flew off before I could get close. He was beautiful." Rhen yawned and stood up. "I'm going to bed Cece. I'm sure Charlie's stench is gone by now."

Ceceta nodded and turned back to her book. Erfce, Crystam, Latsoh and Tgfhi stared after Rhen's retreating form. Rhen had seen a dragon? No one saw dragons. The two organizations, who had permission to handle dragons, had only found three of them over the last ten years. There was no way Rhen just happened to hear one in the Wood Elf Forest.

Ceceta asked her friends about a math question. They turned away from their thoughts of dragons and back to their homework.

As the weeks passed, and Rhen was pestered morning, noon and night by the Thestran Royal Family and the Elfin Royals, Rhen's friends began to pity him.

"What do they want from you," Tgfhi asked Rhen one night, during their private study session.

"I'm not exactly sure," Rhen told him. "Latsoh, do you know?"

"No. My Dad hasn't mentioned anything other than it's important for you to be with us."

"Why?" Ceceta questioned her. Latsoh shrugged.

"Maybe they miss you," Erfce offered.

Ceceta and Rhen laughed. "I don't think that's it Erfce," Rhen told him. He lay down on the floor by the coffee table and closed his eyes.

Tgfhi watched Rhen, settle down on the floor. He had been trying to learn more about Rhen's childhood, but had had no success. Deciding to try, yet again, to learn something about his friend's past, he asked, "Rhen, did you play 'hide and seek' when you were a kid?"

"What?" Rhen inquired.

"Did you play 'hide and seek' on Surpen?"

"No," he responded. He opened one eye to look at Tgfhi. "We don't play games on Surpen."

"Yes, we do," Ceceta contradicted. She kicked at Rhen's foot.

"Yeah? What games did you play? Run away from the butcher before he kills me for dinner?" Rhen teased.

"No, we used to play some hand games, where you clap your hands together and say a rhyme," Ceceta informed him.

"That's so girly!" Rhen snapped back. "Was that what you used to do, while I was off killing Dapags and Yentarians to keep you safe?" Rhen sat up and Ceceta kicked at his foot again.

"It was not girly," she replied with a pout. "It was fun. You should try to have fun sometime. It might make you a more enjoyable person to be around."

"Oh, I think I'm a very enjoyable person to be around!" Rhen replied in a haughty voice. "Ask them," he added, while pointing at their friends.

"Right!" Ceceta laughed out. She turned towards the others. "Who would you rather spend time with…me or Rhen?" No one answered. They sat staring with intense concentration at their books. "Oh, come on! You're not still afraid of Rhen are you? You can tell him the truth!" Still no one answered.

Ceceta watched a grin spread across Rhen's face. "Well, now I have a new game for you Ceceta," he whispered. "It's called, 'run away from the butcher before he eats you for dinner'." Rhen lunged himself towards her from his spot on the floor. Ceceta shrieked and flipped herself over the back of her chair. The two of them giggled with abandon, while Rhen chased Ceceta around the apartment. The others had gotten used to this behavior. In the privacy of their apartment, Rhen and Ceceta were always flirting with each other. When Rhen had succeeded in catching Ceceta and flattening her onto the floor with his body, their giggling turned over into kissing.

"I used to play hand games as a child," Latsoh announced. "That's how elfin children learn about Lord Themrock. We pass down the Genisters' stories through games and…"

Latsoh continued to talk for a full twenty minutes, without realizing that no one was listening to her.

"…and that's how you get your powers if you have them," she finished. The others perked up in the silence that followed.

Tgfhi yawned. "Are you done?"

Latsoh's face flushed with anger. "What do you mean 'are you done'? Didn't you hear what I was saying?" No one answered. "Were any of you listen to me?"

There was a collective, affirmative mumbling sound from her friends, yet none of them would meet her eye. "Right," Latsoh said, the corner of her mouth rising. "So, what do you think?" She was sure that none of them would know what to say.

"Well, of course we believe you," Erfce declared, surprising her. Erfce shook his head for a moment, clearing the vision of him asking Latsoh out. He was going to have to do it soon, since the two of them were going to get married before they graduated from the University. "Themrock," he continued, "created all living things, so if anything has powers, their powers had to have come from him. It's perfectly logical."

"That's stupid!" Tgfhi snapped. "How can one Genister, who's not even around anymore, give me my powers! My powers came from my genetic makeup. My great, great, great grandfather had several powers. I seem to have gotten one of his abilities."

"The Supreme Lord gave you your powers Tgfhi. Powers can be passed down to us genetically, but they all originate from the Supreme Lord. They're gifts from God," Rhen said.

Although religious, Rhen rarely spoke about his beliefs, so they were a little surprised to hear him engage in the debate. He was the only one who prayed on a daily basis to his God. Out of curiosity, Latsoh and Crystam had joined him a few times during his morning prayers. They had found the experience peaceful.

"Who is the Supreme Lord again?" Tgfhi asked.

"He doesn't have a name," Ceceta reminded him.

"So how can he exist, if he doesn't have a name?" Erfce argued.

"He just does," Rhen responded. "He created the entire Universe, as well as twelve other Universes. He gave us the gift of life, he provided us with great powers and he allowed us our free will. We must work hard not to abuse his gifts."

Crystam rolled her eyes. "Twelve Universes? Who ever heard of twelve Universes? There's only one Universe."

"You can't actually believe there are twelve universes. Can you?" Tgfhi asked, sounding incredulous.

"Of course, there are," Ceceta replied. "The Supreme God loves life. Each Universe is its own self-contained celebration of life. The Universes don't mix, the TUB keeps them apart. They run independently of each other in perfect harmony. God is very generous."

"Okay," Erfce stated. "First, there's nothing beyond The Ultimate Blackness that surrounds our Universe or TUB, as you call it. And secondly, your Supreme God is just another name for Themrock." He turned to Tgfhi. "Just as those nameless gods that you worship on Tgarus are the Genisters."

"Hell, no!" Tgfhi protested.

"Themrock is very generous," Latsoh broke in. "Themrock gave us the ability to love, the ability to learn and the ability to experience joy. He was a musician and an artist. The murals, on our castle walls, show him during different stages of his life."

"Anyone can paint a mural, Latsoh," Tgfhi snapped. "Maybe I'll paint one showing myself as an amazing God and you can worship me."

"Latsoh isn't going to worship anyone but me," Erfce responded, without thinking. A moment later, everyone laughed. Erfce blushed and looked away.

"Are you guys going out?" Crystam asked.

Latsoh shook her head and frowned at Erfce. "No," she told Crystam.

"Oh," Crystam replied. She flipped to a new page in her text book. She'd noticed the way the two of them looked at each other and figured it was only a matter of time before they did hook up.

"Hey, my birthday is at the end of the week!" Tgfhi exclaimed. "I'll soon be a man!"

"That's great Tgfhi," Rhen told him.

"We have to celebrate," Crystam insisted. "Let's go out to dinner in Warton and then see a movie."

"Only if we can ditch the Thestran Royals," Tgfhi added. " Rhen and Ceceta are never any fun when they were around."

Rhen laughed.

"Don't worry," Ceceta told Tgfhi. "We'll find a way to get rid of them."

"Great!" Crystam exclaimed. "It's settled. I'll arrange for everything."

On the last day of the week, Tgfhi arrived at breakfast wearing large shorts and a huge shirt over his clothes. His enormous green shirt hung off his shoulders and dangled down around his knees and his big, brown shorts were tied together around his waist with rope, but they kept slipping down to the floor. The students in the cafeteria laughed at Tgfhi as he walked over to his table with his tray. Tgfhi glared at them, while he placed his tray next to Ceceta's. "Can you believe them?" he complained. Turning, he noticed his friends were also laughing at him. "Yeah, yeah, yeah," he told them, with a shake of his little head. "Laugh all you want, but by the end of today, these clothes will fit me just fine."

"Are you sure Tgfhi?" Erfce asked with a snicker. "They seem rather large for you. I mean, let's face it, even if you were to double in mass, you still couldn't fill them out." He reached over to pull on the loose sleeve of Tgfhi's enormous t-shirt.

"You'll see!" Tgfhi snapped. He slapped Erfce's hand away.

Rhen was flanked that morning by Reed and Lilly, so he didn't comment on Tgfhi's clothing, but he knew from experience that Tgarian men were quite large, and Tgfhi, if he did grow into a man today, would easily fill out his new set of clothes.

Tgfhi was teased, without mercy, about his clothes during the school day. At lunchtime, he was still very small and his big clothes were looking rather disheveled. "Are you sure you're growing today?" Crystam asked, when he arrived at their table with his lunch tray.

"Yeah," Latsoh added. "We don't want to go out to dinner with you tonight if you're still wearing a second set of clothing."

"Just wait!" Tgfhi said, his lower lip trembling. He plopped down on the bench and focused on his meal to keep from crying. While he ate, his belly began to bother him. Tgfhi pushed on it with his little hands, but the pain wouldn't lessen.

"Are you okay?" Crystam asked. "Your face seems a little pale."

"No, my stomach hurts. I must have eaten something bad. I think I'm going to throw up," he whispered. Tgfhi crawled off the bench and ran towards the bathroom.

After a few minutes had passed and Tgfhi still hadn't returned from the bathroom, Ceceta turned to Erfce and Rhen. "Come on you guys. One of you should go see if he's feeling alright."

Erfce had just put his hand on Latsoh's arm for the first time. He had no intention whatsoever of moving.

"I'll go," Rhen mumbled, when Erfce didn't volunteer.

"Thanks love," Ceceta said. "If he got vomit on his big clothes, you should help him wash them off. He's very proud of them." Rhen sighed and rolled his eyes, but he could see that Crystam was also concerned, so he stood up to go check on Tgfhi. Reed decided not to follow him. He didn't like the smell of vomit.

Rhen was gone for long time. When they saw him again, he was walking into the room backwards, holding the door open with his back and talking animatedly to someone. A large, muscular man followed Rhen into the dining room through the door he had been holding open. The man stopped and laughed at something Rhen said. Rhen put his arm around the man's shoulders and pointed down towards the floor. The man dropped his head down to look at what Rhen was pointing at and his long, dirty blond hair fell across his face. The man had a blond beard and he was wearing brown shorts and a green t-shirt that looked very familiar.

"No way!" Ceceta breathed out. She and the others stood to get a better look.

When Rhen arrived at their table, the man beside him looked up and smiled. His face was different now. He had lost his boyish charm, gaining a very rugged look instead, but he still had the same twinkling, blue eyes. There was no mistaking his eyes. It was Tgfhi.

"Tgfhi?" Crystam asked in a small, high voice that caused everyone to laugh. She blushed and covered her face with her hands. She couldn't believe how much Tgfhi had changed. He was so…handsome. He had thick, strong looking shoulders, long muscular arms and legs and a strong jaw line that suited his eyes.

"Yes!" Tgfhi replied in a low voice, sitting down at the table next to his tray. They followed his lead and sat down but continued to stare at him in wonder.

Finally, Erfce yelled out, "Holy crap! Now I'm the smallest one here. You look like a man. How did you get all those muscles and that chest hair?" Tgfhi smiled at Erfce's compliments as Erfce added, "You're just so damn…big!"

"I'm a man now," Tgfhi replied in a deep voice. He felt proud of his new body and voice. "What do you think? How do I look?" He stood up again and backed away from the table, turning around, so they could look at his body. "Do you like it?" he asked. Everyone nodded their heads with appreciation. "See," he added, while pulling on his shirt. "I told you it would fit." He had been right. Tgfhi's shirt and pants were tight against his body. He probably would have been more comfortable in a larger size.

When Tgfhi sat back down, he looked at Crystam, which made her blush and turn away. He glanced towards Rhen for support and found him smiling. Tgfhi gave Rhen a lopsided grin, as he pointed towards his new face. Rhen opened his mouth to comment on Tgfhi's looks, but thought better of it. Instead, he reached past Reed and ruffled Tgfhi's hair.

"My hair grows fast like that sometimes," Rhen admitted. "For no reason at all, I'll turn around and my hair will be down past my shoulders. Ceceta has to cut it, before I can go out in public. She's good at cutting hair. Do you want her to give you a trim?"

Tgfhi looked at Crystam. She was gawking at him from over the rim of her glass, while pretending to drink. "Do I?" he asked.

Crystam coughed and put her glass down. "Well, I prefer long hair, but if you want to cut it, so you look like a Tgarian, then you should."

Tgfhi smiled and glanced back at Rhen. "I think I'll leave it like this for a while."

"But you could shave off your beard," Crystam added.

Tgfhi's smile widened. He reached up to feel his cheeks. "Yeah," he said, nodding his head. "Maybe I'll just shave off my beard for now."

Crystam blushed and picked up one of her books to hide her face.

Tgfhi watched as Crystam hid from him. He could tell she liked him, she just wasn't admitting it. When they got up to leave for class, Tgfhi walked around the table and picked up Crystam's book bag.

"What are you doing?" she asked.

"I always carry your books for you!" he answered.

Tgfhi had carried Crystam's books for her when he was a small boy, but now that he was a man, somehow it seemed wrong to Crystam. It would signal to everyone in the school that they were a couple.

Tgfhi had been friends with Crystam long enough to know what she was thinking. He held his breath, waiting for her to make her decision. Without saying anything, Crystam lifted her chin and brushed past him, as she walked out the door towards their class. Tgfhi cried out in victory, before running after Crystam, carrying her books as if they were rare jewels. The others laughed and headed off to their classes accompanied by Reed and Lilly.

That evening, after class, they met up at the school's portal. Somehow, during the day, Tgfhi had found the time to shave off his beard. He had a few cut marks on his cheeks, which Crystam found endearing. They had all received permission from the Headmaster to visit the City of Warton, which was the closest Thestran City to the school. Crystam had picked out a restaurant she thought everyone would like. It was also the only restaurant she could find that agreed to serve raw meat to Rhen and Ceceta. "You ditched the Thestran Royals?" Crystam asked Ceceta, when they arrived.

"Totally," she replied with a laugh. "Let's go."

"Do you want to take my spacejet?" Tgfhi asked.

"Do you know how to fly it?" Latsoh inquired.

"No," Tgfhi replied. "But it's been sitting in the jet port all year, waiting for me to turn into a man. My Dad is going to show me how to fly it when he visits tomorrow."

"Ah...let's use the portal then," Crystam suggested, as Latsoh nodded in agreement.

The restaurant Crystam had found for them was a small, Ventarian restaurant with a well-dressed clientele. They stood in the entranceway talking, until the hostess led them to a round table. Crystam translated the Ventarian menu for them and everyone discussed which dishes they wanted to try. Rhen and Ceceta inspected the items that were offered, but they knew they couldn't try anything. When their waiter arrived, Crystam ordered everyone's meals for them in Ventarian.

The restaurant owner, a native of Ventar, was thrilled to have the Queen's daughter dining in his establishment. He had become famous on Thestran for offering exquisite, Ventarian delicacies and now, to have a member of the Ventarian Royal Family eating in his establishment, he knew he was going to have even more business. He asked them if he could take their picture to hang on his restaurant wall. They agreed and Rhen, Erfce and Tgfhi rose to stand behind their 'girlfriends'. They joked around, saying they felt old, as the manager took several pictures of them.

The waiter brought platters of tantalizing Ventarian delicacies to their table, and Ceceta and Rhen were given some raw meat. They sat watching, as the others sampled exotic, smelling foods. "God, I'd give anything to try some of those," Ceceta whispered, while gazing longingly at the noodles in front of Latsoh. Rhen reached over to rub her shoulders.

"I'm sure it doesn't taste very good," he told her. "Otherwise, the cafeteria would serve it."

Crystam laughed. "Rhen, the cafeteria food is horrible. You have to go out to a restaurant or visit someone's home to get good food."

"Do you really think the cafeteria food is good?" Tgfhi questioned him.

"I thought it was," Rhen replied. "Why would you eat it if it wasn't?"

"Because there's nothing else to eat," Latsoh complained. "We have no other choice."

Rhen smiled and looked away. He was embarrassed. He had thought that they enjoyed the cafeteria food.

Crystam began to talk about the movie they were going to see and the others chimed in.

When they were finished with dinner, they walked to the theater. After the movie, they returned to the University. Rhen and Ceceta bid everyone good night and headed off towards their apartment. As Tgfhi and the others walked down the brick pathway towards the student dormitories, they heard Ceceta calling out to them. Tgfhi turned to find her running down the pathway in their direction. "Tgfhi!" Ceceta cried out, her soft-soled shoes sounding like raindrops on a wooden roof, as they hit the pathway.

"Yeah? What's the matter?" he asked.

Ceceta giggled and bent over to catch her breath. "Sorry," she said. She stood up and placed her hands on her hips. "Rhen and I were talking, and we want to give you a birthday present. So, since you love the Black Angel, we figured, if we could provide you with some information on him, then that would be a good gift, yes?"

Tgfhi smiled at her obvious enthusiasm. "That would be an amazing gift, but you can't provide me with anything Ceceta. The whole world is stuck on the Black Angel."

"Well, actually," Ceceta said with a chuckle. "We can. We know he's a man."

Tgfhi's smile fell, and he stared at her in silence. Eventually, he asked, "How do you know the Black Angel's a man?"

Ceceta pushed a lock of her hair away from her face. "I guess we could have told you this before. But, well, it didn't really seem to matter what sex he was. Anyway, we know he's a man, because, well, the cape he wears is a male Genister cape. You can see pictures of it in: A Tribute to Genisters, by Maryanne Williams. It's an ancient book that's mostly speculative, but the drawings it has of the Genisters' capes are the same as the Black Angel's. You can see for yourself. The book is in the school library. Go check it out."

"He wears a Genister cape!" Latsoh yelled. Ceceta nodded her head yes.

"So, he's a Genister!" Crystam exclaimed.

Ceceta appeared confused for a moment. This wasn't going well. She had thought that Tgfhi would scream with joy and hug her, but instead, he seemed angry and Latsoh and Crystam seemed flabbergasted. "No," she told them with hesitation. "I don't think so."

"You've known this all along and you've never told anyone?" Tgfhi demanded.

"Well, it doesn't really matter what he wears, does it? It won't help you determine who he is," Ceceta replied defensively. She couldn't understand why Tgfhi was getting mad at her? She had just given him an awesome present.

Tgfhi pushed past Ceceta, as he marched off towards the library. "Is there anything else you're not telling us that could help us discover who he is?" he yelled back over his shoulder, while the others ran after him, leaving Ceceta alone.

They left before Ceceta could answer Tgfhi's last question. She was glad they did, because she felt like screaming at them that Rhen was the Black Angel, and if they weren't so blind, they'd be able to see it. Ceceta marched back to her apartment. "And to think I was going to offer him a chance to ride through the sky with the Black Angel later tonight," she hissed through clenched teeth.

The next morning at breakfast, Ceceta and Tgfhi glared at each other. Everyone tried to ease the tensions between them, but nothing seemed to work. James, Reed and Sage were sitting with them this morning. As usual, they were trying to engage Rhen in conversation, but he wasn't in the mood to speak.

Suddenly, Tgonar appeared at the table startling everyone. "DAD!" Tgfhi cried out, jumping up to hug his father.

"Sorry I couldn't get here yesterday. You got my note that I was busy?" Tgonar asked Tgfhi.

"Yes, I got it," Tgfhi told him.

"Well, let me look at you!" Tgonar said, backing up to stare at his son. His face radiated pride, as he took in his son's mature body. "You're much bigger than my side of the family. You look like your mother's brother Tgiis." Tgonar announced, slapping Tgfhi on the shoulders with affection. "Congratulations Tgfhi! You look wonderful! You grew well." Tgonar pulled Tgfhi in for another hug and then kissed him on both cheeks, because he could no longer reach the top of Tgfhi's head. Pointing behind him to a string of servants carrying boxes, he said, "Your new clothes. Where should I have them leave the boxes?"

"My dorm room would be great Dad."

Tgonar turned to speak in Tgarian to the men behind him. When he was done, he sat down at the table to eat breakfast with his son. "Prince Rhen," he said, bowing to Rhen. Rhen nodded his head in response. "Thestran Royals," Tgonar said, giving a nod to James, Reed and Sage.

"Your majesty," James replied.

Tgonar smiled at the members of Thestran Royal Family, who were sitting there trying to get close to Rhen. He had already accomplished that objective with his Tgarus weed. If they only knew. Turning to Tgfhi, Tgonar asked, "So, how was your birthday?"

"It was great! We went out to dinner and then to a movie." Tgfhi paused. Turning to face Ceceta, he added, "And then, I got the most amazing birthday present ever!"

"Really? What was it?" Tgonar asked, while looking over at Ceceta, who had become a vision of the perfect Surpen woman. She was staring at her plate without moving.

"Well," Tgfhi told his Dad. "A friend of mine has been studying Genisters, and she discovered that the cape the Black Angel wears, is actually the cape of a male Genister, so the Black Angel is a man."

Tgonar sat up straight. This was big news, very big news.

James, Reed and Sage seemed just as shocked. "Are you sure?" James asked Tgfhi.

"Yes," Tgfhi confirmed. "I didn't believe her at first, and I was angry with her, but I went to the library and I read through the book she told me about. It showed images of what people used to believe the Genister's clothing looked like. She was right. The Black Angel is a man, and he's wearing a cape that's similar to the ones they believed the male Genisters wore."

"That's incredible!" Reed cried out. "He's a man! That's huge! How do you think he got a Genister cape?"

"He must be a Genister," Latsoh responded. "How else would he get one? How else does he have so many powers?"

"But the Genisters have been dead for almost a thousand years. How could he be a Genister? He couldn't," Sage replied, feeling overwhelmed.

Tgfhi ignored them and continued speaking, "The book claimed that Genister women and Genister men have different capes. There were sketches of what their capes looked like. We think the Black Angel either read this book and is imitating the cape he saw or he has somehow found a real Genister cape."

"What book did you find this in?" James asked. He rose from his seat with Reed. "We'd like to have a look at it."

Tgfhi reached into his school bag, pulling out an old, crumpled, brown book. "I got it out of the library last night," he informed them. He handed the book over to James, who immediately snatched it up and left with Reed.

"I guess, in a few hours, the whole Universe will know the Black Angel's a man," Tgfhi murmured.

"Probably," Crystam agreed, giving Tgfhi a sweet smile.

Tgonar noticed the look that passed between them and was horrified. The Ventarian Princess and his son? This wouldn't do at all. They were Surpens and the Ventarians were Thestrans. Surpens and Thestrans did not mix. He would have to talk to Tgfhi about his relationship with the Ventarian Princess later.

Glancing over at Rhen, Tgonar noticed he was being watched by Sage. He felt sorry for the boy. It was obvious the Thestrans were annoying him. He would have to tell Andres about it when he got home. Clearing his throat, Tgonar asked, "Prince Rhen, would you mind doing the Tgarians an enormous favor?" Rhen looked up at Tgonar with raised eyebrows, but didn't speak, so Tgonar continued. "We can't train Tgfhi to fight, while he's at the Elfin University. If you have any free time, would you please train my son for battle? I will talk to the Headmaster to make sure he's free, when it's convenient for you."

Tgfhi was shocked by his father's question. "Train me for battle?" he asked. "But, I don't need to know how to fight. The Surpens protect us from attack."

"Of course, you need to know how to fight," Tgonar responded. "The Surpens won't always be there to protect you. You are my heir. The Prince of Tgarus. You need to know how to fight, so you can rule properly." He prayed Rhen would agree to train Tgfhi. If he did, Tgfhi would know how to fight like a Surpen, and he could, in turn, train the Tgarian army to fight like the Surpens, thus making them as lethal a planet as Surpen.

Rhen was silent. He glanced over at Tgfhi, while chewing on bloodworms. There was no Debrino Code against training others in Surpen's battle techniques, so his father couldn't get upset. In fact, Rhen thought, it might be fun to train Tgfhi. He hadn't trained anyone in a long time. As Rhen glanced back down at his breakfast, he nodded his head once in agreement.

If Tgonar hadn't of been watching, he would have missed it. "Thank you my Prince," he told Rhen, with barely concealed joy. Tgfhi's new body was perfect. He was tall, broad and muscular. With Rhen's training, he would be lethal. Tgarus would be in good hands, when Tgfhi took the crown. Thank the Gods he had caved into Tgfhi's pleas to attend the Elfin University. It was proving to be the best decision Tgonar had ever made for Tgarus.

Tgonar spent the rest of the morning celebrating Tgfhi's birthday with him by teaching him how to fly his spacejet. Just before lunch, Tgonar bid Tgfhi goodbye, stopped by the Headmaster's office, to have a word with him, and boarded his own spacejet to return home.

Professor Dewey walked into the student dining hall during lunch and sat down next to Rhen. A grimace passed over his face, when he caught sight of the bloody animal parts that were on Rhen's plate. After he had gotten his gag reflux under control, he looked up at Rhen's face and said, "I understand you will now be teaching the Prince of Tgarus how to fight. May I open the course up to other students or is it a private lesson?"

"Private."

Professor Dewey frowned. He had hoped he could add a Surpen Fighting Class to the school's brochure. It would've been a popular course for the students, especially for those, whose planets were located near the Convention members. "Okay," he agreed. "If you change your mind, please let me know. I've arranged for you to train Tgfhi during your arithmetic class. As I understand it, you have a free period then?" Rhen nodded. "Perfect," Professor Dewey continued. "The stadium is free during that period, so use it for your lesson. You can begin tomorrow. Good day!"

Once the Headmaster had left, Tgfhi shook his head. "The best fighter in the Universe is going to train me to fight." He laughed and asked, "What do I need to bring to class tomorrow, professor?"

"Shorts and a t-shirt," Rhen replied.

"Should I bring any weapons?" Tgfhi inquired. Rhen shook his head.

"You're not good enough to fight with weapons yet, Tgfhi," Ceceta remarked.

Tgfhi's horrified expression to her comment made his friends laugh.

That night, during the B.A.C. meeting, most of the male students in the room pressured Rhen into including them in his fight class. Charlie's friend Stanley was the worst. He fell on the ground in front of Rhen, tears streaming down his face, while he begged Rhen to teach him how to fight. When Rhen said, 'alright', the room erupted with cheers.

Rhen arrived at the stadium the next day to find half of the student body milling about in the center of the main field. "No way!" he exclaimed, turning to walk back towards the main school building.

"Oh, no you don't," Tgfhi told him. He grabbed Rhen's arm and pulled him back towards the stadium. "You promised to teach all of us last night. Now you have to deliver."

Shaking his head with dismay, Rhen mounted the stairs to the stage in the front, lower section of the stadium. As he walked towards the microphone, he noticed most of the Thestran Royal Family in the audience, as well as a few elves, wearing what appeared to be military uniforms. 'An elfin army?' he thought, before laughing at the idea. Rhen turned away from the microphone in the middle of the stage, but not before everyone had heard him laughing at them. When he had gotten himself under control, Rhen faced his 'students'.

"You are the sorriest bunch of losers I've ever had to train. If you were Surpens, I'd kick your butts out of here and go to lunch. Pathetic!"

The stadium was silent. Tgfhi was shocked. He wasn't used to being on this side of Rhen.

"This is going to take some time," Rhen murmured. He glanced at the eager Thestran faces in front of him. "I've taught Surpens how to fight for years, but we use our skills daily. I can't understand why most of you would want to learn how to fight? Your soldiers have been trained to do your killing for you."

Rhen sighed and ran a hand through his hair. "I require my men to be flexible. In battle, flexibility can mean the difference between victory and failure. Why don't we start by seeing how flexible you are? Can you touch the ground in front of you, without bending your knees?" Rhen watched as his students struggled to touch the ground. Most of them couldn't even touch their shins. "Well, I guess you have your homework for tonight. Those of you who can touch the ground, move over to my right. The rest of you move to the left."

"For the students on my left, pair up and follow my movements." Rhen turned and handed Tgfhi one of his battle swords. "Attack me."

"Really?" Tgfhi asked. He held up the sword to admire its shine. "You want me to strike you?"

"Yes."

"Ok." Tgfhi rushed forward, but Rhen stepped out of his path. Miscalculating his speed, Tgfhi ran several steps past Rhen, before he could stop himself. Rhen laughed at him.

Flushed with embarrassment, Tgfhi turned and raced back towards Rhen, with the sword held high. Rhen spun around, when Tgfhi tried to bring the sword down on top of him. He knocked the weapon out of Tgfhi's hands and twisted Tgfhi's arm backwards, causing Tgfhi to bend over in pain. "That's the move,"

Rhen told his students. "Try to catch your partner's arm and twist it behind them in this manner. Practice amongst yourselves. One of you attack, the other defend. Then switch off." Rhen released Tgfhi and tapped him on the back. His gesture made Tgfhi feel better. There was no shame in being bested by the best fighter in the Universe.

Pointing towards the right side of the field, Rhen said, "Okay. Let's see how flexible you really are. Follow my movements. If you can't do them, move to the middle of the field." Rhen glanced back at Tgfhi. "Did you touch your toes?" Tgfhi smiled and nodded yes. "Good," Rhen told him, sounding pleased. "Now, follow along."

Rhen reached down to put his palms on the ground. He kicked his legs up, so he was in a handstand, flipped over backwards into a backbend and stood up again. Only half of the students on the right could follow his movements. Rhen laughed at the sight of the students sprawled on the ground in defeat. Like most of them, Tgfhi got into the backbend but couldn't get himself back up. "Work on that," Rhen told Tgfhi in private.

Turning, Rhen pointed at the remaining 35 students. "Let's have some fun, shall we?" He jumped up, did a back flip in the air and landed on his feet. Five students succeeded. Rhen winked at Tgfhi and then did a front flip. Only three students were able to follow him. "Okay," Rhen said, pointing at the remaining three students. "You can join Surpen's military. The rest of you are fired." Rhen laughed and motioned for the three remaining students to come up onto the stage. Rhen demonstrated a defensive move for the students in the middle and right sides of the stadium to practice then turned to greet the students, who had arrived on stage.

"What're your names?" he asked.

"I'm Jack," a young, brown-haired, blue-eyed elf said, putting out his hand to shake. Rhen looked at Jack's hand and saluted. He had never gotten used to the Thestran's habit of touching hands in greeting. Jack was wearing a white t-shirt that had the words 'Air Elves Shine Brighter' on it, so Rhen knew which tribe he was from. He nodded at the two elves standing beside Jack. "And you?" he asked. The man had brown hair that was streaked with blond highlights and light blue eyes, while the woman had long black hair and green eyes. She reminded him of Sage. Rhen guessed she was a Water Elf.

"I'm Aaron and this is Sarah," Aaron replied, pointing at Sarah.

"Nice to meet you." Rhen took in Aaron's well-developed muscles. "You don't go to the University, do you?"

"No," Jack admitted, answering Rhen's question for Aaron. "I'm too young and Aaron and Sarah have already graduated."

Rhen had figured as much. Aaron's muscles were too filled in for him to be a student at the University. "How did you find out about my class?" Rhen asked.

"We heard about it from Charlie. He told everyone you'd be teaching a fight class," Aaron informed him.

"Charlie!" Rhen hissed, through clenched teeth. Of course, it would be Charlie.

Pointing at Aaron and Sarah, Rhen said, "You two pair up and Jack, you get Tgfhi." He showed them a defensive move then told them to practice. Turning, Rhen jumped off the stage and made his way over towards the first group of students, who couldn't touch the floor. He walked amongst them, giving advice and taking a moment to help them with the moves they were practicing. Rhen showed the students different techniques that would work better for their size and shifted them around into proper groups.

When he was finished, Rhen moved over to the other groups, repeating what he had done with the first group. He then returned to the stage, where he fought with Aaron, Jack, Sarah and Tgfhi. Rhen took one more trip around the field, before the end of class. He instructed his students to remember the group they were in for tomorrow's lesson and left to meet Ceceta.

Tgfhi caught up to Rhen, as he entered the University. "That was awesome! We get to do that every day?" he asked.

"You get to do it twice a day."

"What?" Tgfhi asked.

"I promised your father I would teach you how to fight. If I'm going to do that, we need to work on it twice a day," Rhen explained. He climbed the stairs towards the dining hall. When they reached the cafeteria, Rhen went over to their table, as Tgfhi joined the lunch line.

"So," Ceceta asked, when Rhen sat down across from her on the bench. "How was it?"

"Yeah," Latsoh added. "We were watching you from the windows of math class. It looked like fun. How did all of those students get time off to attend your class?"

Rhen shrugged. He didn't feel like talking, because James, Reed, Lilly, Rachel, Sage and William were walking over towards him with trays of food. They sat down around him, while chatting about his class. "Nice class!" Reed complimented.

"Yes," Lilly agreed. "It was a lot of work, but you didn't feel like you were working."

"I loved it!" Rachel told Rhen. "I can't wait to do it again tomorrow."

Rhen nodded his thanks.

When Tgfhi entered the room, he found there weren't any seats available for him at his usual table. He approached his friends with his plastic, green tray in hand and stood beside the table looking morose. Crystam tried to move over to make room for him. Tgfhi would've fit in the space she'd freed up, if he hadn't of grown. He was too big now. "I guess I'll catch you guys later," he mumbled, walking over to another table to sit with some kids he knew from his Chemistry class.

Rhen felt the Headmaster's hand on his shoulder. "I hear you've decided to teach a fighting class after all. Thank you! I understand your first class was amazing. Everyone is talking about it." Rhen nodded his head. "I knew it would be successful, but I didn't realize how popular it was going to be. I'm afraid we have to change the time of your class. It seems too many students want to take it. I've just had complaints from every teacher at the University. Most of their students skipped class today or stared out the window, watching your class. Would you mind if we moved the time of your class to right after dinner?"

"No," Rhen told him.

"No?" the Headmaster asked. "No, you don't mind or no, we can't move the time of your class?"

"Can't fight on a full stomach," Rhen told him. He lifted his fork to his mouth, a piece of raw meat dangling from the end.

"Oh, yes, of course, you're right. Sorry. How about before breakfast? First thing in the morning?"

Rhen shook his head. "Surpen prayers," he told the Headmaster, after swallowing.

Professor Dewey had forgotten that Rhen was a religious man. "What if we did it right after your prayers? You usually work out for two hours before your prayers, right? Will you be too tired to teach in the morning after your prayers?" Rhen snorted. It was all the approval Professor Dewey needed. "Great, we'll move your class to first thing in the morning, before breakfast. We'll just delay the school day by one hour. I'm sure the teachers will be happy to hear that."

As the Headmaster walked off towards his office, he noticed groups of elves practicing defensive moves on the school lawn and wondered about the logistics of charging them for taking one course.

That night, Rhen showed Tgfhi some fighting techniques in his apartment. They wrestled over and over, until Tgfhi was panting with exhaustion and Crystam yelled at Rhen to let Tgfhi study, because he had a test tomorrow. "We'll practice every night during study group," Rhen told Tgfhi. "In time, you'll be as great a fighter as General Bosternd."

Instead of smiling at this news, Tgfhi looked upset. "I wanted to be as great a fighter as you!"

Rhen laughed. "No one will ever be as great a fighter as I am."

Tgfhi grunted and picked up his books. He couldn't disagree.

Rhen's fight class became the most popular class at the University. The Elfin Royals had thought their soldiers were in shape, until a few of them had been placed into the beginner section of Rhen's class. Once that had happened, the Elfin Royals made Rhen's class a requirement for all military personnel. Less than a week passed, before individuals from other planets began to appear to take the course as well.

When Rhen needed a victim for one of his lessons, he glanced up at the seats behind the stadium's stage and spotted a Zorthan boy watching him. "You," he yelled, pointing at the boy. The kid sat up straight and pointed at himself. "Yes, you, come here," Rhen told him. The boy jumped up and ran down the stadium's stairs to join Rhen. "What're you doing here?" Rhen asked, when the kid appeared by his side. He heard several people in the crowd gasp, at the site of the Zorthan on stage.

"I'm watching," the boy replied.

"I know, but why?"

"Well, I wanted to take your class, but the Thestrans won't let me, because we're a part of the Convention."

"I'm in the Convention," Rhen stated. The boy shrugged in response and Rhen shook his head. He moved the kid over to Sarah and showed her how to hold the boy, without hurting him, while she fought to defend herself. Tgfhi, Jack, and Aaron then took turns in holding the boy, while fighting against Rhen.

"Did you like our last Conference?" Rhen asked the kid, while he lunged at Aaron. Rhen maneuvered past the boy with grace, scoring a hit on Aaron's cheek.

"No, it was boring! Didn't you think? I saw you hanging out with the Vivist kids by the pond. That game you play with them looks cool. I can't wait until I'm old enough to join in."

Rhen laughed and moved the boy back to Sarah, to help her with a move she was having difficulty with. "You can join us at the next Conference. I'll let you be on my team. We always need more players on our team. The Vivists have a nasty habit of killing at least one of us during each game." He finished Sarah's lesson and bowed to the Zorthan. "Thank you for your help young Prince. You're welcome to join my class every day, with or without, the Thestran's approval."

"REALLY?" the boy shouted. "Thanks! You're the best! Wait till my friends hear. They already think you're amazing, because you can survive a Vivist's sting."

Rhen paused. "That's not true. You know no one can survive a Vivist's sting."

"But you survived a poisonous Rasack bite," the boy replied loudly enough for all to hear. "Maybe you could also survive a Vivist's sting."

Rhen frowned. No one was supposed to know that he had been bitten by a Rasack. Only a handful of his most trusted men were aware that he was bitten, while saving Bosternd's life. Rasacks were almost as poisonous as Vivists. In the history of the Universe, only a few people had ever survived their bite, and those who had, were known to have amazing powers. Rhen needed to find out how the boy had heard about his run in with a Rasack. Leaning backwards towards the microphone, he announced, "Class dismissed." Rhen picked up the boy and walked out of the stadium towards his apartment, carrying the kid in his arms.

Ceceta decided it was a good thing that Rhen had missed breakfast that morning, because the entire Thestran Royal Family and all the Elfin Royals sat at their table, grilling her about Rhen's run in with a Rasack. Ceceta was starting to get a headache from playing dumb.

As Ceceta sat down in their first class of the day, she was again surrounded by the Royal Family and the Elfin Royals. They wanted to talk to Rhen and were waiting for him to arrive.

Rhen strode into the room, right before class began, feeling angry at himself. The Zorthan Prince had only heard a rumor that he had been bitten by a Rasack. He had panicked for no reason. The boy didn't have any details and knew no more than what he had said. When Rhen noticed the Royals waiting for him, he cringed. If only he had dismissed the Zorthan Prince's comment.

Before Rhen could take his seat, the Royal Family started to ask him questions. Rhen stared at them with a blank expression on his face. He wasn't going to answer. When the Royals realized this, they quieted down to let Rhen's teacher begin.

As soon as class was finished, they leapt forward, cornering Rhen by the classroom door. "Rhen, please," James said to his brother. "Is it true? Were you bitten by a Rasack?"

Rhen nodded his head and stepped sideways to leave. "How long ago was that?" Rachel asked.

"A while ago," he replied. He pushed William, to make him step backwards.

"How did you live?" Reed asked.

"God healed me," Rhen told him, making his way out of the room. He jogged to catch up to Ceceta.

"That's not an answer," William declared. "The Genisters don't heal anyone."

"Well, we've seen Rhen's healing powers," Sage commented. "They're amazing. Perhaps he can survive a Rasack's bite."

"It's possible, but not probable," James remarked. "Rhen must have more powers then he's letting on. We need to know what they are."

Chapter 20

Loreth floated down into Andres' study and zapped him with a small blast of electricity. Andres fell to the floor shaking and gasping for breath.

When the bolt had passed through his system, Andres sat up. "Yes," he asked, while clenching and unclenching his hands to rid them of their numbness. Loreth had been crueler to him lately and Andres wasn't sure why. He figured it had to do with Rhen's continued absence, but he wasn't positive. You never knew what Loreth was thinking.

"It's time," Loreth stated, taking a seat on Andres' chair. Loreth was ready for Andres to retrieve Rhen and declare war on Thestran. Most of the Thestran Royal Family seemed to care about Rhen now. They would be done in by Rhen's betrayal, maybe even die from the shock of his duplicity. Loreth chuckled at the thought.

Andres wasn't sure what it was 'time' for, but he was too afraid to ask. "Of course," he mumbled, rising to his feet.

Loreth could see, from the expression on Andres' face, that he was clueless. Gods damn the Genister's Code Book. If he hadn't of signed the Genister's laws, he would've taken care of the Thestrans himself. The whole thing was maddening. One break of the law and every Genister would come forth to destroy him. 'Damn them,' Loreth thought. It would be so much easier, if he could use his powers to destroy the Thestrans; his puppets took forever to get anything done.

"It's time to remove Rhen from Thestran," Loreth stated. "Bring him home."

Andres breathed a sigh of relief. He wanted nothing more than to bring his son home. He hated knowing the Thestrans were around Rhen all day long. "At once," Andres replied. He reached out for a bell to call his guards. Loreth waited, as Andres told his aides to send word to Rhen that he must come home.

"Excellent," Loreth remarked, when they were alone. "Once Rhen has returned, prepare for war."

"Yes," Andres agreed. He bowed, while Loreth flew up into the air, disappearing through the vaulted ceiling.

An hour later, a letter was delivered into Andres' hands. It was written on plain, white paper and tucked with haste into a cheap envelope. Andres opened it and read:

"Thank you for your note father, but I'll be staying at the Elfin University. We had an agreement, and I expect you to uphold your side of the deal. Although I will not be returning home right now, please remember that if you need me for a specific task, I will be there to assist you. Rhen."

Andres threw back his head and screamed. He had lost. Rhen had become Thestran. He had refused to return home, when Andres had called. Andres threw the letter down onto the tiled floor and marched from the room. He would take care of this.

Two weeks later, the Thestrans noticed that Rhen was acting odd. He had stopped talking, except during his fight classes, and was even moodier than usual. He had also begun to sleep through some of his classes, which angered his teachers to no end, since they couldn't do anything about it.

Rhen wasn't the only problem. It appeared the Black Angel had disappeared as well. No one had seen him or been saved by him for an entire week. Everyone was worried that he might have been hurt or even killed. The Universe's oracles had also started working overtime, spouting out their words of doom regarding Rhen and the Universe. The Thestran Royals were overwhelmed with calls from worried individuals across the Universe. Their staff was working full time to ease people's fears, while the Thestran Royals themselves remained vigilant around Rhen.

One morning, Lilly noticed Erfce was keeping his face averted from Rhen. When Erfce flinched, after Rhen dropped his hand on the table, Lilly knew he had had his first vision of Rhen turning into the Surpen God of War. "You're not the only one," she told him, after hearing about his vision. Lilly had pulled Erfce into a private room to confront him before class. "Every oracle in the Universe is having the same exact vision that you had last night. We've been spending time with Rhen to get him to accept his Thestran heritage so he won't attack us."

"Oh, Themrock!" Erfce exclaimed, his light brown eyes twice as large as normal. "Why didn't you tell us about this before? We could've worked with you."

"Your friendships with him have made more of a difference than anything we've done."

"Why do you think we're all having the same vision?" Erfce wondered.

"Honestly," Lilly confessed. "I think it's because we're about to reach the moment of truth regarding Rhen."

"Do you think Rhen will really turn into that…that beast?"

"No," Lilly told him. "I think you and your friends will stop him."

"Us?" Erfce asked. "I hope you're right," he added, before walking towards his class. He prayed that he and his friends weren't the Universe's only hope for salvation. He hoped the Black Angel would return soon.

Lilly watched Erfce walk off. Turning, she went to the University's portal. She needed to inform James that Erfce was now aware of their situation. As she mounted the steps to her family's private section of the Thestran castle, she stopped a staff member to ask him her brother's whereabouts. The man told her that James had left for Delna to meet with the rulers there, but Reed, Henry and Kate were sitting on the balcony off the third conference room. Lilly nodded and proceeded to the balcony, where she found her parents and older brother chatting about one of her niece's latest antics.

When Reed was finished with his story, Lilly told them about Erfce. "Good," Reed commented. "We'll need his help. Things are really heating up now."

"It'll be fine," Kate replied, pulling on the tassels of her dark brown shawl. "Rhen is here, and we removed the Zorthan robot from his brain. Andres has lost."

"He's here physically mom, but not mentally," Lilly corrected her. "Andres hasn't lost yet."

"If he's here, he's here," Kate corrected Lilly. "Andres has lost."

"There's a difference between being somewhere physically and emotionally," Lilly replied with persistence.

"Obviously," Kate said. "But Rhen is coming around. We've won this battle."

Lilly stared at her mother with disbelief. "Mom, Rhen is not coming around. He's actually…falling behind, if you ask me."

"He hasn't been the same lately," Reed agreed. "Something is wrong with him."

"Precisely," Lilly stated. "And not only should we be asking ourselves if we can do more to help Rhen, but we should be demanding that he see a doctor, so we can find out what's caused this change in his behavior. It's dangerous for us to do nothing."

In a dismissive tone of voice, Kate said, "He'll be fine."

"Like he was for the last ten years on Surpen," Lilly snapped. "Themrock, Mom! He's not fine and this time you can't just abandon him or we'll all die." Lilly saw her mother's lips had become thin lines of disapproval, but she couldn't help herself from speaking her mind. "You screwed up," she told her parents. "You abandoned our brother. You handed him over to a horrible, evil man, and when you had the chance to rescue him, when you could have assisted Ceceta's family in removing him from Surpen, you did nothing. Nothing." Reed had dropped his head down and was refusing to look at anyone. Lilly felt tears forming at the corners of her eyes. "I keep thinking, what if it had been me? What if I had been the one abandoned on that despicable planet at the age of eight?"

A servant walked out onto the balcony, but Henry waved him away. "Darling," Kate said. She rose to hug Lilly.

Lilly stepped back and swatted her mother's hands away. "How could you?" she asked. Tears flowed down her cheeks. "He was our brother. He was a part of our family and you cut him off like some sort of diseased limb." She wiped at her tears with her sleeve. "You know what? I don't blame him for hating us. I'm embarrassed to be a part of this family."

"You don't mean that," Henry told her.

"Yes!" Lilly yelled. "Yes, I do. Look at us. We're horrible. We're worse than Andres."

"Now Lilly," Reed began.

"Think about it Reed. Andres has a passion for Rhen. The minute he knew Max was named Rhen, he focused all of his attention on him. He made Rhen into a great warrior. Would we have done that? I don't think so, just look at Charlie. We ignore him completely. The only reason why we're paying any attention to Rhen right now, is because we're afraid of him. If our futures didn't rest on his becoming a part of our family, we probably wouldn't have ever spoken to him again." Lilly took a deep, shuddering breath. "He deserved better from us." Turning she added, "He was right you know. We are all assholes. At risk to himself, he came to our aid against the Ustarians, and we didn't even thank him properly. We criticized him. What do you think the Surpens would've done? They probably would've thrown him a feast. We let him get beaten instead." Lilly shook her head and moved towards the door. Kate tried to grab her arm to detain her, but Lilly slipped through her grasp. She didn't want to look at her parents. She was too angry with them.

Over the next two weeks, Rhen continued to decline. He even fell asleep during lunch. One moment, Rhen was chewing on some meat, and the next, there was a loud thud, as his head smacked down onto a plate of bloody liver. Ceceta glanced over at him then turned back to Crystam, who was explaining something to her about their astronomy homework.

Reed, Sage, Lilly and Rachel, who were on Rhen duty, felt awkward. "Um, Ceceta. We probably shouldn't leave him in his food. Do you want us to take him to your apartment?" Reed offered.

"No. Just leave him there. If you move him, you might wake him up. Leaving him there will give him more time to sleep."

"But," Sage asked. "Why does he need the sleep?"

"He hasn't been getting enough of it lately. In fact," Ceceta added, in a rare moment of openness, "he hasn't been getting any sleep at all."

Charlie staggered over to their table and plopped down next to Latsoh. "What do you mean Ceceta?" he asked, before burping. Latsoh waved away the stale beer smell from his burp. "He gets a lot of sleep. He sleeps during every class!"

"Charlie," Ceceta commented. She watched him with trepidation, hoping he wasn't going to be throwing up in her toilet later. "You mean why is he sleeping during the day? He's sleeping during the day, because he's up all night with his father."

Her words put the Thestran Royals on alert.

Erfce was the first to recover from her comment. "What do you mean?" he asked. In his dreams, he had seen the King of Surpen torturing Rhen. The man frightened him.

"Andres has been showing up at our apartment every night at 11:30. He stays up with Rhen all night long, talking about the most inconsequential stuff. He doesn't leave until the next morning around 4:00, just as Rhen is getting ready for his workout," Ceceta informed them.

"Wow!" Latsoh exclaimed. "Rhen must be exhausted. How long has this been going on?" She was a little surprised that Ceceta and Rhen hadn't mentioned it to them earlier.

"It started about four weeks ago," Ceceta informed them.

The timing corresponded with when Rhen had begun to act strange.

"I think Andres believes that if he stays up with Rhen every night, it will undo any 'damage' the Thestrans are doing to him during the day. He's in a struggle with you guys," Ceceta told the Royal Family, while looking at Reed, "over Rhen's allegiance. He's planning on keeping Rhen up every night until we return to Surpen."

"What do you mean by any 'damage' we're doing?" Crystam asked.

Reed answered Crystam's question for Ceceta. "The King thinks we're 'damaging' his son by corrupting him to our Thestran ways. Rhen broke the Debrino Code when he fought for us. Andres is worried our 'wild ways' are rubbing off on his son. He doesn't want Rhen to become like us. Wouldn't you agree Ceceta?"

"Definitely," Ceceta answered.

When lunch was over, Ceceta shook Rhen until he woke up. Groggily, he wiped off his face with a napkin, before shuffling off to class with her. The hair on one side of his head was still clumped together with dried blood.

"Why?" James asked, when he met with the others, while Rhen was in class. "Why is he keeping Rhen up?"

"By now, he must know that we've removed the Zorthan mind-controlling device from Rhen's brain. Do you think he's trying to brainwash Rhen?" Reed asked the others.

"Can we ban Andres from visiting the University," the Air Elf King, Chaster, asked.

James shook his head. "He'd declare war on us immediately, if we kept him from Rhen."

"So, what should we do," the Water Elf King, Plos, asked.

They talked for a while, but couldn't come up with any ideas that would keep the peace, while allowing Rhen to stay at the University, and forcing Andres to remain on Surpen.

Over the next week and a half, Rhen continued to decline. He was losing weight and had fallen asleep during his morning prayers and fight class. "I saw him sleeping next to Andres last night, as they sat in our living room," Ceceta told her friends during Astronomy Class. Rhen was sleeping beside her, his head on the desk.

After class, Ceceta woke up Rhen and told him it was time to go home. He blinked his bloodshot eyes a few times, before nodding his head and walking off towards the exit. "Love, I have a question for the teacher about tomorrow's test. I'll meet you back at the apartment, okay?" Rhen waved a tired hand over his head as he kept walking.

When Ceceta and her friends were finished, they took a short cut to return to Ceceta's apartment, hoping to catch Rhen before he fell asleep. As they pushed open the exit door that led outside, they were startled to find Rhen standing on the school's grassy hilltop. His hand was on his chin and he was watching Reed in the distance.

Reed had been riding his jet bike with friends, when he had realized he was late for 'Rhen duty'. It was too late for him to return to the Wood Elf Castle to change first, before meeting up with Ceceta and the others, so he decided to ride his jet bike over to the University. As he came out of the woods onto the University's lawn, he noticed Rhen on the hill watching him. Reed did a few stunts for Rhen to keep his interest. When he saw the others emerge from the building, he turned his jet bike to ride up to them.

Ceceta covered her ears as Reed approached.

Reed lowered his landing gear in front of Rhen and turned off his engine, settling his bike on the ground. "Hey, how was astronomy tonight?" he asked, after he had pulled off his helmet.

Rhen nodded his head absentmindedly, while taking in Reed's jet bike. The bike was an eight-foot long, open, mini jet that flew about four feet off the ground. They were used for traveling short distances and pleasure riding. When the jet bike was on, it had a ten-foot wingspan. When the engine was off, the wings would fold into its main frame. The seat for Reed's jet bike was located before the wings, so his legs hung down on either side of the main frame to steady it before liftoff. When he was flying, Reed would lean forward and tuck his feet up into the foot holds under the main frame.

"Do you want to try it?" Reed asked Rhen.

Rhen took a moment before asking in a tired, whisper of a voice, "What is it?"

Reed cringed at the sound of exhaustion in Rhen's voice. "Don't they have jet bikes on Surpen?"

"Thankfully no," Ceceta informed him. "It's too loud!"

"Jet bike?" Rhen repeated. He walked around the bike, examining it.

Reed handed his helmet to Rhen. "Come on, I'll take you for a ride."

Rhen hesitated. "How's it powered?"

"It uses the same power the portals use," Reed informed him.

"Not fuel?" Rhen asked.

"No. Regular jets use fuel, but the jet bike is small enough it can use the power strain that was left over from the Genisters, the same one we use for our portals. We have scientists working on a new type of spacejet that will also be powered by the Genisters' powers, but it's not yet functional." Rhen nodded his head, his eyes on Reed's jet bike. Reed flipped his leg over the frame and tilted the jet bike into take off position. "Come on," he told Rhen. "I can see you're curious. Swing your leg over and I'll take you for a ride. Just hold onto my back." Rhen continued to hesitate. "You'll love it, trust me!" Reed added.

Rhen took a step forward and swung his leg up over the bike, so he was standing behind Reed. "Maybe you should leave those behind," Reed said, indicating Rhen's swords, which dangled beside the shuddered wings. With effort, Rhen moved to unhook his belt. Ceceta was there at once to take it from him.

Seeing how tired his little brother was, Reed took the helmet from Rhen's hands and put it on him. He tightened the strap under Rhen's chin.

"No," Rhen protested. He reached up to remove the helmet, but Reed smacked the top of the helmet and told him, "No helmet, no ride. You can heal amazingly fast, but if you should fall off onto something that kills you, I'd be dead meat."

Rhen paused then lowered his hands, so Reed could check the helmet's fit. When he was finished, Reed pulled Rhen's arms around his waist. "Hold on, so you don't fall!" he shouted, while starting the engine.

The bike rose into the air. Reed turned it back towards the Wood Elf Castle. They crossed the lawn and entered one of the paths that led into the Wood Elf Forest.

"I can't believe Rhen actually found something he likes on Thestran," Ceceta remarked.

"Thank Themrock!" Lilly exclaimed. She couldn't believe they had been working on Rhen all this time with no results, and just by chance, Reed had appeared with the one thing that Rhen had shown an interest in. Maybe now they would have some success.

"Reed and his jet bikes," Rachel said. She shook her head. "He's obsessed. They have races at his castle every third month. He's very good. You should check it out Ceceta. Their next race happens to be next Sunday."

"No, they're too loud for me," Ceceta replied. She turned to go to her apartment with her friends. They had a lot of homework to do and she wanted to get started.

"STOP!" Lilly yelled, startling everyone. She stepped forward, placing her hand on Ceceta's arm. "Ceceta, I can't take it anymore!"

"What?" Ceceta asked.

"I'm really happy that Rhen has finally found something Thestran he can relate to, but it's not enough. We NEED your help Ceceta."

"With what?"

Lilly hesitated. "We're worried about…you see…when we were dressed as soldiers on Surpen, we heard the King talk about a war between Thestran and Surpen. Do you remember?" Ceceta nodded. "Well, we're worried that Andres is going to turn Rhen into a God of War and we won't be able to stop him. We believe he's going to kill us when he conquers Thestran."

Ceceta caught sight of Erfce nodding vigorously beside her. "No," she told him. Turning back to Lilly, she added, "You don't have anything to worry about. Rhen won't fight you. He may be forced to attack Thestran for Surpen, but he won't kill you."

"You're wrong," Sage contradicted. "He will. It's been predicted by all the oracles in the Universe. He'll be turned into the Surpen God of War, and he'll kill us. Even Erfce has seen visions of Rhen as the God of War."

Ceceta glared at Erfce. He dropped his head in shame. "It's true," he admitted, while his friends gawked at him. "I've been having nightmares about Rhen turning into the God of War every night."

"What?" Latsoh asked. "Why didn't you tell us?"

"Wait," Ceceta interrupted. "You keep mentioning this 'God of War'. You do realize that Rhen is already called the God of War by the planets he's conquered."

"They call him the Surpen God of War?" Rachel asked.

"No, not the 'Surpen' God of War, just the God of War," Ceceta responded. "It's nothing more than a name. That's all." She turned to go, but Lilly tightened her grip, forcing Ceceta to turn back.

"Do you know what the ancient Surpen God of War looks like?" Sage asked.

Ceceta shook her head. Lilly pulled on her arm. "Come," she told Ceceta. "There's something you need to see."

Ceceta and her friends followed Lilly to the school's portal, where they passed through into the Thestran Royal Castle. They mounted the Family's private staircase and entered the Royals' private library. Ceceta and her friends took seats, as Lilly walked through the wooden stacks looking for the book she had shown her family almost a year ago. When she found it, she brought it over to Ceceta and opened it to the pages that displayed the vicious, dragon beast known as the Surpen God of War.

"That's what Rhen looks like in my visions," Erfce told Ceceta, when he saw the fierce looking animal on the pages in front of her.

"Andres is going to turn Rhen into this creature," Lilly explained.

"I've never seen this before," Ceceta told them. She turned the book over to examine the cover. "They don't have this book on our planet."

"Perhaps the King banned it?" Rachel offered.

Ceceta nodded in agreement. "Yes, he's banned a lot of books. They keep a very close eye on what we're allowed to read."

Sage felt impatient. She was pregnant and wanted this whole problem with Rhen resolved immediately. "You have to help us Ceceta," she insisted. "You have to keep Andres from turning Rhen into this God of War. You have to give us information about Rhen that will help us reach the Thestran side of him and turn him away from..." she was about to say Surpen, but at the last minute decided not to, "from his desire to kill," she finished.

Ceceta pointed at the picture in the book. "Don't worry. Rhen won't turn into this. It's just not like him."

King James, who had followed them into the library, stepped up beside Ceceta. Trying to look casual, he reached out to touch the book in front of her. "We think Andres will brainwash Rhen or do something else to him, to force him to change into the Surpen God of War. We don't think he'll have a choice in the matter." Ceceta frowned at the prospect and looked back at the book. After Punishment Island, she knew anything was possible. If Andres had his mind set on it, Rhen could very well be vulnerable.

"Did you know that Rhen is already called the God of War by the planets he's conquered?" Sage asked her brother.

James took off his black cowboy hat and nodded his head. He had heard as much from his spies. Over the last few months, he'd become very aware of the fighting prowess of his younger brother. Rhen's superior abilities on the battlefield terrified him. "Ceceta, I'm worried about Rhen losing control of his sense of self because of the King's tricks. I'm worried Andres will turn him into a killing machine." From the expression on her face, James could see that Ceceta was also worried.

"Ceceta, you know you're in Andres's way. Don't you?" Lilly blurted out. "You're Rhen's connection to...to reality, to humanity, to kindness and to warmth. Andres will have to kill you in order to turn Rhen into the Surpen God of War. Your life is in danger." Lilly paused, waiting for the information she had just given Ceceta to soak in.

James considered Lilly's comment and realized she was right. If he wanted to succeed, the Surpen King would have to eliminate Ceceta. James made a note to put some soldiers around Ceceta to keep her safe.

"You also know," Lilly continued, "that if Rhen turns into the Surpen God of War, we'll have to declare war on Surpen. You don't want that to happen. You don't want Thestran to be at war with Surpen. Please Ceceta," she pleaded. "Will you help us? Will you provide us with information on Rhen, so we can keep him, and Thestran, safe?"

Tgfhi, Crystam and Latsoh stared at each other in shock. They had had no idea that any of this was going on. They had thought the Royal Family was following Rhen around to get to know him, not because they were afraid he would kill them. It was hard for them to believe that Rhen was expected to conquer the Universe as some strange dragon beast. He was their friend, a nice, funny guy, who was shy around new people.

Ceceta stood up and walked towards the door, her friends following behind her. Just like Rhen, she had been raised on Surpen. There were many things about Surpen that she despised, but like Rhen, she still considered Surpen to be her home. She loved her planet. Ceceta felt her skin prickle with anger. How dare they ask her to betray Surpen! Pausing by the library door, Ceceta turned to look back at the Royal Family. "You want me to betray Surpen and Rhen, to help you? You want me to spy on my husband, so you can defeat him?"

"NO!" Kate shouted from the hallway behind her. She had been listening to the entire conversation outside the library door. Kate approached Ceceta with her hands out. "No, Ceceta. All we want you to do, is to work with us to prevent a war that will kill billions of people. We don't want to hurt Rhen. We want to protect him." Kate glanced over at Lilly. They hadn't spoken since Lilly's outburst.

Ceceta stood with her hand on the door, mulling over Kate's words. She hated death and senseless destruction. Perhaps she could help the Thestrans, without hurting her husband or her planet. Perhaps they could protect Rhen from whatever plan Andres had for him. It was worth a shot. "If I tell you a little bit about Rhen, it will stop the war between Surpen and Thestran?"

"Yes!" Kate told her. She hoped that once Ceceta began telling them about Rhen, she might continue, so they could learn what they needed to know about him to stop the war.

"Okay," Ceceta agreed. "But you can't tell anyone what I tell you. He would be furious with me, if he knew I was giving away his secrets."

"Of course," James said. "You have our promise. We will keep the information you give us a secret."

Ceceta pursed her lips, as she considered what to tell them. It occurred to her that Lilly was always asking her why Rhen didn't pay attention in class. Turning towards Lilly, she said, "You wanted to know why he doesn't pay attention in class?"

"Um..." Lilly began. That wasn't necessarily the information they were hoping for. Lilly caught James' eye, and at his prompt, nodded yes.

"Well, he doesn't pay attention in class, because he can't read or write," Ceceta informed them.

"Seriously?" Tgfhi asked, looking stunned. "Rhen's illiterate?"

"Yes. Andres believes that if he can control the information Rhen has access to, he can control Rhen. No one on Surpen, except for Andres, Orpel and Bosternd know that he's illiterate."

"By the Genister Gods," James swore. "How deviously clever of the Surpen King to use illiteracy as a way to control Rhen." Ceceta gave him a nod.

"He doesn't know how to read or write?" Latsoh asked, feeling dumbfounded. She just couldn't believe she had heard Ceceta correctly. She tried to think back on all of her classes and study sessions with Rhen. As Latsoh thought about it, she remembered that Rhen had never written anything in her presence. He had flipped through their textbooks many times, and it always looked as if he were reading them, but maybe he was just looking at the pictures. How had he fooled them for so long?

"No, he doesn't," Ceceta told her with a smile. She thought their reactions were funny.

"But Reed said the Surpen soldiers mentioned he had a special tutor growing up," Sage blurted out.

Ceceta laughed. "A special tutor? That's rich. No, he had no tutor, except a weapons expert and a fighting expert. Those two men trained him mercilessly in all forms of battle and weapons. Why do you think he's such an amazing warrior? They spent every minute of every day for years training Rhen to kill. Andres wouldn't let him learn anything else. They kept him in a room in the dungeon. He was never let out. He ate and slept in that room and he learned how to kill. He can kill every creature in the Universe faster and better than anyone else. He's a killing machine. That's what he was raised to be." Ceceta looked over at Tgfhi. "You're always asking Rhen questions about his childhood. I've wanted to tell you the truth, but he didn't want you to know, so I couldn't. Tgfhi, Rhen didn't have a childhood. Please stop asking him about it."

Tgfhi nodded his head. He had begun to suspect as much.

Ceceta noticed Erfce's face seemed paler than normal. "Are you okay?" she asked.

"Yeah," he murmured back.

"But, how will he pass his exams?" Crystam asked.

"I read and study the textbooks and he pulls the information out of my mind when he needs it. All of those times, when you guys made fun of him for not studying, he's been reviewing the stuff I've been taking in by reading my thoughts."

"He can read your mind?" Erfce asked.

"Yes," Ceceta answered. "He also has an amazing memory, so if the teacher tells us something in class, he locks the information up in his mind for future reference."

"But how will he write his exams?" Sage asked.

Ceceta shook her head. She was finished with the topic. She wanted to tell them how wonderful Rhen was. What an incredible person he could be. "Have I ever mentioned to you that he's an amazing musician. In fact, if he had stayed on Thestran, he probably would have been called the King of Music. He's truly gifted. Unfortunately, we ended up in a society where Rhen was beaten, if he ever attempted to let himself create. Pity, isn't it?" she remarked. "The Universe would be a much more beautiful place today, if he had been free to show his talents."

Ceceta tapped the wooden door with her fingertips, as she considered an idea. "I can't really remember what Debrino's punishment is for playing music. I should check it out someday." She turned to Lilly. "It's sad that you will never get the chance to experience Rhen's gifts." She pushed the library door open a little further and added, "You know, it really is unfortunate that our school doesn't force ALL of its students to learn an instrument. Perhaps if it did, some musician with talents beyond your wildest imagination might burst forth and free himself from the ties that bind him." Ceceta winked at Lilly. "If you know what

234

I mean," she whispered, before walking out the door, with her shocked friends following along behind her.

"What did she mean?" Rachel asked.

"She wants us to find out what the Debrino Code's punishment is for playing music. If it's not something terrible, she wants us to start making music available to Rhen," Lilly explained.

"Interesting," James said, while drawing up a schedule for everyone to keep an eye on Ceceta. "Lilly is absolutely correct in her assumption by the way. When the time is right, the Surpen King will want Ceceta out of the way. She would be a liability to him, as she is an asset to us."

"Where're you going?" Rachel asked Lilly, once James was finished with his 'Ceceta' schedule.

"To talk with the Headmaster about moving the music classes next door to Rhen's classes," Lilly answered, with a mischievous smile. She pushed her medium length brown hair behind her ears. "I want Rhen surrounded by music."

"So he can't escape," Kate agreed.

"Precisely," Lilly replied with a wave, as she left the room.

Ceceta and her friends returned to the University through the Thestran's portal. As they made their way to the lawn, Tgfhi asked, "Rhen is musical?"

Ceceta laughed at the way he said it. It was obvious he didn't believe her. "You have no idea. He's amazing!"

Tgfhi considered her words. "I guess I just never pictured him as a musician," he admitted. "Soldier yes, musician, no."

"What instrument can he play?" Crystam asked.

"Everything," Ceceta told her. They exited the school building and walked out onto the lawn. Ceceta was relieved to find that Rhen and Reed hadn't returned yet.

"Everything?" Erfce repeated.

"Yes, Erfce," she confirmed. "He can play any instrument in the Universe."

"But how did he learn how to play them, if he wasn't allowed to touch any instruments," Crystam asked.

Ceceta glanced around to make sure no one else was on the lawn. "Remember when you asked me if he had any powers?" She waited until Crystam nodded. "Well, that's his power. Music!"

"Genisters' Balls!" Erfce laughed out. "You're kidding me? The musical soldier? How funny is that?"

"Not healing?" Crystam asked. She had already been blown away by Rhen's ability to heal. She couldn't believe that music was his main power.

"No," Ceceta told her. "It's music. He's...well, you'll see. If the Royal Family picked up on what I was hinting at, we'll all be able to enjoy Rhen's powers soon."

"His main power is music," Tgfhi said to himself. "A fighting musician." He chuckled at the idea of Rhen killing people, while playing the violin.

"So, Rhen's illiterate," Crystam stated, in the silence after they had sat down on the grassy lawn outside the main University building.

"Yup. Andres wanted him to be the strongest warrior in the Universe, but he also wanted Rhen to be reliant on him."

"Didn't Rhen want to learn how to read and write?" Latsoh asked.

"Sure," Ceceta told her. "But he loved his father, and like any obedient Surpen child, he never challenged what his father told him to do. He never questioned his father's decisions. He would do anything for his dad."

"Including conquer the Universe," Erfce whispered.

"Yes," Ceceta agreed. "Although, I admit I don't know anything about Andres turning him into a 'Surpen God of War'. That's just...wrong. AND, it was wrong of you not to tell us about your dreams." She added, while jabbing at Erfce's chest with her finger.

Erfce flushed. "I'm sorry."

"Just don't do it again," Ceceta chastised him.

After they had been sitting on the lawn for a while, Ceceta asked Latsoh the time. "They'd better get back soon. I don't want to have to entertain Andres, if Rhen is late," Ceceta murmured. She smoothed her pale blue robes down across her legs and glanced, with apprehension, towards the Teacher's Residence Hall.

"Hey," Charlie shouted out, while walking over towards them from the dorms. He laughed for no reason and fell into a pile on the grass beside Ceceta. "Want a drink?" he asked, pulling a silver flask from his jacket.

"Really, Charlie, why are you always drinking?" Ceceta asked him.

Charlie shrugged, before giving her a lopsided grin.

Sage joined them a few minutes later. As she sat down beside Latsoh, they heard two jet bikes coming down the path from the Wood Elf Castle. The bikes seemed to be moving slowly. When they cleared the woods, Ceceta and the others saw Reed on one jet bike and Rhen, following him, on a second bike.

From the way Rhen's bike kept jerking forward and stalling, it was clear he was having trouble with it. Rhen fell off his bike several times, as he progressed across the school's lawn. After what seemed like an eternity, Reed and Rhen finally arrived on the hilltop in front of them. Rhen fell off his jet bike again right at their feet. He hadn't had a chance to put the landing gear down, so the bike toppled over on top of him. Charlie and Reed jumped forward to help.

"Why's he shaking?" Sage asked, when she noticed Rhen's legs shake underneath the bike, as Reed and Charlie lifted it off him.

Rhen stood up and removed his helmet. He was laughing so hard, there were tears streaming down his face. "That was fun!" he exclaimed.

Reed stared at Rhen with wide eyes. "Yeah," he agreed halfheartedly. He couldn't believe Rhen had enjoyed it. Rhen was terrible at driving the jet bike. If he didn't have healing powers, he'd be dead from all his accidents.

"Can we do it again?" Rhen asked.

"Sure," Reed agreed. "No one else in our family seems to appreciate jet bike riding. I'm glad you do." Rhen nodded with approval and held out his helmet to Reed. "No, you keep it," Reed told him. "I'm giving you this bike too," he added, while tapping its seat.

Rhen paused a moment, and then, in one quick movement, hugged Reed, while slapping him on the back. "Nice!" he declared, stepping back. "Thank you!"

Caught off guard by Rhen's hug, Reed stuttered, "Y..y..you're welcome." He wondered what his mother's reaction was going to be, when she learned he'd been the first one hugged by Rhen. Clearing his throat, Reed added, "I'll give you lessons every night, and maybe next Sunday, you can join me in one of our races. We have them every third month and everybody, except for my immediate family," he threw out, while glaring at Sage and Charlie, "joins in."

"I'd like that," Rhen told him. He was about to say more, but Ceceta coughed interrupting him. Rhen gave her a puzzled look. Ceceta nodded her head at something behind him, while handing him his weapons belt. Turning, Rhen saw his father standing with his legs wide apart and hands on his waist. He was glaring down at them. Rhen sighed. Andres was angry.

"Thank you again Reed," Rhen said. He buckled his weapons belt around his waist. "I need to go." He nodded to his friends then strode off towards the Teacher's Residence Hall, with Ceceta following along behind him at a respectful distance.

They watched Rhen hug his dad in greeting. After they had disappeared into the Teacher's Residence Hall, Rhen's friends bid the Thestran Royals goodnight and left.

Glancing around, to make sure they were alone, Sage blurted out, "You'll never guess what we just found out!" Reed and Charlie gave her puzzled looks. "Rhen can't read or write. Andres kept him illiterate in order to control him. Can you believe it? And, Ceceta thinks Rhen is an amazing musician. Isn't that funny?"

"That's interesting," Reed agreed vaguely, while his blue eyes dropped to the ground. "I've also got something interesting to tell you." He paused, as if considering his words. "Let's...let's keep this a secret for now, okay?" Glancing back up at them, he asked, "Can you do that?" Sage and Charlie nodded yes. "Okay," Reed began. "I decided to explain the jet bike's engine to Rhen, while we were halfway through one of the Wood Elf Courses. When we got off my jet bike, we felt the ground shift....no it, it kind of shuddered underneath us. Both of us nearly fell over."

"Was it a mini-earthquake?" Sage asked. She'd never heard of the Wood Elves having earthquakes before.

"That's what I thought at first, but then I noticed the land around us had changed. The grass appeared greener, fuller and healthier and there were buds and flowers on all of the plants around us. Oh, and get this, this totally shocked me." He reached around his bike to the seat bags. Opening one of the bags, he pulled out several, long-stemmed, scallop-shaped, white flowers with dark blue centers. Sage gasped at the sight of them and grabbed them out of his hands. "Exactly," Reed remarked. "Giy flowers were blooming everywhere we looked. Giy flowers only bloom once a year, during the summer elf festival."

"They do?" Charlie asked.

Reed sighed. "Do you remember the Giy flower story or did you sleep during that part of school?"

Charlie shrugged. Reed realized he was clueless. "Giy flowers are our most sacred elfin symbol. They were created by our God Themrock just for us. Themrock gave us these flowers as a gift. Their smell brings us peace and happiness."

Charlie nodded. "Now I remember that class," he told Reed. "The teacher explained to us that the flower's presence symbolized the elfin race would continue, it would flourish and grow."

"Right," Reed said. He turned to Sage. "Why do you think I would find Giy flowers deep in the woods, months before they're supposed to bloom?"

"I don't know," Sage replied. She held the flowers up to her nose and sniffed their intoxicating scent. "Perhaps it's a new type of Giy flower?"

"Does it smell the same," Charlie asked, reaching up to take one. Sage pulled them away from Charlie in a protective gesture. When she saw Charlie pout, she realized she was being selfish and handed him and Reed one of the flowers.

Charlie smelled his flower and smiled. "Ahh, I feel so peaceful now. It's definitely the same flower I smelled at the last elfin festival. It's like catnip for elves," he added. "I wonder what would happen if you smoked one?"

Reed smacked Charlie on the head with his hand. "Imbecile!" Shaking the flower he was holding at Sage, he added, "This should not be blooming. Something is either terribly wrong or...."

"Or, something is wonderfully right," Sage interrupted. She smiled in a wistful manner and drifted off towards the school building. "I love Themrock," she hummed to herself. Reed watched, as Sage stopped walking, her body tensed and she turned back towards him with round eyes. "OH, THEMROCK!" she yelled.

"Shhh," Reed hissed. He glanced around at the school's grounds. Everyone seemed to be in for the night.

Sage marched back to Reed and stuck her finger in his face. "Are you trying to tell me that you think...that you think that...that Themrock is back?!"

Charlie laughed, but Reed nodded his head. "No, way!" Charlie exclaimed.

"No way is right Charlie," Sage snapped. She paced around them, while cradling her flowers. "I mean, we all know that Themrock promised to return to us one day, but if he's back, why hasn't he contacted us? He would've told us if he was back!"

Reed grabbed Sage by her forearms to stop her pacing. "Sage, think about it. The Giy flower only blooms once a year. The only other time it will bloom, is if Themrock is present. How could I have found blooming Giy flowers, months before the festival, if Themrock isn't around. He must've been walking through the woods before I arrived. As soon as I noticed the flowers, I ran into the woods searching for him. I would still be there now, if Rhen hadn't of gotten bored and asked me to bring him back."

"NO!" Sage yelled. "There must be another explanation. If Themrock was back, he would've contacted us. He wouldn't be hiding from us!"

"Did you see anyone else in the woods around you?" Charlie asked, sounding rather sober.

"No," Reed told him. "Rhen and I were the only ones on the jet bike path tonight."

"And the flowers just showed up?" Charlie asked.

"I stopped my jet bike to talk to Rhen, and after we had gotten off, I noticed the flowers were everywhere," Reed informed him.

"So, you think Themrock was in the woods before you arrived," Charlie recapped.

"Yes," Reed agreed. "That's the only explanation for the Giy flowers."

"Cool," Charlie responded, a goofy smile appeared on his face, as he bobbed his head. He lay down on the grass and placed his Giy flower over his nose, before closing his eyes.

Sage started to argue with Reed. She couldn't fathom the concept of Themrock returning. She was positive Themrock would've notified them if he had returned. After fifteen minutes of fighting, Sage and Reed agreed to disagree. They made a pact that none of them would mention the subject of the Giy flowers, until Reed had gotten additional proof that Themrock had returned.

As Reed and Sage headed home, Charlie leapt to his feet with grace and ran into the Wood Elf Forest.

Chapter 21

When Rhen and Ceceta walked into the student dining hall the next morning, they noticed the tables had been squeezed together on the right side of the room to make space for a stage. Musical instruments were stacked in cases along both sides of the stage and Professor Dewey was tapping the stage microphone to get the students' attention.

"I have an announcement. We received an anonymous donation that will make it possible for you to have music during your meals. Also, as a part of this donation, every student will now be offered musical instruction. All students are now required to take at least two semesters of music to graduate. Mr. Orisco, our highly-acclaimed music teacher, will oversee your instruction. Mr. Orisco, would you like to say a few words?"

A squat man with unnaturally, poufy, brown hair approached the microphone. "Thank you," Mr. Orisco said in a high, nasal voice. "This is a day of new beginnings. You must consider which instrument you would like to learn. I will be visiting your classes today to assign each of you an instrument and to give you your class schedule."

After Mr. Orisco had stepped away from the microphone, four students mounted the stage to perform. They gave their classmates nervous glances, while opening their instrument cases. By the time they were ready to perform, Rhen was half-way through his bowl of bloodworms. The classical composition they were asked to play was much too hard for them and everyone winced, as the students' instruments squeaked out the notes.

Tgfhi chuckled and smacked Erfce's arm. "Look at Rhen," he whispered.

Rhen had covered his ears with his hands and he was leaning over to lick the last few bloodworms out of his bowl.

Ceceta bent over to James and told him, "Andres was furious, when he saw Rhen on that jet bike and then hugging Reed. As usual, I went to bed as soon as they sat down to talk, but last night, they had an argument and it woke me up around 1:30. I was just walking out of our bedroom to check on them, when I bumped into Rhen, who was coming in to go to sleep. He told me he asked his father not to visit us at school anymore. Rhen got a chance to sleep. He slept from 1:30 to 4:00. That's more continual sleep than he's had in weeks. Things should start to improve."

"We noticed he was more alert and talkative during fight class this morning," Reed commented. "He even made a few jokes, which he hasn't done in three weeks."

Ceceta nodded her head. "Just a little bit of sleep makes all the difference."

"Believe me, Ceceta," Reed told her. "I have young children. I know all about lack of sleep."

"Keep us informed of his progress," James requested.

"Don't worry," Ceceta told him. "I will."

A few minutes later, the classical piece ended, when one of the student's instruments groaned in protest and shuddered to a stop. Ceceta giggled in response, causing Rhen to burst out laughing. He tried to stop himself, but couldn't, so he rushed from the room hiding his face behind his hands to quiet his laughter. With vehemence, Mr. Orisco banged his walking stick on the stage for silence, but no one paid any attention to him; instead, the students left the cafeteria following in Rhen's footsteps.

Later that morning, Mr. Orisco entered Rhen and Ceceta's classroom to assign the students instruments and hand out class schedules. After he had spoken with the other students in the room, he sauntered over to Rhen and Ceceta. His face looked pinched, as if he'd been sucking on lemons. He was a handsome man, but years of scowling weren't helping his appearance. "Well," he said in his nasal voice. "Have you decided on which instrument you will be playing?" He was planning on denying Rhen the opportunity to play the instrument he wanted, as punishment for this morning's outburst.

"None," Rhen replied, without looking up from his textbook.

"It's the University's new policy," Mr. Orisco informed him. His finger tapping the silver handle of his black cane. "You have to play an instrument!"

"I am Surpen. I do not listen to, nor do I play, music. You can tell the Headmaster that we refuse. I'm sure he will understand."

"No, he won't you baboon. There are no exceptions to this policy. None!"

Rhen, who had been staring at the pictures in his Women in Intrauniversal Politics text book, closed it and stood up. He was almost double the height of Mr. Orisco.

Reed and James were attending Rhen's class that day. They glanced at each other with concern as Rhen stared down at Mr. Orisco.

Suddenly, Rhen cried out, "Uuha, uuhaa, uuha," imitating a baboon, while scratching his head and belly and jumping up and down. He lurched forward towards Mr. Orisco, forcing him to stumble back.

Reed and James watched, as Mr. Orisco's face turned red and his body began to shake with rage. "You are uneducated and unworldly. You are nothing more than a savage!" he yelled. "Music is the pathway to enlightenment. Without it, you will always remain a stupid, base worm. You have just lost the opportunity to learn from the Universe's best music teacher." With that, Mr. Orisco drew himself up to his full height and marched from the room.

After he had walked out the door, most of the students began to laugh. It took the teacher several minutes to get her class to quiet down.

Rhen flopped down onto his seat and leaned over towards Ceceta. "Did you hear he called me unworldly?"

"That was funny."

"Do you think he's ever been off of Thestran?" Rhen asked her.

Ceceta shrugged. "I have no idea."

"Don't you find it odd that most of these students have never been left Thestran?"

"There's no reason for them to leave," James answered from behind them. "By the way, nice animal impersonation!"

"Thanks," Rhen replied. When the teacher was helping a student on the far side of the room, Rhen leaned over towards Reed and James. "You two travel a lot, don't you?"

James smiled. Rhen was talking to him! "Yes," he answered. "We travel for business and on vacation, but we prefer to stay here, it's our home."

"Oh." Rhen was silent for a moment. "I've traveled a lot for someone my age," he added.

"Yes, you have," Reed agreed. "War takes you to many places you wouldn't normally go."

"That's the truth," Rhen replied. He turned back to listen to his teacher.

Later, during lunch, an upbeat classical piece was played on the piano by one of the gifted musical students at the school. Rhen absentmindedly tapped an interesting rhythm to go along with it while he ate. When the girl was finished, she was treated to a round of applause.

A young boy appeared on the stage next, carrying his new trumpet. He blurted out a terrible rendition of a song that everyone knew. Wincing, Rhen covered his ears and put his head under the table. After ten minutes, he couldn't take it anymore. With his head still under the table, Rhen stood up, but he miscalculated how far under the table he was and his head and shoulders lifted the table into the air. Rhen jerked his body backwards and the table slid off him, crashing to the ground and sending plates and glasses to the floor. The trumpet player stopped in the middle of his song and frowned at Rhen.

"Sorry," Rhen apologized with a half-smile. "It was an accident." Turning, he walked out of the room, as fast as he could, to escape. For a heartbeat, the dining hall was silent and then everyone started to laugh, as they also rushed for the exits.

Professor Dewey, who had been attending the performance, grimaced and chased after Rhen. "Rhen! Rhen!" he called out, when he saw him walking towards the Teachers' Residence Hall. Rhen paused by the stairs to the entrance. Professor Dewey ran up to him and stopped. He leaned over panting, as he tried to catch his breath.

"Are you alright?" Rhen asked.

"Yes, sorry. Just needed a moment there. Listen Rhen, you must stay until the end of each performance. Every time you leave, the other students feel they have permission to leave too. It's disrupting things."

The Headmaster watched Rhen's eyes widen. "I...I can't stay," he confessed. "They're just too awful."

"Yes, yes, they are," the Headmaster agreed. "They need practice and we must let them do it. Please, don't leave the dining hall again until they are finished, alright?"

"Yes, sir," Rhen told him with reluctance, as Ceceta and their friends strolled up to join him.

"Thank you, Rhen," the Headmaster replied. He turned to go back to his office. "I knew I could count on you."

After Professor Dewey had left, Rhen turned to Tgfhi. "What am I going to do?" he asked, sounding desperate.

Tgfhi laughed at the look of horror on his 'hero's' face. He could face down blood thirsty armies, but when forced to listen to a poorly trained musician, he fell to pieces. "Hey, you shouldn't be too upset," Tgfhi replied. "Ceceta told me you got out of having to take music lessons from him. You're both very lucky."

"I'll say," Latsoh agreed. "I asked Mr. Orisco if I could play the guitar, but he gave me the oboe."

"He gave me the violin," Erfce told Latsoh with a groan.

"I asked for the drums again and he gave me a kazoo," Tgfhi confessed with a frown.

"What about you Crystam?" Ceceta asked.

"She's the teacher's pet," Latsoh teased, as Crystam looked embarrassed. "She asked for the piano and she got the piano." Erfce and Tgfhi made fun of Crystam, until she slapped out at both of them with her hand. Sometimes it was good to be beautiful.

That evening, Ceceta sat down in the dining room with her friends and various members of the Thestran Royal Family. About ten minutes later, as the students' performances for the evening were about to begin, Lilly asked, "Where's Rhen? Is he skipping dinner?"

"No," Ceceta replied. She glanced about the room. "I don't think so. He went to the bathroom and I thought he'd meet us here."

Just as Professor Orisco was announcing the performers for the evening, Rhen walked into the room wearing the jet bike helmet that Reed had given him the day before. Several students laughed at the sight of him. Without looking up, Rhen sat down at the table across from Ceceta and started to fill his plate with food.

Reed tapped Rhen on the shoulder until Rhen turned to look at him. "Don't you like the students' performances?" Reed asked with innocence. Rhen shook his head. "Does that help?" he asked, pointing at Rhen's helmet. Rhen smiled and nodded his head.

When the first performance began, it was truly awful. Soon everyone wished they were wearing Rhen's helmet. He sat smiling during the entire meal, oblivious to the hell that everyone else was being forced to endure.

Later, when Reed was teaching Rhen how to ride his jet bike, Ceceta and the others sat outside on the school's lawn, laughing at the fact that Rhen had worn his helmet during dinner. They all agreed that it had been a good idea, and they wished they had thought of it first.

Ceceta was surprised, when she saw Kate and Henry walk out of the University building and approach them. Henry would come by once a month to sit with Rhen for a few hours of 'bonding' time, but she'd never seen him here with Kate.

"Hi, Ceceta," Kate called out in greeting. "I heard the students' musical performances today didn't go over very well." Ceceta laughed and everyone started to give them the rundown of the day's events.

"Watching Mr. Orisco and Rhen during our Politics class was the best," Ceceta told them. "It was like having a dog catcher, who's hungry for power, tell a seasoned king that he can do a better job."

"Do you think, if we keep this up, he'll crack and play some music for us?" Kate asked.

"Definitely! It's the best way for you to break through his Surpen hide. Did you find out what the punishment is for breaking the Debrino Code when you play music?"

"Not yet," James told Ceceta. "It's harder than we thought, to get an accurate copy of Debrino's Codes."

"So," Lilly said, changing the subject. "What have you got for us today?" She was ready to learn more about her little brother.

Ceceta sighed. She was tired and didn't want to talk about Rhen. "I don't know, what do you want to know?"

"What's Punishment Island?" Rachel blurted out.

Ceceta turned a pale blue, as her dark eyes grew very large. "No," she whispered, shaking her head. "I can't tell you about it...I...I can't...I...I'm sorry." She lowered her head down onto her bent knees. It appeared as if she were about to cry. Crystam and Latsoh moved over to rub her back and everyone was quiet while she recovered.

"Tell us how Rhen stopped that Zorthan robot," James asked. "None of us could make a dent in it, yet he just looked at it and it fell apart."

Ceceta's friends didn't know what James was talking about, so Lilly filled them in. Ceceta didn't want to tell them the answer to that question, so she played dumb. "I don't know how he stopped it. Do you have any other questions?" She was hoping they would say no.

The Royal Family was getting frustrated with Ceceta, but they were afraid to push her too hard. They needed her on their side. They didn't want to alienate her. "If he can read your mind, can he read ours too?" Sage asked. She wanted to know if his mind reading abilities were limited. He already had healing and phasing powers. It was hard for her to believe that he also had the power to read minds. She assumed it was a limited power.

Ceceta had already given them this information, so she felt safe talking about it. "Yes," she answered. "But he doesn't. Rhen feels it's inappropriate to intrude on people's personal thoughts. If someone asks him to read their mind, he will, but he won't do it without being invited." She beamed with pride adding, "It's very noble of him, don't you think?"

Everyone nodded their heads in agreement, although Charlie looked perturbed. "Well, that's stupid," he blurted out. "If I had the power to read people's minds, I'd never stop. What a gold mine!"

"Then it's a good thing you don't have that power," Lilly commented.

"It's a good thing you don't have any powers at all, you imbecile," William snarled. Charlie retaliated by throwing grass into William's face. William jumped on top of him and the two of them wrestled like children, until Henry told them to stop.

It was quiet after William and Charlie's outburst. Rachel lay down on the ground and stared up at the starry sky. "Most mind readers are oracles too. Is Rhen an oracle?" She wasn't sure why she was asking. Rhen had three powers. For him to have four powers would be…well, crazy.

"Yes," Ceceta told her.

"Hell," James mumbled under his breath. How many powers did Rhen have?

"But," Ceceta continued. "He doesn't use that power. He doesn't like knowing what's going to happen next. He prefers to be surprised. He blocks his power. In fact, he blocks it so well that when other oracles are around him, they find their powers are blocked too."

"I knew it!" Erfce exclaimed. "I knew it was something like that!" Ceceta gave him a confused look. "Sorry Ceceta, but that's the reason why I started hanging out with you guys. I needed peace of mind. I was going crazy before, with everyone's futures assaulting me. Rhen gave me the peace I needed to learn how to keep my powers under control. It's wonderful to be around him. Simply wonderful!"

"I also find peace of mind when Rhen is around," Lilly mentioned. "Rhen must be a very strong oracle, if he's able to block us when we're near him."

Ceceta shrugged and looked off towards the Wood Elf Forest.

"Are you sure he doesn't read our minds?" Charlie asked, sounding worried.

"Yes, Charlie," Ceceta said, rolling her eyes. "He'll only read your mind after he's received permission. Believe me, he really hates doing it." She didn't add the fact that he had been banned by the Genisters and her from reading minds. Charlie's mouth dropped open and Ceceta thought he was going to ask her another question, but he turned away.

"Fascinating," Kate said to herself. Rhen had an enormous amount of power. More than any elf in the Universe and more than most people in the Universe, too.

"You know," James told Ceceta. "He blocks both of your minds from us, so we can't read your thoughts."

Ceceta tilted her head to regard James. "I knew he blocked our minds, but I wasn't sure if you could break through his powers, since you're a part of his family." Her chest tightened, as she realized what she had said.

"That's right!" Lilly cried out. "We're a part of his family. Don't you forget that."

"That's not what I meant," Ceceta told Lilly, but the Thestrans changed the topic, and for the next hour, they discussed a variety of issues from oracle predictions to the disadvantages of being a member of the Convention.

"I want to talk to Rhen about his illiteracy," Kate announced.

"NO!" Ceceta yelled. "You said you'd keep what I'm telling you a secret. You can't bring it up. He feels he's doing fine without those skills, and if you ask him about it, he'll know I told you. He'll consider your interest in the matter to be an insult. It'd be better to just leave the entire subject alone."

"But how is he going to pass his written exams?" Sage asked.

"It's kind of hard to explain. You'll understand when you see him taking his exams," Ceceta told her. A second later, Rhen and Reed broke through the woods on their jet bikes.

The next morning, Rhen forgot to bring his helmet to breakfast. He suffered through a terrible group of singers, who couldn't hold a note to save their lives.

Rhen remembered his helmet for lunch. He sat smiling at his friends, while the rest of the student body squirmed in their seats to the sounds of the Thestran Royal Family anthem being sung by a Nosduh with no ability to speak, let alone sing, in Thestran.

"Take that smug look off your face or I swear I'm going to hide your helmet," Ceceta threatened.

Rhen gave her an innocent grin and continued to eat his meal. Every now and then, they could see his shoulders shake, as he laughed at their agony.

That evening, when Rhen and Ceceta arrived in the dining hall for dinner, they were arguing in Surpen. *"That wasn't nice!"* Rhen snarled at Ceceta, while sitting down with a thud next to Tgfhi and Reed.

"I didn't do it! I swear I didn't do it!" Ceceta protested in Thestran. She sat down across from him, beside Crystam and Latsoh.

"Didn't do what?" Crystam asked.

"I didn't hide his helmet. I threatened I would hide his helmet, but I didn't actually do it," she informed them.

Everyone at the table laughed. "Seriously?" Tgfhi asked his friend. "You can't find your helmet." Rhen growled at him and reached for some meat. "Ahh," Tgfhi sighed. "I hope you enjoy tonight's performance."

A look of fear settled on Rhen's face, as he watched the first performer for the evening walk onto the stage. Fortunately, the young man was an excellent pianist and his performance was quite enjoyable.

"You're going to choke if you keep eating that fast," Erfce warned Rhen.

"He's trying to finish and leave before the next performance," Ceceta explained.

"Good idea," Latsoh said. She dropped her utensils and shoved handfuls of food into her mouth, making them laugh.

"Ahem." A nasal voice said into the microphone. "I have decided to give you a treat this evening and will be playing the next piece personally."

Rhen glanced over to see the pompous Mr. Orisco on stage. He laughed out loud at the thought of Mr. Orisco's performance being a treat then ducked down to hide from view behind Tgfhi. The music teacher glared in his direction, but he couldn't see who had laughed.

"Nice job," Charlie whispered to Rhen from the next table over. "You're finally learning." Rhen gave him a thumbs up sign, but stayed hidden.

Trying to look dignified and regal, Mr. Orisco made his way to the piano. He spent ten minutes placing the music and moving the bench to the 'right' position. After Mr. Orisco was seated, he made a show of stretching his fingers in preparation of playing. When he began his performance, it was mediocre at best. The piece he was playing was supposed to be performed at a steady pace, but Mr. Orisco sped up and slowed down throughout. He also seemed to be having trouble pressing down on some of the keys, when they were supposed to be played. He played without any feeling or understanding for the piece. When he was finished, Mr. Orisco turned to bow. There was a smattering of applause from some of the students, but most of the room was silent.

Ignoring the students' lack of interest, Mr. Orisco announced, "I will now play a piece by a composer most of you should recognize, Wilhelm Adora."

Several students sighed. Everyone knew Wilhelm Adora's music. It was beautiful, sweet and light but complicated to play. There was no way Mr. Orisco could play any of Wilhelm Adora's pieces the way they were meant to be played.

Rhen remembered several of Adora's compositions, from when he was a child. He glanced about the room, hoping to make a getaway, but dropped his head down onto the table in defeat, when he spotted several of the teachers watching him from the doorways. Rhen couldn't believe he was going to have to sit through Mr. Orisco's performance. Glancing over at Charlie, who was sneaking drinks from a flask he had hidden in his jacket, Rhen wished, for the first time, that he could drink. Suddenly, he had a wicked idea.

Mr. Orisco fixed his jacket, cleared his throat and placed his hands above the keyboard. As he lowered them down towards the keys, the piano jumped three feet away from him, making a loud, screeching sound, as the metal tips on the bottom of its legs scratched against the stage's wooden floor.

"What the hell," Reed swore to Rhen's right, a murmur going up among the students.

Mr. Orisco raised an eyebrow, but decided to ignore the incident. He moved his bench back into place, stretched out his fingers with care and started to lower them once more onto the keyboard. Again, there was a burst of noise as the piano jumped backward. Many of the students laughed. Latsoh hid her face behind her napkin, while Tgfhi shoved food into his mouth to try to stop himself from laughing.

Jumping to his feet, Mr. Orisco glared at the students. "Whoever is moving the piano had better stop or you will all receive detention!" he yelled. "Do you hear me! You will all receive detention!"

"What's going on," James asked a teacher by the door. He, Kate, Henry and the Headmaster had arrived late from a meeting they were having. James nodded towards a few of the Elfin Royals, who were sitting in the room on 'Rhen duty'.

"One of the students is moving the piano so Mr. Orisco can't play," the teacher explained.

"Who's doing it?" Professor Dewey asked. He couldn't remember any of the students reporting that they had the power to move objects with their mind.

"I don't know," the teacher said. They watched Mr. Orisco move his bench back into place.

Mr. Orisco sat down and made a show of flexing his fingers. As he started to lower his hands to play, the piano jumped back five feet. "AHHH!" Mr. Orisco shouted with fury, while the students tried not to laugh.

Mr. Orisco marched over to the microphone. He opened his mouth to yell at the students, but nothing came out. His mouth was wide open, and he was gesticulating with his hands, but he was silent. A look of fear passed over his face.

Everyone quieted down, as they watched him struggle.

"What's going on?" Reed asked, rising to his feet. He was going to go to Mr. Orisco's aid, but stopped, when he saw the Headmaster running towards the stage.

Suddenly, the piano began to play. Mr. Orisco's fear about losing his voice morphed into confusion. He turned to stare at the piano, which was playing by itself. The room quieted down, as a magnificent rendition of Wilhelm Adora's Ode to Sunrise filled the dining hall.

"It's perfect," Crystam whispered, with tears in her eyes.

"Yes," Erfce agreed, sounding equally moved. "I've never heard it played that well before."

"Is Kate doing it?" Latsoh asked Reed. He shook his head no and sat down. "Well, who's doing it?" Reed shrugged in answer. He didn't want to talk, he wanted to listen.

Reed glanced at his family and noticed they were all staring in his direction. Turning, he shifted in his seat to watch Rhen. Since none of them could play music with their powers, it had to be Rhen. Lilly's efforts had paid off. After being buried for years, a part of Rhen that belonged to Thestran alone, had been resurrected only two days into the music program.

"Between this and Reed's jet bikes," James whispered to Henry. "We're going to make Rhen Thestran again." Henry smiled and inclined his head in agreement, while listening to the music.

Unaware of the looks he was receiving from the Royals, Rhen remained still. He stared down at his plate, his hands resting on his lap. Ceceta glanced over to smile at him a few times during the piece, but Rhen ignored her. He ignored everyone as he worked Adora's music.

When the last chords were played, the room shook with applause. Kate was so happy she hugged James and Henry. "We did it," she whispered fiercely to them, before laughing with relief.

"You'd never know it was him," James said. He watched Rhen clap along with everyone else. Rhen's eyes were on the piano, and he had a sad, wistful expression on his face.

"Whoever you are, thank you," the Headmaster announced, when he reached the microphone. "That was a beautiful rendition of Wilhelm Adora's music. It was," he paused to shake his head, "beyond comparison." Pointing over at Mr. Orisco, who was still quite furious, Professor Dewey added, "Now, if you would please release Professor Orisco, we can call it a night and no one needs to get detention."

"BASTARDS, ASSHO..." Mr. Orisco yelled, before he caught himself.

"One more thing," the Headmaster added. "If the student, who performed this piece, would like to join the orchestra, I think we would all be very happy to welcome them!" His words brought cheers from the student body.

"Ready to ride?" Reed asked Rhen, when the commotion in the room died down.

"Yes," he agreed, but when they left the dining hall, they discovered it was raining.

"I guess we'll have to postpone," Reed said. "Sorry." He knew Kate and the others would be frustrated that they couldn't talk to Ceceta, but there was nothing they could do about it. "Tomorrow?" Reed asked Rhen.

"Definitely," Rhen agreed.

"If you're not riding your jet bike, you can come with us to the B.A.C. meeting," Ceceta told Rhen, looping her arm through his. Rhen rolled his eyes for show, while walking with her to the University's library.

"HE'S BACK!" Stanley was screaming from the top of the balcony, when they arrived. Tgfhi ran up the stairs to join him. When Ceceta and the others caught up to Tgfhi, he turned towards them beaming. "There have been reports that he saved 35 people yesterday. He's back! The Black Angel is back!" Tgfhi gave a shout of joy and grabbed Crystam up into his arms, swirling her about in a circle, before planting an impromptu kiss on her lips. As Tgfhi lifted his face from Crystam's, he realized what he had done and flushed a deep red.

"I'm sorry," he told her awkwardly, placing her back on her feet. "I guess I was just so excited about the Black Angel's return that…"

"Don't be sorry," Crystam told him. "We're all happy the Black Angel has returned. It's fantastic news." Crystam's lips felt warm and tingly from Tgfhi's kiss and she wanted him to grab her again, but she was too embarrassed by the looks they were getting to initiate another embrace herself. Crystam gave Tgfhi a nod and walked over to take a seat.

"I didn't even know he was missing," Rhen replied, sounding bored. He moved over towards his favorite chair to sleep.

When the B.A.C. meeting was over, Ceceta invited her friends back to her apartment to study. They opened the door to find Charlie emptying out the refrigerator, stacking the food into teetering piles on the counter beside him.

"Hey," he said. He glanced up at them and his blue eyes widened. "What's with the face stuff?" he asked, while pointing at Rhen and Ceceta, who had scarves wrapped around their mouths and noses.

"It's raining out," Latsoh informed Charlie. She pushed past the others and walked into the apartment.

"So," Charlie commented, without understanding.

Rhen and Ceceta walked into their bedroom, unwrapping the scarves from around their faces as they went.

"How can you not know why they're wearing scarves after all this time!" Erfce yelled. "Haven't you seen them wearing scarves before?" Charlie gave Erfce a vacant look and Erfce sighed. "If they swallow rain water, the bloodworms will kill them," he explained.

"Oh," Charlie gasped. "Wow! That's rough."

"Are you done?" Ceceta snapped. She had returned to the kitchen to rescue her food, so it wouldn't fall onto the floor.

"Yes," Charlie replied, giving her a goofy smile. "I was looking for pickles, but you don't have any." He waved good bye and walked out of the apartment without cleaning up after himself.

Tgfhi stared at the mess on the counter and whistled. "Seriously Rhen, are you sure you're not the older brother? He acts like such a baby sometimes."

"I'm sure," Rhen answered. He walked out of his bedroom carrying a small knife. "Knives tonight," he told Tgfhi. He had just started to train Tgfhi on how to handle weapons.

Tgfhi frowned but moved over to join Rhen. He loved learning about weapons, but he hated when they had to fight. Forty minutes later, he plopped down onto the sofa gasping for breath. He was finished with his training for the night and felt exhausted.

As usual, Rhen looked unfazed from the experience. He lay down on the floor next to the coffee table and closed his eyes to 'study'. They had stopped making fun of Rhen for his 'studying', now that they knew he was reading Ceceta's mind to learn his homework.

The next day, Rhen wrapped his face with a scarf to go on his daily run, because it was still raining out. Ceceta shuffled over, wrapped in their white comforter, to give him a hug. "Have fun," she said. The corners of Rhen's eyes crinkled as he smiled. He kissed Ceceta on the top of her head and left.

Ceceta dressed and wrapped herself up with a scarf, before running over to the main school building to meet her students. Entering the room, she shook the water off her scarf, while nodding hello to Crystam and Latsoh. They'd been doing very well with their Surpen. Tgfhi and Erfce, who had recently joined her class, were having mixed results. Since Surpen occupied Tgarus, Tgfhi wasn't having any difficulty in picking up the language. It felt familiar to him. Erfce, on the other hand, couldn't even begin to understand the complexities of Surpen.

At the end of her class, Ceceta pulled a packet of photos out of her school bag. "Now that you all have a good grasp on the Surpen language," she told them, while giving Erfce a wink. "I thought I'd start to focus our lessons on Surpen's culture. I had Orpel send me some photos from our palace, so you could see what life is like on Surpen. Most of the pictures are of our country, but a few of them are of Rhen and his men." Ceceta handed the photos to Crystam. "We've run out of time for today, so you guys should review them tonight. Rhen and I will be late for study group tonight. When we return, we'll answer any questions you have about Surpen."

"Return?" Latsoh asked. "Where're you going?"

"Oh, Andres has asked us to eat dinner with him tonight. We're going home for dinner, but we'll be back tonight. I promise."

"Sorry," Erfce sympathized.

"Me too," Ceceta confessed. "Don't tell Rhen. I'll see you at breakfast," she said, walking off to meet Rhen for Surpen prayers.

Later that night, in Rhen and Ceceta's apartment, Crystam tossed the photos to Latsoh and moaned, "They have the most beautiful clothing ever!"

Latsoh picked up the pile of pictures and started to flip through them. "You see," Crystam remarked. She pointed at the photo in Latsoh's hands. "Even their merchants in the marketplace wear gorgeous tunics and robes."

"Yeah," Latsoh agreed. She leaned back on Rhen and Ceceta's couch to get more comfortable. "We look terrible compared to them."

"We sure do," Crystam added. She pulled a few of the pictures out of Latsoh's hands and laid them out on the coffee table. "They use so many beautiful, vibrant colors in their clothing."

"And the elaborate designs on the men's tunics are amazing!" Latsoh commented, picking up a new picture from the top of the coffee table.

"And the men's jewelry...it's incredible!" Crystam threw out. Latsoh nodded her head in agreement.

"Did you guys see this one of Rhen?" Tgfhi asked, holding up one of the photos.

In the picture, Rhen appeared to be struggling against a large Dristar Beast, which seemed to have wandered down a city street. Everyone on the sidewalk around Rhen appeared to be frightened, but he was laughing. Dristar Beasts were a cross between Thestran cows and Zorthan Rhinoceroses. They were large and black, had thick skin and three horns. "I thought Dristar Beasts were mean and stupid," Tgfhi added, lifting the picture closer to his face to study it. "Why would Rhen risk his life by wrestling with this animal alone?"

"Yeah," Erfce agreed. "Why wasn't anyone helping him?"

"Maybe there were other people helping him, but you can't see them in the photo?" Crystam offered. She held out her hand for the picture. Tgfhi handed it over to her and reached down to pick up another one.

"I like the one of Rhen wearing his dress uniform and riding the Surpen Beast of War," Erfce told them. "You know, the picture with him sitting on top of a rearing Surpen Beast of War, while holding his swords up in the air above his head and smiling with triumph? It looks like it was taken after he'd just returned from a successful battle."

"That's the first time I've ever seen a Surpen Beast of War," Latsoh admitted. Erfce nodded in agreement.

"Oh, they're scary," Tgfhi told them. "The Surpens brought them to Tgarus."

"They look like dragons only smaller," Crystam commented.

"Yeah," Tgfhi agreed. "I think they're similar to dragons. Their snouts are rounder though and their teeth are smaller, but just as sharp. I think their tails are longer than a dragon's, compared to their body mass."

"Do they come in different colors?" Erfce asked.

"No, they only come in tan, but the black spots are different on each beast. It helps you to tell them apart."

"Can those tiny wings really carry them?" Latsoh asked Tgfhi.

"Yes. They fly all over the place. And they land in a run, so watch out if you don't have enough space. They're amazingly quick and agile in flight. You'd never think it just to look at them."

"I like this one of Rhen laughing and falling into these Surpen Generals. They look so happy," Latsoh commented. She held up the photo for the others to see.

"Do you think they caught him?" Erfce asked.

"He'd kill them if they didn't," Tgfhi told them. Crystam smacked Tgfhi on the arm and he laughed.

Latsoh turned the photo around to look at it again. Rhen was laughing and falling backwards, his left foot was lifted high in the air and his right foot was just coming off the ground, as the soldiers behind him, who were also laughing, appeared to be lunging forward to catch him. She smiled at the joy that was so apparent in the photo. "I like the..." Latsoh paused. Something about Rhen's left boot made her hesitate. For months now, she had been working for the Black Angel Club. Twice a week, she would sit for hours, staring at photos of the Black Angel's clothing, looking for clues. A shiver ran down Latsoh's spine, as she bent her head closer to the picture to examine Rhen's boots. "Tgfhi, do you have a picture of the Black Angel that I can look at?" She was surprised by how calm her voice sounded.

"I always have pictures of the Black Angel," he sassed, while removing a folder from his bag. Tgfhi pulled out a few photos and handed them to Latsoh. She flipped through them, until she located the one she wanted. In the picture, the Black Angel was flipping over backwards to save a child from being killed by a stray laser blast. It was a very clear shot of the Angel's boots.

"OH, MY GOD!" Latsoh screamed. "LOOK! The Black Angel wears Surpen military boots! We did it! We found another clue to the Black Angel's identity!"

Lunging forward, Tgfhi snatched the photos from Latsoh's hands and laid them down on the coffee table to compare them. Sure enough, the boots looked almost identical. Erfce and Crystam waited for Tgfhi to give his verdict, before congratulating Latsoh. "No," he finally said, shaking his head. "No, the Black Angel's boots are similar to a Surpen's boots, but they're not the same."

"You're wrong Tgfhi," Latsoh growled. She grabbed the photos. "They're the same, except the back heel of the Black Angel's right boot has a small tear in it and there's also a red mark down the side of his left boot." Latsoh tossed the photos onto Tgfhi's lap. "I'll prove it to you. Rhen must have a pair of old military boots in his closet. Once I get them, you'll see they're the same. The Black Angel probably spilled something on his left boot and he's torn the heel of his right boot from use, that's all."

"Latsoh," Tgfhi called after her, as she walked away from the sofa. "Don't bother. They aren't the same."

Latsoh stuck her tongue out at Tgfhi, before marching into Ceceta and Rhen's bedroom. She opened their closet and stepped inside, turning on the light. Some old, military boots had been kicked into the back corner of the closet. "Perfect," she said, swopping down to pick them up. Latsoh turned off the light and stepped out into Rhen and Ceceta's bedroom. As she moved into the brighter light of the bedroom, she paused to look at the boots in her hands. The left boot had a red mark down the side of it and the right boot was torn at the back of its heel.

Stopping dead in her tracks, Latsoh felt confused. Why would Rhen have copies of the Black Angel's boots? Hesitantly, she took a step forward then stopped. Her head felt light, and she was having trouble thinking. Latsoh stared at the boots, her throat growing tight. These weren't copies of the Black Angel's boots, these were the Black Angel's boots. But, why would Rhen have them? Taking another hesitant step forward, Latsoh stopped again, her mind swirled, grasping at facts. "Oh, Themrock," she breathed out. A prickling sensation raced across her scalp. It all made sense now. Rhen refused to tell them his powers. He already had more powers than any elf in the Universe. Those weeks, when his father had kept him from sleeping, Rhen was too tired to function and the Black Angel had disappeared. Now he was sleeping again and the Black Angel was back. Rhen had the Angel's boots, because Rhen was the Angel. How could they have been so stupid as to not realize it before? The reality of it all crashed down upon Latsoh. Her eyes fluttered and she collapsed to the floor with a thud.

"What was that?" Erfce asked, rising from the couch. "Latsoh?" When she didn't answer, Erfce rushed into the bedroom to see what was wrong. "Latsoh! Latsoh!" he cried out, when he saw her lying on the ground. Erfce dropped to his knees beside Latsoh and picked her up in his arms.

"I'll get some water," Crystam told him, while running towards the bathroom. She came back a moment later with a wet washcloth that she used to dab around Latsoh's ashen face. "What happened?"

"I don't know," Erfce said, sounding worried. "Should we take her to the doctor?"

"No," Latsoh replied. She reached her hand up to her head and pushed her long red hair away from her face. "I can't believe it?" she whispered. "Can you? It's just so beautiful, yet bizarre at the same time."

"What? What are you talking about?" Erfce asked, his eyes full of concern.

Without warning, Latsoh burst into hysterical laughter. She pushed against Erfce's chest and reached out for the boots that had fallen to the floor. Picking them up, she cradled them to her body, as she cried and laughed at the same time.

"What's wrong with her?" Tgfhi asked the others.

"I don't know?" Erfce replied. He reached out to take the boots from Latsoh, but she jerked them away from him.

"Latsoh, what are you doing?" Crystam asked. She was beginning to feel afraid. "You went to look for some of Rhen's old boots to compare them to the Black Angel's? Why are you acting like this?"

"Compare them to the Black Angel's," Latsoh repeated, with a hiccupping laugh. "I don't need to compare them to the Black Angel's!" She pulled Rhen's boots in closer to her body and bent her head down, to rub her cheek against the side of them.

"Whoa!" Tgfhi said, taking a step back. "That's a little weird." He looked at Erfce. "Do elves ever go crazy suddenly?"

"NO!" Crystam retorted. She couldn't believe Tgfhi was joking at a time like this. It was clear that Latsoh was in trouble. "Latsoh, what's going on?" she begged.

Lifting her face, Latsoh gave them a dreamy smile. She took a deep, shuddering breath and said, "Crystam, I don't need to compare them to the Black Angel's boots, because these are the Black Angel's boots. Rhen is the Black Angel."

The others were silent for a moment and then Tgfhi jumped forward and grabbed the boots out of Latsoh's arms. Lifting them into the air, he studied them. The left boot had the identical red mark down its side as the Black Angel's left boot and the right boot had the same tear at the back of its heel that the Black Angel's right boot had. These were the Black Angel's boots. Tgfhi handed the boots to Erfce and Crystam, who snatched them up with excitement to examine them.

"Why would Rhen have the Black Angel's boots?" Tgfhi asked the room.

"Think about it Tgfhi," Latsoh told him. "He doesn't just have the Black Angel's boots. He is the Black Angel. It all makes sense. Everything was right before our eyes. We were blind! It's so obvious now."

Tgfhi shook his head, refusing to accept what Latsoh was telling him. He walked over to Rhen's closet, opened the door and flicked on the light. "If Rhen's the Black Angel, he would have more than just his boots." Reaching into the closet, Tgfhi started flipping through the clothes that were hanging in front of him. He couldn't believe Rhen was the Black Angel, and he felt satisfied, when he didn't find any of the Black Angel's clothes. "He's not the Black Angel. He doesn't have any other Black Angel clothing," Tgfhi told the others, turning to switch off the closet light. As he put out his hand to flip the switch, he noticed a pile of black clothing thrown carelessly on the floor in the front, left corner of the closet. Bending down, Tgfhi reached out to pick up one of the items on the floor.

"What're you doing," Crystam asked.

Tgfhi didn't answer. He turned towards the room. In his hands, he held the famous long-sleeved shirt that the Black Angel wore. It even had the slight fray at the edge of its left sleeve. "By God," he whispered, as he showed it to them.

Erfce brushed past Tgfhi and grabbed the pile of clothing off the floor. He moved it over to the bed and started laying out each item.

"Do you believe me now?" Latsoh asked, with a triumphant smile. She didn't need an answer. It was obvious he did.

Tears streamed down Tgfhi's face, his nose was clogged, and he was having trouble breathing. Crystam went over to him to give him a hug. He pulled her into his body and bent his head down to cry on her shoulder.

"Where did you find those?" Latsoh asked Erfce, while walking over to the bed.

"Thrown carelessly on the floor of the closet."

"No one would throw the Black Angel's clothes carelessly on the floor," Latsoh commented. "Unless…"

"They were the Black Angel," Erfce finished for her. He turned around so everyone could see that he was holding up the Black Angel's Genister cape. "I'm holding a Genister cape!" He laughed and raised it higher, the black folds of fabric swung in the air in front of him. "A Genister cape," he repeated with wonder.

"Come," Crystam told Tgfhi, pulling him towards the bed. Together they joined Latsoh and Erfce, as they picked through the Black Angel's clothes. Tgfhi lifted the scarf the Black Angel wore to cover his face and head. The Black Angel's gloves had been wrapped up into it. They fell onto the floor by his feet. Bending down, Tgfhi picked up the gloves. He rubbed the black leather between his fingers. They were softer than he had thought they would be and there was a small stain on the back of the left glove. "I wonder where he got that stain."

"Do you think he used those gloves in the military, before he became the Black Angel? Could they be blood stains left over from one of his wars?" Erfce asked. Tgfhi shrugged and placed them down on the bed.

"So, how do I look?" Latsoh asked, tossing her hair over her shoulders. "Do I look like the Black Angel?" She turned around wearing the Black Angel's sunglasses and lifted her chin in the air.

"Oh, Themrock!" Crystam exclaimed, as the reality of what they had just discovered finally hit her. "Oh, dear Themrock!" Her whole body was shaking.

"What's wrong," Tgfhi asked. He pulled Crystam into his arms to try to comfort her.

"Don't you know what this means!" she yelled, her body still shaking. "If Rhen is the Black Angel, he has more power than anyone else in the Universe. He can fly, breathe underwater, make the ground move, catch lightning bolts, disappear, phase...you name it. No wonder the oracles are saying he'll conquer all of us. It's because he can. It'd be easy for him!"

"Wow," Tgfhi breathed out. "You're right. Nobody can defeat him."

Erfce put the Genister cape he was holding onto the bed. "It's funny, when you think about it," he commented. "Rhen's the one person in the Universe that no one would ever suspect of being the Black Angel, and yet he is. Everyone is waiting for him to turn into the Surpen God of War and destroy all of us, but in secret, he's been spending his time trying to save us."

"Ironic," Latsoh said in agreement.

"All those times they attended the B.A.C. meetings. They never said a word," Tgfhi added in a daze. "Rhen would just fall asleep in the corner, as we discussed what he had done the night before." He laughed, envisioning Rhen sacked out on his favorite chair in the back of the balcony, while they worked to discover his identity.

Tgfhi picked up the Genister cape to look at it. "I can't believe it. I mean, I know it's true. These are the Black Angel's clothes, but still, I can't believe that Rhen, Rhen of all people, is the Black Angel."

"Oh, Themrock!" Crystam said again.

"Is it possible that Rhen knows the Black Angel, and he keeps his clothes for him?" Erfce asked the others.

"No," Latsoh told him. "Think about it. Most people have how many powers?"

"One," Erfce replied.

"Right," Latsoh agreed. "Yet every day, we discover that Rhen has a new power. There doesn't seem to be a limit to what he can do. He must be the Black Angel."

"Rhen, who told us when we first met him that he didn't have any powers worth mentioning," Crystam remarked with a laugh.

"I guess he lied," Latsoh said. She took off the Black Angel's sunglasses and put them back into the pocket of the Black Angel's coat, where she had found them. "I guess this also means that the Black Angel isn't a Genister," she added. Erfce was gathering up the clothes on the bed to put them back into Rhen and Ceceta's closet.

"I guess not," Tgfhi agreed. He reached out to take the clothes from Erfce. He wanted to be the one to put them back in the closet. When he was finished, Latsoh tossed Rhen's boots into the closet, where she had found them.

"So," Latsoh said, while closing the closet door. They walked back into the living room. "No one in the Universe, except for us, knows that Rhen is the Black Angel!"

"Ceceta knows," Crystam corrected her, as she sat down.

"That she does," Tgfhi agreed.

"His powers...they're mind boggling," Erfce remarked. He leaned back against the old, blue couch and ran his hand through his medium-length, brown hair. "Even though Rhen isn't a Genister, he has powers that are just as strong as the Genisters' were rumored to be." The others nodded their heads in agreement.

After a few minutes of silence, Latsoh brought up the subject they needed to discuss. "So, what do we do now?"

"We must tell the Thestran Royal Family," Erfce insisted.

"No!" Tgfhi barked. He was proud of the fact that Rhen, his Prince, was the most powerful man in the Universe. One day, Rhen would be his King. For the second time in his life, Tgfhi loved the fact that Surpen ruled his planet. To think that Rhen, his friend, his Prince, was the Black Angel! It made him feel honored.

"We need to tell the Thestran Royal Family," Latsoh concurred with Erfce. "Rhen is supposed to turn into the Surpen God of War. The Royal Family needs to be made aware of the fact that they're dealing with someone who has powers that are greater than all of theirs combined."

"No," Tgfhi insisted. "We can't tell them. Rhen is our friend. It's important to him that his work as the Black Angel be kept a secret. We should respect that. Rhen will tell everyone, when he wants them to know."

"No, Tgfhi," Crystam replied. "If he turns into the Surpen God of War, we'll all be in danger. We need to warn the Thestrans about his abilities."

"He won't turn into the Surpen God of War," Tgfhi assured them.

"Yes, he will," Erfce retorted. "I've watched him turn into the Surpen God of War in my dreams for weeks now. The predictions are true. He will become this beast and he will conquer the Universe."

"You heard Ceceta," Tgfhi told them. "He's already called the God of War. Do you think that Rhen is evil?" Tgfhi paused for a moment to stare at each of them. They shook their heads. "Exactly, so even if his body should change into that...that animal thing, he'll still be Rhen underneath. Rhen is a good person. We need to respect our friendship with him and keep this quiet."

"No," Latsoh snapped. "It's too dangerous not to tell the Thestran Royal Family! Tgfhi, we're talking about saving the Universe."

"Latsoh," Tgfhi replied. He turned to look her in the eyes. "This entire conversation rests upon what type of person you believe Rhen is underneath his Surpen façade. I say he's a good person. How could he not be? He's the god-damned Black Angel! Would an evil person spend his evenings saving people? NO!"

"Why is he saving people?" Crystam asked.

"I don't know, but I'm sure we'll find out eventually," Tgfhi remarked.

"Perhaps because of guilt," Erfce ventured. "He may feel guilty about killing so many people. He could have invented the Black Angel to make himself feel better."

"He did tell us once that God gave us great powers and with those powers came 'great responsibilities'," Crystam said quoting Rhen.

"Exactly," Tgfhi replied. "And our responsibility is to Rhen. He's a good person. We need to respect that. He should be able to count on us, as we have come to count on him as the Black Angel. We must keep his secret. We can't tell the Thestran Royal Family."

"You want us to keep his secret, possibly jeopardizing the entire Universe's safety, because you think he won't turn into the Surpen God of War?" Erfce asked Tgfhi.

"No," Tgfhi told him. "I want you to keep his secret, possibly jeopardizing the entire Universe's safety, because I know that when the moment comes and he has to decide whether or not to kill us, his good side will prevail and he will do the right thing. We know Rhen's personality better than anyone else. We know he's a decent person. He has a good heart. We need to have faith in him. We need to trust him and to offer him our silence. He will not destroy the Universe. His personality won't let him."

Everyone was quiet. Tgfhi's words rang true. They agreed. Rhen was their best friend. They owed it to him to keep his secret. They wouldn't tell the Thestran Royal Family about his powers, nor would they tell Rhen or Ceceta that they had discovered their secret. They would act as if nothing had changed. If he wished it, Rhen's secret would remain a secret forever.

They sat talking to each other about the Black Angel and Rhen, until they heard the front door to the apartment open.

Rhen and Ceceta strolled into the room discussing something in Surpen. They were speaking so rapidly that neither Crystam nor Latsoh couldn't understand their words.

"Hi," Ceceta called out to them, as she joined them. "Sorry. We're much later than I thought we were going to be." Rhen nodded to everyone in greeting, before walking into his bedroom to take off his armor. His friends sat on the couch staring at him. Ceceta noticed their intense interest in Rhen and called them on it. "Okay," she asked, while looking at their faces, which were turned towards her bedroom. "What's going on?"

"Oh, nothing," Crystam said, feeling flustered. "We were just looking at these photos and um…" She didn't know what to say.

Erfce reached over for the picture of Rhen fighting the Dristar Beast. "When we came upon this photo, it kind of freaked us out," he confessed. He handed Ceceta the picture. "We can't believe Rhen is still alive. Why didn't the Dristar Beast kill him?"

"Oh, yeah," Ceceta commented, taking the photo. "I forgot that picture was in there. It would freak you out." Rhen walked back into the living room wearing a simple green tunic. As he bent down over Ceceta's shoulder to look at the picture in her hand, everyone stared at him. They couldn't help themselves. They couldn't take their eyes off of him. The Black Angel was Rhen. The Black Angel was standing right in front of them. Ceceta reached up to stroke Rhen's cheek. He turned his head, gave her a kiss and walked over to sit down on the ground next to the coffee table.

Ceceta handed the photo back to Erfce. "To tell you the truth Erfce, Rhen didn't have any trouble with that Dristar Beast. My husband has a way with animals."

"No kidding!" Latsoh laughed out. She was remembering a time when the Black Angel had communicated with a herd of vicious Yuris. The Yuris had been terrorizing a town and the Black Angel had somehow told them to leave.

"What do you mean, 'no kidding'?" Rhen asked.

"Oh," Latsoh replied, her face blushing. "I was thinking of the time when Charlie gave his horse some Tgarus weed and it freaked out. You did something to calm the horse down and saved its life. Remember?" Rhen nodded. He remembered that incident. Charlie had done some stupid things while at the University, but that had to have been one of his dumbest moves.

Rhen leaned over the coffee table to look at the pictures. He smiled at some of the photos, as Ceceta held up a few of them to explain to the others what life was like on Surpen. While Ceceta was talking, everyone continued to stare at Rhen. They realized their big decision to keep Rhen's secret a secret was going to fail, if they couldn't relax around him. They needed to treat Rhen like they had before they had found out. Ceceta was oblivious to what was going on.

When Rhen was finished looking at the pictures, he glanced over at Ceceta. Realizing she was in her teacher mode, he lay down on the ground and closed his eyes. The others continued to stare at him in amazement. When Ceceta concluded her lecture, she tossed the picture, she was holding, back onto the coffee table.

They sat in silence, with their thoughts, for a couple of minutes.

"So, Rhen," Latsoh sneered, jolting everyone back into the present moment. She studied Rhen, as he lay on the floor in front of her with his eyes closed. "What are you studying now? Politics? Astronomy?"

Latsoh's teasing words broke the tension that Erfce, Tgfhi and Crystam had been feeling. Somehow, she had put everything back into perspective. Rhen was their friend, a normal guy with, well, with super, abnormal powers.

"No," Rhen replied, keeping his eyes closed. "This time, I'm actually tired."

Latsoh laughed. "Well, you could've fooled me. The way you look when you're tired and the way you look when you study are the same." She stood up. "I'm going to bed," she informed them, brushing past Ceceta. "Good night everyone!"

As Latsoh stepped past the coffee table, Rhen kicked out at her in retaliation, but his boot missed her leg by inches.

"And you're the amazing fighting teacher that everyone's talking about?" Latsoh sassed, making everyone laugh.

"I'll walk you home," Erfce said. He jumped off the couch to follow her.

"When will that boy ask that girl out?" Crystam grumbled, after they had left.

Ceceta and Rhen chuckled. The same thing could be said about Tgfhi, who was busy getting himself a drink in the kitchen.

"I guess Latsoh's right," Crystam told them. "It is late. Do you mind if we take off too?"

"No," Ceceta replied. "I'm sorry it took us so long to return. The King had a lot to say to Rhen, since his birthday is coming up soon. Andres is worried, because Surpen Princes always kill their fathers, after they come of age."

In the kitchen, Tgfhi choked on the water he was drinking. "What?!" he yelled, wiping at his mouth with his hand. "Some of your Surpen traditions are just too bizarre!"

"I'm not killing my father," Rhen replied with fatigue.

Ceceta began to gather the pictures. "Rhen told Andres that several times tonight. It seems to be the one Thestran trait of Rhen's that Andres doesn't mind keeping."

Tgfhi and Crystam shook their heads at the irony and gathered their books to leave.

After they had gone, Ceceta walked into her bedroom and flopped down on the bed. She was exhausted. All night long, she had to keep reminding herself to be silent and passive. It took a lot of energy to be submissive. A few moments later, she felt the bed move, as Rhen climbed up on top of her. Ceceta willed herself to keep her eyes closed. She could tell that Rhen was studying her face. Ceceta smiled, when she felt his soft lips brush against hers. Rhen lowered his body onto hers and she breathed out.

"You don't have time. You're public awaits," Ceceta told him, trying to sound as tired as she felt.

"I always have time," Rhen whispered, kissing her throat.

"Rhen, go do your business as the Black Angel. If you miss a night, the students will be grumpy and we'll have a horrible day," Ceceta instructed him. She pushed against his broad chest.

"You have to take care of something for me first," Rhen murmured, pulling on her robes. Ceceta giggled, when his fingers brushed against her inner thigh.

When Rhen unclasped her bra, Ceceta protested again. "No, Rhen! You'll fall asleep and then everyone, especially Tgfhi, will be crabby tomorrow because the Black Angel has disappeared again. We'll have to spend the entire B.A.C. meeting tomorrow night praying for your return."

"I could rescue a few people in the morning," Rhen offered. He kissed her belly and moved up towards her chest.

"No!" Ceceta barked, rolling off the bed.

Rhen lay on the empty bed looking defeated. "Tell me why I do this again?"

"Because it's the right thing to do."

"Ugh, I hate having to do the right thing all time," Rhen complained. With effort, he got up to put on his Black Angel clothes. As he put the sunglasses on his face, he said, "Hey, I was thinking it might be fun to poke my head into a B.A.C. meeting one night." He laughed, thinking about the reactions the students would have if the Black Angel showed up to one of their meetings.

Ceceta laughed as well. "Maybe next semester, my love. I won't make you attend their meetings next semester. That way you can easily pop your head into one of them." Rhen nodded in agreement and bent over to kiss her good bye.

"Love," Ceceta added, "if you're not too late in coming back, wake me up." She winked.

"I'll be home early tonight!" Rhen assured her, before turning invisible and flying out of the room.

Chapter 22

To the Thestran Royal Family's despair, it had been raining for days. Not only had Rhen and Reed not been able to bond over their jet bikes, but they hadn't gotten any more information out of Ceceta. The Thestrans were dying to know how Rhen had used his powers to play the piano and they were growing concerned that they were running out of time. In addition, for the last few nights, Rhen and Ceceta had been disappearing for about fifteen minutes each evening after dinner, and nobody could figure out where they were going.

Tgfhi, though, was determined to follow them. He laid a trap, cornering Rhen and Ceceta on the stairwell, right after they had given the Royal Family the slip. "Okay," he said, his hands on his hips. "What's going on?"

Ceceta glanced around to make sure no one was nearby. "If you can keep a secret, you can come with us," she told him.

"Of course!" Tgfhi reassured them. Rhen put his arm around Tgfhi's shoulders to lead him down the stairs.

"I have to tell Crystam," Tgfhi exclaimed, pulling back. "You know?" Rhen hesitated but nodded his consent, so Tgfhi contacted Crystam. She met up with them in the school's basement, along with Latsoh and Erfce. The group walked down the cool, concrete hallway until Ceceta paused outside a storage-room door. She pushed the black door open and flicked on the florescent lights, as her friends followed her in. Once the room was lit, they saw it contained hundreds of musical instruments stored in black and brown cases. Rhen closed the door behind them and locked it.

"Now I feel like I'm in a horror movie," Latsoh mumbled, in the ensuing silence. "Any minute now, one of you will start killing us." Ceceta laughed and pretended to knife Latsoh, as she shrieked in response.

When they had quieted down, Erfce asked. "So? What gives?"

Ceceta pointed at Rhen. "He gives."

Everyone looked at Rhen with expectation. "I have one power that I'll share with you now," he confessed.

"Oh," Latsoh inquired, in a teasing voice. "Is it something worth mentioning?"

"You can decide," he told her with a dismissive wave. Out of the blue, the instrument cases opened of their own accord and the instruments lifted out of them into the air. They floated six feet above the ground for a moment, before coming to life, playing an upbeat, danceable tune.

"That was amazing!" Erfce exclaimed, when the song ended. "How'd you do that?"

"That's one of my powers," Rhen replied, with a modest shrug.

"What a wonderful power!" Crystam laughed out with delight.

"You're the person who screwed with Professor Orisco!" Tgfhi shouted. He jumped forward and grabbed Rhen in a big hug, shaking him about.

Rhen laughed, as Tgfhi shook him around playfully. "Yes," he admitted. "That was me."

"Wow!" Latsoh said. She shook her head. "That's an amazing power. I wish I had it."

Tgfhi released Rhen then reached out to tap him on the top of his head, the way Rhen used to pat him, when he was little. "Thanks for screwing with Orisco! You're definitely my hero now."

"Please, please, please play another song," Latsoh begged.

"Okay. If you want me to."

"Only if you sing for us as well," Ceceta threw out. "I love the sound of your voice." Rhen winked at her, as a new song burst out of the instruments. When Rhen opened his mouth to sing, his friends forgot to breath. His voice was amazing. The song he invented was ideal, fitting the melody to perfection. When Rhen was finished, everyone sat in silence.

"Did you really just think that up?" Crystam asked. "It was incredibly poetic and beautiful."

"Yeah," Rhen told her. "I have this like…problem. Songs are always playing in my head. It can actually be kind of annoying at times, especially in battle, when a happy song starts to ring out in my brain, as I try to conquer someone's planet." He shook his head, adding, "That's when it's a real problem."

"I can't even imagine," Erfce whispered.

"Will you play another song for us?" Latsoh asked.

"One more," Ceceta told her, holding up a finger. "Then we have to return. We can't be gone too long or someone will figure out what we're doing. As you know, it's against the Debrino Code for Rhen to be making music, and I don't want the Surpen King to find out."

"What happens to you, if you break the Code by playing music?" Crystam asked.

"We don't actually know," Ceceta told Crystam. "When Rhen was young, he played his flute in the Surpen Castle and Andres took it from him. He told us it was against the law to make music and…well, we weren't in a position to question him about it at the time. Rhen's never played since."

"You mean to tell us," Erfce said, his eyes on Rhen. "That you have this amazing power you've kept bottled up and hidden away your whole life? You haven't made music until now?"

"Right. I'm the Prince of Surpen. I shouldn't be breaking our laws. It's not right."

Erfce put his head in his hands in dismay.

"But, it is okay to do it now my love," Ceceta reassured Rhen. She didn't want him to stop just yet. "We're on Thestran in a private, locked room. No one here will tell Andres what you're doing. How about one more song for tonight and then we'll go?"

After a brief pause, Rhen nodded. "Only if you sing harmony with me."

"How would we be able to do that?" Tgfhi asked.

Ceceta laughed and clapped her hands with delight. "Yes, please!" She turned to the others. "Just wait, you're going to love this."

A moment later, they heard the instruments begin a new song, then, unexpectedly, they felt a presence in their bodies, as Rhen somehow manipulated them, so they were singing with him. They sang accompaniment throughout the song, until Rhen finished. As the last notes rang out, the six of them burst into laughter.

"Themrock!" Latsoh exclaimed breathlessly. "That was amazing!"

"Indeed," Erfce agreed. He gripped his sides. They hurt from laughing so hard.

"You have to let us do that again with you tomorrow," Crystam begged.

"Of course, we will," Ceceta told her. "We'll do it every night until the rain stops."

"Woo hoo!" Tgfhi belted out with glee. "I can't wait."

They headed upstairs to the B.A.C. meeting, where Rhen plopped down into his usual chair to sleep, while Tgfhi and the others pretended to be interested in Stanley's latest guesses at the identity of the Black Angel. Leaning over to Crystam, Tgfhi whispered, "I thought I'd find this meeting boring, but it's actually funny." Crystam nodded in agreement, as Stanley insisted that the Black Angel came from the planet of Sastar.

After the B.A.C. meeting, they headed back to Ceceta's apartment to study. When they reached the landing that led to the apartment door, they saw Charlie walk out of the apartment. "Hey, guys! See you later," he called out, strolling past them down the stairs towards the exit.

They entered the apartment to find the refrigerator door wide open and bits of food on the kitchen counters and floor. There was a terrible smell wafting out of the toaster oven as well as from the bathroom. "Nasty," Rhen commented, walking over to open the apartment's windows.

"Maybe we should ban Charlie from using our place," Ceceta suggested to Rhen. She picked up a broom to clean the floor. She didn't want to leave it this way overnight. The servants only cleaned their apartment in the morning, while they were at breakfast.

"Whatever you want to do with Charlie is fine with me," Rhen told her. He sat down on the floor by the coffee table and closed his eyes to 'study'. He knew Ceceta felt sorry for Charlie. She wasn't going to kick him out of his 'home base'.

The next morning, after days of rain, everyone was relieved to wake up to a beautiful, cloudless sky. The warm sun beat down on Thestran, drying out the grass and making everything shine. Reed's jet bike races were scheduled for later that morning, which thrilled the students, because there was always a big party afterwards in the Wood Elf Castle.

Latsoh and Crystam decided to join Ceceta and Rhen for their morning prayers, as an excuse to get outside. Even though neither of them believed in Rhen's God, they still enjoyed listening to Rhen and Ceceta chant. The sound of their voices was soothing and they both found it to be a very pleasant and peaceful way to begin their day.

As usual, when the weather was nice, they prayed down by the lake, facing the rising sun. Rhen always sat in front of the women on his knees, holding his many prayer beads in his hands. Ceceta would sit behind him on her knees, with her hands in her lap, and Crystam and Latsoh would sit behind her. The sound of the water, the birds' morning calls and the quiet, gentle chanting was more peaceful than usual this morning, after so many days indoors.

Towards the end of their prayers, a man, dressed in Surpen military clothing, walked silently through their little group. He stopped to stand beside Rhen. His presence startled Crystam and Latsoh. They looked up at him, wondering why he wasn't saying his morning prayers. The soldier waited beside Rhen, while Rhen chanted with his eyes closed.

The man looked familiar to Crystam and Latsoh. They assumed they had seen his face before in the photographs that Ceceta had loaned to them. He was older than Rhen, and he had a scar across his face. His nose was small and his grey eyes were rather tiny and close together. Something stirred to their right. Crystam and Latsoh turned to find ten more Surpen soldiers surrounding them. It was then that they realized this wasn't a social call.

A large soldier, who looked freaky, because he was so muscular, walked up to join the first man, positioning himself on the opposite side of Rhen. Crystam and Latsoh realized they needed to warn Rhen. Latsoh let out a loud cough and Ceceta, who was bowing down like Rhen, opened one eye to chastise her. As soon as Latsoh had Ceceta's attention, she jerked her head towards Rhen. Ceceta turned just enough to see what Latsoh was indicating. She gasped, when she saw the Surpen soldiers.

Although Rhen didn't move or change the rhythm of his chant, Ceceta knew her gasp was enough to alert him. A few more minutes passed, before Rhen brought his prayers to an end, by lifting his beads up into the air and placing them on his lap. The minute his beads touched his thighs, Rhen jumped forward, throwing his body into the lake. The two soldiers, standing beside him, had been expecting this. They lunged forward, grabbing Rhen's legs. The men struggled against Rhen, trying to pull him back towards the shore, while he thrashed about, sending mud, rocks and water flying.

Ceceta screamed at the top of her lungs, as the King's guards seized her, Latsoh and Crystam.

"Now, now, boy, why fight it!" the man with the scar on his face yelled, while he fought to hold on to Rhen. In desperation, Rhen splashed both men in the face with a large amount of water. They released him to wipe at their faces, before they swallowed any of it.

The University's grounds, which were peaceful in the morning, filled with teachers and students, who had come to help, after hearing screaming. Reed, who had been nearby in the forest, previewing some of the paths that were going to be used in today's races, ran out of the woods onto the University's lawn to see what was wrong.

Earlier, Charlie, who had been drinking his morning cocktail on the balcony of his dorm room, when he had seen Aul, Narseth and nine of the Surpen King's guards walking down the hill towards Rhen, had run to get James. The

Thestran Royal Family was just arriving on the lawn, when they heard Aul yell, "Come back here boy!"

Rhen swam across the lake in less time than it would've taken Sage. He scaled the rocky cliff on the other side and stopped at the top of Death Rock. Rhen laughed at Aul and made a rude gesture towards the soldiers, who yelled insults at him.

Ceceta, Crystam and Latsoh struggled against the soldiers who held them. "Use your knives," Aul barked at his men. The soldiers pulled knives and placed them at the women's throats, bringing their struggles to a halt.

Aul turned back to watch Rhen. The two groups stood in silence, staring at each other. They seemed to have reached a stalemate. Neither side knew what to do next.

"Come on Aul. Let's go," Narseth told Aul. He stepped past the soldier holding Ceceta. "He got away from us. He won this time."

"NO!" Aul barked, startling the soldier, who was holding Ceceta. He jumped, bumped into Narseth and threw Ceceta to the ground by accident.

Ceceta screamed at the soldier in Surpen, calling him an 'idiot', while reaching up to see if her throat had been cut by mistake.

Aul stared at her with disgust, as Narseth bent over and picked her up. Neither man was used to being spoken to by a woman. They found Ceceta's outburst disturbing. A moment later, Aul smiled and turned back towards Rhen. "Rhen has allowed his woman too many liberties. We will teach her some manners."

"Men," Aul shouted, so Rhen could hear. "Take these women back to Surpen. If we can't have what we came for, we might as well enjoy ourselves with these whores." He smiled with satisfaction, as he watched Rhen grow still on the distant cliff. The soldiers started to move up the hill, away from the water, pulling the screaming women with them.

"Time for action," Kate said. She and the others stepped forward to intercept Aul and his men, but James grabbed her arm.

"Wait," James hissed. He pointed towards the right side of the University building. Andres and Bosternd were just walking out the door on their way to the Teacher's Residence Hall. "Let's see if they're acting under Andres's orders."

Kate nodded and the Royal Family hid behind the crowd of students, teachers and elves, who had gathered to watch the scene.

Andres and Bosternd seemed to be deep in conversation, as they walked towards the Teachers' Residence Hall, but when they noticed the entire school was standing outside facing the lake, they stopped to see what was happening just as Aul yelled to his men, telling them they would be raping some pretty Thestran women tonight.

Rhen took the bait that Aul was dangling in front of him. He dove off the cliff into the water.

Seeing that Rhen was returning, Aul held up his hand to indicate to his men that they should wait. They watched as Rhen began to swim towards the school.

"That's right Rhen," Aul shouted. "Come back here and I will entertain you, while my men enjoy the company of your pretty wife."

His words had an unexpected result. Instead of continuing to swim towards the shore, Rhen stopped. He stared at Aul, while treading water in the middle of the lake. Then, unexpectedly, Rhen sank down, underneath the water. Everything was quiet.

BOOM! An enormous eruption sounded from deep beneath the water's surface. It rocked the ground, making the windows on the school's buildings rattle and causing several people to fall. The crowd watched in horror, as a gigantic typhoon lifted up into the air like an angry cobra with Rhen standing still and dry in the middle of it. The look on Rhen's face was cold and his eyes glowed red. When Rhen stepped forward, the typhoon moved. With every step, he brought the typhoon closer and closer to the shore.

The soldiers holding onto Ceceta, Latsoh and Crystam released them and ran towards the University building for safety. The moment the women were free, the typhoon disappeared, the horrendous roaring sound that had accompanied it ceased, and the University's grounds became silent. Looking out over the water, the crowd saw Rhen standing on top of the lake, as if he were standing on land, his eyes glowing red.

Ceceta, Latsoh and Crystam were standing behind Rhen. They appeared confused and glanced to their left and right, trying to get their bearings. Latsoh bent down to touch the water beneath her feet. "It's like glass it's so still," she mumbled, as Crystam reached down to dip her fingers into the cool water.

Andres marched down the hill towards Aul. "You've done more today to hurt our cause than you have any idea," he hissed. Turning towards the lake, he lifted his hands above his head and clapped. "Okay son. You've proven your point, you can come back now!"

Rhen hesitated a moment, before walking across the top of the water towards his father. His feet made smacking sounds, as if he were walking on wet pavement, yet the water didn't even ripple under his sneakers. As Rhen neared the shore, his glowing, red eyes faded back to their normal black color. Ceceta, Latsoh and Crystam follwed him, marveling at the experience of walking on water. Rhen stopped on the shore in front of his father and saluted.

"What have I told you about using your powers!" the King barked.

Rhen stared at the ground, without answering for a minute. "It's forbidden," he replied in a quiet voice.

"YOU ARE FORBIDDEN FROM USING YOUR POWERS!" Andres yelled, slapping Rhen across the face. He regretted his actions at once. They were days away from Rhen's 18th birthday. He needed to control his temper. He had to get Rhen back on Surpen. Loreth had big plans for Rhen. If Andres caused a rift between them, those plans could be jeopardized.

Frowning, Rhen looked out over the water. A red handprint had formed on his cheek, where his father had hit him. Rhen narrowed his eyes and turned his head back towards the University's grounds. For a second there, he had thought that he had heard Loreth's theme music, but he couldn't see his father's advisor anywhere.

Andres turned on Aul. He ripped three bars off Aul's uniform. "You have disgraced our soldiers today! You will return home to be punished and you will remain in your new, lower rank, for one year!"

Aul saluted Andres, before turning to go to the school's portal. "AND," Andres yelled, making Aul turn back. "You are forbidden from ever coming back to Thestran, unless you have my permission. DO YOU UNDERSTAND!"

"Yes, sir," Aul replied with a salute. He and his men marched up towards the University building.

"I'm sorry about that son," Andres told Rhen, after Aul had left. Rhen's eyes held Andres' for a moment and then he shrugged. Reaching out, Andres put his hands on Rhen's shoulders. "You made a very nice typhoon," he added. Rhen gave Andres a blank look. "I didn't even know you could make a typhoon. We should use it when we attack a liquid planet." Rhen didn't respond.

Andres removed the red cape that was attached to his military shoulder plates and draped it around Rhen. "I do hate water," he remarked with a shudder. "Why don't you go change and come back home with me. Today is a Warrior Holiday. We're going to have a big party. You'll have a wonderful time. Bosternd has seen to all of the festivities." Rhen shrugged in response, bringing Andres' ire forward. "Is that a yes or a no?" Andres barked.

Rhen cleared his throat and took off his father's cloak. As he handed it back to Andres, he said, "It's a no."

"Oh," Andres replied, taking the cape from Rhen. He noticed he still had Aul's military bars in his hand. Realizing his son's lower rank had brought on today's mishap, he handed Aul's bars to Rhen. "I now restore upon you, your full military rank. You are once again Commander of Surpen's Military Forces. Congratulations!"

A typical soldier, Rhen snapped to attention, saluting his father, before taking his stripes. "Thank you, sir," he replied, sounding official.

"Will you come home now?"

Rhen shook his head. "Sorry Dad, I have another event to attend."

"What other event?" Andres growled. "I told you, you're not allowed to attend any of the Thestran's functions."

"It's a Universal function," Rhen replied.

"What Universal function?" Andres asked.

"I'm going to a jet bike race at the Wood Elf Castle," Rhen told his father, knowing it would make him angry.

"WHAT!" Andres yelled. He raised his hand to strike Rhen, but caught himself.

Rhen grinned, as he watched his father struggle for control. If Andres hit him, he was going to retaliate. He'd had it with his Dad's attitude.

Instead of lashing out, Andres dropped his hand down by his side and walked towards the University. "Well, if you change your mind, our festival will be going until late into the night. You can join us after you've seen this…jet race," he called out over his shoulder. Andres was pleased he had kept his temper in check. He knew it would confuse Rhen. Turning with a smile, he asked, "Why don't I send Bosternd by later tonight to check in on you?"

Rhen hesitated. "Okay," he agreed. He walked up to stand beside Andres.

Andres threw his arm over Rhen's shoulders, and the two of them continued up to the school. Stopping by the door, Andres said, "Maybe I'll see you tonight Commander?"

"Maybe," Rhen replied, looking bewildered. He couldn't believe his father was going to let him stay on Thestran to go to a jet bike race without a fight.

With a wave, Andres entered the University building with Bosternd on his heels.

After Andres had left, Rhen turned to find Ceceta standing behind him. "Are you hurt?" he asked, reaching out for her.

"No," she told him, stepping into his arms.

"Latsoh, Crystam, are you okay?" Rhen asked. When they said they were fine, Rhen sighed with relief. "I'm sorry that happened," he apologized. "Soldiers aren't allowed to attack women, unless we're at war with their planet. You'll be happy to know they'll be severely punished for what they did."

Latsoh and Crystam weren't sure what to say in response, so they nodded, to indicate they had heard him.

Rhen hugged Ceceta and kissed the top of her head. "Breakfast?" he asked. He knew he had screwed up. Not only had the Genisters told him not to use his powers, but his father had issued a similar rule, for while he was at the University. If he hadn't of been so angry at Aul, none of this would've happened. Now everyone knew he could control water. Rhen was sure they'd be gaping at him all day long because of it. He cringed at the thought. He had wanted to enjoy a quiet day at the races, but now the Thestran Royals would be all over him, again.

"Sure," Ceceta told him. "I'm feeling famished. I might even eat two bowls of bloodworms this morning." She looped her arm around Rhen's waist and winked.

Rhen lowered his lips to her ear. "Thanks for making everything alright," he whispered. Ceceta gave him a quick kiss and the two of them turned to walk into the building. Erfce and Tgfhi caught up to them just as the door was swinging shut. They grabbed Latsoh and Crystam up into their arms and hugged them. "That was way disturbing," Tgfhi announced, before smacking Rhen on the arm. "You never told me you could control water. Do you think you can show me how to do that typhoon thing someday? I've never met a person with water powers, who can make a typhoon."

"Someday," Rhen agreed, without meeting his eyes.

For a moment, Tgfhi couldn't understand why Rhen was avoiding his gaze, and then he remembered, Rhen wasn't allowed to use his powers. He couldn't show Tgfhi anything. If he did, he might be punished and it wasn't worth the risk. Tgfhi was about to ask Rhen why Andres wouldn't let him use his powers, when Erfce said, "So, Rhen, are we really going to the jet bike races today?" Rhen nodded and Erfce fist pumped the air, making the others laugh.

It occurred to Rhen that his friends were like Ceceta. He could rely on them. He felt a connection to them that he hadn't realized he had before. Putting one arm around Ceceta's shoulders and one around Erfce's, he pulled them towards the student dining hall.

The Thestran Royal Family and the Elfin Royals gathered on the University's lawn to discuss what they had witnessed, while Loreth floated above them in his invisible state. Loreth had been angry with Andres for not bringing Rhen home, but after today's display, he was pleased that Rhen had remained on Thestran. Today's incident had been hysterical. The look in the Thestrans' eyes, when they had seen Rhen in the typhoon, was priceless. That young Thestran, known as Charlie, had run for cover, panicking at the sight of Rhen's red, glowing eyes. Loreth laughed in silence. If the boy only knew.

James was speaking, so Loreth floated down to listen to him. "...and his eyes," James said with concern. "Did you see his eyes? I've never seen anyone's eyes glow, when they use their powers. Rhen's powers are different from ours. They're stronger."

Loreth sensed James' fear and clapped his hands in triumph. 'That's right you Thestran scum,' he thought. 'Be afraid. Your doom will soon be upon you.' What luck that Andres hadn't brought Rhen home sooner. Today had been marvelous fun for him.

Everyone in the group agreed with James' statement. They had all noticed Rhen's glowing eyes, and they didn't know what to make of them. "No one's eyes change color when they use their powers," the Water Elf King, Plos, stated in response. "Why did his turn red?"

"His powers are stronger than your's mom," William remarked.

'Yes, they are,' Loreth thought. 'What will self-centered Kate say about that?'

"Well," Kate began. "His powers over water are stronger than mine. But, his other powers are not as strong as mine."

Loreth giggled, while listening to Kate's thoughts. How delicious of her to deny Rhen his due. He was going to enjoy taking her life, even more than he had anticipated.

The Thestrans had become silent, pondering over what they had just witnessed. What powers did Rhen have? What was with his eyes? How had he created and controlled a typhoon? How was he able to stand in the middle of it? How did he walk on water? They had so many questions they needed answers to.

'Answers you will never receive,' Loreth remarked to himself, while flying up into the air. He'd grown tired of them. He wanted to swing by Andres, to hear what he was thinking. Before today, the Surpen King had believed Rhen capable of only one power. What would he think of his son now?

Meanwhile, Charlie raced through the school's portal yelling, "Zorthan Midmeree Mountain." He jumped onto the rocky ledge before him and waved the temporary portal behind him away. "Themrock!" he swore. He had just seen Thaster's glowing, red eyes on Rhen.

Thaster, the cruelest Genister ever, the ruler of Hell! Thaster had been locked into a different dimension by the other Genisters. Although he could become ethereal to slip through the bars of his prison, so he could visit the Universe, Charlie had never heard of him possessing someone before. Thaster's eyes glowed red. Rhen's eyes had just been red. Could Thaster have somehow possessed his brother? It would explain the powers that Rhen had shown.

Charlie walked along the rocky cliff towards the twin peaks in the distance. Was Thaster controlling his little brother? He needed to think about this development, and the best place to do so was in the cultish cave of the Zorthan High Priest. He reached the twin rocks and took the hidden path to the right. Within a few minutes, he found himself in the hidden enclave of the High Zorthan priests. The younger priests bowed to him, as the older ones waved hello. They recognized him from his earlier visits.

Charlie decided to forgo the cave of enlightenment today. He sat down in one of the outdoor pavilions near the pond, closing his eyes and opening his mind to the possibility that Thaster might be controlling Rhen. The oracles' predictions of his little brother conquering the Universe seemed more believable now. If Thaster was giving Rhen his powers, he could defeat anyone who opposed him. Ever since Thaster had been locked into the dimension known as Hell, he'd been trying to find a way out. It was possible he could have found a way to connect to Rhen's brainwaves. He could be living again through Rhen. 'Dear Themrock,' Charlie thought. If it were true, it would be the beginning of the end.

Charlie felt the presence of an elder and opened his eyes. The tiny, wrinkled Zorthan High Priest bowed to Charlie. Charlie nodded politely in response. Without speaking, the Priest presented a small, wooden bowl to Charlie. It contained several, colored mushrooms, also known as Ventarian Delights, the most hallucinogenic drug in the Universe. They were banned, and had the High Priest not consumed these delicious 'delights' with Charlie before, he never would have shown them in public.

Charlie pondered his situation. He needed to meditate about Rhen and Thaster, but he also needed some relief from this morning's activities. One of the mushrooms rolled over in the pot, revealing a dark-brown patch. Dark brown was Charlie's favorite color. 'It has to be a sign from the Gods,' he thought. 'Besides, what better way could there be to meditate about Rhen than under the influence of the forbidden Ventarian Delight?'

"Don't mind if I do," Charlie told the High Priest, reaching out to take the mushroom that had a dark brown patch on it. 'This is going to be good,' he thought, as he popped the entire mushroom into his mouth, while the younger priests around him gasped. The High Priest smiled and sat down beside Charlie. A moment later, he had placed a tiny piece of purple-blue mushroom into his mouth.

Charlie would have commented on the size of the priest's mushroom, but he was already floating along to a different dimension. His thoughts and concerns regarding Rhen and Thaster had slipped away.

In the student dining hall, Rhen and his friends ate breakfast, while chatting about the upcoming races. Erfce and Latsoh seemed very excited about attending. Latsoh announced that there were many elves from all four elfin castles, who would be in attendance, and Erfce added that people from other planets competed as well.

Half an hour later, they finished breakfast and rose to leave. They followed the other students across the University's lawn and down the lengthy path that led to the Wood Elf Castle. As they stepped out of the woods into the clearing near the Wood Elf Stadium, they heard an announcer reading the program for the day over the intercom system. Many elves and foreigners, from other planets, stared at Rhen, as he approached. They knew about him from the oracles' predictions and had heard the news of what he had just done at the University. Curious to see what he looked like, they craned their necks and jostled each other to get a better view.

Almost at once, Rhen and his friends bumped into Princess Lilo, Reed's wife. She was standing near the stadium greeting people. "Hi!" she called out, when she saw them. Lilo latched onto their group, telling them which races Reed would be in, while guiding them up to her family's reserved seats.

When they arrived at the Wood Elf King's tier, Lilo separated Rhen and Ceceta from their friends and walked them over to her parents. "Mom, you remember my brother-in-law Rhen and his wife Ceceta?"

"Yes, of course," Queen Ralis said, greeting them with a smile. She felt sorry for Rhen. He hadn't been given a proper elfin upbringing, and in her opinion, suffered from it.

"Dad," Lilo called out to King Estan. "Rhen and Ceceta are here." Estan nodded in their direction but turned away. After a few minutes had passed, during which Estan continued to ignore them, Lilo apologized, "Sorry, he's still having trouble with your eating meat and...well, stuff." She couldn't believe her father was acting this way, when they all knew how important it was to bring Rhen into the fold.

"No need to apologize," Ceceta told her. "We'd be breathless, if we had to apologize to everyone Andres insults." Lilo laughed and walked them back to their friends, who had sat down on the left side of the balcony. She took a seat next to Rhen and glanced around her at Ceceta and Rhen's friends, wondering what it was like to know the Surpens personally.

Behind her, Lilo noticed the Thestran Royal Family lurking about. They were seated near Rhen, and from their posture, it was obvious they were trying to listen in on his conversation with his friends. Lilo frowned. She knew they had to bond with Rhen, but somehow the way they were going about it, seemed annoying, even to her. Rhen must have felt the same way, because he was ignoring them.

The stadium's stands were filled to maximum capacity, as the first race was about to begin. In anticipation, Lilo leaned over to Rhen and said, "This first race is really between Reed and Aaron, the son of the Fire King. They've had a rivalry for years."

Latsoh was Aaron's sister. She laughed in agreement adding, "Since they were born." Latsoh waved across the stadium to a well-dressed man and woman, who were taking their seats. "My parents," she explained, when Ceceta craned her neck to see who she was waving to. Ceceta decided that Latsoh looked like her mom, Queen Reman, which was a good thing, because her dad, King Naci, wasn't that good looking. Queen Reman was tall and thin, and she had bright red hair like Latsoh's.

Sage, who was sitting with her husband Ryan in front of Rhen and Ceceta, leaned back towards Lilo and said, "Don't forget, we Water Elves are in this race too. Sarah, King Plos and Queen Neka's daughter, is also challenging Reed and Aaron."

Shaking her head, Lilo replied, "But she's never won a race on a dry course, she doesn't stand a chance."

"She's very good, and one day she'll beat your husband," Sage retorted.

"I know Sarah and Aaron," Rhen told them, breaking their good-natured rivalry and causing them to stare at him, since he had never spoken to them before. "They're some of my better students." He searched the field, to see if he could pick them out.

Lilo laughed at something beside Rhen. Turning to see what she had found so funny, he saw her pull her daughter, the little blond girl in the green dress who had tried to look under his tunic on his first day, up onto her lap. The girl stared at Rhen for a minute and then surprised him, when she pushed herself off her mother and crawled up onto his lap. Rhen sat very still as she mounted him, afraid that any movement on his part might dislodge her, causing her to fall. With raised eyebrows, he stared down at her, as she settled herself on his lap.

"You never said you were sorry," she informed him, once she was comfortable.

"You say it first," Rhen replied with a hint of mirth. Ceceta appeared confused, but Rhen knew what the girl was talking about. She wanted an apology for his shoving her way from him after she had tried to look up his tunic.

The girl stuck her tongue out at him then turned to watch the race. A horn blew somewhere in the stadium and the riders took off. It was an exciting race, because Reed and Aaron were well matched. Sarah kept up with them, but she didn't take the same risks they took. Reed won the race by one jet bike length and the Wood Elves cheered.

"Just wait until the water course. Sarah will beat them both there," Sage told Rhen with confidence.

Lilo snorted at Sage's remark. "As if!" she declared.

In retaliation, Sage swung her popcorn upwards, so it flew into Lilo's face. Lilo laughed and threw some of the popcorn she was holding down into Sage's brown hair.

Bored by their behavior, the girl on Rhen's lap lifted her head to look at him. "My daddy's the best," she informed him. Rhen nodded in agreement. He had no quarrel with that. He had ridden with Reed several times and knew firsthand how talented he was. Something caught the girl's eye and she climbed up to stand on Rhen's lap. Holding onto his shoulders, she smiled and waved behind Rhen at both of her grandmothers, who stared at her with shock. The little girl grinned and leaned backwards, releasing Rhen's shoulders. Rhen caught her at once, so she wouldn't fall. Nestled between his strong hands, she smiled, as her grandparents watched with open mouths.

A minute later, she grew tired of their scrutiny and turned back to Rhen. "I play the piano very well. Mommy and Daddy say I'm a natural."

At that comment, Lilo stopped picking popcorn out of her hair and focused on her daughter. "Alexa, get down. It's not nice of you to stand on people, unless you're invited to do so, and it's also not nice to brag about your abilities."

With a shrug, Alexa flopped down onto Rhen's lap. "I'm not moving," she replied. "He's taller than you, so I can see the races better from his lap."

Lilo gave Rhen a sympathetic look. "Is it alright with you if she sits on you?"

"It's fine," Rhen told her. He liked children, although he'd never been comfortable around foreign children. They always seemed undisciplined.

The next race began and it was just as exciting as the first. A woman from Jeniper beat Reed and Aaron by a millimeter. When the race ended, Alexa turned around and reached her small hand up to Rhen's chin, grabbing it with her little fingers. "You look familiar," she told him.

Lilo laughed. "Of course, he looks familiar. He's your uncle. He looks just like Uncle James and Grandpa Henry, only with elfin ears." Someone in the stands above them yelled out Lilo's name, so she turned around to wave at one of her many cousins.

"No," Alexa said. She continued to examine Rhen's face. "You look like someone else. A picture of someone I've seen before." She paused. "I know. You look like the man painted on the ceilings and walls of our castle, only you have shorter hair and no beard." A servant with treats walked past their seats and Alexa forgot what she was talking about. She asked her mom for candy. When Lilo said 'no', Alexa turned her attention back to Rhen. "Do you play the piano?"

As soon as she asked the question, Tgfhi and Crystam had coughing fits and Latsoh started to giggle. Their reactions indicated that Rhen's friends knew something about his abilities. While no one was looking, Kate closed her eyes and felt the chill of her powers, as she pushed them into Latsoh's mind. She saw Latsoh's memory of playing music with Rhen and smiled. "What?" Lilly whispered next to her mother. Kate pushed Latsoh's memories into the minds of Lilly and the other members of Thestran Royal Family, who were sitting around her. She shivered when she was finished using her powers. The Royals were amazed by the beautiful songs they heard Rhen and the others playing in the University's storage room.

"Did Latsoh say you could go into her mind?" Lilly whispered. Kate shook her head. Lilly rolled her eyes with annoyance.

"I had to do it to help Thestran," Kate whispered back, justifying her actions.

Lilly couldn't take it. She stood up and moved over next to Queen Susan, James' wife.

Meanwhile, Alexa persisted in badgering Rhen. "So, can you play the piano?" she asked him for the twentieth time.

It occurred to Rhen that she wasn't going to give up without an answer. "On my planet, music is forbidden, so no, I don't know how to play the piano. But, if I lived on your planet, I would say yes, I can play the piano."

Alexa laughed. "That's not an answer. Yes or no is an answer, not yes and no at the same time."

Without responding, Rhen stared past Alexa, down at the races. He hoped, by ignoring her, she would get the hint that he was done with their conversation. Unfortunately for him, Alexa repeated herself over and over, until her whining annoyed Lilo enough that she yelled at her to stop. After Lilo had disciplined Alexa, she quieted down. Her silence lasted only a minute. She stood up on Rhen's lap and stared into his eyes. "You do play the piano, since you're living on Thestran. That's the answer," she told him. Satisfied, she plopped back down and reached over to pick up his left hand to study it during the next race. Reed, Aaron and Sarah tied in that race and everyone in the stadium cheered.

The announcer told the audience that the next batch of races would be held on the water course in half an hour, so the stadium began to empty, as everyone made their way to the Wood Elf Lake.

"Have you seen the lake yet," Lilo asked Rhen. He shook his head. Lillo sighed. "It's not pretty. Since Themrock's been gone, the lake has deteriorated to a point where nothing can live in it. The water has turned a dark brown color and its consistency is rather soupy. We know it's not polluted, but we have no idea why it's in the state it's in. The priests think it might be tied to Themrock, which means it will only go back to its original splendor when he returns. For now, our lake is useless. The only time anyone visits it is during Reed's jet bike races."

"That's unfortunate," Rhen told her. "I hope your God Themrock retur..."

"I can see," Alexa said, interrupting their conversation, while waving Rhen's hand back and forth in the air. "That you're actually an amazing piano player. It's written all over your hand. Can I hear you play after the races?"

Rhen laughed at her insightful comment and replied, "No." He picked her up off his lap and placed her down on the ground beside him. "Go play with your friends," he added, with a dismissive gesture.

Alexa frowned and reached out Rhen's hand. "No," she told him.

As Rhen regarded her, memories from his childhood on Surpen raced through his mind. If he had said 'no' to his father, he would've been punished.

Yet here, on Thestran, this child felt no repercussions from speaking back to an adult. Without realizing it, he began to feel sorry for himself. Rhen tightened his grip on Alexa's little hand and walked with her towards the water course.

When they were about halfway there, Reed ran up to join them. He was wearing a green and brown racing outfit, the official colors of the Wood Elves. Reed hugged Lilo, as she congratulated him on his win. Turning towards Rhen, his expression changed from joy to surprise, when he noticed Alexa holding Rhen's hand. "So, did you like the races?" he asked with hesitation.

"Very much so," Rhen commented. "You rode masterfully."

"Thank you." Reed was pleased that Rhen approved of his skill. He glanced down and saw that Alexa had taken another step closer to Rhen. Her body bumped into his side, as she swung their hands back and forth, while staring out across the lawn at the attendees for today's event. "Is she bothering you?" Reed whispered to Rhen. "She can be very…persistent."

From Alexa's sudden change in posture, Rhen realized she had heard her father's words but was pretending that she had not. Remembering how his father used to do the same thing to him with his advisor, he understood Alexa's frustration. "No," Rhen told Reed. "I like Alexa. We're friends." He felt Alexa's grip tighten on his hand and grinned.

Reed gave his little brother an odd look, before turning to greet the rest of his family, who had walked over to join them. "What are you doing here? You never watch my races."

As the Royal Family talked to Reed, Rhen glanced down at Alexa to find her smiling up at him. They had formed a bond.

"So," Reed began, walking over to Rhen's side. "When are you racing little brother?"

Rhen couldn't help himself from laughing. "What? I can't even stay on my jet bike. I don't think it would be a good idea for me to race."

"But it would be funny to watch," Ceceta mumbled, receiving a frown from Rhen in response.

"Why don't you race with the Children's Division?" Reed offered. "They're all learning how to ride. You'd find it fun."

Rhen raised an eyebrow at Reed in mock horror. "Are you trying to make me look like a clown?" he asked. "Thank you. No."

Reed laughed and turned to go back to his jet bike, adding, "I'll put your name onto the children's line up in case you change your mind. After all, you are my LITTLE brother."

"No!" Rhen yelled at his retreating back. They could hear Reed laughing, as he ran back to prepare for the water race.

The water races took the riders through the Wood Elves' dead lake. Both the jet bikes and the riders were outfitted with special, clear, plastic forms, so they could fly underwater. At certain points in the course, the riders jumped obstacles that would bring them out of the water. On the far edge of the lake, the course ran up the side of a cliff, before plunging back down into the water. The cliff part of the race was where most of the riders tried to pick up the speed they would need to finish in first place.

Instead of going into the stadium to watch the races, Rhen and the others found a grassy spot on the bank of the lake to sit down. Alexa asked Rhen to put her up into the apple tree that was above them, so he lifted her onto one of the tree's branches. She giggled, while trying to hold onto the branch. In no time, she slipped. Rhen caught Alexa with ease and tossed her back up into the tree, which brought forth a scream of delight. This time, she caught the branch and held firm. "Come up here with me!" Alexa yelled down to him.

"No, I'm too big," he told her.

"And you're not wearing shorts, right?" she added.

Rhen smiled at her jab. "Yes, I am."

"Then you're not a true Surpen man or we are assholes visiting your country," Alexa mocked in a low voice, calling forth what he had told William the morning of his first day on Thestran.

Rhen laughed out right at her gaul. "Alright, you win," he told her, pulling himself up into the low crook of Alexa's tree. "I wasn't that bad," he added.

"Yes, you were!!!" she yelled back.

"Then you're right, I should apologize." He bowed to her from his branch. "I'm sorry."

"I'll forgive you if you play the piano for me."

Rhen shook his head. "Sorry, I can't do that. You'll have to come up with something else."

The announcer declared the riders in the first race and everyone quieted down to watch. The race started to the sound of a loud horn. The riders took off, struggling through the water. Their jet bikes groaned under the strain of the pressure. Sarah took an early lead, which no one could lessen. She won the race hands down. There were eight more races through the lake and then the audience was asked to move back into the main stadium for the final set of races.

Sage decided to take this opportunity to announce to her family that she was pregnant. As everyone congratulated her and Ryan, Rhen jumped down from his seat in the tree and gave them a Surpen salute. "May God bless you and the child you carry," he told them, before turning to help Alexa out of the tree. Rhen swung Alexa up onto his shoulders and followed the others back to the stadium.

Half way back, Lilo noticed Alexa was eating an apple. "Where did you get that?" she asked. The servants hadn't brought them any food, so she couldn't imagine where Alexa might have gotten an apple.

"From the tree," Alexa told her mom, while taking a bite. "It's really good."

Lilo frowned. "Don't lie to me Alexa. We all know those trees don't bear fruit."

Rhen took Alexa off his shoulders and put her down on the ground by her mother.

"But they do!" Alexa exclaimed. "There were tons of apples in the tree that I was sitting in."

"Alexa, go to your room for lying."

"But Mom, I'm not lying," Alexa replied in protest. She turned to Rhen. "You saw them, didn't you?"

Rhen paused to think. "Yes, you're right Alexa. There were apples in the tree, when I helped you down." He turned to Lilo. "She's not lying."

"But that's impossible! Those trees haven't bore fruit in a thousand years, not since our Lord Themrock was imprisoned," Lilo remarked, sounding flabbergasted.

"Let's go check it out," Reed said by her side. He was finished with his races for the day and had joined the group in time to hear about the mysterious apples.

They walked back down to the waterfront to find that Alexa hadn't lied. Not only was the tree that she had been sitting in bearing fruit, but the trees around it were too. Reed reached up to pull off an apple from the tree closest to him. He bit into it. "Wow, this is amazing! Have one," he told the others, while grabbing an apple for Lilo. Everyone, except for Rhen and Ceceta, started to pull apples down from the trees.

"They're the best tasting apples I've ever had," Sage remarked.

"I have to tell my parents. This is a miracle!" Lilo exclaimed. She ran off towards the castle, where her parents were now entertaining their special guests.

"Why is Lilo so excited?" Ceceta asked.

"Because it's a miracle!" Reed told her. "These trees stopped producing fruit the day that Themrock was imprisoned. The fact that they're blooming again means he may have found a way to escape. He may be returning to us!"

"Wow," Ceceta said. "That would be amazing, if your Genister God returned!"

Reed nodded his head, noticing for the first time that Giy Flowers had begun to bloom around the trees. He smiled to himself as the others talked. This was the second sign that proved their God Themrock could be returning.

As everyone continued to talk about Themrock and the trees, Rhen became bored, so he and Ceceta excused themselves to go back to the University.

After they had left, Estan and Ralis arrived. When they saw the apple trees, they declared it to be an elfin holiday. That night, the elves celebrated with abandon over the possible return of their God Themrock.

Chapter 23

"You need to ride with Rhen tonight," James instructed Reed, while putting down his empty wine glass. "We have to talk to Ceceta to find out how many powers Rhen possesses. He's off the charts with his water powers, music and healing. We need to know what else we may be facing."

"Tonight?" Reed groaned, rubbing his aching head. He'd been drinking, since the end of the jet bike races.

"Yes," Kate agreed. The Royal Family had been celebrating with the Wood Elves for a good part of the day, but they were now ready to refocus their energies on Rhen.

"Fine," Reed moaned. He downed the rest of his drink and rose to his feet. "Let's go find them."

James waved towards his brothers and sisters to tell them it was time to leave.

They searched for Rhen in his apartment and in the common areas of the school. Charlie took them to a dorm party, where Rhen and Ceceta's friends were celebrating, but no one there had seen Rhen since the jet bike races.

"So where to now?" Rachel asked. She threw her arm around Charlie and pulled him in towards her to give him a hug. Charlie laughed and Rachel reached up to tussle his dirty-blond hair.

"Look," Reed said, nodding towards the University's main school building. Bosternd and Nk were just walking out the door onto the path that led to the Teachers' Residence Hall. "Come on." He jogged towards them, calling out, "Hey!"

Bosternd and Nk paused, when they saw the Thestran Royal Family running towards them.

"Hi," Reed repeated, when he got closer. "I'm Reed, this is King James, my father Henry, my mother Kate, Lilly, Rachel, Sage, William and Charlie."

Bosternd and Nk remained silent.

"We just wanted to meet you," Reed explained. "We know you're friends of Rhen's."

"It nigh a mee ooh," Bosternd told them in broken Thestran. He saluted their out stretched hands. "No lng ere. Tac Rhen om fur olidy."

"Oh, you're here to take Rhen home for that Warrior Holiday King Andres mentioned," James stated. Bosternd paused for a moment, as he thought about James' words, then nodded.

"Dude, you may have trouble with that," Charlie told Bosternd, while giving Nk a goofy smile. He had returned from Zorthan only a little bit sober. After the Zorthan Delight he had swallowed had worked its way out of his system, he could no longer remember why he had gone to Zorthan in the first place but he was really happy.

Bosternd wasn't sure what a 'dude' was but he did understand the rest of Charlie's comment. Nk, on the other hand, didn't speak any Thestran, so instead of looking confused by Charlie's words, he just grinned at Charlie with an equally goofy look on his face.

"We've been looking for Rhen for an hour," James clarified for Bosternd. "We can't seem to find him or Ceceta anywhere." James tilted his cowboy hat back on his head, so it was off his forehead. He shrugged to add emphasis to what he said.

Bosternd stared at James' hat. He had never seen anything like it before. With a shake, he pulled himself back to the task at hand. Bosternd reached into his shoulder bag, lifting out a blue, metallic, circular disk. Flipping it open, he watched, as the two dials on the disk spun in circles. When they had settled, he said, "E dis ay." Bosternd turned and walked back towards the main University building.

"What's that?" Charlie asked, bumping into Nk to get a better look at Bosternd's blue disk.

"Ocaying devys," Bosternd informed him. The Thestrans appeared confused. "A pek Nepchn. Ooh?"

Again, the Thestrans hesitated in confusion. Charlie pinched his lips and repeated, "A pek Nepchn ooh."

"Charlie!" Rachel admonished. "Don't make fun of his Thestran!"

"Good," Bosternd told Charlie in Neptian. "I'm glad you can speak Neptian. I'm really bad at Thestran. This is a locating device." He held it up, so Charlie could see it. "Rhen gave it to me, when we fought the Dawpars. Their planet is always dark and we were losing the war because we couldn't see anything. Rhen handed me this and told me to join him in two hours. The men and I waited for two hours. After which, I opened the device and we followed it right to Rhen. As we shined our lights in front of us, we found Rhen standing among hundreds of bowing Dawpars. They had surrendered their planet to him.

It was amazing." Bosternd shook his head with wonder and smiled at the memory.

"*Prince Rhen is amazing*," Nk slurred in Surpen, while bumping into Charlie on purpose. They both chuckled.

Bosternd smiled at Nk then turned back to Charlie. "Does anyone else in your family speak Neptian?"

"We all do," James informed him. "I'm surprised you do too."

Instead of answering James' inferred question, Bosternd said, "I've kept this device for times like these, when I need to speak with Rhen and no one can find him."

"*We use the locating device to find Rhen a lot*," Nk told Charlie in confidence. Bosternd shook his head.

"He can't speak Neptian," Bosternd told them, while nodding towards Nk. "He said it happens to us a lot." Turning, Bosternd continued down the hallway, following the directions the locating device was giving him.

Charlie grinned and nodded his head at Nk. Nk laughed and put his arm around Charlie's shoulders. Together they walked behind Bosternd, grinning like fools. Every now and then one of them would bump into the other one and they would both laugh.

"Are they both…," Lilly whispered to Rachel. She looked from Charlie to Nk. "Well, you know."

"I think so," Rachel said in response, while Reed shook his head with dismay at their condition.

They followed Bosternd up to the astronomy classroom. Although they couldn't see Ceceta and Rhen in the room, the locating device indicated they were there. As they entered the room, they heard a sigh from somewhere near the base of the room's enormous telescope. Peering down over the seats, they saw Rhen lying on the floor with Ceceta straddling his hips. Before any of them could move, Rhen laughed and said, "You're such a tease."

Ceceta giggled and dropped her body down on top of his. "I know," she told him, giving him a kiss. Rhen wrapped his arms around Ceceta and rolled the two of them over, so he was on top. "No, no, no! I want to be on top," Ceceta demanded. Rhen rolled them back over again.

Silently, Bosternd and Nk stepped back, out of the astronomy classroom, into the hallway. They moved a few feet down the corridor and sat down on the floor to wait for Rhen and Ceceta to finish. The Thestran Royals followed their example, sitting in the hallway across from them, except for Charlie, who sat down next to Nk and fell asleep. No one spoke as they waited, pretending not to listen.

Rhen and Ceceta kissed for awhile. They heard Ceceta's clothing swish, as she sat back up on top of Rhen. "How many Universes are there?" she asked him.

"Huh?"

"How many Universes are there?"

"Uh, 13," Rhen murmured, while reaching out for her.

The Royal Family members looked at each other. They had heard from Lilly that Rhen and Ceceta believed there were thirteen universes, but they still couldn't understand why.

Ceceta slapped Rhen's hands away from her. "And who's the most powerful man in all of the 13 Universes?"

Rhen chuckled. "Uh… me?"

"You? Ceceta asked. "First of all Rhen, I think that if…"

"Ceceta," Rhen said with a heavy sigh, interrupting her. "Do you want to talk? I thought you wanted to make out? It wasn't me who insisted we come up here."

"I do, I do," Ceceta declared. "Lie down again. My mind is just mixed up tonight."

Rhen hesitated. "What's wrong?"

"Nothing," Ceceta insisted. "Go ahead and lie down." They heard Rhen shift about. "Here let me relax you."

"I'm relaxed," he told her. "You're the one who's not relaxed."

"I'm fine. Let me relax you more with one of my Neptian tricks." They heard Ceceta move about. Rhen jerked, and a moment later, a red light poured out of the doorway to the astronomy classroom.

Bosternd and Nk, followed by the Thestran Royal Family members, stood up to peer into the room. A bright red light was shining out of Rhen's eyes. The light was so intense, it illuminated the entire room. Ceceta was sitting next to Rhen's head, looking angry. She slapped him across the face and yelled, "STOP IT!"

The red light plunged back into Rhen's eyes, disappearing. "What the hell! Do I have a sign on me today that says, 'please slap hard'? Would you like to slap me again for fun? Maybe I'll just have Narseth come back. He likes to dish out punishments."

"You were glowing," Ceceta chastised him. "You know you're not supposed to do that."

With a heavy sigh, Rhen sat up. "Whatever," he grumbled.

"You've been told not to use your powers," Ceceta reminded him. She hesitated and then asked, "Rhen, you were just glowing red and today, on the lake, your eyes lit up in red. I've never seen you light up in red before. Why do you think you're doing that?"

Rhen shrugged, "I don't know."

As Ceceta brushed the hair out of her face, she thought about Rhen's red eyes. "Rhen, I think something might be wrong with you. You shouldn't be glowing red. It's just not right. We should talk to them about it."

Rhen rose to his feet and adjusted his tunic. When he was finished, he put out his hand to help Ceceta stand. "I don't want to talk to them. It's been nice not having them around. Come on, let's go to bed."

Ceceta reached over and pulled down on the back of Rhen's tunic, where it had been caught in his shorts. "Sorry," she apologized. "It's been an emotional day. I thought Aul was going to rape me."

"No one is ever going to touch you!" Rhen growled. He pulled Ceceta into him and lifted her face up with his finger, to make her meet his eyes. "No one. You know that."

Ceceta sighed. "I guess I'm just tired of all the danger. We never seem to catch a break. I want to go somewhere, where we can live a quiet, calm life and all we have to worry about is making sure the colors of our clothes don't bleed together on laundry day."

Rhen laughed. "Well..." he began, but he broke off, when he saw the concern on her face. "Ceceta, before we got married I warned you that life with me was going to be difficult. I love you more than anything in the Universe. But if you've decided you need a break from me, you're free to go. I would rather see you happy than miserable."

"I know, I know," Ceceta replied, while punching Rhen on the arm. "I don't want to leave you...yet."

"Yet?" Rhen groaned. "Oh, God, I got a yet." At that, they both laughed and started walking towards the door.

Realizing it was time for action, Bosternd entered the classroom, pretending he had just arrived. He held his locating device in front of his face and appeared surprised to see Rhen standing before him, when he dropped it down. *"Oh, here you are Rhen! The King sent us to see if you would like to come home for the tonight's festivities."*

Nk sauntered through the doorway. He saluted Rhen, before giving him a hug.

Rhen smiled at his two best friends. It'd been a while since he had spent any real time with them, and he realized he would rather go to Surpen than home to bed. Before answering, Rhen gave Ceceta a questioning look.

"Go. Have fun! I'll see you later," she told him.

"Thanks love," Rhen replied, bending down to kiss her.

As Rhen was putting his arm around Nk to leave, the Thestran Royal Family walked into the classroom. Rhen nodded hello to them but kept on walking. When Rhen reached the door, he heard Bosternd call out, *"I'll catch up with you in a minute."*

After Rhen and Nk had left, Bosternd turned to Ceceta. *"Ceceta,"* he said, keeping his eyes averted from her face. "You need to know your life is in danger."

"What?" she asked. She was surprised that Bosternd would break Surpen protocol by speaking to her.

"I have a man in the King's Guard, a good man. He's told me that they have been given orders to kill you, when Rhen turns eighteen," Bosternd informed her.

"And you believe him?" Ceceta asked.

Bosternd nodded. *"Yes, I do. He's been giving us a lot of useful information lately."*

"Who is it?" Ceceta asked.

Bosternd shifted on his feet and glanced at the Thestrans, before saying, *"I don't want to put his life in danger."*

"They don't understand Surpen. I need to know who it is."

After a brief pause, Bosternd replied, *"Jet Turner."*

Ceceta smiled at the name. Jet was one of Rhen's friends in the military. He had trained Jet, when Jet had entered the service. Rhen had always spoken well of Jet. There wouldn't be any reason for her to suspect him of lying. *"He's a good man, very talented,"* Ceceta remarked in Surpen, using Rhen's words.

"Promise me Ceceta that you won't, under any condition, return to Surpen. Stay here on Thestran. The Thestran Royal Family can protect you here. Don't let the Surpen King kill you."

Ceceta raised her eyebrows. Whatever the Surpen King had planned for her must be terrible or Bosternd wouldn't be here. *"Don't worry Bosternd,"* she reassured him. *"I promise I'll stay here. Please go with Rhen. Keep him safe."*

Bosternd hesitated, as if he wanted to say more. He changed his mind, saluted Ceceta and marched from the room.

"What was that all about?" James asked Ceceta, after Bosternd had left.

Ceceta shrugged and walked towards the door. "It's nothing." She glanced with curiosity at Charlie, who Reed was struggling to keep standing.

"It wasn't 'nothing'," James persisted.

"Just a little Surpen gossip," Ceceta sang out, making her way out of the room.

The Thestran Royals followed her out of the building. Before Ceceta could turn to walk to her apartment, Kate grabbed her arm and guided her over to a comfortable spot on the lawn.

"Sit," she told Ceceta.

As Ceceta lowered herself to the ground, she wasn't surprised to see the rest of the Thestran Royal Family sitting down on the grass around her. When they had entered the astronomy classroom, she had assumed they had been looking for her. Rhen had displayed his water powers today, which meant they'd have questions for her.

"We haven't spoken with you in several days because of the weather," James began, taking off his cowboy hat.

"So, you owe us a lot of information," William added.

Ceceta laughed at William. "You're getting greedy."

"No, we're getting desperate," Lilly informed her. "Rhen's almost eighteen. We need some assurance that we aren't going to have a serious situation on our hands."

"Fire away," Ceceta said in an off-handed way, although she was feeling rather tense.

"What other forms of control does the King of Surpen have over Rhen?" James asked.

"Like the King informs me of his plans," Ceceta replied in a snarky tone.

James chose not to be insulted by her quip and continued, "We understand you and Rhen have been playing music after dinner."

Ceceta's face contorted with shock. "Who told you!"

Kate shook her finger at Ceceta and said, "We have our ways."

Frowning, Ceceta turned on Kate. "You read my mind?"

"No, not yours, Latsoh's," Lilly informed her. She was still mad at her mother for abusing her mind-reading power.

"Oh, you're good," Ceceta laughed out without humor. After a brief pause, she replied, "Yes, we didn't play tonight, but for the last few nights we've been playing a lot of music. It's good for Rhen. He's been opening up a lot more. I'm sorry you can't join us."

"Why can't we?" Sage asked. She had hoped to join them for their next session. She could play a mean oboe.

"Because Sage, if the King finds out that Rhen's playing music, he'll be in serious trouble," Ceceta replied. She rubbed her temples, wondering why she had to keep explaining it to the Royals. "The fewer people who know the better."

"But we can keep secrets," William replied. "Can't we join you?"

"NO!" Ceceta snapped. "How would you explain it to Rhen? Would you tell him that you were there because one of our friends broke his trust or would you tell him you read his friend's mind without permission?"

"She's right," Reed agreed. "Listen everyone, now that the Wood Elves' apple trees are blooming, maybe Themrock is coming back to us. If he is, we won't have to worry about Rhen."

"That's true," Sage said. "If Themrock returns, he'll restore our powers, so we can stop Rhen if he attacks."

"It'll be fun to see what powers you elves get," Rachel said, leaning over to give her sister a hug.

"Rhen won't notice much of a difference," Lilly replied, sounding thoughtful.

"What do you mean?" Ceceta asked.

"Well, he already has enormous powers. What more could he possibly get from Themrock?" Lilly hoped to draw out Ceceta into telling them more about Rhen's powers.

Ceceta turned her face away from the Royal Family. It was clear they were waiting for more information about Rhen's powers. She knew she had to give them something, even if she didn't want to. Suddenly, she had a thought. Perhaps she could make them believe that Rhen had no powers. She'd have to show them more of her and Rhen's past than she'd like to, but it just might do the trick in getting them to leave her and Rhen alone.

"Actually," Ceceta said with hesitation. "He doesn't have strong powers. She does." With that, she knew she had their attention. Ceceta giggled to herself, as she watched their eager faces turn towards her, looking for more.

"Go on," James urged, after they had sat in silence for a few minutes, waiting for Ceceta to continue.

Ceceta had been wondering how she could explain it to them, without giving away too much information. "Well, you see, there's a woman living inside him," she began, feeling rather naughty for ratting out Layla. But then, Layla was a bitch and she deserved whatever Ceceta was going to do to her. "I don't think I can explain it," Ceceta said. "Perhaps, Kate, you could just show them my memory."

Kate was stunned. She couldn't believe Ceceta was going to let her into her mind. "Okay," she agreed. "Assuming Rhen hasn't blocked my ability to transmit your thoughts, when you give them willingly." She moved over to sit down beside Ceceta, reaching out to touch her face. "Relax and think about what it is you want us to see. I'll project it to the others."

"WAIT!" Ceceta cried out, pulling away from Kate's hand. She was having second thoughts. What if Kate stumbled onto one of the secrets that Ceceta was holding. One of the ones that couldn't be made public. "This isn't a good idea," Ceceta told them. "What if another image that I don't want you to see, pops into my mind?"

"If you want me to stop, just say it and I'll stop. I won't pry into any of your memories. I'll simply take the one you're willing to share and broadcast it to the others," Kate explained, shifting her legs to the side to make herself more comfortable.

"No, this isn't a good idea. I don't know why I even mentioned it," Ceceta replied, feeling ashamed. "Ask me a different question." She couldn't risk the chance of their seeing any of the secrets she was holding.

No one said anything. They wanted to learn more about this mysterious woman living inside of Rhen. After a while, their silence began to bother Ceceta. Her guilt, at throwing out a morsel and not explaining it, was making her uncomfortable. "He's really ticklish," she offered, to break the silence.

"Oh, great," William snapped. "So, when he's killing us, we can just tickle him and he'll stop. Good plan!"

Ceceta glared at William, as if he'd slapped her. She had thought that the Royals cared about her, but from William's comment, it appeared they didn't. They just wanted to know how to stop Rhen. Well, if that was the case, they needed to think Rhen was powerless. If they thought Layla had all the power, perhaps they would leave Rhen alone.

"Okay," Ceceta agreed, turning to Kate. "You can look into my mind, but only at the part about the woman, right?!"

"Yes," Kate answered. She placed her right hand onto Ceceta's forehead, closed her eyes and forced her powers to seep into Ceceta's mind. Ceceta jerked away from the cold that flowed out of Kate's fingers but then sat still. An instant later, everyone felt an odd, swirling sensation, and then they found themselves in a small, dark, stone cell. The room was cold and there was water running down one of the walls into a drain on the floor. A small cot was located on the right side of the room. As the Thestrans looked out through Ceceta's eyes, they could just make out the figure of a boy lying on the floor in front of them. Before they could register who it was, they felt Ceceta crying and they heard her sob, "Oh, they killed you. They killed you." Ceceta bent down over Rhen's head and kissed him on his forehead, as tears dripped from her eyes into his matted hair.

"No," Rhen answered in a hushed voice. "I'm okay. I just want to sleep."

"No, don't sleep. You'll never wake up. Please, stay awake, please," Ceceta pleaded.

"I'm so tired," Rhen whispered in the dark.

Ceceta moved closer, pulling Rhen's young body up into her arms. She was crying so hard she could barely speak. "Please," she choked out. "Don't sleep. Don't die. Don't leave me here alone."

Rhen didn't answer. He was already unconscious. Ceceta held onto him for awhile longer, sobbing into his hair. Eventually, she grew concerned and lowered his body down onto the floor, before leaning over to listen for his heartbeat.

A rustling sound passed through the cell, startling Ceceta. She gasped and felt chills run down her arms. Ceceta wondered if Rhen's spirit was leaving his body. Looking up, she froze, when a ball of light entered the room through the stone wall. The white light moved towards her, changing shape in the air. She watched in astonishment, as it misted into the form of an elfin woman.

The woman was gorgeous. Ceceta found herself speechless in the apparition's presence. The ghost woman floated closer to her and gave her a smile. Ceceta was too stunned to move. She watched as the ghost woman hovered over Rhen's body. From the glowing light that she gave off, Ceceta saw that Rhen's left arm was broken. He was bleeding from his mouth, nose and ears and there were large bruises forming on his chest and stomach. "He's dying," Ceceta whispered.

The elfin woman shook her head and her eyes began to glow whiter. She formed a ball of white light in her hand and placed it above Rhen's battered chest. Placing her palm on top of the light, she pushed the ball down towards him. The ball touched Rhen's naked chest, but instead of entering his body, as it appeared the woman wanted it to, the ball split in half and flowed out from under her hand, up into the air and back into her body.

The woman seemed puzzled. She formed a new ball of light and again tried to push it into Rhen, but once more, it wouldn't penetrate his skin. She tried repeatedly to push a ball of light into Rhen's chest, and every time, it flowed back into her. By the end of her seventh attempt, she gave up. Forming a larger ball of light, she held it over Rhen's face to study him. Suddenly, she made a strange gesture that looked like a gasp. Her expression changed from annoyance to delight and before Ceceta could blink, she plunged her entire body into Rhen's. Rhen glowed white, as the wounds on his body healed. When he was healthy, the light within him faded and the room grew dark. Ceceta bent down over Rhen and placed her head on his stomach. "Thank you," she whispered to the woman inside of Rhen. She curled up beside Rhen for warmth and fell asleep.

The transmission of Ceceta's past became black, as Ceceta fell asleep in her memory. Kate felt Ceceta push against her, to end the transmission. Instead of releasing Ceceta, as she should have, Kate sped up Ceceta's memory. She wanted to see what happened next, so she decided to take the liberty of continuing.

The Royal Family watched, as the next morning, Ceceta felt Rhen move underneath her. She opened her eyes. "You don't have to wake up yet," Rhen told her in Neptian, his prepubescent voice startling the Royal Family. Many of them had forgotten what his youthful voice had sounded like. Yawning, Ceceta lifted her head. Her muscles were sore from the position she had slept in. She looked over at Rhen, who was illuminated in the thin ray of electric light that came from underneath the cell's metal door, and smiled. The Royal Family stared at Rhen through Ceceta's eyes. They had been so taken, with the glowing elfin woman, that they hadn't realized his condition before. Rhen was filthy. His cheeks were gaunt and his ribs stuck out too much for a child of his age. He and Ceceta were wearing nothing more than drab half tunics that hung low on their thin waists.

Turning sideways, Rhen stood up. As Ceceta's eyes glanced over his chest, she remembered what had happened during the night. "You've got something inside you!" she blurted out in Neptian.

Rhen seemed confused. When Ceceta failed to continue, he stretched his tired body. "No. There isn't anything left in me. Besides, if I did have some food, you know I would've shared it with you. It's my fault that you're in this mess. I'm sorry."

"NO!" Ceceta yelled. She was angry, hungry and tired of always having to tell him that she had chosen to join him. He had apologized to her so often about their situation that she now found it annoying whenever he said he was sorry. "You don't understand. You were dying last night and this woman came and entered your body. She healed you, but I think she's still in you. I didn't see her leave."

"A woman is in my body?" Rhen asked. The corners of his mouth turned up, as if he were going to laugh.

"I think she's a power goddess. You know? One of those gods who decide what powers a person receives," Ceceta exclaimed.

This time Rhen did laugh. "They've been giving you too many experimental drugs Ceceta. There's no such thing as a power goddess."

"But there is Rhen. We Neptians worship them. She exists and now she's inside you! You have powers now!"

"Right!" Rhen said, although Ceceta could tell he didn't believe her. He turned to the stone wall behind him and held up his hands. "Open a portal to Neptian," he bellowed at the wall. Nothing happened. He looked back at Ceceta with a mischievous grin and asked, "Shall I try again?" Ceceta frowned feeling confused. She had thought that Rhen had received his powers last night. Rhen misunderstood her silence and turned back to the wall saying, "Someone please rescue us and take us the hell away from this place!" Although Rhen's back was to her, Ceceta could hear him snickering.

"Rhen, you have to learn how to use your powers," Ceceta informed him. "Nobody knows how to use their powers right away. You need to practice using them. Also, you may not have the ability to open a portal. Try something else. See if you can fly!"

Rhen laughed out loud at Ceceta's suggestion.

"Stop it," Ceceta hissed.

Rhen turned towards her with a wicked smile, saying, "I know what I'll try." Raising his face to the ceiling, he said, "I will now use my powers to make my wife be quiet." He waved his hands about and laughed, while gesturing towards Ceceta with his left hand.

Ceceta's face grew dark. In a tired voice, she said, "You used your left hand again. You have to stop doing that! They're going to rip it off you if you don't stop."

Rhen's shoulders dropped, as every ounce of joy left his face. He had been trying so hard to stop himself from using his left hand. "I know, I know," he agreed. "That seems to be the hardest thing for me to let go of. I can do everything else they want me to do. I've become the perfect Surpen for Mom and Dad. I'm obedient, I can kill without remorse, I can eat people without hesitation, I enjoy the taste of blood and I love to fight." He paused looking down at his left hand. "I just can't seem to remember to use my right hand over my left."

Ceceta knew all too well how hard it had been for him. Last night was the third time they had broken his left arm. She stood up and walked over to sit down on the cot. "You really are done with them, aren't you?"

"What?" Rhen asked.

"When you told the wall to become a portal, you asked to go to Neptian, not Thestran. You're really done with your family. You weren't joking, when you told me you never wanted to see them again."

"No. I wasn't joking," Rhen confirmed. "They're dead to me."

Ceceta shook involuntarily from his words. The Surpens had placed them on Punishment Island to remove their Thestran habits. The guards had worked Rhen over, until they had convinced him that he hated his family. She wanted Rhen to realize his family still cared for him, but how could she explain it to him, when she wasn't even sure if she believed it herself. They had heard nothing from the Thestrans, since Kate and Henry had left. Who would do that to their child? "Rhen," Ceceta began. "The Surpens want you to think that. They tell you horrible things about your family every day, over and over again. In the back of your mind, you need to remember they're doing it to you for a reason. What they say isn't true."

"They 'were' doing it to me," Rhen corrected her. "Not anymore. They haven't mentioned the Thestrans to me in months."

"Because you believe them now," Ceceta whispered.

"Don't you?" Rhen asked.

Ceceta didn't respond. The Surpens hadn't been slandering her family or the Neptians the way they had the Thestrans. She had to admit, she was beginning to believe their stories. But she and her family were a part of Thestran, and her deep love for her family, made her trust that the Surpens' stories were false. They were nothing more than propaganda, created to turn Rhen from Thestran towards Surpen. Ceceta wondered if she would have lost faith in her Neptian family, if the Surpens had slandered them as they had Rhen's.

At that moment, the door opened and Rhen rushed to take her into his arms. He spun them around, so his back was towards the door, his body a shield, blocking Ceceta from whomever was entering. A jet of water blasted across the cell into Rhen's back. Ceceta heard Rhen grunt in pain, as he threw his left arm out, to try to take some of the pressure from the water off his back. The water pushed them both back against the wall, pounding them into the cold stones.

When the water stopped, they heard a gruff voice call out, "Rise and shine!" A younger version of Aul walked into the room. He was dressed in a non-military tunic and wore a great deal of jewelry around his neck. His face had not yet acquired its jagged scar. Aul was holding a metal rod, which he tapped against his leg. "Narseth, come here," he demanded, while staring at Rhen.

Narseth, who was already rather muscular, walked into the cell. Aul asked, "What arm was our boy here using to block his bath with?"

Narseth grinned. "His left arm boss."

"That's right," Aul agreed. He tapped the pipe against his leg. "And what is the Debrino Code's penalty for using your left arm?"

"A proper flailing!"

"Correct!" Aul replied. He raised his pipe and brought it down on Rhen's left arm. There was a sickening crack, as Rhen's arm broke from the blow. Rhen screamed, causing Narseth to laugh.

Narseth grabbed Rhen's broken arm and pulled it backwards, increasing Rhen's agony and forcing Rhen to double over.

Ceceta reached out for Rhen, but Aul shoved her back into the wall with his pipe. Aul leaned over to rub the back of his hand up Rhen's bare stomach, until he reached Rhen's throat. Rotating his hand, he grabbed Rhen's neck and lifted Rhen's head. "What's the matter boy?" he asked. Rhen gritted his teeth to keep himself from crying. Aul leaned his face in closer and whispered, "Didn't you enjoy last night's class?"

As soon as Aul released his throat, Rhen spat into Aul's face. Aul swung his arm back and struck Rhen in the ribs with his pipe. The Thestrans heard another crack.

Rhen cried out, doubling over as much as possible in Narseth's grip.

Aul was expecting Narseth to laugh. When he didn't, Aul turned to see what was wrong. Narseth's brow was furrowed in confusion, as he stared at Rhen's arm. Aul stepped back to see what had gotten Narseth's attention. Rhen's arm had healed. Aul shifted his gaze to Rhen's ribs and watched, as the skin that had torn over Rhen's ribs, sealed closed without leaving a mark.

"Give me your knife," Aul barked. Narseth handed him his knife. Aul stepped forward and slashed Rhen clear across the throat, cutting deep into his jugular veins. Ceceta screamed. Blood gushed out of Rhen's throat, hitting the cement floor below him.

Rhen reached up to grab his neck, a surprised expression on his face. A second later, his surprise turned to curiosity. He took his hands down from his throat and looked at them. The blood on his hands had dried. His throat had healed. Rhen smiled to himself. Ceceta had been right. He did have powers. Healing powers.

"Hold him against the wall with his left hand in the air," Aul ordered. Narseth pinned Rhen to the wall with his left hand out. As soon as he was secure, Aul stepped forward and chopped off four of Rhen's five fingers. Ceceta screamed again, as Rhen cried out in pain. He tried to free himself from Narseth's grasp, but couldn't. Aul watched Rhen's hand. Within a few seconds, the four fingers he had removed, grew back.

"Well, well, well. It appears they were right about you after all. Release him," Aul snapped. As soon as Narseth let go of Rhen, he fell to the ground, clutching his aching left hand. Aul nodded his head towards the door and Narseth left. Once he was gone, Aul said, "Your breakfast today is your fingers." He put his metal pipe under Rhen's chin and lifted Rhen's head, forcing Rhen to meet his eyes. "Life for you has just gotten a lot more interesting," he added, before turning and marching towards the door. "Enjoy your breakfast!" he yelled over his shoulder. Aul slammed the door behind him, leaving Ceceta and Rhen in the dark.

When Rhen's eyes had readjusted to the darkness of the cell, he glanced over at Ceceta. "I guess you were right. I did get some powers last night. Can you tell me what happened?"

As Ceceta told him the story, Rhen picked up his fingers and walked over to her, handing her two of them. Ceceta turned away from him. She wouldn't take them. Rhen sat down on the cot and gestured for her to sit next to him. "But, how do I use these powers?" Rhen asked Ceceta. "Will the goddess tell me?"

Ceceta shrugged. She had no idea. No one in her family had ever had powers.

Rhen felt defeated. "I have no idea what to do," he confessed. He looked away from her to gain control of his emotions. With a heavy sigh, he turned back to Ceceta. Grabbing her hand, Rhen forced her to take two of his fingers. She squealed in protest. "Eat your breakfast!" he yelled.

Ceceta dropped his fingers onto the cot and put her hand up to her mouth. "I can't, they're your fingers!" she wailed.

Rhen laughed. He held up his left hand, with four of his fingers bent down, so they were hidden, and screamed 'aaarrgh', while swinging his hand about to make it look like he was in pain.

"That's not funny," Ceceta snapped.

"Neither is starvation," Rhen snapped back. He grabbed her skinny shoulders. "Ceceta, they're food. Food! We don't get enough of that to be able to pick and choose what we eat!" At the look of horror on her face, he was hit by a wave of guilt. "I'm sorry," he added, releasing her shoulders. He put one of his fingers into his mouth and took a bite. "Mmm," he said, giving her an encouraging smile. "It tastes like chicken."

Despite herself, Ceceta giggled. She knew Rhen had never eaten chicken before in his life. After a few minutes, she reached out and took one of his fingers. Closing her eyes and grimacing, she took a bite.

"Remind me, if we ever get out of here, to never eat chicken again!" she told him with a grimace.

Rhen laughed and took a bite out of his second finger. "Agreed. We'll never eat chicken again," he promised. He didn't add the fact that he expected them to die on Punishment Island.

After they had finished their breakfast and tossed the bones into the drain in the center of the room, the cell door opened and five men entered. They grabbed Rhen and dragged him out. Ceceta waited in the cell for the entire day. No one brought her lunch or dinner. Eventually, the door to the cell opened and the guards carried Rhen back in, dumping him on the cot. Rhen's body was limp but his eyes were open. Other than his head having been shaved, there were no visible marks on his skin. Once the guards had released Rhen, Ceceta rushed to his side. He gazed up at her with unfocused, bloodshot eyes.

"Take her," one of the men said, indicating towards Ceceta. They grabbed Ceceta and hauled her out of the room, walking down several dark passageways, up two stairways and through two rooms, until they arrived at a dirty, white, metal door, where they paused for one of the men to knock.

"Enter," someone said from inside. The soldiers obeyed, pulling Ceceta into the room. Ceceta glanced around her and panicked. They had taken her to an operating room. There was blood everywhere, on the floor, the operating table, the instruments, everywhere. An older man stood with his back to her. He removed his bloody gloves and threw them into the sink in front of him then took off his bloody apron and threw that into the sink as well. Turning towards Ceceta, he smiled. His teeth were crooked and black, his head was too large for his body and he had scars across his cheeks and neck. His eyes looked almost purple in color.

"Hello, Ceceta. It's nice to see you again. How's Rhen doing? Did he speak yet?" the man asked in a gentle voice. Ceceta shook her head. "Oh, well, he's new at healing. I'm sure it won't be long until he's his old self again." The man stepped closer. "What happened last night? Why does he now possess powers?"

Ceceta shook her head. "I ddd...don't know, sir" she stammered. This man had hurt her before. He enjoyed causing her pain.

"You wouldn't be lying to me, would you dear? You know from our last meeting that I don't like it when you lie to me." He reached out one of his cold, damp fingers to touch the blue skin of her cheek. Chills passed through Ceceta's body and she felt like vomiting.

"No, no, sir, I'm not lying to you," she told him. "He woke up healed. We can't figure it out. Does he have powers now, sir?"

The man laughed. "He's always had powers Ceceta! We've been working hard to wake up his powers these last few years. It looks like we've finally gotten their attention." He stepped behind Ceceta and leaned over to whisper into her ear, "What other powers does he have besides his healing powers?"

Ceceta swallowed before stammering, "N...None, sir."

"Are you sure?" he asked, his lips touched her ear in a gentle kiss.

Ceceta nodded. "Yyyes sir."

The man walked around Ceceta surveying her. "Has he tried to do anything with his powers yet?"

"He, he, he tried to make a portal in the wall, sir, but nothing happened."

The man laughed and clapped his hands together with delight. "He tried to escape," he declared. "That's rich. No one can escape from Punishment Island Ceceta. Remember that my dear, no one can escape—not man, nor beast, nor even," he paused to touch Ceceta's face again with his long, cold finger, before whispering, "God."

Ceceta nodded. She believed him. She'd been on Punishment Island long enough to know that no one had ever escaped.

"Very well," the man said. "Come with me, there's something I need to show you." The jailers grabbed Ceceta's forearms and pulled her along behind the man. They walked through two rooms, until they arrived in a dark room that stank of decay. The man stopped and turned back to look at Ceceta. "Someone tried to rescue you. Did you know that?"

Ceceta shook her head feeling afraid. "Your family I presume?" the man said with a smile. He stepped aside, while one of the jailers flipped on the room's lights, illuminating the mass of mutilated Neptian bodies lying on the floor. Ceceta screamed in horror. Her father, her mother, her grandparents, her brothers and sisters, cousins, aunts, uncles, everyone was dead. Massacred by the Surpens and left to rot on Punishment Island. Ceceta fell to the ground in defeat. Her body numb. She wanted to cry, but she couldn't. She couldn't do anything but lie on the ground with her mouth open, gasping the horrid, rotting air, as she stared at her desecrated family. In the distance, she could hear the sound of the man laughing at her misery.

"STOP!" Ceceta screamed. "STOP!" she screamed again.

The Thestran Royal Family was confused. Where had that scream come from? Ceceta wasn't screaming in her memory, yet they could hear her screaming 'STOP'.

Again, Ceceta screamed, "STOP!"

This last scream sounded close by. There was a swirling in their minds and they found themselves back on top of the University's hill. It was then that the Thestrans realized Ceceta had been screaming at Kate to stop.

Sobbing, Ceceta screamed, "STOP", once more. She looked up at Kate, her face wet with tears of sadness and fury. "You said you'd only look at the woman part. How dare you continue on past her!" Feeling like she was going to be sick, Ceceta staggered to her feet and ran disjointedly towards her apartment.

Rhen returned to the University from Surpen feeling great. Neither Andres nor Loreth had bothered him about his new powers, while he was home for the holiday. They had talked about the ongoing festival and had praised him for his decision to remain at the Thestran's school. He wasn't sure why they weren't fighting with him, but he didn't feel like thinking about it now. After he had left their company, he had joined up with his good friends Bosternd, Nk and Ngi. They had partied until Nk had passed out. Bosternd and Rhen had carried Nk back to his home, dumping him on his pregnant wife, before walking out into one of the paddocks to be with their Surpen Beasts of War. It wasn't long before Bosternd had started falling asleep himself. Rhen had carried him back to his bunk in the barracks and then taken his leave. 'Yes,' Rhen thought. 'It had been a perfect night.'

Rhen stepped out of the University's portal, humming a tune and holding up a small, blue vial on a silver chain. He kissed the vial and tucked it inside his tunic, before pushing open the door to go outside. As soon as he opened the door, he heard Ceceta yelling 'STOP'. He hesitated in the doorway to watch Ceceta run away from the Thestran Royal Family towards their apartment. All of the warmth and joy that he had been feeling evaporated, as he watched his distressed wife running away from the Thestrans. What had they done to her? Rhen bolted from the doorway, running after his sobbing wife. "CECETA!" he cried out, trying to get her attention to let her know he was there.

The Royal Family jumped at the sound of Rhen's voice. They hadn't expected him back so soon. They watched in dread, as Rhen chased after Ceceta. "What's she going to tell him?" Rachel asked the others with concern.

"That's her problem. We need to talk about what we've learned," Kate announced. She rose to her feet and brushed the grass off her pants. "Let's go home."

Rhen's brothers and sisters followed Kate back to their castle. They walked into one of their private conference rooms and sat down around the room's table. "We don't wish to be disturbed," Kate told the castle's staff, closing the door and locking it.

Reed put his hand on his father's shoulder. Unlike Kate, Henry looked devastated. He sat low in his chair, with his head in his hands. "I always assumed he acted like a Surpen, because he'd been living there for so long," he told them, raising his head. Tears ran down his cheeks. "I never knew they...they were hurting my child to turn him into a Surpen. I was such a blind fool to allow this to happen, if only I'd been less greedy."

Lilly stared at her father. It was the first time they had ever seen one of their parents express true remorse for what they had done to Rhen. His words made Kate's silence almost unbearable.

"They tortured him," Reed remarked. He couldn't imagine someone torturing his son. The idea of it made him sick to his stomach. He would kill anyone, who tried to hurt his children. Reed clenched his hands in anger.

"Years," Rachel said in a hushed voice. She cleared her throat. "The doctor said to Ceceta that they'd been torturing Rhen for years to get him to show his powers."

"Oh, Themrock," Sage whispered. Ryan pulled her into his arms.

Lilly turned away from Sage to stare at her parents. They had abandoned Rhen to men who had tortured him. What kind of people were they? She had always considered them to be perfect, but this…this was anything but perfect. This was a tragedy. Lilly considered her own happy life on Thestran. While she had been enjoying herself, worrying about simple idiotic things, like what dress to wear to a party, her little brother was being tortured and starved. Had he ever experienced a carefree day in his life?

"He should kill us," Sage hissed. She glanced up at everyone with red, puffy eyes. "We deserve to die for abandoning him to such butchers. I can't believe that he's been nice to us over this last year. Why would he be nice to us? I wouldn't. If you had done that to me, I would've killed you already."

"This is an outrage!" James screamed, startling everyone. "How dare they treat one of our family members that way!" He slammed his hand on the table for emphasis. "To torture and starve a member of the Thestran Royal Family! It's unthinkable! How dare they do such a thing! We should declare war on Surpen today for this atrocity! I want to kill all of them for what they've done!" He was shaking with rage, as he hit the table repeatedly with his hand.

"Start with Aul and Narseth please," Rachel remarked. "I'll kill that doctor myself."

James started to march about the room, screaming obscenities at the King of Surpen and kicking the furniture. His actions unnerved the rest of his family. They had never seen him lose control like this before. James' fury came from his realization that he was, in a way, responsible for what had happened to Rhen. When Rhen had been left on Surpen, he had been the acting King of Thestran, which had made him responsible for Rhen's safety. He should've checked in on his youngest brother. He should've made sure that Rhen was safe. He shouldn't have left it to his parents. Guilt overwhelmed James, turning him red with frustration and anger.

When James started breaking apart a chair, Reed went to him. The two men talked for a while in the corner of the room, until Reed calmed James down enough that he could sit at the table. Once he was seated, Reed asked the room, "So, who was the elfin goddess that jumped into Rhen's body? Do you think she's still there?"

"Lilly, who was that woman?" James asked.

"How should I know?"

"Because you majored in Neptian History," James retorted.

"Listen, I don't remember ever hearing about a goddess, who visits people granting them powers. I don't know where Ceceta got that. It sounds like a very old, local belief, definitely not one that was planet wide."

"Have you ever seen her before Mom?" James asked Kate.

"No," she replied, with a shake of her head.

"What was that ball of light she was trying to put into Rhen?" William asked.

"His powers," Lilly and Kate answered at the same time. That part of the memory seemed clear.

"So, she was a Power Goddess, just like Ceceta said? Does that mean she gave all of us balls of light when we were babies?" William asked.

"Maybe...who knows," Reed replied. "We aren't really sure how a person's powers are determined, but from Ceceta's memory, it appears we're given our powers." Reed hesitated and looked down the table at Sage. "Actually, we've got pictures of a woman, who looks somewhat like that goddess, in the Ancestor Room of our castle. The pictures we have are of Themrock's wife, Layla. Sage, is it possible that that could have been the same Layla?"

Sage nodded her head looking thoughtful. "Yes, yes indeed. Now that you mention it, she did look a lot like Layla, didn't she? We have pictures of Layla in the Water Elf Castle too. Do you really think it's the same woman? Do you think Layla is performing Themrock's duties while he's gone?"

"Perhaps," Reed replied with a shrug. "I'd like to talk to the Wood Elf Priests, to see what they have to say on the subject.

"Does this mean that Rhen has a Genister living inside of him? Does that make him a Genister too?" William asked.

"No, William," Sage replied. "Rhen isn't a Genister nor does he have a Genister living inside him. It's blasphemous to speak that way."

"But the woman inside him can give people powers," William commented. "Doesn't that make her a Genister?"

"He has a point Sage," Reed agreed. "We really don't know enough about our own history to rule out that possibility. Layla could have been a Genister."

"Does Rhen have any powers?" Rachel asked. "It seemed as if his body wasn't accepting the powers she was giving him. Do you think his healing powers and his mind and water powers come directly from the woman inside him? Maybe he has no powers, but he uses hers?"

"That makes sense," Lilly agreed.

The room was silent, as they thought about the ghostly, elfin woman. The Thestran Royal Family had so many questions and so few answers. It was late, when they broke for the night. They needed to get some sleep, before they confronted Rhen in the morning. It was time to ask him to leave Surpen once and for all. They were planning on using the information they had gathered from Ceceta's memory to prove to Rhen that he was Thestran. The Surpen's had brainwashed him into becoming Surpen. It was time for Rhen to face the facts. He needed to denounce Surpen.

Chapter 24

"Have you seen them yet?" Lilly asked Reed. She stood up on her toes in the doorway of the student dining hall to search for Rhen and Ceceta.

"No. They cancelled both of their classes and they haven't attended any of their lessons," Reed informed her. He pulled off his leather riding gloves. "I assume they're still in their apartment."

"Because of us," Lilly mumbled, dropping her gaze to the floor. "I feel awful about last night."

"So, do I," Reed agreed, reaching out to give his sister's shoulder a squeeze. "Let's go meet up with the others." Lilly nodded and the two of them headed towards the school's portal.

As they walked down one of the school's corridors, a classroom door opened in front of them and Latsoh stepped out into the hallway. Her red hair was tied up in a pony tail and she was carrying two notebooks in her arm. "Hey," Reed called out. "Have you seen Rhen or Ceceta today?"

"No. Are they okay?" Latsoh asked.

"We hope so," Lilly told her.

"Did you see the bandstand that Professor Orisco set up down by the lake front?" Reed asked. "Do you know what's going on?"

"No," Latsoh replied again, while Lilly answered, "I think Mr. Orisco has organized a concert for tonight."

"Tonight? Huh. Well, it looks nice down there," Reed told them. "He did a good job setting it up."

"I'll have to check it out," Latsoh commented. She said goodbye to the Thestran Royals and walked off towards the dining hall.

Tucking her notebooks under her arm, Latsoh stopped at the stairwell window to take a quick look at the bandstand that Lilly and Reed were talking about. "That thing is huge," she murmured to herself, taking in the tennis court sized, rasied wooden stage. A sound system had been installed on the left side of the stage and instruments and stools had been set up in sections for the musicians. Latsoh turned to go down the stairs to the dining hall, but paused, when she noticed black sneakers sticking out from under the apple trees. "That's where you've gone. Hiding in plain sight." Latsoh smiled at the thought of Rhen and Ceceta, as she walked the rest of the way to the dining hall. "Hey," she whispered

311

to her friends, so William and Rachel wouldn't hear her at the adacent table. "I found them. Come on."

Together, they sneaked away from the dining hall, making their way down to the apple trees. "So, this is where you two have been hiding?" Erfce remarked, while he and the others sat down on the ground around Rhen and Ceceta. "Why did you skip your classes today?"

"We were busy," Rhen replied. He had been lying on his back, but when his friends arrived, he sat up.

"So busy that you've decided to fall behind?" Erfce asked.

"Yup," Rhen agreed.

Ceceta looked tired. They could see she'd been crying. Her eyes were red and her nose was running. Crystam put her arm around Ceceta's shoulders and hugged her. "Are you okay?" she whispered. Ceceta nodded, while keeping her eyes on the ground.

Last night, Ceceta had confessed to Rhen that she had not only told his family about their past, but she had also allowed them to watch a part of her memory from Punishment Island. She still felt sick to her stomach for allowing the Thestrans to see that part of her life and for letting Rhen down. Ceceta had expected Rhen to scream at her for being an idiot, but instead, he had just shrugged and held on to her, as she had cried all night long, over the memory of her murdered family and the breaking of his trust.

"Did you guys see the Black Angel didn't save anyone last night?" Tgfhi commented. When neither Rhen nor Ceceta answered, he added, "I wonder why?"

"Something must have come up," Erfce snapped. He was pissed that Tgfhi was talking about the Black Angel, when it was obvious that something major was bothering Rhen and Ceceta.

Neither Rhen nor Ceceta were looking at Tgfhi, so he mimed to Erfce that he was only trying to help. Erfce rolled his eyes in disbelief, before shaking his head. 'What?' Tgfhi mouthed back. Erfce mimed back that he should stop talking. Tgfhi stuck his tongue out at Erfce then turned to swipe the black dagger that Rhen had begun to dig at the ground with.

"Nice," Tgfhi said, examining the weapon. The dagger was heavy, small and black. The tip of it curved upward at a slight angle. "It's heavy. I bet it could do some serious damage to someone." Rhen nodded and reached over to take his dagger back. "Not just yet," Tgfhi said, jerking it out of Rhen's grasp. He flipped it over in his hand and handed it to Erfce. "Check it out."

Ceceta started to cry, so Erfce handed the dagger back to Rhen. "Sorry," he apologized. Rhen shrugged his shoulders and went back to picking at the ground.

Latsoh and Crystam held onto Ceceta, until she got herself under control. In the heavy silence that followed, Rhen cleared his throat and everyone looked over at him, expecting him to speak. "No," he said, pointing to his neck. "Just a little something in my throat." A moment later, they all laughed.

"You were lucky you missed class this morning," Latsoh began, hoping to change the dismal mood that had settled over the group. "Our homework assignment for tonight is to try something new? We have to write a report about it and present the report to class tomorrow morning? How are we supposed to try something new at school?"

"I know," Erfce remarked. "Rhen, can I ride your jet bike? I've never ridden a jet bike before."

"Sure," Rhen answered.

Crystam clapped her hands together. "Let's all do that. Except for you, of course, Rhen. You've already ridden a jet bike. What are you going to do?"

Rhen didn't care. The assignment sounded stupid to him. Ceceta wiped at the tears that had sprung to her eyes again.

Feeling uncomfortable, Tgfhi blurted out, "Hey, why don't you play something for Ceceta." He pointed over towards the instruments on Mr. Orisco's bandstand. "That would be something new." Rhen stared at him. "What?" Tgfhi asked, sounding defensive.

"It's too risky Tgfhi. There are too many people who could see me." Rhen picked up his dagger and poked at a rock, to free it from the grass.

Narrowing her eyes, Ceceta snapped. "Do it!"

"Ceceta?" Rhen asked, raising his head to meet her gaze.

Ceceta was feeling guilty for doing something wrong, so she wanted Rhen to be guilty of doing something wrong too. "I said, do it! Please Rhen? Play an instrument for me."

Rhen studied his wife. Why did she want him to play music, when it was forbidden? They had been playing music in the University's basement for days now and no one had found out. He had enjoyed it more than he had thought he would. It made him feel free. But, why would Ceceta want him to play in public? Rhen thought about their last jam session and he felt a longing to let his powers over music out. He'd love to play in the open, even if it was for only one song. Was anyone even around to see him play? Rhen glanced about the University's grounds for signs of life, but there wasn't anyone in sight. "Is everyone still at lunch?"

"Yes," Crystam told him.

"Okay," Rhen agreed.

In a flash, Erfce ran over to the bandstand to grab a guitar off the stage. Unfortunately, at that moment, Mr. Orisco was telling the Headmaster about the concert for that evening. They were both looking out the windows in the student dining hall. Mr. Orisco was gesticulating with his hands, while explaining his plans for the evening, when he saw Erfce run over and jump onto the stage. "What's that student doing?" he asked. He knew the students didn't appreciate him. He had caught several of them attempting to play practical jokes on him. Fearing Erfce was going to try to sabotage this evening's performance, Mr. Orisco studied him with apprehension.

Several of the students in the dining hall heard Mr. Orisco. Curious to see what was going on, they stood up and moved over to the windows. They watched as Erfce returned to the apple trees and placed the guitar he had taken, down onto the ground in front of Rhen. Rhen hesitated a moment, before picking it up.

"Oh," Mr. Orisco huffed, turning to march out of the room. "If that Surpen oaf thinks he's going to touch one of my guitars, he's got another thing coming."

As soon as Mr. Orisco said the word 'Surpen', the Thestran Royal Family, who had gathered in Rhen and Ceceta's seats to wait for them, moved to the windows. "There they are," James remarked, opening the window in front of him.

Most of the students in the dining hall were now crowding around the windows. They were eager to see the upcoming confrontation between Mr. Orisco and Rhen. Hopefully, Rhen would head butt Mr. Orisco, as he had Mr. Balot.

James sighed and turned to his siblings. "Will you guys go keep Rhen out of trouble. The last thing we need is to have Rhen attack a teacher."

"Sure," Lilly said.

As James turned back to the window, an enchanting melody floated into the room. It was a magnificent piece that left him mesmerized. James couldn't take his eyes off Rhen. The melody flowed in a gentle manner, became complex and detailed then tapered off, turning sweet again. When the piece was over, James realized his nose was pressed against the window's screen.

"Oh, Themrock!" he heard Latsoh and Crystam exclaim down below on the grass.

"Oh, Themrock is right," James whispered, listening in.

"That was pure genius! Your music takes my breath away," Latsoh told Rhen.

Rhen laughed at the compliment. It seemed odd to him to be getting praise for something he wasn't supposed to be doing. He placed the guitar on the ground and kicked it over towards Erfce. "I don't know what you're talking about? I don't play music! I'm Surpen," he told them, an innocent look on his face.

Tgfhi couldn't help himself. He grabbed Rhen's shoulders and shook him around playfully. Something moved near the school building, catching Tgfhi's eye. He looked up to find Mr. Orisco rushing down the hill towards them. "Oh, damn," he sighed. "Here comes the party pooper."

Mr. Orisco's short legs were working overtime, as he made his way to Rhen at top speed. "I didn't realize he could move that fast," Tgfhi commented.

"I saw that! You have detention!" Mr. Orisco yelled, his finger pointing at Rhen. "Actually," he added, "all of you have detention!"

No one replied. Mr. Orisco began to march around their little group, yelling insults. Ceceta dropped her head, covering her face with her hands. Her gesture made Rhen's anger flare. When Mr. Orisco was behind him, he leaned back and said, "Who cares."

Tgfhi's eyes widened. He pushed Rhen's leg with his foot, warning him to be quiet.

"I don't like you Surpen! You're a freak. A freak of nature. You belong locked up. They should have left you on your miserable planet!" Mr. Orisco yelled.

Due to the ground's acoustics, everyone in the dining hall could hear what Mr. Orisco and Rhen were saying. Several of the students and teachers gasped, when Mr. Orisco continued to shout obscenities at Rhen.

Taking his time, Rhen stood up and stared down at Mr. Orisco. "I don't like you either weasel face," he told Mr. Orisco, while the music teacher was taking a breath between his tirades.

Fury surged through Mr. Orisco. "How dare you speak to me with such disrespect?" Raising his hand, Mr. Orisco slapped Rhen across the face.

Rhen smiled at Mr. Orisco, daring him to continue. Without another thought, Mr. Orisco slapped Rhen again. "Thestran must have flies Ceceta, because I think I felt one whiz by," Rhen told her.

Any sense of control that Mr. Orisco had was now lost. He started to pummel Rhen with both of his hands, hitting him repeatedly, as hard as he could. Rhen stood in front of him smiling. With a scream of rage, Mr. Orisco picked up his walking stick from where he had dropped it and raised it in the air to strike Rhen on the head. As he brought the stick down towards Rhen's forehead, Rhen grabbed it with his right hand and yelled, "BOO!"

Startled, Mr. Orisco tumbled backwards, falling onto the ground. Rhen dropped the walking stick and bent over to grab Mr. Orisco by his poufy, brown hair. He twisted his grip so that Mr. Orisco's face was looking up at him, balled his right hand into a fist and raised it above his head. "This, you pathetic fool, is how you hit a man."

Rhen started to swing his arm down to punch Mr. Orisco but Reed arrived in time to grab his fist with both of his hands. Rhen stopped himself the minute he felt Reed, but the force of his movement was so strong that Reed lost his balance and fell onto Mr. Orisco, causing him to scream out in pain.

"Sorry," Rhen mumbled. He held out his hand to help Reed up.

"Thanks," Reed replied, as Rhen hauled him off the whimpering music teacher.

Although she didn't want to, Lilly helped Mr. Orisco up. She listened to his never-ending complaints, while walking him back towards the school.

"Pathetic fool," Rhen snarled, watching Mr. Orisco's retreat. "He should've been eliminated in infancy." Reed laughed, but when Rhen frowned at him, Reed realized Rhen wasn't joking. Charlie and Sage were just sitting down next to Crystam and Erfce, so Reed turned to join them. Rhen hesitated a moment, before sitting back down next to Tgfhi.

"So," Charlie said. "We heard your piece. It was amazing!"

"What?" Rhen asked. Charlie was looking right at him, but Rhen couldn't understand what he was talking about.

"We heard your piece," Charlie repeated. "It was fantastic!"

"My piece?" Rhen asked. A shiver of dread started to crawl up his spine. With increasing trepidation, Rhen asked Charlie, "You heard me play?"

Charlie nodded with enthusiasm, while pointing up at the windows of the University behind him.

Rhen and his friends looked up at the school to find thousands of faces in the open windows of the dining hall staring at them.

"We all heard you," Charlie informed him.

"Oh, that can't be good," Ceceta moaned, raising her hand to her mouth. She had wanted Rhen to break the rules, but not to get caught doing it. Now he was going to be punished because of her.

"It's fine," Sage reassured Ceceta, when she saw the fear in her face. "We can always say that Erfce was playing. The guitar is in front of him, isn't it?" Sage's words were empty comfort. They knew everyone had seen Rhen play.

"How long have you been playing the guitar?" Reed asked Rhen.

Realizing he had been caught and there wasn't any reason why he should hide it anymore, Rhen said, "A couple of days?" He glanced at Ceceta for confirmation, and she nodded her head.

"I don't understand. How did you play that piece?" Sage asked. "It was so complex."

Rhen shrugged in response. Answering Sage's question would've required him to speak about himself, and he still didn't like to talk to the Royal Family about his personal life, even if Ceceta had shown them his dirty laundry.

"The music is always in his head. When he has an instrument, he can get it out. Otherwise, it just swirls around, entertaining him during the day," Erfce explained. Rhen glared at Erfce and tossed a stick in his direction. It bounced off Erfce's hand. Erfce stuck his tongue out at Rhen in retaliation.

"Can you play other instruments?" Charlie asked.

"He can play anything and everything, singly or all together," Ceceta told him. "He's amazing. In fact, that's how I first fell in love with him." She gave Rhen a glowing smile. "He was so cute with his little flute. He would play and all of the women would sit around him sighing and looking at him with love in their eyes, but I got him!"

"Lucky you," Rhen answered with sarcasm.

"Well, come on then, forget the Debrino Code. Get your butt over to the bandstand. Let's hear some more music," Charlie blurted out.

"No," Rhen replied. "I don't think that would be wise."

"They've all heard you play," Tgfhi answered, pointing towards the University building. "It's just a matter of time before your father shows up. Why not enjoy yourself before he comes?"

It was a tempting suggestion. Rhen glanced over at the bandstand. Turning to Ceceta, he asked, "What's the punishment for playing music?"

"Your hands get cut off," Latsoh replied. After she had first heard Rhen's music, she had been motivated to find out what the Debrino Code's punishment was for performing. She wanted to know how much trouble Rhen would be in if he was ever caught.

"Oh, dude!" Charlie grimaced in horror. "Oh, well, I guess we aren't going to hear you play."

Rhen and Ceceta grinned at each other. "Just your hands? Are you sure?" Rhen asked Latsoh. She nodded. Rhen winked at Ceceta. "Well, let's get going before the King gets here!" He shifted his legs to stand up but stopped short. "No, wait. I didn't wear my shorts today." With a quick glance at the height of the stage, he added, "I can't play without them."

"I'll get them," Ceceta piped out. She jumped up and ran towards their apartment. Ceceta had been waiting for this moment for a long time. She couldn't wait. Now everyone would know how gifted Rhen was.

No one said anything, while they waited for Ceceta to return. In boredom, Rhen leaned over and scooped up the guitar that was resting on the ground in front of Erfce. The movement caused his tunic to hitch up and Reed noticed a black mark on his thigh. "What's that?" he asked.

Rhen nestled the guitar on his lap and looked over at Reed, "What?"

"That on your leg," Reed said, pointing towards Rhen's thigh.

Putting the guitar back on the ground, Rhen pulled his tunic up to show his upper thigh, which had the tattoo of a dagger.

"Wow!" Tgfhi exclaimed, leaning over to look at it. "It's amazing. It looks exactly like your dagger." Tgfhi snatched up the dagger from beside Rhen and held it next to the tattoo on Rhen's thigh. The two were identical. In fact, they looked so much alike, it was hard to tell which one was the real dagger and which one the tattoo. Latsoh felt like her eyes were playing a trick on her. Without thinking, she leaned over and touched Rhen's thigh. Rhen laughed at her, as she snatched her fingers away from his warm skin. "What, did you think it was real?" he teased.

"I can't believe it's not. It looks so real. Can I touch it again?" Rhen shrugged in response, so Latsoh reached out to touch it again.

"My turn," Tgfhi announced. He reached over and tapped Rhen's tattoo with his fingertips. Soon everyone was touching it. The thing was too realistic to believe.

"Damn that's good. Who did it? I want one," Tgfhi commented.

"The person who did it isn't doing tattoos anymore," Rhen told him.

Tgfhi frowned. "That's too bad. If they were still doing tattoos, I would've gotten a picture of the Black Angel." Rhen laughed and Tgfhi flushed with embarrassment. "What's the matter with that?" he asked, sounding defensive. "The Black Angel is amazing! He's a much better tattoo than a stupid dagger. Why did you choose a dagger anyway?"

Before Rhen could answer, Ceceta raced up to them panting. She tossed Rhen's military shorts onto his lap and glanced down at his tattoo. Crystam was poking at it with her finger, so Ceceta realized Rhen had been telling them about it. "That's cool, isn't it? I loved it when he showed it to me," she told them. Ceceta plopped down onto the ground next to Rhen to catch her breath. Her golden robes looked disheveled, as they fell to the ground around her. "I once asked him to keep taking daggers out of it to see if it would ever run out. We had 3,865 daggers before we finally just gave up." She laughed at the memory. "There were daggers everywhere. We didn't know what to do with all of them. Rhen hid some of them in our bedroom, until the King found them and thought he was stealing daggers from the armory." Ceceta smiled and shook her head. When she glanced back up at her friends, she found them staring at her with confused expressions on their faces.

Rhen rolled his eyes and shook his head. "I didn't show them that part, dear," he hissed.

Ceceta gasped. Guilt washed over her again. Her guilt turned to anger and she poked Rhen in the ribs to indicate he should show them what she was talking about.

Rhen slapped Ceceta's hand away and sighed. "Okay," he told them, after a long pause. He dropped his hand down towards his tattoo. "It looks realistic because it's…well, like magic." Rhen's hand had been resting against his tattoo. He twisted his wrist, so his palm was facing upward. A black dagger rested in the center of his hand. The dagger in his hand was the same as the one that Tgfhi was holding.

"NO WAY!" Tgfhi shouted. "Do it again!"

319

Rhen gave the dagger he was holding to Ceceta and dropped his hand back down to his tattoo. He twisted his wrist to reveal a new black dagger resting in his palm. His friends laughed with surprise at the sight of it.

"Okay," Reed began. "How does that work? I've never heard of 'magic' tattoos before."

There was nothing to do but tell the truth. No one had ever heard of magic tattoos before, because they didn't exist. Reed and the others would realize Rhen was lying, if he fabricated some story. Rhen knew he would be opening an enormous can of worms, when he told them the truth, but for some reason, he didn't care. Maybe it was because he was about to break one of Debrino's Codes by playing music, maybe it was because his 18th birthday was tomorrow, maybe it was because last night Ceceta had opened the door to his life for the Thestrans to walk right in, whatever the reason, he realized he didn't care anymore.

"Actually, it's a Genister tattoo," he admitted. He watched their faces become blank.

"Did you say Genister?" Sage asked. Rhen nodded. "But there are no Genisters. They're all dead."

"They aren't *all* dead," Rhen corrected her. "Some of them are dead but there are others that are still alive." Everyone was silent, as they contemplated what Rhen had just said. Realizing they were having trouble comprehending him, Rhen added, "Is Thaster dead?"

"Thaster gave you that tattoo?" Charlie snapped, while thinking to himself that there was something about Thaster and Rhen that he was supposed to remember.

"No," Rhen replied. "I was just proving to Sage that not all of the Genisters are dead."

"So, who gave you that tattoo?" Charlie demanded. Ceceta stared at Charlie. She had never seen him looking so cognizant, let alone forceful before.

"A Genister named Thellis gave it to me and he is dead," Rhen informed Charlie. Charlie nodded his head, as if it made sense.

"Rhen..." Sage began. "There are no Genisters. Someone is tricking you. The Genisters are gone."

"Well, Sage, if the Genisters are all gone, then how did I get a Genister tattoo?"

"If Thellis is dead, how did he give you a tattoo?" Erfce asked, feeling confused. "It doesn't make any sense?"

Rhen smiled at Erfce, who was trying to put the pieces together to make some sort of logic out of what he had just told them. "It appears that dead Genisters still have powers," Rhen informed him.

"Why did he give you the tattoo?" Reed inquired, in a monotone voice. He was staring, dumbfounded, at the grass, where the three daggers were lying.

"I was..." Rhen paused, remembering the night he had met Thellis. With a shake of his head, he told them, "I was having a rough night and he took pity on me. He wanted to give me the tattoo, so I'd always have a weapon to defend myself with."

"Why were you having a rough night?" Sage asked. "Were you in a war?"

"We'd just finished a war and...." he shrugged, as if the rest were obvious.

"How'd you do?" Tgfhi asked. Rhen gave him a curious look. "With the war," Tgfhi continued, "Did you lose? Is that why you were having a rough night?"

"No," Rhen laughed out. "We never lose Tgfhi. You should know that. We were fighting the Ellorians. We beat them after only three days. I had done really well and was awarded two bars that afternoon for my skill in battle."

"Oh, you weren't the head of the Surpen military yet? Who was in charge before you?" Latsoh asked.

The smile fell from Rhen's face. In a quiet voice, he told them, "Aul and Narseth."

The reason why Rhen was 'having a rough night' became clear. TheThestrans sat in silence. Thinking over everything that Rhen had told them.

"Did the Genister who gave you that tattoo, also give you the Genister Box that you gave to me for my wedding?" Sage asked.

"No. I got that another time. Do you still like it? I have a bunch of them at home."

"NO WAY!" Tgfhi cried out. Everyone had heard about Rhen's amazing wedding gift to Sage. Many of them had even seen Sage using it. "Can you give me one?" Tgfhi asked.

321

"Sure," Rhen said, before standing up. A large spacejet flew over their heads, leaving behind enough noise to make them all want to cover their ears. As Rhen looked up towards the spacejet, he saw Lilly and Rachel in the distance. They were walking down the hill to join them. Rhen figured Mr. Orisco was complaining to the Headmaster, so if they wanted to play music, they'd better start or they would lose their window of opportunity.

"Rhen, you can't have a bunch of Genister boxes at home," Reed stated, interrupting his thoughts. "The Genisters only ever made five of them."

"Five?" Rhen asked, turing to face Reed. "Who told you that? There are hundreds of them out there. They made them for their lovers."

"What?" Sage laughed out, feeling somehow slighted. "Why would they do that?"

"The Genisters were all related, right?" Rhen commented. At the blank look on their faces, Rhen shook his head. "The Genisters, who created our Universe, were all related. Since they couldn't date each other, they would take us as their lovers. Themrock," Rhen said, glancing down at Latsoh. "You'll be happy to know, made the first Genister box for a lover he really enjoyed. That lover was thrilled with her box, so ever since then the other Genisters copied him and made boxes for their lovers as well."

Reed gazed up at Rhen, as if he were a priest. In less than a minute, he had learned more about his Genister Gods than he had ever known before. His eyes fell on Sage, who's mouth was open, and he knew she felt the same way.

"How did you learn about that?" Lilly asked. She and Rachel had arrived in time to hear Rhen's speech.

Rhen sighed. Lilly and Rachel hadn't been there for his tattoo discussion, and he didn't want to have to review it all over again. He just wanted to play music before Andres came. "It's a long story," Rhen told her. He took a step towards the bandstand but felt his left foot drag something. Glancing down, he saw Latsoh clinging to his sneaker. "What're you doing?"

"You…you know Themrock?" Latsoh gasped out. Her green eyes were twice their normal size and her red hair fell down onto the grass at Rhen's feet.

"No," Rhen replied with a laugh. Of course, Latsoh would think something like that. "Sorry Latsoh."

"Did you learn where Themrock was imprisoned?" she asked, with desperation. "Do the other Genisters know? Could we possibly release him?"

Rhen bent down and took Latsoh's hands in his. "I'm sorry Latsoh, no one can rescue him. One of the other Genisters locked him into a void box. The only way for him to return is if that Genister releases him, and according to Thellis, that's not going to happen." Tears formed in Latsoh's eyes. "I'm sorry," Rhen told her again.

"So, Themrock's still locked up," Reed asked. He had hoped that Themrock had escaped. They'd had so many miracles in the last few days that he had thought it was a sign of Themrock's return.

"That's what Thellis told me," Rhen informed him.

"This just totally blows my mind!" Charlie shouted out. "Like, are you friends with Genisters?"

From their reactions, it was clear to Rhen that they couldn't handle the truth. "No," he told Charlie. "I met a Genister once and he talked a lot, while he gave me my tattoo." Rhen helped Latsoh to her feet. "Come, let's play some music. It'll make you feel better."

Before they left, Sage blurted out, "What does it say on my box?"

Rhen had no idea what her box said. He couldn't even read Surpen, let alone Genister. "Usually a box tells you who made it, who it was made for and how much that Genister loved that person. That's about it." Rhen pulled Latsoh forward, towards the bandstand. "Let's play before we lose our chance."

The others followed along behind them, a million questions racing through their minds.

When they reached the steps to the stage, Rhen released Latsoh's hand and ducked behind the stage to pull on his military shorts. Once he was done, he jumped up onto the stage to join the others. He cruised around the floor, inspecting the instruments on hand. As he touched them, he would gain an understanding of what sounds they were capable of and how to play them. When he was finished, he approached the control panel for the sound system. Rhen placed his hand on it, absorbing the knowledge of how it worked. Satisfied that he had learned what he needed to know, he walked over to Ceceta, who was sitting on a stool at the back of the stage.

"Which instrument would you like to play?"

Ceceta gave him a secret smile and batted her eyes. "I've always wanted to play the flute." Rhen laughed. He knew Ceceta liked the flute, because that had been his first instrument. Leaning over to give her a kiss, he reached out to pick up the flute that was beside her. "There you go," he said, placing it into her hands.

"Can I play the keyboard?" Crystam asked.

"Of course! All of you, pick up the instrument you want to play," he called out to the others.

Tgfhi threw himself down onto the seat by the drum set. "I can play the drums!" he yelled out. Without any rhythm, whatsoever, he started to bang on them.

"Okay, stop," Rhen told him, while holding up his hand. "You're going to give us all headaches." Tgfhi gave Rhen a sheepish look and mouthed 'sorry'.

When everyone seemed settled, Rhen glanced up at the University. The windows to the dining room were still filled with students' faces. "I hope they're not disappointed," he mumbled, before turning back to the Thestran Royals. "Just do me a favor and keep yourselves relaxed. I can move your bodies much more easily if you're relaxed."

"What do you mean?" Reed asked, but then he felt a presence inside him, as his fingers began to race up and down the guitar he was holding, so that he was jamming like a professional. "No, way!" he shouted with enthusiasm, before settling down to watch his body perform. A few seconds later, everyone joined in. They played a five-minute instrumental. When the last note was struck, Rhen released their bodies and the air was filled with laughter and cheers.

"Did I just do that?" Lilly asked, staring with awe at the violin she was holding. "That was awesome!"

"I've never had so much fun before in my life," Sage told the others.

"It's better than jet bike riding!" Reed exclaimed. Rhen raised his eyebrow and gave Reed a look. "Okay, it's just as much fun as jet bike riding," Reed acquiesced.

"Let's do another!" Charlie shouted out.

Rhen snatched up their bodies and they tore into another piece. Picking up the microphone, Rhen began to sing. When the song was over, no one had time to react, because he pushed them into another piece. Students were now running out of the building towards the bandstand, while the Wood Elves, who could hear the music in their castle, were flocking to the school to watch the performance.

"Do you want to keep going?" Rhen asked Ceceta. They had played four songs, and he was worried that they might be tired of performing.

"Are you kidding!" Charlie shouted. "This is amazing! Don't stop!"

"Alright," Rhen replied. "Why not? I'm going to get punished either way, right?" He pushed them into a new song that had the audience singing along. When Rhen needed to harmonize, he would pull their voices right out of their bodies. It made them feel breathless and odd, as he manipulated them, but they didn't mind, the end product was worth the strangeness of it all.

Many of the students had contacted friends and family members about Rhen's concert. The school's portal was packed with people arriving to watch the Surpen Prince sing. "I think there might be close to twenty thousand people here," Henry told Kate, as he glanced about the lawn.

"More than that," Kate declared, while dancing to the newest tune.

"He's really getting into it," Henry remarked. He watched Rhen march about the stage as he sang. Rhen was holding the microphone with his left hand, while his right hand grasped and released the hilt of one of his swords or punched out into the air for emphasis. After awhile, Rhen released himself completely and danced about the stage, while singing. From fight class, they knew that Rhen was flexible, but some of his moves seemed downright impossible, and when Rhen started playing with the weapons he was wearing, tossing them in the air and catching them, the crowd went wild.

When Rhen's friends and the Royal Family members became tired, Rhen would either take over the instrument they were holding and play himself or he would use his powers to make the instrument perform. The stage looked enchanted with the instruments floating in the air, while Rhen danced about singing.

"I'm hot," Rhen announced, after a particularly long song. He wiped the sweat from his face onto the sleeve of his turquoise tunic.

"You're dressed too heavily," Erfce told him. "Take my shirt." He pulled off his yellow t-shirt and tossed it over to Rhen. "You might not look as stylish, but you'll be a lot cooler."

"Thanks," Rhen said. Erfce's t-shirt was much lighter than his full tunic. Rhen took off the guitar that was hanging around his shoulders and placed it on the piano, along with his weapons belt. Pausing, he stared at the t-shirt in his hands. "Um, Erfce," he said with laughter in his voice. "There's no way your shirt is going to fit me." He lifted it up to his chest and laughed at the tiny shirt that he was holding next to his body. Rhen had never realized before how much smaller Erfce was. Tossing the shirt back to his friend, he said, "Thanks, but it's not going to work."

"Try mine," Reed called out. He stood up and pulled off his black t-shirt, to the thrill of the female Wood Elves. "I'm your size." Reed tossed Rhen his shirt and Rhen stepped out of view, behind the piano, to change. For added relief, Rhen took off his black sneakers and placed them on the piano beside his weapons belt and tunic. Glancing down, he saw Crystam sitting at the piano. She was finished with her break and wanted to play again. With a smile, Crystam lifted her hands up and placed them on the keys, while she waited for Rhen to move her body. Rhen laughed at her boldness and sat down beside her on the bench.

"Go ahead then," he teased, "play." He knew she couldn't play without him. Crystam frowned and shoved Rhen, making him laugh. When he still didn't command the music to begin, she pouted and dropped her hands into her lap, looking up at him with sad eyes. "I'm only teasing you," Rhen said. He reached over and grabbed her hands to put them back on the keyboard. For some reason, Crystam felt embarrassed. She wrestled playfully with Rhen, trying to pull her hands free from his grasp.

"Why are you being difficult," Rhen laughed out, as he fought with her.

Kate, like most of the audience members, was chuckling at the interplay between the two of them, when she felt the presence of someone powerful standing beside her. Before she could turn, to see who had arrived, she heard the person say in a rich, melodic voice, "My daughter seems to be taken with your son." Kate raised her eyebrows in shock. She knew that voice. The Queen of Ventar was on Thestran! With hesitation, Kate turned towards Chara. It was rare for Chara to leave Ventar, because her powers were so strong; they caused the men and women around her to lose control. In fact, to the best of Kate's knowledge, Chara had never left her palace, let alone her planet.

"Queen Chara," Kate announced with surprise, while noticing that James was walking over in Chara's direction with an impish grin on his face. 'Oh, no,' she thought. James had been hit by Chara's powers.

When James reached Queen Chara's side, he leaned over to sniff the sleeve of her floor-length, blue dress. James had an enormous smile on his face and his eyes appeared unfocused.

Queen Chara glanced in James' direction, before turning back to Kate.

"What an honor to have you on Thestran," Kate told Chara, hoping to distract her from James. She could feel Chara's powers starting to work on her, so she turned away from the Ventarian Queen and focused her mind on the distant bandstand.

"I heard my daughter was putting on a concert with her friends. Since she hasn't any musical ability whatsoever, I decided to see what she was doing," Queen Chara explained. "I ran into Erfce's parents and King Tgonar, Tgfhi's father, on my way here from the portal," she added, pointing towards Kate's left.

Kate glanced in the direction in which Chara pointed and saw that Erfce's mother was fanning his father. It appeared he had passed out after meeting Chara. Behind them, she caught sight of Tgonar, the King of Tgarus. His entire body was soaking wet. Kate wondered if he had doused himself with water, in order to keep control of his senses, after meeting Chara.

With a shake of her head, Kate peered back at Chara, to see how James was doing. Unfortunately, her eyes met Chara's and Kate felt herself losing control. With haste, Kate used her powers to float up into the air. The coldness of her powers lessened, to some degree, Chara's effect. Kate willed herself to look away from the Queen. She was relieved when Rhen distracted her by announcing that his next song was in honor of his good friend, Crystam. Everyone clapped as the song began.

Out of the corner of her eye, Kate saw several men and women crawling on their hands and knees towards Queen Chara. She would have laughed at the sight of them, but she noticed James' wife, Susan, glaring at James and realized the situation really wasn't that funny. Thank goodness Henry had moved down by the stage to watch the performance.

Sneaking another quick peak back at Queen Chara, Kate noticed that the King of Mercioles was now licking her right shoe and the Elfin Royals, Naci, Chaster, and Reman, had joined the throng of people kissing her dress. Chara seemed unphased by their behavior. It appeared she was used to it. Kate felt sorry for her. A life like hers couldn't be easy.

Rhen's song for Crystam was magnificent and everyone applauded when it was over. Queen Chara was startled to find herself moved by the song. Music did nothing for her, but something about Rhen's voice was…different. It touched her in some manner that she couldn't quite grasp. She felt she could listen to him for days and days and never tire of it. She had caught a glimpse of Rhen's powerful shoulders, as he was changing his shirt, and she wondered what it would be like to run her hand across Rhen's chest. BANG! An alarm went off in Chara's head, knocking her back to reality. Rhen had powers! She couldn't quite figure out what his powers were, but whatever they were, they had mesmerized the entire audience and everyone was left wanting more. Rhen had control over everyone watching. His powers were similar to hers, so she was able to detect them, but no one else seemed to have any idea how much they were under his influence. Chara smiled to herself, as she looked around at the audience. Yes, they were under his power, but what power did he have that could cause a reaction like this?

Shaking her head, Chara glanced away from the bandstand. She told herself it was better not to watch Rhen too closely. She didn't want to fall under his spell. Chara stared down at the King of Geis, who was holding up wilted blades of grass he had ripped out of the ground to give to her as a gift. With a disgusted shake of her head, she looked away from him. She had learned the hard way that it was better to ignore her admirers than to encourage them. Any kindness on her part would only make them more desperate for her attention. Chara glanced up at the University, while thinking about the reports waiting for her on her desk and saw something that made her skin crawl. There, on the third floor, were at least fifteen Zorthans hanging out of the University's windows watching Rhen, and if her eyes weren't mistaken, she thought she saw the tail eyes of a Vivist or two peering out of the windows next to them.

King James had now fallen to his knees and was rubbing himself against her left leg. Chara felt he needed to know about the Zorthans and Vivists, so she waved her powers away from his body. When James' eyes came back into focus, and he glanced over towards his wife looking guilty, Queen Chara knew she could speak to him. "James," she said, waiting for him to finish getting control of himself.

After a moment, James nodded, but he kept his eyes trained on his wife. He knew that if he looked at Chara again, he would turn back into a sex-starved idiot.

"Look over at the third-floor windows on the right side of the building. Do you see a number of Zorthans watching Rhen?" Chara asked.

James's head jerked around, as he scanned the building. Chara was right. On the third floor, he could see several Zorthans, wearing military gear, hanging out of the windows. Some of them seemed to be dancing, and as he squinted his eyes, he saw they were also singing along to Rhen's music.

"Themrock's Balls!" James exclaimed with anger. The people near him glanced over at him. James pointed up towards the Zorthans. "Look! Zorthans, dancing and singing to Rhen's music, as if they'd been invited!"

"And a Vivist," Queen Chara added.

Everyone gasped. They searched the University's windows for the Vivist. "Not *a* Vivist," William told them, walking up behind them. "I counted at least six of them, when I came out of the portal." William was careful to keep his eyes averted from Chara. He had noticed the horde of people lying at her feet and he had no intention of becoming one of her victims.

"They can't stay!" James snarled. "We are NOT entertaining Vivists and Zorthans!"

"You're not," the Fire Elf Prince, Aaron, said, while struggling to pull his parents, Naci and Reman, away from Queen Chara's long skirt. He stepped on Mr. DiGrego by accident, as he worked to haul his father away from Chara, adding, "Rhen is. He's like a God of music." With effort, Aaron removed his father's hands from Chara's skirt and dragged him towards the Teachers'

Residence Hall, dumping him onto the ground by the stairs before returning to get his mother.

James watched the Zorthans, as they laughed and sang to Rhen's music. "No," he said, shaking his head and turning to go. "I can't allow this."

Kate stopped him, putting her hand on his sleeve. "Ceceta told us that Rhen is the 'King of Music'," Kate reminded him. "Let them watch, let them adore him and let them realize that he's one of us. It will help us in the long run."

"But he doesn't consider himself to be one of us and they know that!" James argued.

"I know, but watch him with his friends. Rhen's one of us, whether he wants to admit it or not," the Water Elf Queen, Neka, replied. She pulled on her husband, Plos, to try to remove him from Chara.

James struggled to keep himself from having the intruders arrested. He hated the Vivists and Zorthans with a passion. They, along with the Rasacks, were a plague on the Universe. He realized Kate's advice was wise and slowly calmed himself down. Motioning for several of his soldiers to approach, James told them, "Surround the rooms where the Vivists and Zorthans are located. They're not allowed to wander the University's grounds." After his soldiers had left, James marched over to his wife. "I'm so incredibly sorry," he began.

Susan lifted up onto her toes and to kiss him. "Really, James," she said, while watching King Plos, who loved his wife more than anything else in the Universe, kiss the hem of Chara's dress. "If Plos can't control himself around Chara, then no one can. You have nothing to apologize for."

"I love you," James told her. He took Susan into his arms and danced with her to one of Rhen's songs.

Several hours later, Rhen was starting to tire. During his last two songs, he sat on a chair and slid himself back and forth across the stage, which drove the teenage girls, who were watching him, crazy. Every time Rhen would near the edge of the stage, they would reach out to try to touch him, but he would slide away from their grasp.

Rhen paused after his last song and fell silent. Then, unexpectedly, he leaned back in his chair and started to sing an old Surpen war song. Rhen's performance, up until this point, had been spectacular, but now his audience was starting to fidget. It seemed as if Rhen had lost track of what he was doing. When the final chords of the war song began to repeat themselves for the fourth time, some of the students giggled uncomfortably.

Suddenly, everyone felt a cold, swirling, dizziness in their minds. When it cleared, they were left with an image of the back of a Surpen Beast of War in their heads. They realized they were looking at the beast through Rhen's eyes, as he was riding it high into the sky. Someone was transmitting Rhen's memory. Whatever Rhen had been thinking about, when the Surpen song was repeating itself, was now in their minds.

The audience watched as Rhen looked up into two suns. The light blinded him for a moment. He turned his head to the right, to clear his eyes, and stared down at a battle scene that was playing out below him. With a tired sigh, Rhen clicked to his Surpen beast. The animal turned and dove towards the ground at a sickening speed. Rhen's eyes scanned the battlefield, assessing his army's strengths and weaknesses and taking in his enemy's battle plan. The Surpen Beast of War that he was riding, tilted its wings and skimmed over the battlefield with grace. Rhen's arms were resting at his sides. His swords were in his hands. Rhen knew where he needed to strike, and he was waiting for his beast to get closer.

When they arrived above the weak spot in his ranks, Rhen flung himself sideways over his beast, clutching to his saddle with his thighs, as he dangled almost below his beast's stomach. With vigor, he lashed out with his swords, slashing and stabbing at his enemy, butchering and decapitating countless numbers of soldiers as he flew over them. Rhen's men cheered. He barked out orders to them in Surpen, while his beast spun in a circle above their heads, flipping Rhen back up into the saddle. They had reached the end of the weak spot and needed to turn around to have another go. Rhen clicked to his beast. The animal flipped about, its wings beating against its own draft. When they drew closer to the weak spot, Rhen flung himself over the side of his beast again, so he was almost upside down, as he slashed out at the enemy soldiers.

By now, the opposing forces realized they were unable to defend themselves from Rhen's attack, so they fell back to regroup. As Rhen pulled himself up into his saddle, he glanced towards his right to determine his enemy's next move and his eye caught sight of a woman and child being chased by a group of men. Rhen couldn't figure out where they had come from, perhaps the farm house to the left of the battlefield? If they were the farmer's family, why hadn't they left earlier, before the war had begun? Rhen kicked his war beast and barked to it with urgency. The beast shot forward, as Rhen leaned down over its shoulder, urging the animal to fly faster.

Deep over enemy territory, the soldiers below Rhen fired at him with their blasters. Rhen swung around his beast in circles, while using his swords to deflect the blasts. As he neared the woman and child, he sheathed one of his swords, leaned over in his saddle and scooped them up into his right arm. Making a clicking sound, he told his beast to climb straight into the sky. A blast from one of his enemy's weapons caught Rhen on his side. Rhen grunted in pain and looked down at the hole that had been blown through his abdomen.

At that moment, the woman and child struggled against Rhen. He lost his grip on them and they started to fall. Rhen swung himself down, underneath his beast, catching them, and tossing them back up on top of his beast. Rhen let go of his saddle and made a loud cluck sound. His Surpen Beast of War swung its tail forward, hitting him and sending him sailing through the air towards Surpen's side of the battlefield. Rhen landed on the ground near his tent, rolling several times, until his momentum slowed. With a shake of his head, Rhen stood up. He searched the sky for his beast. The animal was headed straight for him. Rhen smiled and looked back down at his side to check his wound. Although his clothes were a tattered mess, his body was fine. He had healed.

Rhen's beast landed in a run, coming up alongside him. Rhen helped the woman and her child down from his saddle. Turning towards his tent, Rhen was about to tell them to wait for him, and he would release them after the battle, but a sword lashed out from Rhen's left, striking the woman and child and killing them both. As Rhen watched them fall to the ground at his feet, fury filled his young body. He pulled out his own swords to kill the person responsible for their deaths, only to find his father glaring at him.

"We're at war!" Andres shouted. "What do you think you're doing saving slaves? Get back to business!" His father growled and raised his sword, as if he were going to hit Rhen.

Rhen ignored Andres. He looked down at the woman and child lying on the ground at his feet. The people watching Rhen's memory could sense something strong building within him, but they never knew what it was, because at that moment, everyone at the school felt a blow to their face. Snapping out of the memory, they looked up towards the stage to find Rhen standing over Erfce. Erfce's nose was bleeding and he had fallen to the floor. He stared up at Rhen in shock.

"I'm so, so, so very sorry. I don't know how that happened," Erfce apologized, his hand cupped his nose, as he shivered from his powers. "You've never opened up your mind to me before. It was so unexpected. Your mind has always been silent and then, suddenly, there was this overwhelming image flowing out of you." Erfce lifted both of his hands towards Rhen. "Please forgive me. I didn't know how to block it. I haven't learned how to block such powerful images."

Rhen raised his hand, as if to strike Erfce again, but before he could, twenty Surpen soldiers marched onto the stage. They had been sent by Andres to bring Rhen home for his punishment for playing music.

Angry at Erfce's betrayal, Rhen threw the microphone down onto the ground beside his friend. He released the instruments that were floating in the air, causing them to crash onto the stage. Snarling several Surpen curses at Erfce,

Rhen turned and walked off the stage into the University building, surrounded by the Surpen soldiers.

The crowd was silent, as they digested the images Erfce had sent to them. Picking up Rhen's discarded clothing, Ceceta and her friends made their way up to her apartment to escape. Lilly, Sage, Reed and Charlie joined them. As Lilly healed Erfce's broken nose, he apologized again. "I'm really sorry. I didn't mean to do that. The images were just too strong for me. I couldn't stop them." Lilly patted Erfce on the shoulder. She understood. He didn't need to explain it to her.

When it was dinner time, they left Ceceta's apartment for the student dining hall, pushing their way through the remaining crowds of people. The entire Wood Elf Army was present now, organizing people into groups and ushering them to both the school's portal and the portal in the Wood Elf Castle.

As Ceceta and the others arrived in the dining hall, they heard Rhen's music playing in the back of the room. One of the students had recorded Rhen's performance and was playing it for the student body, while taking orders for copies. His table was surrounded by students and teachers.

"Unbelievable," Tgfhi mumbled. He sat down next to Ceceta, who was eating her meal. A gust of air blew past them. Tgfhi turned around to find a Surpen soldier in full military gear standing behind him. "Uh, Ceceta?"

Ceceta swallowed the food in her mouth and shifted in her seat. As soon as she saw the Surpen soldier, she paled and dropped to the floor in a bow. The soldier tossed the scroll he had been holding, down onto the floor in front of her. Ceceta whipped her hands out, grabbed it and pulled it in towards her body. While she was reading the scroll, she realized the student dining hall had become quiet. The students and teachers had noticed the Surpen soldier's presence, and they were approaching him, hoping to learn if Rhen would soon be arriving.

"Where did you come from?" Charlie asked the soldier. The man stared at Charlie with a blank expression, before turning back to Ceceta, who was pulling a pen and paper out of her bag on the floor.

"Ceceta, how did he get here?" Sage asked loud enough for her to hear.

"Rhen sent him," she whispered from the floor, while writing a note to Rhen.

"What?" Sage asked.

"Rhen has the power to appear and disappear where ever he wants to. He can do it not only with himself but with others," Ceceta clarified in a louder voice, hoping the soldier wouldn't report her to Andres for speaking in public.

"You mean he doesn't need a portal?" Sage asked. She'd never heard of someone not needing a portal.

"No," Ceceta replied. "But you already knew that. He used this power of his on Latsoh, Crystam and me after he made his typhoon. Remember? He brought us out onto the lake to stand behind him." Sage frowned. They had been so taken with Rhen's powers over water that none of them had considered how he had moved Ceceta and her friends. "The number of times I would be walking down a corridor or reading with his mother and then POOF," Ceceta continued. "I'm standing next to him on a hill or sitting in front of him on his war beast or lying down…" she paused and blushed, giving the table a furtive glance, before turning back to the scroll in her hands. No one needed to hear her finish that thought. From the look on Crystam's face, she could see they already knew where she had been going.

"So, if he doesn't need a portal, why does he use it?" Charlie asked.

"You heard the King the other day, he's forbidden from using his powers. BUT," she added, "he can use them if we are at war. Which means," she held up Rhen's letter, "we will soon be at war. Surpen is close to declaring war on the Planet of Milow. Rhen won't be returning until the war is over." She could smell Loreth's influence on this one and it made her nervous. Why would Loreth declare war on Milow?

Reed leaned down to Ceceta and whispered, "How did Rhen write that?"

"He didn't write it," she replied. "It was written by one of his scribes, but it contains his thumbprint to mark its authenticity." Ceceta gave Rhen's scroll to Reed, so he could look it over. Turning back to the floor, she pushed the letter she had written towards the feet of the waiting soldier. The man bent down to pick it up, there was a tremor in the air and he disappeared.

"That's amazing!" Charlie declared. "Poof!" he gestured with his hands, as everyone laughed at him. "Poof, poof!"

A few minutes later, without any warning, the soldier reappeared beside Ceceta. She dropped down to the ground again, as he flung a new scroll onto the floor in front of her. Ceceta snatched it up and read it, before pulling the paper and pen back out of her bag.

While Ceceta was writing, Lilly reached over and picked up Rhen's letter. She pulled out an oval, translating sphere and held it over the words. Without permission, she proceeded to read the letter aloud to the others. Ceceta glanced up at her with a frown, but kept her mouth shut, as she continued to write her response.

"...and you should know that I'm not mad at Erfce," Lilly read to the group around her. "After I got home, I had a few minutes to think about what had happened and I realized he couldn't have stopped himself. Really, if I were to be mad at anyone, it would have to be me. I should've known better than to let my guard down. It was a stupid mistake on my part, one that I will not make again. Thanks for your birthday wishes. I hope to see you soon. Love, Rhen." Lilly paused at the last part of the letter. "Birthday wishes? I thought his birthday was a month away," she commented, in a hesitant voice.

"Why would you think that?" Ceceta responded, without looking up.

Lilly shook her head with disappointment and gazed over at Reed and Sage. She should've known that her mother had lied about the date of Rhen's birthday. It should've occurred to all of them to look it up, instead of relying on Kate's memory. Her mother had hesitated way too long, before giving them his birthday date. Once again, her family had messed up regarding her little brother.

"When is his 18th birthday Ceceta?" Reed asked, dreading her answer.

"Tomorrow," Ceceta replied. She folded up her letter and pushed it forward, towards the Surpen soldier's feet.

"TOMORROW!" Sage and Reed shouted. They stood up abruptly.

"Yes," Ceceta replied, turning to look at them with concern. Their reactions were unsettling. She waited until the Surpen soldier had disappeared, before standing up herself. "I thought you knew it was tomorrow, because you've been hanging out with us more than you usually do. I thought you were here to protect us."

"We are," Reed informed her. "We just didn't know that it was tomorrow." He turned towards Lilly and Sage. "Let's go to the palace to inform the others." With a nod to Charlie, who was giving them a dumb smile, Reed said, "You stay here and keep Ceceta safe." He paused to make sure that Charlie had understood him and was coherent, before leaving the room with his sisters.

After they had gone, Charlie turned to Ceceta and grinned, while bobbing his head. "Cool! Happy Birthday little brother!" he sang out, oblivious to the others' panic.

Reed called an emergency meeting in the Thestran Royal Castle. "Rhen's 18th birthday is tomorrow!" he told his family and the Elfin Royals, when they arrived. "He's been in communication with Ceceta to tell her that he will not be returning to Thestran, until after Surpen's war with Milow is over."

"Surpen's at war with Milow?" James asked.

"Apparently, they will be declaring war any minute now," Lilly answered for Reed.

"We must go to Surpen now, to get him back," Kate exclaimed, running from the room. She stormed into the Thestran Council Chamber and halted before one of the many portals. "SURPEN!" she bellowed, but the portal did not respond. "SURPEN!" she repeated. Again, nothing happened.

James put out his hand to stop her from screaming again. "Surpen," he said. Nothing happened. It was as if the portal was broken.

Just as James was about to ask the portal to open to Surpen a second time, the King of Meircoles stepped out of a second portal beside them. "It won't work," he snarled. "I've been talking with the other Council Delegates for almost an hour. The Surpens are rejecting all forms of communication. It seems as if the prophecies are about to become true." He stepped closer to James in a threatening manner. "Tell me, why is Rhen back on Surpen? Weren't we supposed to keep him here in order to stop Universal warfare?"

James ignored his rude comment. "Do you know why the portal won't work?" he asked.

The Meircoles King raised his hands into the air and shook them. "Because the prophecy has begun," he hollered. "Surpen has closed its portals to all visitors until further notice. I've heard from the others that they won't even let you fly into their space. Universal war is on our doorstep and we lost the one person we needed to secure our victory."

"We haven't lost anything," James told the Delegates who were present. "We've been working to soften Rhen towards Thestran. If we succeeded, we'll be safe."

"Have you succeeded?" the Delegate Te of Neptian asked in a confrontational manner from across the room.

"We need to talk to Rhen," Kate murmured to her family, ignoring Te's comment.

"Portal, open to the Elfin University," Sage said. The portal's blue light flickered on and the University's portal room appeared on the other side of the frame. Sage pulled on her mother's sleeve. "Come on. Rhen is sending letters to Ceceta. If he's still doing it, we can get him a message." With a curt nod, Kate followed her through the portal. They raced through the University, barging into the student dining hall just as an armed Surpen soldier disappeared in front of them.

Kate stumbled to a stop. "How did he...?" she began.

Lilly pushed her mother forward. "Rhen sends him back and forth. He doesn't need a portal. We saw him use that power right after he made the typhoon, but none of us focused on it, since we were all surprised by his powers over water."

They arrived at Ceceta's table to find her holding four scrolls from Rhen. She looked up at them with concern, as they surrounded her. "Is everything okay?" she asked, when none of them spoke.

Charlie appeared to be sleeping beside her. His head was down on the table and his eyes were closed. Reed kicked him in the leg until he woke up.

"Ceceta, can we see Rhen's letters to you?" Lilly asked, when James and her parents remained silent. "It's very important." Ceceta hesitated, before nodding yes. She held up three of the four letters. The Royal Family reached for them at once.

"Is that soldier coming back with a response to your last letter?" Sage asked.

Ceceta shrugged and replied, "I don't know. Rhen doesn't need to respond if he doesn't want to."

The first two letters Lilly had already read, so she took the third letter. In the third letter, Rhen told Ceceta that the Surpen army was planning on mobilizing within the next hour. He mentioned that, in response to the end of her last letter, she was a mush, and in true Surpen form, he was going to have to eat her the next time he saw her.

Lilly reached for the fourth scroll, but Ceceta tucked it away into her golden robes. "That one's a little more personal," she commented, while blushing. Before Lilly could insist they read the scroll, the Surpen soldier reappeared. He saluted Ceceta, as she dropped to the floor. The soldier tossed Rhen's scroll down onto the floor beside her. William was standing next to them, so he reached down to take it. The soldier drew his sword and placed it at William's neck. The scroll was meant for Ceceta and his orders were to give it to her and no one else. A tense moment passed, until William backed away.

When William was no longer in danger, Ceceta reached out for the scroll. She read it in silence, before handing it to Lilly. There was no point in hiding it from her; the Royals had seen the scroll arrive. Ceceta began to write her response, as the Surpen soldier waited, sword in hand.

As soon as Lilly had Rhen's letter, she used her translation sphere to read it out loud. "Yes, you are funny my dear. Now it's my turn. Do you remember how we got to that island in the first place? Need I say more? Why don't you come back to Surpen and greet me when I finish this war? Or, you can meet me in Crithnians, whichever. Regarding the war, I've never seen Dad so nervous before a battle. He's pacing back and forth about the encampment, as if his walking will ensure our victory. Perhaps he thinks I've lost my edge. Nothing I say seems to reassure him. He keeps drinking this odd flavored drink that Loreth made and he insists that I share it with him. It's becoming a bit of a bore. The Milow's latest dispatch has just arrived. It doesn't matter what they say. Dad's made up his mind about this battle. See you soon. Love, Rhen."

Ceceta was just finishing her return letter. Before she could fold it to send it to Rhen, Sage asked, "Would you tell us what your letter says and perhaps let us send him a message too?"

"Sure," Ceceta agreed, handing her letter to Lilly. She had assumed they would be reading it, so she had made it less personal.

In a loud voice, Lilly read Ceceta's letter for the others. "Sorry dear, I have no interest in returning to Surpen right now. You do realize that exams are coming up and somebody in this family has to start studying. You could get me to Crithnians in a minute, of course, but not until after the Astronomy finals. I'm sorry your Dad is acting like a pain. Is he getting drunk off the drink? Are you? I always told you he needs to try more recreational activities." Charlie laughed. Everyone stared at him until he shut up. Continuing, Lilly read, "Are the Milows nice people? Why are we at war with them again? How's Bartar? I love you more than anything, Ceceta."

Lilly dropped the letter down to Ceceta. "So, do you want to add anything?" Ceceta asked them.

"No," James told her, after he had checked with the others. "We'll send a message with the next letter." They watched as Ceceta handed the letter to the soldier and he disappeared.

Five minutes later, he returned with Rhen's response. Glaring at William, he tossed the scroll down onto the floor before Ceceta.

"Would you read it out loud to us?" Kate asked Ceceta.

"Sure," she told them. Ceceta gave the letter a quick scan for content and began, "I love you more than anything too. Within the next few minutes, we go to battle. Sorry I can't get you back to Surpen, but I will keep Crithnians in mind for future reference. Dad has only gotten worse, and no, the drink is not acting as a soothing elixir. It tastes terrible, so I'm not sure why he's drinking it, except for the fact that Loreth made it. Need I say more? The Milows are nice people. Dad's declared war because he wants them to provide us with more food for the beasts of war. Why we're going to war over this and not simply negotiating it is beyond me and I think the Milow's too? Go figure, Dad is Dad. Did I mention that Loreth is here? Need I say more? Bartar is great. I didn't realize I would miss Bartar so much. By the way, Nk is going to get into trouble soon. His forward thinking has caused him to be beaten many times over the last few weeks. Hopefully, he'll come back to our Surpen ways before we have to kill him. Okay, time to go. All my love, Rhen."

At once, Ceceta began to write a response. "What are you writing?" James asked. He lifted his cowboy hat to scratch his head. "It sounds as if he's already gone into battle." They were too late to send Rhen a message now.

"He has," Ceceta told them. "But I always send him my love, so when he comes out of a battle, he can read it and remember not to get too carried away with conquering things. If Andres and Loreth had their way, one battle would lead directly into another and there would be no rest. Rhen usually tells them he needs a break after a battle, so he can come back to me."

"Thank God," Rachel said.

Ceceta sealed her letter and pushed it towards the waiting soldier. He saluted her and disappeared. After he was gone, Ceceta got up off the floor.

"Okay," Reed asked her. "Who is Bartar?"

Ceceta laughed. "Bartar is his Surpen Beast of War. You saw him in Rhen's flashback, the one that Erfce transmitted to everyone." She looked up at the clock on the dining room wall. "Whoops, I've got to go to Astronomy. See you." Turning, she walked out of the dining hall with her friends, as the Royal Family headed back towards the portal.

There was nothing more to be done.

Chapter 25

"I want Ceceta here, in the castle, for the next two days," James barked at his family. "If Lilly is right and Andres tries to assassinate her, she'll be safer with us."

"I'll get her," Lilly offered. She rose from her chair in the Thestran Council Chamber.

"Now, what's going on with Surpen," James asked his Delegates, turning back to the Council Chamber.

"Surpen has closed its borders," a Delegate announced.

"It's a damned nightmare logistically," another Delegate declared. "They have the largest territory, six solar systems. The fact that no one is allowed to cross their space...it's a nightmare!"

"It's wreaking havoc with everyone's trade routes," a Delegate to James' right informed him.

The room filled with conversation, as everyone complained about Surpen's actions. While the Delegate from Xhingo discussed his need for new space jet refueling stations, now that Surpen's borders were closed, an emergency message flashed on the viewing screens above the Council Delegates' heads. The fuzzy image of the King of Milow and his military advisor appeared on the screens above them. The Milowian King's face had aged a great deal, since the last time they had seen him. "Thestran Council," he called out over the screen. "The Surpens have wrongfully declared war on Milow. We beg you to come to our aid. Milow requests Thestran's protection immediately. The Surpens have slaughtered most of our army."

James rose to his feet, while pointing at his assistant. "Send the King of Surpen a message NOW! We demand he stop his war on Milow and request that he meet with us here in this chamber at once!" Turning towards the screens, where the Milowian King was waiting, James added, "Hold on, I've sent the message."

"Thank you," the King cried with relief.

It was obvious that Andres had been expecting their message, because three minutes later, one of the portals in the Council Chamber flashed to life and he sauntered into the room, escorted by his guard and an invisible Loreth. Andres was dressed in his military clothes, although it was clear that he had not been involved in the fighting. He smirked at the Delegates, while he strolled into the middle of their chamber, stopping just before the crescent desk that was used by the Thestran Royal Family. The Surpen King glanced around the room and smiled in a condescending manner. "You called?"

Behind Andres, Loreth chuckled in silence at the sweat on the Thestrans' faces. They were frightened. Perfect. If they were frightened now, they would be terrified later, when Surpen attacked.

"Stop your war against Milow!" James ordered Andres, while slamming his fist down onto the table in front of him for emphasis. "The Milowians have asked for our protection, and by Order 367 of the Thestran Code, we will offer it to them."

Andres looked up at the screens over their heads, where the Milowian King was watching him. He smiled and gazed down at his fingernails, making them wait a full minute, before answering, "I'm afraid you're too late to invoke Order 367."

As if on cue, there was a blur of movement on the screens above their heads. When the picture became clear, the Delegates realized they were looking at Rhen's back. He was holding the King of Milow and his Chief Military Advisor in the air by their throats. Both men were squirming in his grasp, as they struggled to breathe. Rhen made a 'humph' sound, before saying, "Game Over!" He dropped them onto the floor. "I win."

The Milowian King and his advisor clutched at their necks, gasping for air. Their eyes were round with terror.

"You were much too easy to beat. I had hoped to find this battle challenging. What a waste of my time. I could've crippled your planet with half the force I brought." Turning towards his right, where the door to the room was located, Rhen made a motion with his hand. Several Surpen soldiers ran into the room, dragging the Milowian King's family and his top lords. As the Surpen soldiers were securing the Milowians into groups, Rhen motioned for one of his men to approach. "Send word to my father that victory is ours," he told the soldier.

"RHEN," Andres barked.

Rhen swung about, pulling his sword from his belt in a smooth motion and pointing it at the screen. His Surpen military outfit was covered in blood. Even though Andres had just startled him, the Delegates could see that he was relaxed. Today's battle had been easy for him.

Realizing his father and Loreth (Loreth never missed one of their battles) were not directly behind him, but on a viewing screen, Rhen dropped his sword down and resheathed it. He saluted his father, before declaring, "Your majesty. Surpen is victorious."

"Well done Rhen," Andres praised. He turned away from the royal viewing screens to look at Kate. "I win," he announced, while facing James. "According to your law, if one solar system has already defeated the other, the losing solar system cannot legally invoke Order 367. You are too late." Andres gazed back up at the screens, where Rhen was awaiting his orders. "In more ways than one, I think you'll find," he added, in a sinister way, before yelling, "Rhen, finish the job!"

Rhen saluted his father and turned away from the screen. He told his soldiers to behead the Milowians and started towards the exit.

"No," Loreth hissed in Andres' ear. "Have Rhen kill them himself. It will strike fear in the hearts of the Thestrans."

"RHEN, WAIT!" Andres bellowed.

Rhen waved his hand to stop his men from executing the Milowians. "Your majesty?" he asked, turning back towards the viewing screen.

"I want you to personally finish this job. Kill them yourself!" Andres demanded.

Rhen nodded and ordered his men to release the Milowian King and his military advisor. He pulled two swords from his weapons belt and tossed them to the Milowians. Grabbing a dagger from one of his men, he braced himself to fight the Milowians in hand to hand combat.

"No, not that way," Loreth growled into Andres' mind.

"NO!" Andres shouted, while racking his brain to figure out what Loreth wanted. "Do it executioner style." He hoped that would please Loreth.

It must have, since Loreth didn't bother disguising his gleeful laugh at the prospect of Rhen executing unarmed men in front of the Thestrans.

Rhen paused. "Father, you know I don't like to kill that way. There's no sport in it. Where's the fun?"

"EXECUTIONER STYLE NOW!" Andres bellowed. He couldn't believe Rhen was questioning him. God help him if Rhen refused. Loreth would kill both of them.

Rhen's shoulders dropped, as he considered his options. He hated killing people in executioner style. As he lifted his head up, to look at the viewing screen again, he caught Reed's eye. Rhen started at the sight of his brother. "Okay, Dad," he told Andres a moment later.

Reed blinked and shifted some papers around on his desk, keeping his face blank.

Rhen stared at his father on the viewing screen. He couldn't see Loreth, but he knew his father's advisor was there. He'd have to use his powers on this one. It was imperative that he trick not only Andres but Loreth too. Rhen held out his hand for his sword. His men knocked the Milowian King and his advisor to the ground, so they were kneeling before Rhen. Lifting one of his swords into the air, the Thestrans watched in horror, as Rhen swung his weapon through the neck of the Milowian King. They heard the slicing sound of metal on bone and screamed, when Rhen held up the Milowian King's severed head. "One," Rhen declared. He tossed the head to one of his men and repeated his actions with the Milowian advisor. "Two," Rhen told his audience, holding up the second head. Regarding the screen with half-closed eyes, Rhen asked, in an aggravated voice, "Do you want to watch me decapitate the rest of them or can I end transmission and finish my work?"

Andres laughed and waved at Rhen to end transmission. He was thrilled with his son's performance, and from the chuckling he could hear to his right, so was Loreth. Fantastic! They would have an enjoyable celebration tonight.

"I believe," Andres stated, while walking towards the portals. "That tomorrow, you will find the Surpen God of War has been born." He turned to glare at Kate. "Your efforts have failed. You had best prepare yourselves for war. Although," he added, "I guess it doesn't really matter what you do, because no one can defeat my son Rhen. No one!" With a victorious laugh, he and his men stepped through the portal and vanished from sight.

Everyone in the Council Chamber started to shout at once: "What should they do?" "How were they going to stop Surpen?" "Had the Surpen King just declared war on them?" "Where should they send their armies?" "Who would be attacked next?"

Reed turned towards James. His brother looked terrible. Fear and defeat were etched all over his face. James considered their work with Rhen to have been a failure. "Hey," Reed said.

"What?" James croaked. He cleared his throat and asked again, "What?"

"You're not going to believe this," Reed told him. "But, Rhen didn't kill them." Kate gave Reed a look. "Seriously," Reed told her. James banged the Council bell for silence.

"My brother has something to say," James told the room, when it had quieted down.

Reed stood up to address the Delegates. "Rhen did not kill the King of Milow or his advisor."

There was a loud murmur in the room and someone yelled, "Preposterous! We just saw him do it with our own eyes." James banged the bell again for silence and Reed continued, "I know this sounds unbelievable, but I assure you, he did not kill them. The Surpen King does not fully control Rhen." Again, the Delegates murmured in disbelief, as James rang the bell for quiet a third time. Reed turned to James and said, "Just before Rhen was about to assassinate the King of Milow, he caught my eye and he told me he was going to play a trick. Rhen did slice off a head, but it was not the head of the Milowian King or his advisor, it was the head of a Milowian cow!"

The Delegates in the room started to jeer at Reed: "We saw their heads!" "It didn't look like a cow's head to me!" "What's the Royal Family going to do to stop the Surpens?" "Can Rhen conquer us?" "What powers does Rhen possess?"

Before Kate or James could answer any of their questions, the King of Milow, his entire family and his advisors and lords, popped into the center of the Council Chamber. They were kneeling with their heads bent forward and their eyes closed.

"Your highness?" James asked with surprise, as a silence fell over the room. The Milowian King lifted his head. His brown eyes filled with relief at the sight of the Thestrans. "What happened?" James asked. "We saw Rhen decapitate you."

Rising to his feet, the Milowian King approached Reed with a note. "He asked me to give this to you first," he told Reed.

Reed took the note and read it aloud. *"You did me a favor once. I've released the Milowians as a gift to you Reed. I hope you'll consider my debt to you paid in full. Rhen."*

"What does that mean?" someone asked.

"Whatever you did for him," the Milowian King said. "Thank you for doing it. Thank you for our lives."

"Yes, thank you," the other Milowians called out.

"Please," James asked. "Will you tell us what happened? We saw you decapitated."

The Milowian King cleared his throat. "Actually," he began. "I thought my head had been cut off. I felt Rhen's sword pass through my neck, but when there was no pain, I opened my eyes to see Rhen holding a cow's head above me, as he spoke to his father. He did the same thing with each of us." A few of the Milowians nodded in agreement to the King's words.

"Does that mean Rhen was fooling his own soldiers as well as his father?" James asked. "He doesn't trust his men enough to let them know he didn't follow Andres' orders?"

"Yes. The only people, who knew what he was doing, were two soldiers named Bosternd and Nk. Bosternd and Nk helped Rhen carry us to a separate tent after our 'beheading' so Rhen could send us to you." He pointed at the note in Reed's hands. "Bosternd wrote that, while Rhen healed our injuries and Nk kept watch to make sure that no one knew what they were doing. Unfortunately," the Milowian King added, "Another soldier named Aul found out about us right before Rhen sent us here."

James shuddered at the thought of Aul having damaging information on Rhen. That was something they could do without. "We need to move you. Quickly," he barked. "In case Aul tells Andres." Turning, James motioned for Rachel. "Take them to our private residence." Rachel nodded and gestured for the Milowians to follow her. "Delegates," James announced. "It appears we've had some success with Rhen after all. Now, let's discuss our defences."

The next day, the Thestran Council waited in its Chamber with trepidation. According to Ceceta, Rhen turned eighteen that morning, and according to the oracles, he would also turn into the Surpen God of War. The Thestrans wondered if Surpen would attack them right away or if they would wait a few days. Would Rhen fight with his father or would he oppose him? Ceceta was now living in the castle with the Thestran Royal Family. She'd agreed to leave the Elfin University for her own protection.

That afternoon, one of the Council's portals flashed to life and twenty Surpen soldiers marched through it. James stood up and yelled at them to 'HALT', but the soldiers ignored him. They focused their attention on Ceceta, who was standing beside Reed and Lilly, on the far side of the room.

Just as James was raising his hand to tell his soldiers to attack, a soldier from the back of the Surpen's line broke file and ran past the others, placing himself in front of the lead men. *"Halt!"* the Surpen soldier yelled.

The Commander, in charge of the Andres' private guards, ordered his men to stop. He stepped forward, to see who was blocking their path. *"Well, well, well, Jet. I knew we had a traitor among us. I was hoping it was going to be you."*

"In the name of the true Surpen King, I command you to stop. You will not touch the true King's wife," Jet ordered. There was a rustling in the room, as

some of the Delegates ran for safety, while others grabbed their translating devices.

The Surpen Commander motioned for his men to circle Jet. "*What are you going to do? There's no way you can beat all of us.*"

Watching them, Jet dropped one of the daggers from his weapons belt down onto the toes of his left boot. The dagger fell backwards, so it was facing his shin. "*I am one of Rhen's elite guards. You don't stand a chance against me and you know it,*" he told them. Jet took another dagger from his weapons belt and dropped it down onto his right boot. "*Surrender now or die.*"

The Surpen soldiers chuckled at his bravado and raised their swords. Suddenly, Jet flipped into the air, lashing out with his swords, while kicking the knives on his boots into the necks of two of the soldiers across from him. As he fell downward, Jet spun to his left and severed the legs off another soldier. Rolling, he rose and stabbed forward with his swords into the chests of two more soldiers.

The Surpen Commander stabbed Jet in his back. As he pulled his sword out, Jet rolled away from him, as if he hadn't been injured.

Jet plunged his swords into more of the soldiers and kicked himself up into the air, doing another flip, while slashing at the throats of the Surpen soldiers behind him.

A soldier stabbed Jet in his stomach. Jet landed on the ground with a thud, while grunting in pain. When another soldier lunged forward to stab him again, Jet rolled out of the away, twisting his body sideways in time to stab the man in the eye with a dagger from his own weapons belt.

Jet ducked under the Commander's swinging sword, pulled another dagger from his belt and plunged it into the Commander's stomach. Three soldiers, who had been on the perimeter of the fight, rushed Jet. He swung his swords about and brought them to the ground.

Panting, Jet crouched over in pain. He coughed up blood. The last two soldiers lunged forward with their swords, when they saw the blood on Jet's lips. Jet spun his body, so they missed him, while impaling them with his own weapons.

Jet coughed again and spat out more blood. He tumbled to his knees, clutching his stomach.

The Surpen Commander glared at Jet, from where he had fallen on the floor. "*Fool! Look what you've done!*"

Jet coughed again. Blood was flowing from his mouth, down his chin. "*I'm not finished yet,*" he wheezed. He took off one of his military wrist guards and pushed a button on it. A sharp blade emerged from its edge. Jet leaned over towards the Commander. The man turned sideways and thrust his own dagger up towards Jet's neck. Jet knocked the dagger out of his Commander's hand and slammed the knife part of his wrist guard down into the man's neck, killing him.

Coughing, Jet fell backwards onto the floor.

Throwing Surpen protocol out the window, Ceceta rushed to him. "*Jet!*" she cried. She bent down over him. Rhen was always telling her stories about Jet, and although she'd only seen him from afar, she felt as if she knew him. "*Jet!*" she repeated, tears welled up in her eyes. "*Come on Jet. You can't die.*"

Lilly appeared beside them on the floor. She reached out to unbuckle Jet's armor.

"*My Queen,*" Jet breathed out. "*I die honorably today. I have saved you.*"

Lilly chuckled at Jet's Surpen stoicism, while reaching under his bloody tunic to touch his chest. "Nobody's going to die today," she told him. When her fingers touched Jet's body, he jerked with surprise. Surpen law forbade men and women from touching each other, unless they were married. Jet had never been touched by a woman other than his mother before. He felt a coolness pass from Lilly's fingers into his stomach. Jet breathed in, as a tingling sensation passed over him. He recognized the feeling at once. It was the same way he felt, when Rhen healed him after battles.

"You can heal? Like Rhen?" he asked Lilly in Thestran. He looked down at his body to find his wounds were gone.

Lilly smiled at Jet, surprised that he could speak Thestran. "It's one of my two powers," she told him, while removing her hand from his tunic.

Jet rolled over onto his knees and bowed before her. "Will you marry me, my lady?" he asked.

For a minute, everyone was confused by his proposal, but then Ceceta laughed. "Jet, she's from Thestran. In this solar system, men and women are allowed to touch each other, even if they aren't married. You don't need to marry Lilly to restore her honor."

Jet glanced up at Lilly's blue eyes and heart-shaped face. He felt something stir within him, as he watched a lock of her medium-length brown hair fall forward over her face. He didn't know what it was, but he did know that Lilly was beautiful, and he would be honored, to have her as his wife. Pulling off his military helmet and bowing down before her, Jet said, "I wish to marry you, if you will have me."

Lilly thought the young Surpen soldier bowing before her was the cutest thing she'd seen in a long time. The fact that he wanted to marry her to restore her honor was endearing. She gazed at his short, brown hair and smiled, as she remembered the look he had given her before he had proposed again. Jet's smooth, tan skin on the back of his neck looked enticing and Lilly wanted to reach out and touch it. Something about Jet called out to her. She couldn't quite fathom what it was, but for some reason, Jet appeared familiar.

Ceceta broke the silence. "She's Rhen's sister. Her name is Lilly."

Jet fell flat onto the floor with his hands raised above his head. "I beg your pardon your highness. I didn't realize you were a part of the Royal Family. Forgive me for my impudence. Of course, if I had known your station, I never would have insulted you by asking you for your hand in marriage." He kept his face pressed into the ground, as he waited for his punishment for insulting a member of the Royal Family.

"Jet," Ceceta told him. "You're on Thestran. It's okay. You haven't insulted Lilly. You aren't going to be punished. You can stand up."

As Ceceta spoke, Lilly realized why Jet looked familiar to her. He was the man she'd seen in her dreams. He was her future husband, the father of her three children. Lilly gasped and dropped down onto the floor beside him. "Yes! I'll marry you!" she cried out, taking his hands in hers. The Royal Family members watched the scene with surprise.

Jet pulled his hands from Lilly's grasp. He had no land and no inheritance to his name. He was the third son of a poor Surpen farmer. Why would a princess marry him?

Ceceta laughed in misunderstanding at his gesture. "Jet, you can hold Lilly's hand! You're on Thestran. Congratulations, both of you, on your engagement!" Jet's mouth dropped open. "Really, Jet, it's fine. You're engaged now."

With wide, disbelieving eyes, Jet rose to his feet. Lilly could see that he was uncomfortable, so she did her best to be encouraging, by giving him her warmest smile. With hesitation, Jet returned the smile. He held out his hand to her and Lilly took it in hers. Once they touched, Jet relaxed and his smile broadened, as his shoulders straightened.

Jet couldn't believe it. He was going to marry the most beautiful woman he had ever seen, and he was also going to be related to Rhen, his best friend and the true King of Surpen. Life couldn't get any better. Jet's smile was infectious and soon everyone in the room was laughing and congratulating the young couple. Lilly seemed the happiest of all. As soon as Jet's face had filled with joy, she had known, without a doubt, that Jet was her man. She had seen that same smile on his face a thousand times before in her dreams and it had always brought her happiness.

When the room began to quiet down, Ceceta asked Jet, "How's Rhen?"

Dropping Lilly's hand, Jet returned to soldier mode, standing erect and surveying the progress the Thestran soldiers were making in removing the dead Surpen soldiers. Jet told Ceceta diplomatically, "He's not feeling well, my Queen."

"What do you mean?"

"He has started to transform into…something," Jet wasn't sure what to tell Ceceta. As a part of the King's Guard, he knew all about their work to transform Rhen into the Surpen God of War. He wasn't sure what Ceceta and the others knew of the situation.

"He's transforming into the God of War?" Rachel asked.

Jet stared at Rachel, nodding once to confirm her words. Several people in the Chamber gasped, as others talked about the upcoming destruction of the Universe. James rang the bell and told everyone to be quiet.

"Does it hurt him?" Ceceta asked in a whisper.

James was just bringing the room to order, when Jet replied, "It doesn't…tickle my Queen."

"Why is he transforming?" James asked. "How is the King getting him to transform?"

"While the King was here visiting Rhen on Thestran, Rhen was tired, I think?" Jet began. The Royal Family nodded in response. They remembered how tired Rhen had been during the King's visits with him at the University. "Well," Jet continued, "Rhen would fall asleep, while the King was with him. When he did, King Andres would give Rhen shots of a virus that his advisor created. The virus was designed to change Rhen's body. There's this drink…"

"The drink that Andres is giving Rhen?" Ceceta asked Jet with growing dread.

"Yes," Jet agreed. "The drink is somehow helping the virus, causing Rhen to change."

"Oh, Themrock!" Sage swore. "Andres was doing it right under our noses."

"We never even knew," Kate remarked. "All our efforts to connect with Rhen meant nothing. Andres mocked us by causing the most damage to him, while he was here on our planet. Andres must have been laughing at us every time he stepped onto Thestran."

"But, if it's a manufactured virus, then certainly we can find a way to get rid of it," Rachel told them. "All we need is a sample of the virus to find a cure. If I could get a copy the virus, I could make an antidote."

"The virus would be in his blood," Jet offered. "Do you have any of Rhen's blood?"

"We don't," Reed replied, sounding defeated. The situation was hopeless.

"Ceceta?" Jet asked. "Did Rhen bring you one of those Surpen fertility charms from the last Warrior Holiday? I know all of the married men were making them that night because of the moon's perfect location."

Ceceta flinched, as Jet asked her about the fertility charm. "Yes, he did," she mumbled. She reached into her robes and pulled out a blue vial attached to a silver chain that was hanging around her neck.

"There's your blood," Jet told Rachel. "It's recent, so the virus will be found within it."

Rachel waited with impatience, while Ceceta fumbled to unhook the chain from around her neck. The minute that Rachel had the vial in her hand, she called for her assistants and rushed off to her laboratory.

"What's the Surpen fertility charm?" Reed asked Ceceta. Instead of answering him, Ceceta kept her eyes on the floor.

"It's an ancient Surpen custom," Jet told Reed. "If a couple can't have children, the man cuts himself during the Spring Warrior Holiday and a spell is said over his blood. The blood is then worn by the woman to increase their fertility."

"You were trying to get pregnant?" Lilly asked Ceceta.

"Aren't you a little young to be having children?" Kate remarked.

Realizing his mistake, Jet dropped to the ground, bowing before Ceceta. "Forgive me my Queen. I thought the Thestrans knew, since it's known on

Surpen. I will gladly accept any punishment you feel is appropriate for the lack of respect that I have shown you."

"Jet, get up," Ceceta told him. She sounded weary. "And stop calling me your Queen. I am not your Queen." Ceceta turned to Lilly. "Rhen and I have been trying to have a child for years. We can't. All of Surpen knows about it, so I guess it doesn't matter if you know too. I mean, it was only a matter of time before…"

"TIME!" Jet yelled, as the last Surpen soldiers were hauled out of the room by Thestran's soldiers. "Quick, bring them back," he hollered, racing after them. "The King will be expecting his report. I'm late. Bring them back! The King will be checking in on the situation at any moment, we've run out of time…"

Realizing what Jet was implying, the Thestrans raced to bring the dead Surpen soldiers back into the room, before Andres discovered that Jet had double crossed him. Jet ordered them about, placing the soldiers and Thestrans into position, so it would appear to the Surpen King, as if a major battle had taken place in the Council Chamber.

As James was lying down to hide on the far side of the room, he asked Jet, "Won't it hurt Rhen more if he thinks that Ceceta is dead? It could further his transformation."

"He's already transforming. There's nothing you can do to stop it. The King is in control of the situation right now. He's too powerful for our Opposition Force to stop. We need to wait until the proper moment to strike against him. We need to keep Ceceta safe. She will help us more, if we use her at the appropriate time. We must maneuver properly to win this battle. We will act when our leader tells us to act." It sounded like Jet was repeating what he had been told.

"You have an organized opposition force?" James asked. That was news.

"Yes," Jet told him. "They had me learn Thestran for this very moment. Please, let's hurry. My orders were to keep Ceceta safe and to trick the King into believing we had killed her." Jet seemed to know what he was talking about, so the Thestrans finished preparing the room to deceive the Surpen King. Most of the Delegates left the Chamber. Those who stayed, disguised themselves, so they appeared to be murdered. Ceceta hid behind one of the tables in the back of the room.

Jet jogged over to Ceceta's location. "Your life necklace, please," Jet asked her, while holding out his hand.

"No," Ceceta replied, shaking her head.

"I need it," Jet told her. "It's the only way I can prove to the King that you're dead."

"I...I can't," Ceceta croaked. "It's too cruel. If Rhen were to receive it, he would think that I'm dead."

"My Queen," Jet began. "The Surpen King is playing a game with Rhen that will take him to death's door. If we're to save him, we need to play along until we're strong enough to stop him." Jet held out his hand again. "Your life necklace, please."

Slowly, Ceceta reached up to her neck to unhook a thin golden necklace. With care, she handed it to Jet. "I hope you know what you're doing."

"We can't beat the bastard yet. We need to play along until we're strong enough to strike. It's our only chance," Jet explained. He took the necklace and moved over towards the portals. Jet pulled a dagger out of his weapons belt and slashed his cheek and arms just as one of the portals began to shimmer and open.

Sage leaned over to Ceceta and whispered, "What's a life necklace?"

"When you're born, you're given a life necklace. When you die, it's taken by your loved ones. No one ever takes off their life necklace. It's just...bad luck."

"Bad luck? That's not what we need right now," Lilly whispered behind them.

A moment later, the King of Surpen stepped out of the glowing portal. He took in the remains of the battle and turned to Jet. "Well, is it done?" he demanded.

"Yes, my King," Jet replied with a bow.

"What took so long?"

"The Thestrans put up a fight," Jet responded. His head remained lowered.

"Of course, they did," Andres snapped. "You didn't expect them to just hand her over, did you? I thought you were going to kill the Thestran Royal Family too." He glanced at the 'deceased' Thestrans finding only William, Sage and Charlie lying 'dead' on the floor.

"I'm sorry my Lord, but most of them were elsewhere."

Andres made an impatient sound and snapped his fingers. "Give me the necklace."

Jet stepped forward with Ceceta's life necklace. King Andres held it up in the air, examining it. "Perfect!" He pocketed the necklace and walked back to the portal. As he was stepping through it, he added, "You know what to do."

"Yes, sir," Jet replied, watching the Surpen King depart.

The Thestrans waited a few minutes, after the portal had closed, before standing up. "So," James asked, as he walked down to the center of the room. "What are you supposed to do now?" His soldiers had returned to remove the Surpen's bodies.

"I'm supposed to kill myself," Jet told James. He walked over to stand beside Lilly and carefully took her hand in his. "But," he added, while staring into his fiancée's blue eyes, "I've had a change of heart." Lilly laughed and squeezed his hand.

After Jet had explained the situation on Surpen to the Thestrans, Reed said, "So, you're saying that Surpen has an active Opposition Force. That it's been in place for years, but it's only now gaining true momentum?"

"Yes," Jet replied. "As I mentioned, most Surpens believe Rhen is our true King. He is stronger than his father and he controls the military, so in keeping with Surpen tradition, he should have been crowned King years ago. There is a great deal of anger among my people at the present King's policies. We believe Rhen will change Surpen's path, when he becomes King."

"Will the Opposition Force be able to protect Rhen?" James asked.

Jet shook his head. "No, Andres is still too powerful, but they will cause Andres a lot of grief, which will weaken him and make him vulnerable."

That night, after all of the Delegates had left, Reed, Sage, Ryan and Kate were walking down the second-floor hallway on their way to their bedrooms, when they heard people arguing in Ceceta's room. Feeling concerned for her safety, they stopped to listen.

"I'm furious with you!" Ceceta screamed. "After everything I've done for you, how could you let this happen? What the hell is the matter with you?"

"They caught us off guard," a man responded.

"We're sorry Ceceta," a woman added. "Really, we are."

"We knew he was there plotting with the King," another man commented. "But we couldn't figure out what he was doing."

"That's no excuse!" Ceceta yelled. "Think of what's at stake here. Your behavior is inexcusable. I can't believe you're leaving it up to us to clean up your mess!"

"We're helping you," a woman told her defensively.

"Zorthans crap!" Ceceta screamed at the woman. "You're doing nothing! Use your powers, if you want to help us. Take control of the situation! Make yourselves known and save Rhen for Themrock's sake."

"We can't, he's too powerful for us," one of the men replied.

"You should be ashamed of yourselves," Ceceta yelled.

Suddenly, Ceceta's door swung open and she stepped into the doorframe, blocking the view of her room with her body. The Thestrans were a little surprised by how put together she appeared, considering she had just been screaming her head off. "Is there something wrong?" Ceceta asked them. "Why are you standing outside my door?"

"Oh," Kate started. "Um, we thought we heard voices coming from inside your bedroom."

"You did," she told them. "I was watching a movie. Would you like to come in and watch it with me?"

Reed peered, above Ceceta's head, into her room. There wasn't anyone in sight. Could all of the people they had just heard, be hiding in her bedroom? Was it even possible for them to have gotten in there, before she had opened her door? "No, Ceceta, thanks," Reed told her. "Perhaps another time."

"Okay," Ceceta replied.

The Thestrans nodded good night and walked off towards their bedrooms, as Ceceta waited in her doorway watching them until they disappeared. In her heart, she begged them to return. She was tired of dealing with the Genisters by herself, and she wanted help in resolving the problems they were having with Rhen. Why didn't the Thestrans have more of a backbone? Why hadn't they forced themselves into her room? Thellis was standing right behind her door. They would have caught him, and then they would be the ones forced to deal with all of this instead of her. Themrock did she need help with this one. Feeling depressed, Ceceta leaned against the door frame. She wanted Rhen. She needed him to tell her that everything would be alright.

Thellis pushed on the door, so Ceceta stepped back into the room of waiting Genisters.

Chapter 26

After weeks of silence, the Thestran Royal Council received a report that Surpen had declared war on Solar System 27. Before the Council could mobilize to help System 27, word arrived that Surpen had conquered it.

"They now control eight systems," James murmured to himself, while shaking his head with disbelief.

As expected, as soon as System 27 was defeated, communications between Surpen and the rest of the Universe were once again severed.

"Shouldn't Andres be gloating?" a Delegate asked James.

"You would think," James replied. "That's his personality." He rubbed his forehead with his hand then glanced up at his Delegates. "Alright, let's get down to business. This complicates trade routes again."

"System 27 was one of our major hubs," someone declared.

"I know," James snapped, while reaching out to ring the bell to begin their official session. "We have our work cut out for us."

Two weeks later, it happened again. Surpen declared war on Solar System 26. As soon as the Thestrans had received word of the war, they received another communication, declaring that Surpen was victorious, and their borders had been sealed again. "How can they possibly conquer an entire System in minutes," a Delegate demanded, in the quiet after the announcement.

James glanced over at Reed, who mouthed 'Rhen'. Rhen was the only way Surpen could accomplish such amazing feats.

As the months passed, the same thing happened four more times with Solar Systems 29, 24, 23 and 40. Surpen now controlled thirteen systems.

"Surpen is unbeatable," a Delegate moaned, during an evening Council session.

"The speed with which they can conquer other solar systems is mindboggling," another Delegate announced.

"Even the other Convention members are afraid of them now," a Delegate declared, while walking to his desk.

"What makes you say that?" James asked.

"Before I left my home to attend today's session, I received a message from the Zorthans, asking if they could join us for one of our meetings."

"Seriously?" Reed asked. The man nodded yes and sent the papers on his desk to the Royal Family for review. After a quick perusal, Reed and James glanced at each other. "Should we allow them to join us?" Reed asked his brother.

"Could it hurt?" Kate remarked.

"I guess not," James said. By the end of the day, the Zorthans, Rasacks and Vivists had joined Thestran and her allies in an uneasy truce, as they worked to find a way to stop Surpen.

Two weeks later, Surpen's military forces once again followed Rhen's large, green, reptilian body, as he carved his way through the soldiers protecting Solar System 28. Rhen no longer resembled a man. He looked more like an animal, something between a Surpen Beast of War and a dragon. His long tail swished back and forth, hitting unsuspecting enemy soldiers and killing them, while he blasted jets of fire out of his mouth, incinerating everything in his path. When Rhen wasn't reducing his enemy to ash, he was slashing through them with razor sharp teeth. By now, Surpen's soldiers knew the drill. They followed Rhen's path, stepping over the dead bodies of their foes, as they made their way to the enemy command post. If Rhen got tired of walking, he would jump into the air and fly ahead of them, burning an alleyway through the opposing forces for his men to follow.

"This is so easy," a soldier called out to Bosternd, while following Rhen towards the King's castle on System 28.

"Too, easy," another soldier yelled back. "We never get to fight anymore. Why are we even here?"

Bosternd frowned and stared up at the looming castle. He noticed System 28's King and Prince watching them from their balcony. "RHEN," he called out, pointing towards their audience. With a snort, Rhen spread his wings and jumped into the air. He flew towards the balcony, as Andres, riding a Surpen Beast of War, came up behind him, following him as he made his way towards the King.

Rhen landed in front of the King of Solar System 28 with a thud. "Get to Thestran! You'll be safe," the man yelled at his son. The boy bolted through the closest door.

"There isn't anywhere in this Universe where one can be 'safe'," Andres remarked with a laugh. He watched, as the terrified King, pulled his sword.

The young Prince ran through his castle until he reached the portal room. He hesitated, waiting for his father. He didn't want to leave him behind. After a while, the Prince realized his father wasn't going to be joining him. As he turned towards the portal to go to Thestran, Andres marched into the room, his sword was wet with the blood of the boy's father. "Going somewhere?" Andres taunted the Prince.

The boy jumped forward towards the portal, but Rhen, who had come up behind him, smashed it to pieces with a flick of his tail, before the Prince could escape.

Andres smiled, when he noticed the boy was shaking with fear. "He should join his father," he remarked. "Kill him Rhen."

The shivering boy turned to gaze up into Rhen's red, glowing eyes. At that moment, Bosternd entered the room to announce that Surpen was victorious. Andres turned away from Rhen. He was ready to move on. "Aul," Andres called out. "Close the borders to Solar System 28 and ordered Narseth to pillage the castle."

Bosternd was about to leave, when he noticed that Rhen was still staring at the Prince. He hadn't carried out Andres' order. Bosternd watched Rhen cock his reptilian head and ask the boy in Thestran, "Stanley?"

Andres rounded on Rhen at once. "What!" he bellowed in Surpen. Loreth had given Rhen a collar that would force Rhen to obey, but Andres hadn't used it very much; most of the time Rhen did as he was told. It was when they were alone that Rhen tended to disregard Andres' orders. Andres had been attacking minor solar systems to test Rhen's loyalty. His main prize, Thestran, would be taken as soon as he knew he had complete control over his son.

"He looks like someone I know," Rhen told his father in Surpen. "Someone from school."

Bosternd watched Andres' face turn red. "KILL HIM NOW!" the King screamed.

Rhen stepped forward towards the boy, but hesitated. He looked so much like Charlie's friend Stanley that it was hard for Rhen to believe it wasn't him. Rhen wondered if the boy had attended the Elfin University with him. For all he knew, he might have had Astronomy with the kid. "No," Rhen told to his father. He turned to walk away. "He's too young to kill."

Bosternd held their breath, as he watched Rhen turn his back on Andres. It was the first time, since Rhen had turned into a beast, that he had seen him disobey the King. Was the old Rhen back? Would Rhen turn on his father? Would the Opposition Force finally be able to destroy Andres?

"YOU WILL KILL HIM NOW!" Andres shrieked at Rhen.

Rhen ignored his father, as he walked towards the exit. Andres grabbed the silver, controling device for Rhen's collar, from where it hung on his weapons belt. He pointed the four-inch, rectangular box at Rhen's back and pushed a button on it. A loud, zapping sound filled the room. Rhen howled in pain and fell to the ground. He lashed about, trying to rip the blue collar off his neck. Rhen's front claws dug deep marks into his flesh, as he struggled against the collar and the painful electric shock it was emitting. When Andres released the button, the sound stopped and Rhen lay still on the ground, gasping for breath. His entire body ached from the shock.

"Kill him," Andres told Rhen.

Rhen didn't move, so Andres lifted his controlling device and pushed the button again. Howling in pain, Rhen blew flames from his mouth against the far wall, causing it to ignite. He flipped and twisted about on the floor, digging at his neck to remove the collar, a pool of blood formed underneath him.

This time, when Andres released the button, Rhen rose to his feet and charged the young Prince, roaring like an angry animal. The boy ducked down into a small ball, as Rhen lunged himself onto the Prince, ripping the child to pieces. "Good," Andres remarked, watching Rhen eat the boy. He turned to Aul and Narseth to give them their orders.

When Rhen was finished, he stood up and walked out of the room. Bosternd ran a hand over his face. He had thought that the old Rhen might be returning, but it looked as if Andres had won yet again. Ceceta's death had crushed the man he had once called friend.

After Bosternd had received his orders from Andres, he headed outside towards his makeshift command tent. He was surprised to find Rhen waiting for him on the grass in front of the entrance to his tent. Rhen's body was blocking the tent flap, so Bosternd couldn't enter. "Rhen," Bosternd said, with a tired sigh, pausing beside him. "Would you please move? We need to break camp and return to Surpen."

Rhen rolled his reptilian head over towards Bosternd and looked up at him with red, glowing eyes. "Why are you so sad?" he asked.

"It's complicated and this isn't the right place to talk about it," Bosternd told his old friend.

Sitting up on his back haunches like a dog, Rhen glanced about. Bosternd was the only one in the area. Rhen swung his neck back towards Bosternd and lowered his head to look him in the eye. "I did something…bad," he confessed.

"What?" Bosternd snapped. He checked himself and asked, in a softer tone of voice, "What are you talking about? You followed orders. That's what we do. You didn't do anything wrong."

"Well," Rhen mumbled, while swinging his head back and forth. "I didn't really follow orders." He lowered his head to look Bosternd in the eyes.

"What?" Bosternd repeated. "Rhen, you followed all of Andres' orders on the battlefield today. Let's talk about whatever it is that's bothering you later. I have a lot of work to do, before we can return home."

"Um," Rhen began, but he nodded his head and stepped aside so Bosternd could enter his tent.

Bosternd stepped through the canvas door flap into his tent and came to a halt. Solar System 28's Prince, the same Prince he had just seen Rhen devour in front of the Surpen King not more than twenty minutes ago, was sitting on a chair beside his mother, along with most of the nobles and their families from System 28. A slow smile crept across Bosternd's face. Rhen was coming back. Bosternd stepped backwards, out of his tent, and turned to Rhen. The Surpen Prince was lying on the ground, his head rested on a large tuft of grass. Rhen's red eyes gazed up at Bosternd in a questioning manner. Bosternd stepped over towards Rhen and crouched down by his head. "So," he whispered. "It looks like you have a bit of a problem."

Rhen sighed, blowing out a blast of hot air. He blinked his scaly, green eyelids. "Are you going to tell on me?"

"No," Bosternd told him, while motioning for Nk and Ngi to come over. "But I hope you know what you're doing." He patted Rhen on his reptilian snout and stood up. The three men dressed the nobles and royal family members up as commoners and took them out of the city into the countryside, where they would be safe.

"Do you think he's back," Nk asked Bosternd, as they worked.

"I hope so," Bosternd told him.

"I miss Rhen," Ngi remarked wistfully.

"I hope he disobeys Andres again," Bosternd said. NK and Ngi nodded in agreement.

When Bosternd informed the Opposition Force about Rhen's actions, they were thrilled, but their leader insisted they remain focused. Rhen needed to give them additional signs that he could be counted on, before they could approach him.

Four weeks later, Rachel and her assistants identified the virus in Rhen's blood. This breakthrough offered the Thestrans hope. By now, Surpen controlled fourteen solar systems. It was only a matter of time, before Thestran would be attacked.

Ceceta attended her classes at the Elfin University, as if she were in a trance. Her body performed the functions it needed to to get through the day, but her mind was elsewhere. "It's so sad," Crystam commented to Latsoh after Astronomy class.

"It's tragic and not just for Ceceta," Latsoh agreed. "Everyone's feeling desperate. The Surpens are knocking on their door and they've lost the Black Angel as well."

Crystam nodded. "During their time of greatest need, he disappears."

"It's too bad Rhen couldn't have kept it up."

"Yeah," Crystam agreed. "At least Tgfhi's weekly Black Angel prayer sessions are giving some of them hope."

On Surpen, the Leader of the Opposition Force was feeling depressed. Over the last few weeks, Andres had conquered many smaller planets. During each invasion, Rhen had followed his father's orders without question. It was beginning to look like his earlier behavior on Solar System 28 had been a fluke. Rhen was lost to them.

A week after Surpen's victory over Solar System 32, Bosternd was ordered to bring the prisoners from Cell Block B to Andres. By now, Surpen had conquered so many planets that their jails were overflowing. Bosternd and Nk walked the prisoners up to Andres' throne room. They ordered them to wait on the far side of the room, behind the pool of fish, then approached Andres' throne. "The prisoners from Block B, your Highness," Bosternd announced, while bowing.

Andres was busy signing papers that Aul was holding for him. With a few last flourishes of his pen, Andres waved Aul away. He stared at the prisoners, on the far side of the room, and frowned. Andres was tired of dealing with them. As he debated what to do with the men from System 32, the sound of claws scraping against stone permeated the room's silence. Rhen was coming.

Andres turned towards his right and waited. The sound got louder, as Rhen grew closer. When the scraping sound was almost unbearable, Rhen emerged from a darkened hallway into the Throne Room. The prisoners gasped at the sight of him and huddled together in a tight pack. Rhen wandered across the room towards his father's throne, as Andres snapped, "How many times have

I told you that you make too much noise when you walk? Place your feet down gently on the stone. Stop scrapping it or I'll have Loreth rip off your talons."

Ignoring his father, Rhen stopped a few feet away from Andres' chair and snorted, blowing out a blast of steam from his nose. He flopped down onto the floor behind Andres' throne and stretched out his legs and arms, while arching his back.

Bosternd and Nk hadn't seen Rhen in the castle since his transformation. They had only ever seen him outside on the training fields or during battles. They watched his movements with surprise. He was acting like a pet.

The Queen, who was bowing on the floor in a corner of the room, peeked through her grey hair to watch.

Rhen rolled over onto his back, and with his legs in the air, wiggled back and forth to scratch his back against the stones. When he was finished, he flipped over onto his side, tucked his legs up into his body and rested his head on the foot of his father's throne. Rhen closed his glowing, red eyes. It looked as if he were going to take a nap.

Andres shook his head with disapproval and turned back to the prisoners. "What do you think Aul?" he asked, breaking the silence. "Slaves or food?" Aul snapped to attention and approached the King to give his opinion.

Bosternd and Nk were shocked. Andres should have asked Rhen that question. Rhen was his son, his heir. They knew Aul had been rising in power, but they hadn't realized how far he had come.

"Whatever you wish sire," Aul replied, with a bow.

"I don't really know," Andres told him with disinterest. "We've had so many prisoners these last few months that our jails are overflowing. Why don't you choose what to do with them for a change?"

Aul smiled at Bosternd and Nk's reaction. "These soldiers are weaker than those from System 27 and 28's. I say we eat them."

"Yes," Andres concurred. "Let's eat them." He glanced down at Rhen's head, then leaned over to smack the flat part of the hilt of his sword onto Rhen's reptilian snout.

Rhen made a small sound of protest and growled, before opening his eyes. He shook his head, tilting it, to look up at his father. "Yes, your majesty?" he asked, sounding weary.

"We're eating this lot. Do you want to pick one out for dinner?"

Rhen rolled away from the throne onto his other side. With the top of his head on the stone floor, he gazed upside down at the prisoners. "I'm so hungry I could eat all of them."

"Well, then, they're your's child," Andres offered. "Take them away quickly though. They're beginning to stink." A few of the prisoners had peed in their pants at the sight of Rhen.

Rhen climbed to his feet and sauntered over towards the prisoners. "Come with me," he told them. Bosternd and Nk moved behind the prisoners, following Rhen out of the room. The group walked towards Rhen's bedroom, but Rhen made a sharp turn to his left and led them into the portal room instead. He paused in front of the portal and said, "Planet Elyk in Solar System 32." Bosternd and Nk's eyes widened, as the portal opened and Rhen stepped away from it. Turning to Bosternd and Nk, Rhen announced, "They're not fat enough for me. Drive them home so they can fatten up. I'll eat them later."

Bosternd raised his eyebrows with surprise. Rhen was releasing them. The prisoners looked at him and Nk with apprehension. "Go," Bosternd yelled at them. The men ran through the portal, back to their own solar system. When the portal closed, Bosternd and Nk turned towards Rhen.

"Are you going to tell on me?" he asked. It was the second time that Rhen had disobeyed his father, but they knew not to get their hopes up.

"That depends," Bosternd answered. "What're you going to do now?"

"Eat a cow," Rhen said. He gave them a reptilian grin and started to walk away.

"Rhen," Bosternd called after him. "You can undermine your father all you want to in private, but unless he knows what you're doing, it won't make a difference. You need to confront him in public."

"Who said I wanted to confront him," Rhen tossed back over his shoulder, as he left the room.

Bosternd and Nk reported the incident to the Leader of the Opposition Force, who commented that at least Rhen wasn't Andres' complete pawn, yet.

Five days later, Surpen conquered Solar System 37. The Zorthans were unsettled by this news, since they controlled Systems 38 and 39. On numerous occasions, they had tried to conquer System 37, but they'd never had any success. The King's Guards on Solar System 37 had great powers. For Surpen to have overwhelmed them, in less than a day, was unthinkable. "They're unstoppable," a Zorthan General announced at the Thestran Council meeting.

The Vivist beside him clicked, "They're like an amoeba moving from solar system to solar system, absorbing everything they touch."

"We must declare war on Surpen," the Zorthan General demanded.

"No," James told him.

"If we act together, we might have a chance to defeat them," the General continued.

James shook his head. "Not yet!"

After the meeting, the Zorthan General pulled some of his people aside. "Try to contact Surpen again. See if we can get through. If you do, ask Andres to confirm that he will not be attacking his fellow Convention members."

"He won't answer," one of the aides informed him. "He won't answer for anyone."

Back on Surpen, several generals stood beside a table covered with military plans outside the Surpen Castle's walls, discussing the day's events. Rhen had surprised them during battle. Solar System 37's guards had fired their powers at Rhen repeatedly, but he had been unaffected by them. The guards' blasts had hit Rhen's hide without mercy to no avail. It appeared that Rhen was invincible to power blasts.

Bosternd smiled, when he saw Rhen sauntering up to them with his reptilian gate. "Hey," he greeted Rhen.

"What?" Rhen asked, stopping in mid-stride. He had been thinking about something else and hadn't heard Bosternd.

"I just wanted to tell you that you did a nice job out there today."

Like a cat, Rhen swung his tail back and forth, as he thought about Bosternd's compliment. "Thanks," he replied, sitting down on his back haunches.

It was unusual for Rhen to talk with the generals these days. Andres kept him busy with various duties, so he couldn't mingle with his men, as he had in the past. Bosternd knew it was a ploy to keep Rhen away from his friends and to curb his support among the men.

Stepping closer to Rhen, Bosternd whispered, "Is it true you didn't kill their King?" He'd heard from Ngi that Rhen had thrust the King of Solar System 37, along with his entire family, through their portal just before Andres had arrived.

Rhen barred his five-inch long, sharp fangs in a gruesome looking smile. "Yes," he admitted.

"That will make your father angry."

"If he were to find out," Rhen replied. "Are you going to tell him?"

Losing his temper, Bosternd yelled, "Why do you keep asking me if I'm going to tell on you. I'm your friend. You know I would never tell on you. None of us would." He gestured towards the other generals standing around the table.

Rhen shrugged his massive green shoulders in response.

"Rhen," Bosternd began, holding out his hand. "Why don't you sit with us for awhile? We haven't had a chance to talk to you, since you became sick with that virus."

Rhen shuddered at the thought of his week-long bout in bed. It had been horrible. "I don't have time," he answered. Rhen closed his eyes and turned away from the generals.

"Rhen, why don't you stop him? Why don't you fight back? You know you could end this," Bosternd asked.

"What's the point?" Rhen mumbled. He gazed, through the dusty, dry air, at the Surpen palace's stone walls.

"It's wrong and you know it," Nk told his friend.

Swinging his long neck to see Nk, Rhen bared his fangs in another smile. "Careful Nk or we'll be eating you for supper." He laughed, accidentally spraying a jet of fire out of his mouth, which ignited the dry grass beside him. "Crap," Rhen mumbled, moving over to stamp out the flames. When he was done, he turned and walked off towards the castle.

The generals remained silent, watching him walk off. "Everything's changed since Ceceta's death," General Ngi commented. "He won't talk to us anymore."

"Yes," Bosternd agreed, lifting some papers off the table. "I was told by 'our leader' that we should reach out to the Thestrans. If we keep them informed of the situation, they may be able to help."

Nk scoffed, "You believe that?"

Bosternd shrugged. "We're running out of options. It's worth a shot."

"How?" Ngi asked. "How can we possibly keep them in the loop?"

"When I figure that out, I'll let you know."

Chapter 27

"We've been summoned," Bosternd told Nk a few weeks later. They arrived in the throne room, with a battalion of soldiers, to find the King of Solar System 25, along with his generals, bowing before Andres. Since they had yet to declare war on System 25, Bosternd and Nk were surprised to see its rulers pledging their allegiance to Andres. After a brief pause, the two men pushed their way past Solar System 25's men, so they, too, could bow to Andres. When they lifted their heads, they were shocked to see Aul and Loreth sitting on thrones beside Andres, while Rhen lay on the floor behind them like a filthy animal.

They hadn't seen Rhen since the battle for System 37, and they couldn't believe the state he was in. Heavy metal chains had been hooked through his collar into rings that were embedded in the stone floor. The leathery skin around his neck was raw and oozing. He slept fitfully, snarling every now and then or lashing out in his dream with one of his taloned feet.

Bosternd gave Nk a look. Someone must have caught Rhen disobeying and brought it to Andres' attention.

"Really, this is priceless, isn't it!" Andres announced. He glanced over at Loreth, who smiled in return. "So," he continued, turning back to stare at the King bowing before him. "Tell me. Why did you decide to surrender to us for no reason?"

The King glanced past Andres to Rhen's sleeping form. Following his gaze, Andres leaned over to look behind his chair. When he spotted Rhen, he laughed and settled back down on his throne. "You surrendered to us, because you were afraid of my pet?"

"Your pet?" the King of System 25 asked, sounding confused. "No, not because of your pet, because of your son, Rhen, the Surpen God of War."

Andres chuckled. "No, not my son...my pet." He pushed a button on the electronic controlling device that was resting on the arm of his throne. They heard a buzzing sound from Rhen's collar a moment before Rhen howled out in pain and struggled to his feet. Rhen turned to gaze at his father with glowing, red eyes. When the collar had stopped buzzing, he snorted, blowing a blast of steam out of his nostrils. Rhen yawned and stretched out his front legs, while arching his back and curling his shuddering tail behind him. After stretching, Rhen flexed his long claws, so they broke through the stones beneath him. The cracking sound they made caused everyone to shiver.

"STOP DOING THAT!" Andres yelled. He rose to his feet and turned to face Rhen. "I hate it when you do that. It's driving me insane! How many times do I have to tell you to step lightly on the stones? Your claws are destroying the floors! I have an entire crew of slaves, working ceaselessly, just to clean up after you!" Andres grabbed his remote and lifted it to zap Rhen again, but stopped short, when Loreth cleared his throat. Turning towards his advisor, Andres saw Loreth pointing towards the rulers of System 25.

Taking a deep breath, Andres dropped the remote onto the armrest of his throne and sat down. "Here, Rhen!" he ordered, while pointing at the space on the floor next to his throne.

Rhen swished his tail back and forth, before walking towards his father, scratching the floor loudly with every step. By the time Rhen reached Andres' throne, Andres was gripping the fabric of his chair with white knuckles and grinding his teeth. He turned and raised his hand to strike Rhen, but lowered it, when he saw Loreth glaring at him. There was a dangerous game of tug o'war going on between him and Rhen. Loreth had agreed to stay with them to help Andres get Rhen back under control, so they could attack Thestran.

Loreth rose to his feet and approached Andres. Rhen gave a slight shake of his head, as his father's advisor passed by, making the chains around his neck clank. Reaching down, Loreth picked up a jug, which had been on the floor beside Aul's chair. He handed it to Andres. The Surpen King took another breath, to calm himself, then reached over to scratch Rhen's head near his ears. Rhen seemed to like this, because he closed his eyes and pushed up against Andres' hand with his head.

"Have a drink," Andres offered. He lifted the pitcher up, over the armrest of his chair, and waited. Rhen lowered his head and tilted it sideways, so Andres could pour the black liquid into his mouth. As the cool, dark liquid hit his tongue, Rhen swallowed, his tail swished back and forth with pleasure. Rhen drank the mixture greedily, his long, black tongue darting into the pitcher for more. When the pitcher was empty, Andres handed it to Aul and scratched Rhen around his pointy ears. When Andres felt Rhen push up against his hand, he knew he was in control. "Do you know what my pet?" he asked his son.

Rhen didn't answer. He was content with the scratching. His hide itched all over. In the past, he had had the slaves scratch him, but after one of their fights, Andres had forbidden the slaves from coming near him. Now Rhen had to resort to rubbing himself against the stones, which wasn't the same. He didn't want to talk to Andres. He wanted itch relief. Rhen pushed up again on the King's hand, asking for more. "These people have just given us their solar system because they don't want to fight you," Andres told Rhen, removing his hand from Rhen's head.

Rhen dropped his snout downward and opened his eyes. Scratch time was over. The King was finished with him. Tilting his head to see the prisoners, Rhen replied, "They're wise. I wouldn't want to fight me either." He rose to his feet and walked back behind the King's throne, circling a spot on the ground several times, his chains protesting loudly, until he plopped back down on the floor.

"No, no, my pet," Andres chastised him. "Kill them."

The rulers of Solar System 25 began to protest, but they were silenced by Loreth's powers.

"Why?" Rhen asked his father, sounding lethargic.

For a second, Andres looked lost. He hadn't expected Rhen to question him. "You don't need an answer. I asked you to kill them. That should be enough," he snapped.

Rhen shook his head back and forth with vigor. The chains around his neck made a deafening, clanking sound. Bosternd was alarmed by his actions, but when Rhen reached up to scratch his nose with his claws, he realized Rhen only had an itch. When Rhen had finished scratching, he looked up at Andres and asked, "Why?"

"Damn it child, because I asked you to! What the hell's the matter with you? Are you losing your mind?" Andres roared. "Are you becoming as stupid as the Beasts?"

Rhen ignored his father's outburst. Surpen Beasts of War were rather smart, so Andres had given him a compliment. He yawned, making sure to show his father his sharp fangs and lay his head back down onto the stone floor. "They would make excellent slaves," Rhen mumbled. "They've already got a slave's defeatist mentality and they're strong. Why don't you sell them to the Sastarians as slaves and use that money to give our soldiers the bonuses you've been promising them?" The room was silent, as everyone stared at Rhen.

Andres loved the idea, except for the part about giving his soldiers a bonus. He would put the profits in his own coffers. Andres glanced over at Loreth, to see what he thought about Rhen's suggestion. When he saw Loreth smile, he said, "Aul, return to their solar system and sell their army to the Sastarians."

"Sell this lot to the Sastarians first," Loreth told Aul. He liked the idea of a King being a slave. Aul searched Andres' eyes for confirmation and found the approval he needed. Turning, he motioned for Nk and Bosternd to seize the prisoners and follow him. Bosternd and Nk glanced at each other. They couldn't believe that Rhen had just tricked Loreth and Andres into saving the lives of the rulers of Solar System 25. Rhen might be in danger, but he was still smarter than the rest of them, if only he would fight Andres.

Several weeks later, the Thestran Royal Castle's spacejet control tower notified James that an old Surpen spacejet, was requesting permission to land. James ordered his army to surround the jetport, as he and his family went to greet their Surpen visitor.

When the spacejet door opened, a young man, wearing civilian clothing from Solar System 41, crawled out of the cockpit. He saluted James and announced, "I have been sent from the Surpen Opposition Force. They want you to review my memory of the evening after our loss. They asked me to inform you that they are working on Rhen. They hope to turn him to their side, before any further damage is done."

James exhaled with relief at the news and called for an emergency Council meeting.

When the Council had assembled, Kate put her hands on the man's head. She closed her eyes and pushed her cool powers into his mind. The Delegates in the room felt a cool, swirling sensation in their minds. A moment later, they saw Bosternd, Nk, Ngi and Authe outside Surpen's military headquarters, celebrating their victory over Solar System 41. It was evening and the generals were sitting in a circle on low chairs around a small fire. Nk and Authe were imbibing in a little Tgarus weed, as Bosternd and Ngi recounted certain episodes of their day. They discussed Rhen's amazing skills, before turning to their growing problem with prisoner storage.

Surpen had run out of room in its prisons, so Andres had set up large, outdoor pens, in which to keep prisoners. The idea had worked well at first, but now they had run out of room in their holding pens. As Bosternd and the others celebrated, they were watched by a group of prisoners, including the man who was sitting in Thestran's Council Chamber. The prisoners were sitting on the desert sand. Their ankles and wrists were chained together. Buckets of water had been placed in random locations among them and platters, with the remains of their dinner of bread and fruit, sat between them collecting flies. Unsure of their fates, the men were silent as they watched the Surpens.

"So, what are we going to do with them," Ngi asked Bosternd, while nodding towards the man, whose memory the Thestrans were watching. Ngi was busy unhooking his armor. He had come late to the gathering and was still suited for battle. He dropped his chest and back plates onto the ground by his chair and stretched.

"That's up to Aul," Bosternd replied. "He wanted to be in charge and now he is."

"But he's useless," Nk complained. He inhaled on his Tgarian cigarette, holding his breath for a minute, before letting the smoke roll out of his mouth.

The Thestrans had only just learned about the Surpens' use of Tgarus weed. Although they were not surprised to see the weed, they were shocked to see Surpen's generals partaking of it.

"Not only is he useless, but he's dumber than an ass," Nk added. The generals chuckled in agreement.

"I asked Aul what he wants me to do with the prisoners," Bosternd told the others. "But I don't expect to get a reply back from him for at least a week."

"Figures," Ngi grumbled, while unhooking his shin guards.

"Hey," Bosternd whispered. He sat up in his chair. "Would you look at that?" In the distance, he could see Rhen walking across the field.

"What?" Nk asked, in a cloud of smoke, as he exhaled.

"Rhen's not chained up anymore," Bosternd told him. The other generals shot to their feet to get a look at Rhen. He was walking towards the Surpen Castle with his head down. It appeared as if he had been visiting with the Surpen Beasts of War and was now on his way back home. The generals hadn't seen him walking around on his own in a long time. "Andres must have released him," Bosternd remarked. "I wonder why."

"HEY, NOT GOING TO STOP AND SHOOT THE BREEZE WITH SOME OLD FRIENDS?" Ngi yelled in Rhen's direction.

Rhen stopped walking. They watched, as his pointy ears turned towards them. He lifted his head up, to see who had spoken, and turned to walk towards them. "Crap," Ngi whispered. "I didn't expect him to come over here."

"What do we do?" Authe asked the others. He didn't feel comfortable around Rhen anymore, so he was hoping the others would tell him he could leave.

"Nothing," Bosternd said. "We treat Rhen like nothing has happened." The generals nodded in agreement, while sitting back down on their chairs. Out of the blue, Bosternd turned towards the prisoners and pointed at the soldier, whose memory the Thestrans were watching. "Listen to what we say and watch what happens. If you do, I will find a way to set you free," he told the man. "Do you understand?" The man nodded his head, so Bosternd turned back to face the fire. A moment later, Rhen wandered down a small slope to join them.

The Thestrans were shocked, when they saw Rhen. He had become the animal in the book that Lilly had found. His body was two times larger than a horse's. He was green in color and had a thick, scaly hide and long neck. Rhen's head was large and he had glowing, red eyes and pointy, fuzzy, green ears. There were sharp fangs sticking out of his mouth. He had small wings, which were tucked into his body and a row of spikes that ran down his spine all the way out to the tip of his green tail. Rhen's front and back feet had vicious looking talons. He flexed them, as he walked across the sandy grass towards the generals' fire.

Stopping by Ngi, Rhen gazed at his old friends, before sitting down on his back haunches. The generals regarded their Prince in the glow of the fire light without speaking. His red, glimmering eyes looked menacing. The horrible blue collar around his neck caught the reflection of the flames from the fire, making him appear like a creature from Hell.

"They let you out for a stroll?" Nk asked Rhen. Authe slapped at him to be quiet.

Rhen gazed at them in confusion. He couldn't understand why Authe would slap Nk for his question. With a bob of his head, Rhen replied, "I did well in battle today, so Dad is letting me take a walk before dinner."

"How…generous," Ngi remarked with sarcasm, while Authe flailed about in his chair.

Rhen stared at Authe, as they sat in silence. He didn't see the need to comment on Ngi's sarcasm. After a few minutes, he asked, "Has Authe been…"

"Yes," Bosternd told him.

Rhen grinned, showing off his long, sharp fangs. Authe always acted strange, when he partook of Tgarus weed. Rhen watched Authe in the hopes of seeing him flail about comically, but Authe remained still. He was too afraid to move, while Rhen's red eyes were boring into him.

After five minutes, during which no one spoke, Rhen stood up to leave. "Thrilling conversations you guys have," he hissed, turning to go.

"Well, we were talking about the Thestrans," Bosternd lied. "But we thought you might be uncomfortable discussing them, considering you knew so many of them."

Rhen turned around to face the generals. He swished his tail back and forth with vigor, before sitting down on his hind legs, as he waited for them to restart their conversation.

"I still think Thestran women would be better in bed than Surpen women," Authe announced, while scratching at his left armpit.

Rhen chuckled at the sight of him. He loved watching Authe, when he was high. Feeling himself relax for the first time in months, Rhen dropped his body down onto the ground to rub his head in the dirt. He stroked his head back and forth, pulling up large clumps of grass in the process.

Bosternd's mouth dropped open at the sight of him. Rhen looked like an animal taking a dirt bath to rid itself of fleas and ticks. After a brief pause, during which the generals stared at Rhen with disbelief, they continued their conversation. "Surpen women are just as good as Thestran women, if not better!" Nk declared. He handed his cigarette over to Authe.

"You're just tied up by your woman," Ngi told him. Nk replied with a rude hand gesture.

For no reason, Authe hiccupped with laughter. The sound was so bizarre that all of them laughed. Rhen bared his long sharp fangs in a smile. It had been a long time, since he had had so much fun.

"So," Authe said. He went from laughing to sobbing. "D...D...Did you hear that the Black Angel is g...g...gone?" Ngi handed Authe a towel for his face and Authe sobbed into it. As he cried, he would fling his left leg out into the air at unpredictable moments.

"Did someone kill him?" Ngi asked. He already knew the Black Angel was missing, but they didn't have anything else to talk about with Rhen, so he played along.

"No," Nk replied, gesticulating with his cigarette. "The Angel has disappeared. No one has any idea why, but he hasn't saved anyone in months."

"Some say you killed him Rhen," Bosternd murmured in Rhen's direction. The other generals stared at Bosternd with wide eyes. They had all heard that rumor but were too afraid to mention it.

During their conversation, Rhen had returned to rubbing his head in the dirt. A large, dust ball had formed around him. After Bosternd spoke, Rhen jerked his head up from the ground to look at his old friends. An inch of dirt cascaded down his snout onto the grass. Despite themselves, the generals laughed. Rhen smiled in response, baring his long fangs. He snorted, blowing the remaining dirt off of him and onto them. The generals jumped up and stared at their clothing in horror. Rhen laughed and they joined in, hitting at their clothes with their hands to get some of the dirt off. Authe was smacking his back with such force that he was going to give himself bruises. "We all need baths now!" Nk declared, while pounding on his chest to remove some dirt that had lodged under his tunic.

"Yeah!" Ngi agreed, doing the same.

Authe turned his dirty face towards Rhen. "So, Rhen, did you kill the Black Angel?"

Without hesitating, Rhen nodded. "Absolutely," he told Authe. "During our battle on Solar System 24, I saw the Black Angel heroically dive down to save some jerk, so I ate him. Yup!" Rhen replied, while patting his side with one of his claws. "He was delicious!"

A silence followed Rhen's words. It wasn't until Bosternd started to chuckle, followed by Rhen, that the generals realized Rhen had been teasing them. "Oh, my God, I thought you were serious!" Ngi yelled out, while wiping at his dirty face with his hands. He was feeling ashamed of the fact that he had believed Rhen.

"He's not?" Authe asked. Ngi swiped at him with a hand.

"No, Authe," Ngi said. "He was teasing us."

"Just like he used to," Authe replied in a dreamy voice. "Do you remember how he used to tease us?" Authe asked Nk. Nk nodded and turned back to Rhen.

"Have you ever seen the Black Angel?" Nk asked.

"Nope and I hope I never do," Rhen told him. "I mean really. What a load of crap! Running around the Universe saving people, who the hell cares? What's the point? We're all going to die soon anyway. Why prolong the misery?"

The generals fell silent again. They knew Rhen was thinking about Ceceta. They hoped Jet had saved her, but there was no way for them to find out. Just as the Thestrans couldn't get any information about them, they had no idea what was going on in the rest of the Universe.

"I don't want to die. My wife is pregnant with our 9th child. I want to see if I get another boy or a girl this time!" Nk told the group.

"What on Surpen would you do with a girl Nk?" Ngi teased him.

"I'd love her forever and ever and ever," he told them. "She'd be my little angel."

Rhen snorted and glanced towards the prisoners. He would never have a family. He would never marry again. He was jealous of Nk and had grown annoyed by his company. "Why are they here?" Rhen barked at the generals, when he saw the prisoners watching them. "I thought my father ordered you to put them in the dungeon."

"The dungeons are full," Ngi told him. "The jails are full. Punishment Island is full and the holding pens are full. We can't fit them anywhere."

"Well, then put them in their own dungeons on System 41 or release them. They can't stay here or someone will decide to kill them," Rhen snapped.

"Rhen," Bosternd began with hesitation, "you've been killing so many people lately…"

"I'm not killing anyone!" Rhen interrupted with a snarl.

"Uh, yes, you are," Bosternd contradicted. He hoped he wasn't making a mistake by antagonizing Rhen.

"My father is killing people," Rhen growled. "I'm just doing my job by carrying out his orders. My role is no different than yours. You told me that yourself, after we conquered Solar System 28."

Bosternd was caught. Those had been his words to Rhen, but now he needed to push Rhen into realizing that he was enabling his father's success. Rhen could end Surpen's reign of terror today if he wanted to. "Yes, you're right," Bosternd replied. "But what we're doing is wrong. It must end."

Rhen snorted. "Really Bosternd. I'm surprised by you. I thought you wanted Surpen to be glorious."

"It is glorious!" Bosternd yelled. He held up his hand in the ensuing silence. He knew from experience that yelling at Rhen wouldn't work. Taking a breath, he continued in a quiet, calm voice, "Now, it can stop. Remember what we used to talk about?"

"I don't remember anything," Rhen replied, sounding tired as he rose to go. "All I remember is…pain."

Bosternd lunged forward, putting his hand on Rhen's scaly shoulder to stop him from leaving. "So, stop it!" he pleaded with Rhen in a fierce whisper.

Rhen looked at him with his glowing, red eyes. "I can't."

"Yes, you can. You're the only one who can. You're invincible. Stop this craziness!" Rhen didn't answer for a moment. Bosternd grew concerned that he might have gone too far. Back peddling, he asked, "What pain are you talking about?"

At that comment, Rhen turned to leave. "No! Wait Rhen. Please!" Bosternd urged.

Rhen paused to look back at him. "I misunderstood you. Can you help me?" Bosternd asked, his eyes pleading.

Rhen shook his head. "Bosternd, I can't help anyone or anything. It's over for me."

"No, it's the beginning Rhen. It's not the end. You can stop it, all of it," Bosternd reiterated. "You're in control, not Andres."

"You don't understand," Rhen growled.

"Well then help me. I'm your friend. Help me, help you!"

Rhen was quiet for a moment. He gave a sad chuckle. "I think I sang a song about that once," he commented. Turning away from the group, he walked towards his father's castle.

Bosternd's shoulders dropped and he sighed. "We almost had him. He was so close to speaking openly with us, but then he just shut down and walked off."

After a few minutes, Nk asked, "So, what do we do now?"

"I don't know. It's always so difficult to get a chance to speak to him alone, and now, when we had the opportunity, we didn't accomplish a thing. I wish I knew what to do next."

"We need to report to the Opposition Leader," Nk mentioned.

"I think Rhen is ready for a change," Authe announced.

"No," Ngi replied. "I think we waited too long and he's lost hope. I don't think that we'll be able to get him back."

"The Leader insists there's still hope. The Leader is closer to Rhen than the rest of us, and according to the Leader, Rhen is still fair game. That's why Andres hasn't attacked Thestran yet. He's afraid of losing control of Rhen, when he challenges the Thestrans. Andres and Rhen have been fighting so much lately that Loreth showed up to bring them together, so we can attack Thestran."

"But Rhen does whatever Andres asks," Authe said. "He's not fighting Andres."

"Rhen does whatever Andres asks of him, when we're at war with solar systems that he has no ties to," Nk replied.

"Correct," Bosternd agreed. "He follows Andres' orders, when we're at war with solar systems he doesn't care for, but here at home, in private, he sticks it to Andres. We've all seen him do it. He's very subtle about it, but Andres knows what's happening. That's why Rhen's been chained to the floor in the Throne Room. Andres knows Rhen isn't under his control. He also knows that

Rhen may have second thoughts, if he's asked to attack a solar system, where his friends are the rulers."

"He won't attack Thestran," Authe remarked soberly, while scratching at his left armpit again.

"Who knows," Bosternd replied. "That's the problem. Who knows where his heart lies. He won't open up to anyone. If the Opposition Force were to act now, he could very well turn against them to protect Andres. If Andres were to order Rhen to eliminate Thestran, he could turn against Surpen. No one knows what's going on in that thick skull of his."

"We're in a stalemate," Nk commented.

"Yes," Bosternd agreed. "And the ones who will suffer the most are the smaller planets that surround us."

"Is the Leader still considering the possibility that we will have to kill Rhen?" Ngi asked the others. Bosternd nodded his head. Ngi exhaled. "How do you kill Rhen?"

Nk gave him a strained smile. "Very, carefully."

"No one is killing Rhen," Bosternd snapped. "We still haven't used our greatest weapon in this battle."

"The Ceceta factor," Authe whispered.

"Yes, assuming Jet did his job and she's still alive," Bosternd told them.

Bosternd turned to stare at the soldier, whose memory the Thestrans were watching. To the generals, he said, "I'm going to take a chance and send that one to Thestran. The Thestrans need to know we're trying to stop this situation from the inside. Take the others and release them on Solar System 41."

Nk laughed. "You're following Rhen's orders? You're not going to wait for Aul?"

Bosternd gave him a wicked grin. "That's right. I am going to follow Rhen's orders. I want to make Rhen's relationship with Aul and Andres as difficult as I can. As Loreth works to heal the rift between them, I'm going to do whatever I can to make it deeper." He was feeling desperate. Rhen needed to come to a decision. They couldn't keep waiting forever.

"You're just going to get Rhen punished," Ngi complained. "I don't agree with your plan. I don't want Rhen to get in trouble."

"Maybe it will force him to choose a side," Nk replied. He rose to his feet. "Things can't continue like this anymore." He regarded the prisoners from System 41 and waved for a battalion of Surpen soldiers to approach. They had work to do. They had prisoners to release.

There was a swirl in the minds of the Thestrans and they felt themselves returning to the present. "Wow!" Reed exclaimed.

"Wow, is right," James replied.

None of them could believe what they had seen. Aul was in charge, Rhen looked terrible and the Opposition Force was desperate.

"Sounds as if they want us to wait," the Zorthan King said, from his temporary seat on the Council Chamber.

"Yes," James agreed. "It does."

"Shall we vote?" the Vivist King mocked. He thought it was ridiculous that James was King of Thestran and yet he followed his Council's decisions, even if he disagreed with them.

James stared at the Vivist King. His large, hairy, grey, scorpion body looked offensive in the Council Chamber. Both sets of his beady eyes were pointing towards James. James wished he could throw the Convention members out of the Council, but he needed them as much as they needed him right now. "Does the Council have any objection to waiting, until we hear from the Surpen Opposition Force, before we mobilize?" James asked the room. No objections were made, so James rang the bell to signify the decision had been made. He was pleased the Zorthans had stopped asking everyone to attack Surpen. It seemed they had finally realized the futility of attacking Surpen at the present time. No one could beat Rhen or his army. This was one battle that needed to be waged internally.

Later that week, Rachel developed an antidote to the virus in Rhen's blood. The Thestran Royal Family was overjoyed by the news. They could save Rhen. The only problem was that the antidote had to be administered over six days, one shot for each day.

A few weeks later, the Thestran Council received word that Surpen had conquered Solar System 43. It seemed the Opposition Force had yet to connect with Rhen.

Bosternd hadn't seen much of Rhen in recent days. He barked at his men to keep the prisoners from System 43 in line and wondered if he would see Rhen, when he passed the Throne Room. Peering in, Bosternd noticed the room was empty. He felt himself flush with anger at the sight of the chains for Rhen's collar. When they reached the room that led to Andres' meeting room, Bosternd heard people arguing, so he told his men to halt. They stood in silence in the anteroom, waiting for the King's meeting to end, while listening in on his conversation.

"I already told you! One month!" a man yelled. "I want them all dead in one month!"

"But he's not ready yet," Andres replied.

"He's not ready? Or you're not ready?" the man snapped. There was a moment of silence and then man continued, "I've done what I can to fix the division between the two of you. It's time. You owe me. I told you when I got him for you that I would reclaim him as mine one day."

"You never said that!" Andres retorted.

"The Thestrans held him out to you, dangled him in front of you as a gift and you did nothing. Nothing. It wasn't until after I told you about his potential and made you aware of his future that you snatched him up. Do you remember what I said to you, as you held his hand, the day his parents left?"

Quietly, Andres replied, "Yes."

"Do it then! Strike Thestran now! Kill them all," the man yelled at Andres. "I demand it!"

"I tell you, I still don't have complete control over him yet," Andres responded. "He won't kill the Thestrans."

"That's why I'm giving you an additional month. Get rid of his final resistance and strike."

"A month's not long enough," Andres complained.

"I've waited years for this! I won't wait any longer."

"We couldn't act until he became a man," Andres threw out in his own defense.

"You stupid fool!" the man barked. "You could've turned him into the God of War, when he got his powers at the age of 11. I told you that 'coming of age' doesn't mean anything to his kind. You stalled!" There was movement in the room and Andres cried out in pain. Bosternd's men tensed and looked to him for orders, but he knew the man speaking to Andres was Loreth, and he didn't want to get involved. Let Andres deal with his advisor himself. He had invited Loreth to rule Surpen with him. He should deal with the consequences.

"I forgive you," Loreth said a moment later, in a soothing voice. "Now finish what we started all those years ago. Kill the Thestrans. Annihilate them. Have Rhen blow up their damn planet!"

Andres cried out in pain again, before mumbling, "Yes."

"What?" Loreth asked.

Once more, Andres cried out. A second later, he screamed, "YES, SIR!" As soon as he had agreed, they heard him grunt with relief, as whatever Loreth was doing to him stopped. After a few minutes passed, Andres asked, "What if I can't break him down the rest of the way in one month?"

"Then give him my newest concoction. He'll lose his mind and die a day afterwards, but at least he'll be able to destroy the Thestrans before then," Loreth answered.

"Yes, my Lord!" Andres replied.

Bosternd decided it was time to move. He motioned for his men to advance. They walked the prisoners forward into the King's meeting room. Bosternd saluted Andres, as his men lined the prisoners up against the far wall. Glancing to his left, Bosternd saw Loreth regarding the prisoners with anticipation. Whatever he had planned for them wouldn't be pleasant.

"Your newest prisoners, my Lord," Bosternd told Andres. He bowed then rose for the King's response.

Andres' face was pale and drawn. His right arm seemed to be shaking of its own accord. "Thank you," he told Bosternd, his voice sounding hoarse. "Put them in holding Cell 693 for now. We'll...interrogate them later." Bosternd saluted Andres and barked at his men to remove the prisoners.

As they stepped out of the building, into the sunshine of the courtyard, on their way to Cell 693, Bosternd saw Rhen standing in one of the castle's fountains. He was moving his body back and forth rhythmically, scratching his back on the foot of the statue of Andres that was in the center of the fountain, while making satisfied grunts.

Nk was standing near the fountain laughing at him. He had just finished delivering his prisoners to Cell 256B and was on his way back to report to Aul. When Nk spotted Bosternd, he called out, "Look Bosternd! Rhen has fleas!" All of the soldiers in the courtyard chuckled. Bosternd smiled and held up his hand to tell his men to wait. He wanted to watch Rhen. He missed him. It was good to see Rhen on his own, away from Andres.

Rhen didn't seem to like Nk's comment, because he smacked his tail down into the water, causing it to splash up onto Nk. The soldiers laughed at the expression that passed over Nk's face, as wiped the water away from his mouth and nose.

Bosternd sighed. It had all been a plot from the beginning. He had never realized that before. Rhen had always been the victim. Since the moment he had first set foot on Surpen, Rhen had been cast as the pawn in the Surpen King's game. He had lost his childhood, his family and his friends, to satisfy Andres' need for power. Bosternd felt an overwhelming sadness for the man he had once called friend. He watched as Rhen walked around the fountain, circling the statue a few times. Rhen's tail swung back and forth with contentment. A few minutes later, Rhen settled himself down into the water and rolled over onto his side. He grunted and flipped himself up onto his back with his legs in the air then wiggled about. His tail crashed down to the left and right, as he scratched his back. The water in the fountain was very high, due to Rhen's body mass being submerged. It lapped out of the fountain, cascading across the stone lip and falling to the path below. Rhen threw his head backwards, submerging it. He snorted, sending a blast of steam up out of the fountain then lay still.

After a few minutes had passed, the soldiers, who were watching, became curious. "What's he doing?" the soldier beside Bosternd asked. Bosternd shrugged and moved closer to see.

"Why is he free?" a different soldier asked Nk, approaching from the opposite side.

"Time off for good behavior during battle," Nk told the man. He stared down into the water at Rhen.

Rhen was lying still. He had bared his teeth in a gruesome smile and his eyes were closed.

"Is he dead?" one of the soldiers asked, as they surrounded the fountain. A few of the soldiers laughed with hesitation, unsure of the answer.

"No," Bosternd told them. He studied Rhen's body under the water and noticed Rhen's rib cage was rising and falling.

"He can hold his breath a long time!" Nk declared.

"Yes," Authe agreed, walking up to join them. He had been watching the scene from the window in Aul's office.

"No, he's not dead," Bosternd replied, stepping closer to the fountain. "Look. I think he can breathe underwater."

"NO WAY!" Nk shouted.

The soldiers leaned in to get a better view of Rhen. "Cool," a few of them remarked, as they watched Rhen breathe underwater.

Suddenly, Rhen opened one of his eyes. The soldiers jumped back in surprise at being caught. A bunch of them laughed, before returning to their duties. Only Bosternd leaned in closer. Rhen's eye, which these days was bright red, had, for the moment, turned back to black. His normal black eye was visible beneath the water. A few seconds later, Rhen's eye gradually started to glow red again. Straightening, Bosternd noticed Nk standing beside him. "Did you see that?" he whispered to Nk. Nk nodded.

"It was black," Nk whispered. "His eye had turned black again."

"Which proves they're doing something to him to keep his body from healing itself," Bosternd mumbled, so only Nk could hear. "I wish we had been able to debrief Jet, before he had been sent to Thestran to kill Ceceta. There are so many parts to this that don't add up." Nk nodded again and patted Bosternd on his shoulder, before heading up towards Aul's office.

Bosternd waved his hand at his men, telling them to continue to Cell 693. As they walked through the stone passageway out of the castle towards the newest cells, Bosternd looped his hand through one of the prisoner's arms and pulled him into a dark stairwell. He walked the man down into the dungeon, stopping beside a dysfunctional portal. When Bosternd was positive that they were alone, he asked the man, "Did you hear the King's advisor?" The prisoner nodded. "Tell the Thestrans that we will act soon. In case we're unsuccessful, they should prepare for war." Bosternd turned towards the portal, said a prayer to the Genisters, and waited until the portal came alive. Turning back to the surprised prisoner, Bosternd remarked with a wink, "I always found the Genisters liked a good Surpen prayer every now and then. Now go." The man leapt through the portal to safety. Bosternd closed it behind him. He was taking a risk, but it was vital that the Thestrans knew what was happening.

James was surprised, when a man from Solar System 43, stepped into Thestran's Council Chamber. After reviewing the man's memory, the Council began to prepare for war. It was clear that Thestran would be Surpen's next target.

Later that night, as the Royal Family sat in Kate's living room discussing their war tactics, they talked briefly about the Surpen King's advisor? They couldn't figure out who the man was or why he would want them dead. What powers did he have over the Surpen King? How had he known that Rhen would get his powers one day? What had Andres promised him regarding Rhen? None of them could make heads or tails out of the situation, and despite their best efforts, they all went to bed feeling less secure than ever before.

Chapter 28

When Bosternd informed the Opposition Force about Loreth's demands, it galvanized the movement. They were running out of time. Their Leader told Surpen's generals to visit Rhen daily. They needed to put pressure on Rhen. Perhaps, if they visited him throughout the day, they could convince him to take action.

The Opposition Force wasn't the only one feeling pressure. King Andres had found himself with a tight deadline. He had only one month to remove the last of Rhen's restraints regarding attacking Thestran or his advisor would kill him. He was furious with Rhen for putting him in this position, and he couldn't understand why Rhen wouldn't obey.

The next morning, after the slaves had cleared away the remains of his breakfast, Andres wandered into his Throne Room to chat with Rhen. As he entered the chamber, he found Orpel sitting on the floor beside Rhen reading to him. Rhen's eyes were open and his head was resting on the stones at the Queen's feet. Andres nodded with approval towards his wife. Rhen had always been fond of his mother. Perhaps, with her assistance, he would be able to bring the boy around. Together, they might be able to make Rhen see the wisdom of attacking Thestran. Andres made a mental note to speak with Orpel later about helping him with his efforts.

As Andres entered the room, Rhen's left ear rotated towards him. It was the only movement Rhen made, but it was enough to signify to the King that Rhen knew he was there. "Good morning," Andres said cheerfully, while walking over towards his wife and son.

"Good morning," Orpel replied. She closed her book and bowed down onto the floor before her husband. Rhen shut his eyes and rolled his head away from Andres. The chains attached to his collar creaked, as his movement strained them against the floor's rings.

"What are you reading?" Andres asked Orpel. He sat down on one of the cushioned benches in the room.

"Some writings by Debrino my lord," Orpel responded, while inching her way across the floor towards the exit.

Andres nodded. "I haven't read his material in years," he commented. "Why don't you stay and read to both of us?"

"No," Rhen told his father. "I don't want to hear anymore. He was a terrible man."

Andres found himself bristling with anger over Rhen's comment. He was trying to make an effort here and Rhen wasn't helping. Keeping his temper in check, Andres replied, "Very well. I suppose we could talk." Rhen didn't answer, so he continued, "I think it's time for us to focus our energies on Thestran. For centuries, they have been subjugating us. We've had to grovel at their feet, but now the tables have turned. We are more powerful than Thestran. It's time for us to show them who's in control." Rhen didn't respond, so Andres stood up and walked over towards him. "Rhen?" he asked, waiting until Rhen opened one of his eyes to look up at him. "I want you to attack Thestran and conquer Solar System 3 for us."

With a snort, Rhen lifted his head. Orpel had backed far enough out of the room that she could now stand and walk away. As she raised herself up to her knees, she heard Rhen say, "No."

"Wrong answer," Andres snarled.

"No, sir," Rhen mocked.

"Why do you persist in fighting me on this? We will attack Thestran and you will lead our army into battle," Andres told him. "There will be no further discussion on this topic."

"No," Rhen repeated. He dropped his head down onto the cool, stone tiles. "I don't feel like it, and you can't make me do it."

The Opposition Leader peered into the room to look at Rhen. He was so close to joining them, but as hard as the Leader tried, Rhen still wouldn't commit. He would not overthrow his father. The situation was very frustrating. If only they could make Rhen angry enough at Andres that he would take over.

In the Throne Room, Andres had lost his temper. He reached for the controlling device that was hanging from his belt and pushed the button on it. Rhen howled in agony, as his collar shot a bolt of electricity into his neck. The Queen hurried away from the doorway. She couldn't watch her son being tortured. Everywhere she went in the palace, she could hear Rhen's howls of pain. It appeared as if Andres was trying to torture Rhen into submission. Feeling overwhelmed with despair, Orpel ran from the palace to escape the sounds of Rhen's cries. As she crossed the palace's courtyard and walked out into the city, she realized she could still hear Rhen as far away as Surpen's military headquarters. Orpel looked towards the bunker's entrance. She watched the soldiers moving about haphazardly, their eyes turning every now and then towards the palace, as they listened. They were upset with Andres for torturing Rhen. They wanted to go to him, to help him. Orpel smiled to herself and sat down on a bench in the shade of the palace wall. The generals, who had been reluctant about following the Opposition Leader's orders to visit Rhen, would now risk their lives to stop by the Throne Room to check on him. The King was losing ground. Orpel hoped her son would be able to stand up to Andres when the time came.

Later that afternoon, Bosternd entered the Throne Room. Rhen was lying on his side on the tan stones, staring up at the ceiling. No one was around, so Bosternd approached him.

Rhen rolled his eyes over to look at Bosternd, before flipping his body upwards, so he was lying on his stomach.

"What?" Rhen growled, when Bosternd stopped beside him. He wasn't in the mood for company.

Bosternd hesitated a moment, taking in the dried blood on Rhen's neck. He hadn't realized the collar was cutting Rhen. Bosternd had thought it was just electrocuting him. "You want me to get someone to clean you up?" Bosternd asked Rhen, pointing at his neck.

Rhen tried to turn his head to look at his neck, but he couldn't see what Bosternd was pointing at. He stuck out his black tongue and licked his throat. The coppery taste of blood filled his mouth.

Bosternd watched, as Rhen licked his neck to clean himself. "Here," he said, moving over to the small, blue pool. Bosternd bent down to wet a part of his tunic in the water then walked back over to Rhen's side. With care, he rubbed at Rhen's green scales. When the blood had been removed from both sides of Rhen's neck, he stepped back and patted Rhen on his snout.

"Thanks," Rhen told him, before lowering his head onto the stone tiles.

"Why is your father zapping you?"

Something about Bosternd's question seemed funny to Rhen. He laughed. "He's 'zapping' me," Rhen replied. "Because I won't agree to fight the Thestrans."

"Why won't you?" Bosternd asked.

"I...I don't know why," Rhen replied. "It's not like I owe them anything. My friends are at the University, so they wouldn't be involved in the fighting." Rhen rubbed his snout against the stone floor and turned his head away from Bosternd. "You aren't supposed to be here. You should leave."

Bosternd had been dismissed. He stood beside Rhen, debating what to do. If he left now, no one would've seen him and he wouldn't have to worry about being punished by the King. But he had only spent a few minutes with Rhen, not enough time to make an impact.

Someone walked past the room and Bosternd tensed. Looking up, he saw the Queen checking in on Rhen. She nodded towards them and moved on. Bosternd realized his presence in the room had kept her away. Feeling guilty, he leaned over into Rhen's side and put his head down onto Rhen's thick hide.

Rhen turned his head towards Bosternd. "Um," he said, with a hint of mirth. "What are you doing?" He wasn't used to contact. People didn't touch him.

"Resting," Bosternd replied. Rhen's scales were warm to the touch and Bosternd liked the sound of his breathing. "How do you blow fire?"

Rhen snickered and moved his head over towards Bosternd. "I'm not really sure," he confessed. "That virus I had did some wicked things to my body."

"You're not kidding," Bosternd agreed. He'd seen the King scratch Rhen's head before. Rhen seemed to like having the area around his ears scratched. Reaching forward, Bosternd felt the skin around Rhen's ears. Although it looked scaly, it was, in fact, soft and warm. Bosternd scratched Rhen, watching as he closed his eyes with pleasure. After a few minutes, Bosternd asked, "Will you fetch a ball if I throw it?"

Rhen laughed out unexpectedly, blowing flames past Bosternd onto his back quarters. The flames danced across Rhen's scales before fizzling out. "No," Rhen told Bosternd. He turned his head away and dropped it back down onto the stones.

Bosternd wiped the sweat off his forehead. He wasn't sure if he was sweating from fear at almost having been incinerated or from the heat of Rhen's flames. "Rhen," he said, squatting down by Rhen's head. "If..." he wasn't sure what to say. He wanted to yell at his friend to kill the King and take control of Surpen, but he knew Rhen wouldn't do it. Everyone was pushing Rhen back and forth, trying to get him to obey, but no one was having any success. "Screw it," Bosternd said with frustration. He plopped down onto his bottom by Rhen's head.

"Screw what?" Rhen asked.

"They want me to convince you to overthrow your father, but you won't," Bosternd told him. "So, screw it. There's no point in talking about it."

Rhen blinked at Bosternd. He smiled, barring his teeth. "You're funny," he commented. Rolling over onto his side, he added, "We always had a lot of fun together." He scratched at his neck with his claws, pushing his collar back and forth.

Bosternd noticed open sores on Rhen's neck. The collar had inner metal spikes that dug through his thick hide. "I miss you Bosternd," Rhen added. "I'll be happy when Dad is finally satisfied, and I can hang out with you and the others again."

"We'll have to change our headquarters," Bosternd remarked. "You'll never fit through the doorway. Perhaps I should ask Nk to begin enlarging it today?"

"No," Rhen replied. "Don't bother. I...I..." He rolled away from Bosternd and hissed, "Leave now."

Bosternd watched Rhen for a moment. It was time to go. Standing up, he patted his friend on the neck. "I'll try to sneak in tomorrow to visit you again, if you want," Bosternd offered. As he was turning towards the door, he saw Rhen nod his head. 'Well,' he thought. 'It's a start.'

Several weeks later, Nk asked Bosternd, "Did you learn anything today, when you talked to Rhen?" The two men were walking into the General Meeting Room in Surpen's military bunker.

"Rhen's definitely tired of the wars. He feels Andres should be satisfied with Surpen's current territory, and he's angry that Loreth has convinced his father to chain him to the floor of the Throne Room."

Nk nodded his head. They'd all been hearing the same thing.

"Why won't he do something," Authe asked the others, while reaching for Nk's Tgarus cigarette.

"I don't know," Bosternd replied. "For some reason, he's loyal to Andres. He refuses to stand up to him."

"We just have to keep trying," Ngi told them.

"And hope it has some effect," Bosternd added, while picking up Aul's latest orders from the top of the table.

Chapter 29

"Here," Loreth said, handing Andres a loaded shot.

"I still have one week," Andres replied, while taking the needle from Loreth.

"You haven't had any success yet. Why would you think a week would matter?"

Andres shrugged in response, causing Loreth to strike him on the head. Andres stumbled but caught himself. "Careful," Loreth said, as he watched the Surpen King. "If you drop that syringe, I'll have to make up a new batch of serum and I don't have anyone left to test it out on." He grinned, before floating up into the air and disappearing.

Andres placed the syringe on his desk. He had one week to convince his son to conquer the Thestrans before he'd have to kill him.

"It's the last day of the month," Nk told Bosternd, while Bosternd was stretching on the training grounds. "Do you think Andres and Loreth will succeed in getting Rhen to attack Thestran or do you think they'll resort to poisoning him to get him to obey? And, if they do try to poison him, do you think we can stop them?"

"By God, I hope we can stop them," Bosternd told him. He finished his exercises and the two of them walked towards Surpen's castle. Seeing Ngi, Bosternd asked, "Where's Rhen?"

"Andres released him after breakfast for good behavior. He immediately made his way down to the private courtyard, where he climbed into that fountain that he likes. He's still there now, sleeping under the cool water."

"He's not to be left alone," Bosternd reminded Ngi and Nk. "Someone must keep an eye on him at all times."

"We know," Nk told him. "Don't worry. We'll do our best to keep him safe. We love him as much as you do."

Around mid-morning, Ngi wandered into the Surpen Castle's inner courtyard, where Rhen was located. He walked over towards Bosternd, who was doing some paperwork, and remarked, "Seems our boy likes his fountains?"

"I'm glad he's finally getting some relief," Bosternd replied, while glancing towards Rhen, who was still submerged. "The flies have been doing a number on his neck wounds. I bet the water makes them feel better."

"Yes," Nk agreed, from his spot by the pillar. He had been cleaning swords in the courtyard all day. "I tried to knock them off yesterday, but as soon as I got them off, they would swarm around a different wound. It must have itched like..." Nk hesitated, when he saw Andres enter the courtyard. He snapped to attention, with the other soldiers in the area, and watched, as the King ignored them and approached Rhen.

Stopping by the edge of the fountain, Andres stared down into the water, where Rhen was resting. After a few minutes, he lifted the controlling device and pushed the button on it. They heard a muffled, zapping sound a second before Rhen jumped up in the fountain howling, an enormous steam cloud rising around him.

Snarling, Rhen said, "You didn't have to do that! I was awake."

"Really?" Andres snapped. "Then why didn't you get up when I arrived."

"I deemed it unnecessary," Rhen snapped back. He blew a short blast of steam out of his nose into the air.

"I AM YOUR KING!" Andres roared.

Rhen was quiet for a moment, his eyes on Andres. "Funny," he stated. "I thought you were my father."

"Of course," Andres hissed. "But first and foremost, I am your King."

"No," Rhen replied, shaking his head. "First, you are my father. That's the way it's supposed to be."

"First, I am your King," Andres told Rhen with conviction, misunderstanding his son's needs.

Rhen stared at Andres with his red eyes. The tip of his tail began to quiver. It was clear to everyone watching that something was up.

Andres began to worry that he might have gone too far. Rhen's tail only quivered, when he was about to do mischief. As Andres lifted his foot to step backwards, Rhen lashed out with his talons, grabbing the controlling device out of his hand and throwing it to the bottom of fountain, where he stepped on it, smashing it to pieces.

Bosternd heard Nk gasp. Had Rhen made a decision? Was he finally going to stand up to his father?

"First, you will be my father. Take this damn collar off me!" Rhen growled. He lifted his front feet up onto the edge of the stone fountain. "I'm not an animal. Stop treating me like one."

"No," Andres said, his right hand disappearing into his pocket. He grasped the metal syringe that Loreth had given him. Rhen was out of control. As soon as he had an opportunity, he would inject Rhen with the poison to make him obey.

"Loreth told you to put it on me, now I'm telling you, if you love me, TAKE IT OFF!" Rhen yelled at his father.

Andres waited for Rhen to turn his head. If he could jab the syringe into Rhen's neck, he could inject the potion before Rhen could retaliate.

Instead of turning away from his father, Rhen leaned back into the fountain and sat down on his back haunches. He grabbed the collar around his neck with his front claws and pulled on it, scratching at the skin around his neck. Try as he might, Rhen couldn't remove the collar.

"We have a war to fight. You need to mobilize our army now. We're attacking Thestran within the hour," Andres told Rhen. He felt something brush against his tunic and looked to his left to find Loreth watching.

"No! Take this collar off me Dad!" Rhen growled. He struggled to remove the collar, falling over sideways in the fountain, then lunging upward, in an attempt to remove the collar from around his neck.

"STOP!" Loreth ordered.

Rhen hadn't realized that Loreth was present. As soon as he heard his father's advisor, he turned in Loreth's direction. Seeing that he had Rhen's attention, Loreth added, "Your 'father' has just given you an order. Move out!"

Rhen barred his fangs. "Go to Hell!"

Loreth bared his teeth in response. "I already have. Get the troops ready. We eliminate Thestran today."

"No," Rhen told him. "I don't feel like it today. Ask me tomorrow."

Loreth's face began to turn red and his eyes started glowing purple.

Hoping to get his son to see reason, Andres said, "Rhen, we're attacking them today to surprise them. It will give us the advantage we need to easily win the war."

"Tomorrow sounds better to me," Rhen replied dismissively. He dropped back down onto four legs and turned his back on his father and Loreth. Rhen took two steps away from them, then settled down into the remaining water in the fountain.

Loreth nodded to Andres. The Surpen King pulled the syringe out of his pocket. It was time.

As the Surpen generals advanced around them, Loreth flicked his hand forward and the electronic controlling device that Rhen had smashed, flew into the palm of his hand in one piece. He pushed the 'punishment' button, causing Rhen to howl in pain. "MOVE IT!" Loreth yelled at Andres. The Surpen King leapt forward, plunging the syringe into the wound on Rhen's neck.

Nk reached the King first. He wrenched Andres' hand off of Rhen's neck, pulling out the syringe, then wrestled Andres to gain control of it. Andres screamed and tried to strike Nk, but Loreth beat him to it. He blasted Nk in the chest with a purple power ball, sending him flying backwards across the courtyard. Nk crashed into the far wall and fell to the ground dead.

Andres turned on the rest of his generals with his swords drawn. Bosternd and the others hesitated before falling back. There was nothing more they could do. Andres had succeeded in poisoning Rhen. Their attempt to save their friend had failed.

"NO!" Rhen screamed, when he saw Nk's collapsed form. He jumped from the fountain, but fell on the gravel path with a thud. He was dizzy and had trouble controlling his legs. Crawling, Rhen got part way to Nk then lay still. Before Rhen fell unconscious, they heard him say in a faint voice, "You want me to kill them? Ask me tomorrow."

"Is he dead?" Andres asked, when Rhen stopped moving.

"No," Loreth replied. "He's absorbing my little mixture. He'll be ready to go in five minutes." Loreth tossed the controlling device into the fountain. "You won't need that anymore. He'll obey your every command. He won't have any thoughts of his own."

Bosternd walked over to Nk and knelt down beside him to feel for a pulse. Nothing. He motioned for some soldiers to approach. With care, he looped Nk's arms over his chest, so the soldiers could remove him. When Bosternd moved Nk's right hand, he found the syringe held tightly in Nk's grasp. There was still about a quarter of the potion remaining. Nk had succeeded in stopping Andres from injecting the entire dose into Rhen. Bosternd felt a glimmer of hope. Could Nk have saved them? Would Rhen survive? Leaning over, he kissed Nk on the head, while pulling the syringe from his hand and sliding it into his pocket. "Thank you my friend," he whispered.

Chapter 30

King James was expecting Surpen to attack at any minute. He had ordered his Council Delegates to supply him with additional soldiers and had brought Ceceta and her friends to the castle, hoping their presence might stop Rhen. As he paced around the Council Chamber, Reed walked into the room. "The Convention Members are gone," Reed informed him, while tossing three knives onto his desk.

"That's not surprising," James commented. "Surpen is after us. If they're caught defending us, Surpen will turn on them. They'd rather not risk their 'friendship' with Surpen."

"Idiots," William breathed out. He sat down on a chair beside Henry. Henry had two blasters in his hands, so he offered one of them to William.

"Do we know how the Surpens are going to attack?" a Delegate asked James.

"No," James replied. "They attack differently every time. They change their tactics with each planet." The man nodded and walked off to join his waiting army. James wished he had some information to give his Delegates. He also wished someone from the Surpen Opposition Force would let him know if they'd been successful.

Half an hour later, they heard an explosion and screaming outside the castle. James ran outside the Family's wing of the castle to find Surpen's army had blown up his main artillery bunker and was engaged in hand to hand combat with his soldiers. Kate was in the middle of the battle, throwing power blasts at the Surpens and knocking them backwards. As James watched the Surpens fall back, he felt hopeful. Perhaps they might stand a chance.

A moment later, Rhen appeared on the scene, howling like a crazed animal, while walking out of the burning rubble that had once been Thestran's artillery building. James watched in horror, as Rhen marched right through his men, the flames from his mouth burning them to ash. Kate, Sage, Rachel and William unleashed every power they had on Rhen from their spot near the bunker, but their blasts bounced off his hide. He seemed to be impervious to their powers. Behind Rhen, his men looped about, forming a well-organized net, catching the Thestrans around the entire castle, and forcing them to retreat inside. Rhen's eerie howls echoed throughout the interior of the castle, sending chills down their spines, as James and the others drew back for safety, locking the doors with spells so Rhen couldn't enter.

James heard a crash in the Delegate's wing of the castle and rushed down the Grand Hallway to the center fountain. Smoke billowed out of the wing to the

Delegate's offices, filling the concave glass ceiling above them. The Delegate's soldiers streamed out of the wing in retreat. "He's broken through the windows in the main conference room," a Delegate told James.

Screaming came from the other wings, as people began to stream out of them. "His men have broken into all of the other wings. The only secure wing is the Royal Family's," a Delegate yelled to James, while fleeing down the Royal Family's wing of the castle to escape.

"Hell!" James swore. He ran after the man then watched in shock, as the mass of people in the castle, who were rushing to escape the Surpens, crushed and trampled each other in their attempt to exit through the doors that had been spelled shut. "Retreat through the Council Chamber!" James screamed at them.

Kate used her powers to open the heavy, wooden doors to the Chamber and the flow of the crowd shifted, pulling everyone with it into the Council Chamber. The portals were open, so the crowd surged towards them. They didn't care where they were going. They just needed to get off Thestran.

"Lock the doors!" James yelled at his mother.

Kate used her powers to slam the wooden doors shut. They heard pounding on the other side. "I'll just zip through and rescue those people who are on the other side."

"No!" Lilly screamed at her mother, but Kate had already phased through the wall into the Grand Hallway. She reappeared a moment later, covered in ash and shaking.

"What happened?" James asked her.

Kate turned towards him. Her eyes looked stunned in her soot covered face. "I was too late."

There was a loud thump on the doors. They shook, but held firm.

"Everyone's dead," Kate added in a far-off voice.

BANG! The doors shook again.

"Faster!" James yelled at the civilians, who were pushing each other to escape. He noticed his family still in the room. "GO!"

"Not without you!" Reed yelled at him.

BANG! Dust fell from the ceiling, as the doors shook again.

Henry grabbed Kate and pulled her behind the crescent desk. She fell. He reached down to pick her up but was knocked aside by panicking civilians.

CREAK! The wooden doors were now bowing inward.

"HELL!" James swore again. He watched the metal jambs on the double doors groaning under the pressure of the weight that was being applied to them. A moment later, they popped and the doors caved inward, crashing to the floor of the Council Chamber.

Rhen stood on top of them, his soldiers running into the room around him. Roaring and lunging forward, Rhen swung his tail out sideways, destroying the Thestran's portals, so they couldn't escape.

He was about to light William on fire, when a shout stopped him in his tracks. Although Rhen was no longer advancing on them, he moved with agitation, his hide and tail quivered, his head bobbed back and forth and thick saliva flowed from his mouth and nose. The Thestrans watched, as Rhen's red eyes darted about without focus, while a strange, low, whining sound came from his mouth.

"Something's wrong with him," Lilly said.

"The King must have given him that potion," Reed answered. "It's the only explanation for his behavior. Rhen is under Andres' command."

"What potion?" Ceceta asked. She was standing behind Tgfhi, hidden from view, not more than thirty feet from Rhen.

Sage, who was to her left, said, "The Surpen King's advisor made a potion that would force Rhen to follow the King's wishes for twenty-four hours." Ceceta nodded, waiting for Sage to continue. With hesitation, Sage added, "After that time, the potion will…kill him."

"No," Ceceta breathed out. Her head snapped around to look at Rhen. "NO," she said louder, stepping forward towards her husband.

Bosternd appeared out of nowhere and pulled her back. "Wait," he hissed. "Nk stopped the King from giving the entire potion to Rhen. We may still have a chance. Remain hidden." Before Ceceta could respond, Bosternd dashed back to Rhen's side, just as Andres and Loreth entered the room.

Laughing, Andres gazed at the cowering Thestrans. "I win!" he announced. He walked over to James' desk and sat down in James' seat, putting his feet up onto the Thestran King's desk. "I told you I would win."

Loreth remained by Rhen's side. "I want Rhen to kill them one at a time in the center of the room, so they can watch their loved ones die," he instructed Andres.

"As you wish," Andres replied. He dropped his feet to the ground. "Who do you want him to kill first?" Andres noticed Kate cowering on the floor. "Her?" he suggested with anticipation.

"Oh, my," Loreth said, while gazing at the crowd of terrified faces with his beady, brown eyes, before turning to take in Kate's stunned expression. "No. I want to save her for last. Hmmm. Who do I want to eliminate first?"

"I'll go first," Reed said. He stepped forward from beside James and walked down towards the center of the room.

"Yes," Loreth agreed. "Yes, you would be perfect; the son of the Thestran King and Queen and the Prince of the Wood Elves." He approached Reed, circling him like a vulture. "Yes, I like it. Kill the Wood Elf Prince first. After that, I want you to kill the King and Queen of the Wood Elves, followed by..."

Rhen gave a loud snort, interrupting Loreth. He bobbed his head up and down erratically, as his breathing became more labored.

Turning, Loreth glared at Rhen. "That's not right," he mumbled, returning to Rhen's side. Rhen was now leaning to his left and his head was bouncing up and down, as he breathed in short, quick breaths. "That's not right at all," Loreth repeated. He turned back to Andres. "Did you inject the entire solution into him?"

"Yes," Andres replied. "Why, what's wrong?"

"It's not strong enough," Loreth snapped, marching towards Andres. "I made it strong enough, but he's fighting it. You didn't inject all of it. I bet that idiot Nk stopped you from injecting the full amount." He screamed with rage, as he realized that Andres had failed. "You never do anything right!" Loreth bellowed at Andres. "From the very beginning, you've failed me!"

"It's still working," Andres reassured him, while gesturing towards Rhen. "We've won. We beat the Thestrans. Why are you so upset?"

"Because he's fighting it you imbecile," Loreth screamed. "I gave you the greatest gift in the Universe and you've ruined it...."

While Loreth was yelling at Andres, Tgfhi walked down the stairs towards Rhen. He stopped beside Reed, just in front of his friend, and said, "Hey buddy. How are you? You don't look so good. I thought I told you to stay off that weed."

"T…" Rhen breathed in, "T…" another breath, "T…T…Tgfhi," Rhen breathed out, as if he couldn't get enough air.

"Look," Tgfhi replied with a grin. "I brought your sneakers. You left them at school." He held Rhen's prized black sneakers up in front of him.

Rhen grinned, displaying his long fangs. He was about to respond, when Loreth noticed that Tgfhi was interfering. Screaming, Loreth shot a blast of his powers at Tgfhi. Rhen lunged forward, putting himself between Loreth and his friend. Loreth's powers struck Rhen on his side. He tumbled over, landing on top of both Tgfhi and Reed, pinning them to the ground.

"THEMROCK!" Reed cried out in agony, as he was crushed underneath Rhen's body.

Rhen moaned in pain. The blast had left a large hole in his side.

"Rhen kill Reed and Tgfhi," Andres yelled out.

The pain in Rhen's body was so intense that he had fallen back under the effects of the potion. He spun his torso around and lunged at his friends with his mouth, but Erfce had grabbed Tgfhi and Sage had seized Reed the minute that Rhen had rolled off of them. They succeeded in pulling both men out of Rhen's reach.

Hurt by Loreth's blast, Rhen wasn't moving very well. He tried to rise to his feet to go after his prey, but he was having trouble.

"See," Andres told at his advisor. "He's still under the potion. He's going to kill them."

"Yes," Loreth agreed. "Tell him to hurry."

"Rhen," Andres yelled, while watching the hole in Rhen's side close. "Hurry up and kill Reed and Tgfhi. When you're done with them, I want you to kill the Wood Elf King and Queen."

With great effort, Rhen jumped forward. He scooped Reed up into his mouth. Reed screamed in pain, as Rhen closed his mouth, but before Rhen could clamp his jaws shut, severing Reed's body in half, Ceceta stepped forward and held up her hand.

"STOP!" she commanded.

Rhen stared down at Ceceta and froze. With hesitation, he lowered his snout towards her. His quick, sharp breaths blew her hair and robes back and forth around her body. Andres and Loreth were so shocked by the sight of Ceceta that they remained silent.

Rhen took a tentative step towards Ceceta. With caution, he sniffed the air in front of her, as snot rolled down his snout and dropped onto the floor at her feet. Suddenly, he made a wounded animal sound and jumped back ten feet. Bobbing his head up and down, Rhen stepped from foot to foot, before dropping Reed out of his mouth and asking, "C…C…C…Ceceta?"

Ceceta was horrified by the way her husband looked. Doing her best to smile, she said, "Yes, Rhen, it's me."

The room was filled with a disturbing, crunching sound, as Rhen turned from the Surpen God of War, back into his elfin form. He looked horrible. His skin had turned green, his fingers and toes had claws, his upper and lower teeth protruded from his mouth in sharp fangs, his pupils were red, a long, thick, green tail stuck out of his back and his hair and beard were uneven, as if someone had chopped at them months ago with a knife. Rhen was wearing a filthy military uniform that was stained and ripped, and an unholy odor wafted from his body, filling the room with a stench so foul it made their noses run.

"His collar," Nk whispered beside Bosternd. The blue collar that had been around Rhen's neck, while he was an animal, had shrunk in size to accommodate his elfin form. The prongs within it bit deep into his flesh, causing blood to seep down his throat.

Everyone was stunned at the sight of him. No one had known that he could change back into his elfin form. Loreth seemed the most confused. He stared at Rhen with an open mouth and a blank look on his face.

"You look tired my love," Ceceta told him.

"I…I…I thought you were dead," Rhen said. He stepped back and forth, while bobbing his head up and down. Rhen's breathing was still labored and shallow and it was clearly an effort for him to speak. "After Milow I…I got sick with this, this, this, this virus. It…It changed me into this," Rhen told Ceceta. "I…I…I c…couldn't leave my bed, n…not even to go to t..t..the b…b…bathroom. When, when, when they told me you were d…d…dead, I…I t..t..t..tried t..t..to g…g…get up t..t..to g…g…go t..t..to you. I…I c…c…couldn't move." Out of breath, Rhen dropped his head down to try to get the air he needed.

It was at this moment that Andres and Loreth returned to their senses. "KILL CECETA," Andres yelled at his Surpen soldiers.

396

Bosternd motioned for his men to stop Andres' guards from advancing on Ceceta, while Rhen shook his head, fighting against his father's order. His eyes darted back and forth and he took an unsteady step forward towards Ceceta, as if he were going to follow the King's demands.

The Thestrans could see the battle going on inside of Rhen, and they realized they were on their own. With nothing to lose, they lunged forward towards Andres and his advisor. Andres fell to the ground, as James hit him with his powers. Loreth blasted his powers about the room, killing people at random, before turning his energy blasts on Rhen. He shot Rhen in the shoulder, throwing him clear across the room.

Ceceta ran towards her wounded husband screaming, "HELP HIM, HELP HIM, HELP HIM," over and over again.

The people around Ceceta gave her confused looks. Who was she yelling at?

A shimmering, misty image of the Black Angel swooped into the room. He flew over to Ceceta and gave her something. "The key to his collar," the Angel said. "Remove it and he will heal." The Angel disappeared as quickly as he had arrived.

Ceceta took the key and removed Rhen's blue collar. A moment later, Rhen healed. He was still affected by the virus, but the potion that Andres had injected into his system, and the wound he had received from his father's advisor were gone.

Rhen rose to his feet and ran down the stairs towards Loreth.

His father's advisor saw him coming. Laughing, he threw a power blast in Rhen's direction. Rhen put his arms up and blocked the blast with a power shield. Trying again, Loreth blasted at Rhen's shield with his purple powers.

Rhen poured every ounce of his strength into his shield. It glowed so white, that everyone, except for Loreth, had to shade their eyes. "Damn it!" Loreth screamed, when his purple powers refused to penetrate Rhen's shield. He flew up towards the ceiling, surveying the room.

"SAVE ME!" Andres screeched, from where he was cowering behind a burning chair.

Loreth glanced in his direction and sneered. Using his powers, Loreth lifted Andres up into the air. The Thestrans watched with surprise, as Loreth proceeded to use his purple powers to form a noose around Andres neck and choke him, while he dangled helplessly in front of them.

Rhen threw a blast of his white powers at his father's advisor to stop the man, but Loreth evaded his efforts.

Just as Andres was beginning to lose consciousness, Loreth hissed, "No, that's too easy a way for YOU to die." His purple powers flashed out towards Andres. The King cried out in pain, before being thrown through the ceiling of the Council Chamber.

"DAD!" Rhen screamed.

"Too late," Loreth mocked. "I've sent him into the TUB, where he'll die a slow, painful death."

"NO," Rhen howled. He threw up his hands and sent an enormous power blast at Loreth that exploded in the man's face. The blast blew off most of the Council Chamber's roof. There was a quick flash of purple right before Rhen's powers incinerated the Surpen King's advisor.

Rhen dropped to his knees. His body shuddered, as he released himself, turning back into the Surpen God of War. "Dad," he whispered into the roar of the remaining fires.

When Rhen turned towards Bosternd, he found his friend, as well as the other Surpen soldiers, bowing before him. "Huh," he mumbled. He had forgotten. With his father gone, he was now the Emperor of Surpen. As he stood up, the Surpens in the room rose with him. Before Rhen could say anything, they cheered.

Rhen shook his head. He would have to mourn the loss of his father another time. His first responsibility was to heal Surpen. He needed to go home.

"I'm sorry," Rhen told James. "We'll be leaving immediately. If you have trouble healing anyone, please let me know and I'll return to help."

"Rhen," James said, stepping forward. "We won't hold Andres' actions against you. You're innocent in our eyes. Also, Rachel has found an antidote to the virus in your system. Why don't you stay on Thestran and we will heal you?" He didn't want Rhen returning to Surpen just yet. He wanted to keep an eye on his little brother. Everything had happened so fast, the Universe needed time to recover.

"An antidote?" Rhen asked. "Really?" James nodded. Rhen dropped his reptilian head downward to consider his situation. "Yes," he said, lifting his head to meet James' eyes. "That would be good, but first I must go home to Surpen. There's a lot that I need to take care of on my planet. Later, I will seek out Rachel for this antidote."

James hesitated, before dipping his head in Rhen's direction. "Spoken like a true King," he told his little brother. He didn't like Rhen's decision, but he knew he would've done the same thing.

Rhen turned towards Ceceta. "Are you...are you..." he wanted to ask her to return to Surpen with him, but he wasn't sure how she felt about him. A lot had happened over the last year.

"I'm coming my love," Ceceta reassured him. She rushed down the stairs to be by his side.

Rhen sighed and turned to Tgonar, who had entered the Council Chamber with his army in time to see Rhen destroy Loreth. "What are you doing here?" he asked the King.

"When I heard you had opened a connection from Surpen to Thestran, I knew I had to come. It's been too long since I've seen my son."

Rhen frowned at Tgonar's words. He would never see his father again. Without responding, he transported his military force back to Surpen.

"No way!" Charlie laughed out. "How does he do that?"

Before Tgfhi could make his way down to his waiting father, Erfce grabbed his arm. "Hey, I guess the Black Angel saved the day."

"But he wasn't the same," Lilly commented beside them.

"No," Jet agreed, reaching out for his wife's hand. "It was like he was a ghost, as if he had died and come back."

Tgfhi was confused by what had happened. He and his friends knew the Black Angel was Rhen; so if that was the case, who had just impersonated the Angel? Turning, he saw his father waiting for him at the bottom of the steps, arms open. It was over! Rhen had stopped Andres. Tgfhi ran down the stairs into his father's embrace. He would deal with the question of the Black Angel another day. Today, they would celebrate.

Chapter 31

"I just heard that Rhen has removed all of Debrino's Codes," James told his family, while sitting down to join them at the dinner table a week after their battle with Surpen.

"That's amazing!" Henry exclaimed. "I didn't think that would happen in my lifetime."

"We did well with Rhen," Kate declared. "He's taken on many of our Thestran ways. Freeing his father's prisoners and returning all of the captured Kings and Queens to their thrones, is exactly what we would have done. He's definitely following in our footsteps."

Reed chuckled. "Yeah, I'm not so sure about that mom. Every planet that he's freed has pledged itself back to Surpen. You may think he's being 'Thestran', but I think he's just being clever."

Kate stiffened. "He's not that clever. If he was, he would've returned for Rachel's antidote. He's making many of our allies nervous, staying in his present form."

"All in due time mom," James told her.

Three months later, Rhen sat down on his back haunches next to Ceceta on the balcony of the Surpen Palace. When he had returned to Surpen, after his battle with the Thestrans, he had offered his mother the throne. Her role as Surpen's Opposition Leader had helped the country fight against Loreth's influences and Rhen felt he owed his mother, but Orpel was content to sit on the sidelines. Her only request was that he keep her involvement a secret and he remove the restrictions placed on women, which he did at once.

"It's been three months," Ceceta told Rhen, interrupting his thoughts. She reached out to pat her husband's thick neck. "I think it's time for us to visit Rachel." Rhen nodded his head but didn't respond. "I miss you," she told him, her fingers dancing across his scales.

A crunching sound filled the air as Rhen changed back into his elfin form. He pulled Ceceta up into his body. His skin and claws hurt her, but she remained quiet. She didn't want to frighten him. Rhen had been acting odd around her ever since they had returned to Surpen. This unexpected show of affection on his part was rare for him these days.

After Rhen had gotten Surpen under control, the two of them had argued in private about Ceceta's role in tricking Rhen into believing she had died. Rhen had been angry with her. Ceceta had assured him that, at the time, she hadn't had any other choice, but Rhen had disagreed.

Ceceta kissed Rhen on his bearded cheek, while fighting against her gag reflux. He spent most of his time in his beastly form and still hadn't cleaned himself up yet. Rhen looked and smelled disgusting in his elfin body. Trying not to make a face, Ceceta breathed in the smell of old urine and rotten blood. By chance, Rhen's eyes were closed, so he missed seeing her displeasure at being held by him.

Closing her own eyes, Ceceta concentrated on listening to Rhen's beating heart. This was the first time he had held her in his arms since the war had begun. It was hard to believe they had survived the King's wrath and come out on top. Andres had hurt both of them for so long that neither of them felt safe anymore.

"Okay," Rhen whispered. He kissed Ceceta on the top of her head.

"Okay what?" Nk asked, walking out onto the balcony to join them.

Rhen released Ceceta and turned back into his beast like form.

When they had returned to Surpen, they had found Nk partially healed by the Black Angel. Even though it was Rhen, who had finished healing him, the only thing Nk could talk about these days was the fact that he had met the Black Angel. Tgfhi had been rather interested in Nk's 'Angel' meeting, and during Rhen's coronation, he had grilled Nk without mercy about his experience, until Tgonar had told him to be quiet or leave.

"Hey," Rhen said, greeting Nk. "Ceceta said it was time to go to Thestran for the antidote and I agreed."

"No! Really!?" Nk replied with sarcasm, as Bosternd and Authe wandered out onto the balcony to join them. "You mean you don't want to look like a lizard for the rest of your life?"

"I thought I looked like a dragon," Rhen remarked, feeling slightly offended by his friend's comment.

"Lizard," Nk teased.

"Surpen Beast of War," Bosternd commented.

"Worm," Authe added, making everyone laugh.

"Do you want us to come with you?" Bosternd offered, while patting Rhen's shoulder.

"No," Rhen answered. "But, thank you for the offer. Everything is still too raw. I don't want to leave Surpen unattended. Stay here to keep the peace. You can meet with me in the Thestran's castle whenever you have questions."

"How long will it take them to give Rhen the antidote?" Nk asked Ceceta. The ban on speaking to women had been lifted, so Ceceta was free to speak to whomever she wished.

"Six days. There are six injections, one for each day," Ceceta told them. "I don't know how long it will take for the injections to work after they give them to him."

"Probably not long," Bosternd remarked. "We know from Rachel's analysis of that black stuff Aul was making you drink that it was hurting your healing powers. You should heal quickly now that you no longer drink it."

Rhen stiffened at the sound of Aul's name. Aul had blackmailed Rhen into drinking Loreth's black mixture, after he had seen Rhen release the Milowian prisoners. When Rhen had returned to Surpen after his battle with the Thestrans, he had wanted to punish Aul for his part in turning him into a beast. Rhen was positive that Aul was working for Loreth. But, upon his return, Rhen had found Aul and Narseth missing. No one seemed to know where they were.

"Yeah," Rhen remarked. "This whole thing has been a nightmare. I'm glad it's over." Ceceta placed her hand on his side. Rhen turned to face her. "Ceceta is right. It's time for the antidote. We need to get on with our lives."

Later that day, Bosternd found Ceceta alone in the Throne Room writing a letter to one of her school friends. "Um, Ceceta. Could I speak with you, please?" he called out to her, as she stood up to leave the room.

Ceceta chuckled and moved back to her seat. "Old habits die hard, I guess," she told him. "I was just about to leave the room for you."

"Yes," Bosternd agreed, while sitting down in a chair beside her. "It's going to take all of us some time to adjust." He paused and pulled at his uniform for a minute before continuing, "Ceceta, there were several things that happened on Thestran that I didn't understand. I need you to explain them to me."

"I will if I can."

"Do you know why the Thestrans' power blasts didn't work on Rhen but Loreth's did? Also, how did you know the Black Angel would come when you called?"

Ceceta sat in silence for a moment, studying Bosternd's face. She released the breath she was holding and smiled. "Bosternd," she began. "That wasn't the Black Angel on Thestran, but a Genister dressed like the Angel."

"What?" Bosternd asked. "A Genister...? I don't understand."

"Ahh, Bosternd," Ceceta sighed, leaning back in her chair and smoothing her violet robes. There was a twinkle in her eye. "There are so many things you don't know."

"Like what?"

Ceceta shook her head and reached for his hand. "As Rhen's right-hand man, you need to know the truth, so you'll be prepared for future complications."

"Complications?" Bosternd asked.

"Bosternd. The Black Angel is Rhen."

Bosternd felt his mouth drop open. Before he could come up with something to say, Ceceta continued, "On Thestran, you saw a Genister dressed as the Black Angel. He was helping Rhen fight Loreth. The Thestrans' power blasts or anyone else's blasts for that matter, won't work on Rhen. Only a Genister's power blast can hurt him."

"What?"

"Bosternd," Ceceta said with a smile, while patting his hand. "Haven't you figured it out yet? Loreth was a Genister. That's why the other Genister helped Rhen and that's also why Loreth's blast affected Rhen."

"But," Bosternd began. "I don't understand. Why would only a Genister power blast affect Rhen?"

Ceceta chuckled and shook her head. She released his hand and leaned back in her chair. "Because," she told him in a teasing voice. "Rhen is a Genister."

A coldness descended upon Bosternd's body, as he felt his head grow light and his vision roll black. Everything he'd seen Rhen do, it all made sense now. He could hear Ceceta chuckling in the distance as a man said, "Well, now you let the cat out of the bag. I'll talk to him when he wakes up."

"Thank you, Thellis," Ceceta replied. "I'll see you later."

Acknowledgments

Thank you to my readers Maryanne and Alexandra, as well as my husband, Stephen, and my sons, Jack, Reid and Aaron. Without your support, Rhen never would have moved beyond the pages of my two a.m. notebook scribblings.

RHEN is the first book in a five-book series called THEMROCK. Book Two – THE SURPEN KING – will be released in the fall of 2017.

Made in the USA
Middletown, DE
08 April 2017